# BLACK TEARS

## KAREN WOODS

EMPIRE
PUBLICATIONS

First published in 2010
This edition published 2013

This book is copyright under the Berne Convention. All rights are reserved. Apart from any fair dealing for the purpose of private study, research, criticism or review, as permitted under the Copyright Act, 1956, no part of this publication may be reproduced, stored in a retrieval system, or transmitted, in any form or by any means, electronic, electrical, chemical, mechanical, optical, photocopying, recording or otherwise, without the prior permission of the copyright owner. Enquiries should be sent to the publishers at the undermentioned address:

EMPIRE PUBLICATIONS
1 Newton Street, Manchester M1 1HW
© Karen Woods 2010

ISBN 1901746 720

Printed in Great Britain.

# Acknowledgments

I would like to thank so many people in Manchester for the support I have been given following my first book. Firstly, my four beautiful children Ashley, Blake, Declan and Darcy. Also my Grandson Dolton and his mother Toni, who has been patient with me while I have been writing. Also my parents Margaret and Alan who have supported me and believed in me.

Writing is a lonely business and my friend Helen has been with me all the way, helping and supporting me. My mentor, fellow author Paul Kennedy, has also helped – we have laughed along the way and I know he has been near strangling me a couple of times but his support has been incredible.

I would also like to thank Nicola Murphy and Lee Kyte from the band Northern Icon, and Martin Finnigan from The Rainband, who have both recorded songs about my first book Broken Youth.

Also John Ireland and Ashley Shaw from Empire publications who have believed in me from the start and made all this possible. Many thanks also to Delennyk Richardson for her editing skills.

My Niece Brogan Woods deserves a mention, for being an inspiration to me and showing me that no matter what happens in life, we can get through it with a smile on our face. Also to all my facebook friends thanks for the support.

To James who has stood by me and supported me. My last thanks is to my son in heaven Dale, I'll never forget you and somehow writing these books has helped me say goodbye to you, even though you are always in my heart.

# Chapter One

Gordon clenched his fist tight, as the judge passed sentence, his knuckles turning white as he clenched them together. He now knew he had to serve the next five years of his life in prison. The judge peered over his oval glasses and looked at him as he stood tall, looking like he was about to explode. The noise inside the courtroom subsided as everyone listened eagerly.

"You are a menace to society young man, and especially to women. You're a bully and prey on young, defenceless people who know no better. I hope the time you spend in prison will help you reflect on the crime you have committed and try to change the monster you have become." Gordon raised his head and tugged at his white fitted t-shirt. His solicitor had advised him to wear a suit for court but Gordon had told him to 'fuck off' and came to court in his everyday clothing. He stared directly into the judge's eyes before he spoke.

"Do ya think jail will sort me out ya wanker? I'll do my time on my fucking head. Fuck you and fuck the system ya tosser." Gordon looked at the people sitting in the wooden dock facing him and started to shout at each of them like a wild man, he was pointing his finger at them. Security tried to eject him from the courtroom as quickly as they could but he was like a man of steel and stood tall. "You load of wankers," he continued, "who the fuck do ya think you are, messing round with people's lives. Fuck the lot of ya, because I'll do my time and I'll be back out before ya know it, watch ya fucking back the lot of ya's."

The judge sprung out of his large black leather chair and ordered security to take the prisoner down to the cells. He could see the jurors were terrified and he didn't want them to feel any more intimidated. "Take him down," he shouted. The two stocky Group Four guards, dressed in white shirts and black trousers, grabbed Gordon's hands and tried to restrain him as he struggled to break free.

"Get off me you daft cunts!" Gordon snarled.

Everyone watched the battle between them and one jury member hid her face behind her shaking hands. She was on the verge of breaking down and you could see her lips trembling as the convicted man tried to escape. Gordon head-butted one of the guards and tried to grab the radio from his hands so that he couldn't call for help, but it was too late. The door opened from behind him and in ran more staff to restrain him. Immediately they twisted Gordon up and carried him away kicking and screaming at the top of his voice. The courtroom felt cold and the members of the jury looked agitated as the reality of it all hit home. One of them stood up and made it quite clear he would never sit on a jury again as he now feared for his own safety. He told the courtroom Gordon had gotten a good look at them all and wanted to know what protection they would have when this man was finally freed. Every member of the jury felt the same way and they were up in arms. The way this man had looked at them left them afraid and they believed every word he said to them. Gordon's screams could still be heard as they dragged him to the cells. The jury members all left with the usher to go to the judge's chambers.

The police officer who'd given evidence against Gordon tried to calm the jury members down. They all gave him their names and addresses and were promised protection once this man was back on the streets. Gordon had been found guilty of the rape of his ex girlfriend, Misty Sullivan, possession of a firearm and ABH on the officers who arrested him.

The team of Group Four security guards threw Gordon into the holding cell and slammed the door behind him as quickly as possible. He was like a caged animal frothing at the mouth and the abuse he shouted out shook the cell walls. Pacing the floor he dragged his hands through his hair as he screamed out.

"Fucking bastards! Takes a team of you to hold me down does it? Well let's see when you have to let me out who the big men are, I'll wipe the fucking lot of you right out!" Gordon laughed as he kicked the cell door before walking slowly back to the small wooden bench on the opposite side of the room. The platform was situated across the back wall and the smell of sweaty feet lingered all over it. Gordon's nostrils flared as he inhaled deeply. The lighting was poor in the cell and he found it hard to read the things people had engraved all over the walls. He felt like he could conquer anything as he lay on the bed cracking his knuckles, his chest was rising frantically. Gordon knew the next five years of his life would be hard, but the one thing that kept him strong was the thought of knowing Misty would pay for every day he spent in jail. "Bitch" he whispered under his breath.

Gordon had seen Misty during the trial. Her boyfriend Dominic was never far from her side. As she walked into the courtroom, his heart melted at the sight of her. She looked so defenceless and innocent but he still felt the urge to hurt her badly. Misty still looked as stunning as ever to him and the red fitted dress she wore showed off all the curves he'd once caressed when they were together. He loved the way her dark hair shone under the courtroom lights. Her locks had always attracted him and today was no different. Gordon closed his eyes, he could still remember the smell of her hair and he inhaled deeply remembering their time together.

Misty looked tired as he searched her face for any signs of love for him. No matter how much he studied her, her face remained the same. She hadn't made any eye contact with him as she gave her evidence to the courtroom. He knew everyone believed her story regarding the shotgun and he just shook his head in disbelief as he listened to her speak. As he cast his eyes over to where she sat, he wanted to shout out that she still had his money, the money he'd stolen from the armed robberies he'd committed before he was arrested. He bit hard on his tongue as he knew nobody must ever know the truth. He couldn't chance any connection with it, as he knew that would definitely give him more time in prison. So, for now, he just gazed at her with malice in his eyes praying for the time when he would seek his revenge.

Dominic looked straight at Gordon as he stood in the dock, their eyes locked like gunslingers at dawn. Gordon screwed his face up as he snarled at him and nodded his head slowly letting him know his time would also come. Surprisingly Dominic didn't flinch and stood his ground. He knew if he showed any sign of weakness Gordon would have laughed in his face and considered him an easy target. Dominic's face slowly nodded back at Gordon letting him know he was ready for whatever he had to throw at him.

Gordon's mother was also in the courtroom. Her face was filled with grief and her grey hair was held back from her face by two rusty old clips. She'd tried to dress smartly for the trial but her heart was like a lead weight and she had no interest in the way she looked anymore. His mother felt so ashamed of her son and couldn't believe that he was the person they were all talking about in the courtroom. When they took Gordon down to the cells, ranting and raving, tears filled her eyes as the members of the court all gazed at her. The tears she cried were the tears of a mother who still couldn't help feel love for her son, but she was also relieved that he was out of her life for the next five years. She could relax knowing he wouldn't be knocking on her door late at night making her life a misery.

Francesca slowly rocked her body as Gordon was carted away. He'd been her life for so long now, and without him she felt empty inside. She also held a secret deep in her heart and was hoping he would have walked free today so she could have shared the news with him. Francesca had made the unusual effort that day to look respectable for court. Her black pants suit now looked like bags of rags as she tried to wipe the fluff from it. She'd borrowed ten pounds from Gordon's mam to go to Primark to get something to wear, hoping it might help his case. Her once seductive auburn hair was held in a ponytail and the roots were more than half way down her head; she was a walking wreck. The happy times she'd imagined in her mind seemed so far away now and she questioned herself whether she could care for a child on her own. Gordon's mother struggled to stand to her feet as they left courtroom nine in Manchester Crown Court. She held onto Francesca's arm for support. Francesca slowly followed behind her, making sure she didn't keel over as her gammy leg had been playing up lately and she was finding it hard to walk. Francesca's world was shattered into a thousand pieces and life without her boyfriend just seemed unbearable. At that moment, she hated her best friend Misty more than ever for making her lose the man she adored. The walk to the exit seemed long and both of them looked exhausted. As they walked down the red carpet stairway, Francesca's heart sank as tears appeared on her cheeks like a river of sadness.

The hours passed and the Group Four employees were ready to confront Gordon to see if he'd calmed down. As they looked through the small window on the iron door, a man lay on the platform in front of them staring into space. His six-foot body looked a threat to anyone who crossed him. Gordon had been busting the gym for the last few months and his muscles bulged from head to toe. He looked as if he'd calmed down and he seemed in a world of his own. Cautiously, the guards slowly opened the door and stood facing him ready for whatever he had to give. The officer spoke to him with a stern tone.

"Right lad, we don't want any trouble. It's up to you. You can do this the hard way or the easy way. What's it to be?" The men now stood at the door like soldiers getting ready for war. They watched his every move as they slowly entered his cell. Gordon thought about wiping the four of them out, but he knew one way or the other he was fighting a losing battle. He chuckled as he stood up. Stretching his hands above his head he spoke.

"Listen, I was fucked off before. Fuckin hell I've just had five years shoved up my arse, what do ya expect? Anyway, I'm sorted now and won't give ya any more trouble. Where am I going anyway?"

The men looked relieved but they were still cautious as they approached the prisoner knowing he could be having them over.

"Strangeways mate. That's where they're sending you for now, unless you're shipped out. So you should be alright as long as you keep your neck out of trouble." Gordon grinned and thought he'd got a result in going to the 'Ways. He knew a few lads in there already. Gordon feared he would have been shipped to another jail leaving him miles from home. This was a result for him because if he'd been sent far away his visits would have been few and far between, as he knew his mother and Francesca didn't have a pot to piss in. His sentence had knocked him for six deep inside but he tried to remain calm as the guards approached him.

The men placed the cuffs round his hands and the group headed down the long corridor where a few other lads were waiting to be shipped out too. All the convicts had that hard knock look in their eyes and some of them looked as if they'd already lost the plot. Gordon knew he would have to kick some arse to show them he was no nobhead once he got to the 'Ways.

All the paperwork was completed at the main desk and each of them in turn were put into the large white van, known as a sweatbox. All that was behind each door was a small window and a seat, which didn't give you enough room to swing a cat in. Gordon was led into the van and once he was seated, the door was slammed behind him. His head fell into his hands and anger filled his body as tears trickled down his face. Gordon listened to all the doors being closed in the vehicle. As he held his ear to the door he could hear one lad crying his eyes out. He was shouting loudly that he was innocent and proclaiming that he 'shouldn't fucking be here'.

Gordon gripped his arms around his body as he

looked out of the window. Tears fell now and he cried like a small child holding his hands over his mouth so nobody could hear his heartache. This was the real Gordon now, rather than the gangster he pretended to be. This was his life and he knew he'd have to get used to doors being slammed behind him. Prison life was hard, everyone had told him so in the past. From this day forward Gordon would have to watch his back because by the look on some of the criminals' faces he knew they wouldn't think twice before they rammed a blade into his body.

## Chapter Two

The journey didn't take long from Manchester Crown Court to Strangeways and it wasn't long before Gordon's door was opened. His eyes squeezed together as the daylight hit them. He watched the other men being lined up outside and the lad who had been crying previously was still declaring his innocence to the group. The screw now looked at the bag of bones in front of him and laughed.

"Oh, not another fucking innocent man. Tell ya what mate, if I had a pound for every time an inmate had said that to me, I would be a rich man. So take a bit of advice, shut the fuck up and just do ya time like everyone else has to." The inmate yanked his over sized jeans up from his waist and followed the officer to the main office still moaning. All the doors were opened and locked behind them as they were escorted through the gates of the prison. The inmates finally found themselves in a small room with a prison warden stood behind a tall wooden desk. Gordon's eyes focused on the man he saw in front of him and listened to him as he asked them each to fill out a form with medical questions on it. A smack head was now shaking desperately, telling the screw he was a heroin addict and that he needed medical attention straight away to stop him going cold turkey. The screw told the addict he would have to wait until the doctor came on duty in the next hour. The bag head now held his stomach and started to roll about as if he was going to shit himself. He knew the nights that lay ahead would be long and hard without any drugs to feed his addiction.

One of the new inmates who stood next to him looked at him and started to speak in a sarcastic manner. "Listen, ya fuckin smack head. Stop being a mard arse and do ya fucking roast." The screw heard the conversation and stepped in telling him to move along. The rattling drug addict walked past the inmates and started to fill out a doctor's request form with a trembling hand. The snide remarks kept coming at him as they watched him from a distance. The bag head knew they thought he was the scum of the earth and the lowest of the low and hung his head in shame. The comments kept on coming.

"Fucking junkie! Low life fucker! You better not get padded up with me, keeping me awake all night crying for fucking drugs." You could tell the addict was at breaking point and it was only the sound of other screws' voices that made the inmate stop his insults. The convicts were all issued grey trousers and red t-shirts. They were also given several pairs of socks and boxer shorts. To some of them it brought a smile to their faces. It was as if they'd never owned as much clothing in their lives and they held on to them as if they'd been given bars of gold.

The next step was a body search and each prisoner had to go into a small room to be searched from top to bottom. As Gordon took his turn, he noticed the screw putting on plastic disposable gloves. He was made to strip down to his bare bollocks and then the screw started to run his fingers through his thick crop of dark hair. Gordon was now asked to squat down over a mirror to make sure he hadn't shoved anything up his arse. He chuckled and told the screw to fuck off at first but when the other two screws moved towards him, he had no choice but to follow orders. Gordon was moaning as he started to squat.

"Fucking joke this. What the fuck could I possibly shove up my arse? Do ya think my mobile phone's up there or something?" The screw laughed out loud now and told him he would be surprised what convicts had previously shoved up their arse-holes. As he continued, he casually leant back against the wall and reminded the other screws of a previous inmate's misfortune. Apparently, a previous criminal had shoved a small mobile phone up the crack of his arse and forgotten to turn it off. Eventually, when he was due to be searched, someone decided to phone him. They all laughed from their bellies as the screw continued his story doing all the actions.

"There I was doing my normal search, and when I asked the fucker to squat down, the fucking glory, glory Man United ring-tone came playing out of his arsehole. The cheeky bastard looked at me and he could tell I was onto him". They were all laughing their heads off now as he finished his story. "Before we knew it we were all screaming laughing as he tried to pull it out of his arse. He was laughing too. It was a memorable day I can tell you and one of the funniest things I have ever witnessed since I've been doing this job." Gordon at that moment seemed to forget about the humiliation of it all and chuckled as he bent down to get his arse searched. Just before the search took place, Gordon started singing 'Glory, Glory

Man United' at full pelt and they all laughed with him taking the pressure off the moment.

The searches were all done and the screws escorted the prisoners through some great big wooden doors that looked ancient. Once the doors were opened the chill of the place made the new inmates realise that this was where they were going to live for the rest of their sentences. Gordon rubbed his arms as goose-bumps appeared all over them. The prison walls were painted in a dull cream colour, the bricks still visible through the paintwork. The metal staircase in the middle of the prison led to a landing. You could see silver guardrails secured around it. Gordon stretched his neck looking about at his new surroundings.

Prisoners shouted from their cells as they heard the new inmates approaching. Some of them were singing at the top of their voices. The screw escorted the first two men to a grey door and opened it slowly before he spoke.

"Right you two, this is your pad. Unpack all ya shit in the morning, just get ya heads down for now." Gordon peered into the cell and could see two beds with grey blankets thrown over them and a small wooden cupboard situated in the corner of the room. The walls were the same as the landings but painted in a battleship grey colour. The side light in the cell barely lit the room. The two inmates, who were in their mid twenties, trudged into the pad and the screw quickly locked the door behind giving them no time to speak. The rest of the prisoners followed behind him to another cell a couple of doors down. The officer now told Gordon and another prisoner that this was their pad. Gordon took a deep breath as he watched him slowly unlock the door and escort them inside. The room was the same as the one he had just seen and he made eye contact with the other criminal for the first time. Within seconds, the screw was gone and all you could hear was the door being banged from the outside. Gordon felt suffocated and found it hard to breathe. He poked his head through the small window that was secured by bars and gasped for breath. The window was between the two beds and it was the only view they had from their cell. Gordon felt the cold night air on his face. His eyes scanned the area as he clocked the other wings inside the prison grounds. As he stood there, he closed his eyes and felt his emotions rising from his body. Gordon knew he couldn't break down and cry because he could feel the other inmate's eyes drilling into the back of his head watching his every movement. After a few more deep breaths, Gordon turned to face the man for the first time. Words were few between them at first but as soon as they both lay on their beds, they started to talk freely.

"Well what you in for then?" Gordon asked with a serious face hoping the lad was not in for some big time murder. The other man fidgeted about for a moment and folded his wafer thin pillow under his head before he began to talk.

"Fucking drugs mate. I was caught with a load of sniff in my car. They got me bang to rights; there was nothing I could do about it. They'd been watching me for weeks and had loads of evidence, like photos and video evidence" Gordon watched as his pad mate looped his arms behind his head. "I'm fucking gutted mate, I can tell ya. If the cocaine had hit the streets, I would have been on a right little earner. But ay, all good things come to an end don't they?" He blew a laboured breath as he continued. "Anyway, three years isn't that long when ya think about it. It could have been a lot worse, but I threw a guilty plea in as soon as possible, and probably saved some time being shoved up my arse if it had gone to trial."

Gordon listened to his every word and the word cocaine made him realise that his own addiction was now over. It was a blessing in disguise and he knew the next few weeks would be hard without his magic dust to help him along. The inmate now introduced himself as Joey, but he told Gordon all his mates called him Tigger and he preferred that name. It was only his mam and close family who'd ever called him by his Christian name. Gordon now introduced himself and told Tigger he was in for fighting and nearly killing someone. He didn't mention it was his ex girlfriend who he'd tried to kill, or the rape episode. He wanted to keep his cards close to his chest because he knew if word got out that he had raped someone, the prisoners would make his life a misery. He'd heard so many stories about what happened to rapists and nonces in jail. Gordon didn't really class himself as a rapist and could never understand why he'd ever been charged with it. After all, she'd been his girlfriend at the time, or so he thought, and what was the harm of a bit of slap and tickle for old time's sake. It couldn't really be classed as rape, could it? Both men leant over to each other and shook hands. Lying on his bed, Gordon pulled the scruffy, stale smelling blanket over his body. The cover hid away his sins and the real person he was inside.

Sleep came easily to Gordon and Tigger, they were both knackered and within minutes, they were both sound asleep. The midnight air crept in through the open window as they slept and caused them both to bury their heads deep under their covers. The noise of shouting throughout the prison eventually eased off and silence filled the cell.

Morning came with the sound of banging doors that woke Gordon from his sleep. As he listened carefully, he could hear people shouting from outside and footsteps going past his door. He stretched his arms above his head and the reality of where he was hit home. His stomach felt like a lead balloon and the ache he felt in his heart was like nothing he'd ever felt before. Misty was still on his mind every minute of the day and his feelings were mixed about her. Half of him wanted to cherish her forever and the other half wanted to destroy her. It was her fault he was in prison and somehow he knew she would pay big time. Looking across the room, he noticed Tigger waking up, and smiled as their eyes met before he spoke.

"Wakey! Wakey! Welcome to hotel Strangeways. Should I go and put our towels on the sun loungers by the pool, while you order breakfast?" Tigger smirked but you could tell he'd realised where they were. This was no holiday camp and the years that lay ahead would be no picnic.

The door opened and a screw shouted in to them. "Come on lads, time to get ya brekkie." The man looked just the same as all the others and he was wearing black pants with a white shirt. The keys that he had hanging from his trouser pocket were the size of a football, and you could see that they were a strain to carry. Gordon was the first to jump up out of bed, shortly followed by Tigger. As they left their cell for the first time, they could see hundreds of bodies scattered about the prison. The landing looked so much bigger than it had the previous night, and Gordon couldn't believe that the inmates were cleaning it so early in the morning. The screw led them to the dining area; hundreds of tables were placed about the room. The officer showed them where to queue up for their breakfast and left them alone, looking like lost sheep. Gordon continued in the line and when it was finally his turn the older man behind the serving counter asked him what he wanted for breakfast. Gordon's eyes scanned the contents of what was on offer and he couldn't make up his mind, it all looked like shite. The porridge looked like mush, and the eggs looked like they had been cooked three weeks before. The server, who was also an inmate, now looked at him and you could tell he was losing patience.

"Fucking hurry up ay, there's not just you who's hungry. I've got all these other people to feed so make it quick." The server was pointing at the big queue behind him. Gordon looked at him as his blood boiled with anger. He knew there was nothing he could do at the moment, so with a cocky face he shot his eyes at him and told him he'd have egg on toast. The fat sweaty inmate now threw two eggs on two pieces of burnt toast and slid it under the glass-serving hatch.

"Next!" he shouted looking straight at Tigger, who knew not to hang around and ordered the same as Gordon. They both got a brew each and found two seats at the end of a table. As they sat down the other men stopped eating and looked at the two new inmates. Gordon could feel fear in his body and hoped there wouldn't be any trouble, he clenched his fists as his nostrils flared. Tigger broke the silence and introduced himself to the others sat at the table.

"Alright lads, don't mind if we sit here do ya?" The men looked at each other and carried on talking. Tigger and Gordon were now accepted as inmates. Gordon dug his fork into the egg, and looked at Tigger.

"Fucking food is shite. Look at my egg. It's as hard as

that mean looking fucker sat over there." Tigger laughed as his eyes focused on a large man facing them on the next table. The man looked about twenty stone and his t-shirt barely covered his hairy stomach. The prisoner's face looked as hard as nails and they both knew not to mess with him. Tigger watched as Gordon played with the food on his plate. He laughed out loud and told Gordon he better get used to the menu because five years was a long time to start being fussy about prison scran.

The noise of everyone eating was deafening. The canteen was filled with talking and knives and forks being clashed together. The men seemed to be on edge all the time. Gordon sipped his brew and scanned his eyes about the prison. He was taking in all the different faces and characters present. As he looked at them, he wondered why on earth they were in prison. Some of them looked angelic, as if butter wouldn't melt in their mouths. However, deep down inside he knew everyone had a story to tell and before long he would be wiser to everyone's crimes and previous antics. When breakfast was finished, everyone seemed to leave in a rush.

The screw that had brought them in earlier now came over to them. "Come on lads. It's induction time for you both. You'll spend all this week learning about the prisons routines, rules, and regulations." Tigger nodded and hurried the rest of his brew, he stood to his feet waiting for Gordon to finish his. As they left the kitchen staff, who were also inmates, moved in to clear up after breakfast. You could hear them shouting at each other and the sound of pots and pans being flung around filled the room. The kitchen was a large area and all the surfaces were made of steel. You could see the shine on them and the place looked immaculate.

Walking towards the far end of the landing, more inmates joined them. There were a few lads that Gordon recognised from the previous day; he nodded his head slowly at them. Some of convicts looked tired, as if they hadn't slept for days. The smack head that was by their side was trembling from head to toe as he tried to hold his body up to walk. The young man's eyes looked black, like someone had drawn dark circles underneath them. Sweat was dripping from his forehead like a running tap and he kept lifting his hand to his brow to wipe it away. Gordon shot a look at the other lads and no words were spoken until they reached a side room just off the main corridor. Inside the room were about forty chairs, a large white notice board sat in the corner not far from them. The men took their places and sat waiting for the induction to begin. About ten minutes passed and the last of the new inmates came inside the room to join them.

The induction began and most of the rules were explained. They were told they would get one visiting order each month and how to process it. The screw explained that these visiting orders could be taken away at any time for bad behaviour such as fighting. The officer now spoke about inmates making the most of their time in jail. He told them they could get jobs inside the prison, and earn more money towards their canteen. Canteen was what they could order for themselves, things like deodorants and toothpaste could be bought from the wages they were paid. The screw explained canteen was something all inmates appreciated. He also told them they could even become a trustee in time which meant they would have the freedom to walk about the prison with no one bothering them. When Tigger heard the word trustee, he chuckled to Gordon and covered his mouth as he whispered to him.

"Fucking trustee my arse, brown noser more like. Those kinds of jobs are for the grasses in here so I can't see myself ever becoming one, can you?" Gordon shook his head slowly but secretly he would have loved to have the freedom of walking about the prison, but if the job was labelled an arse licker, it would definitely be a no go area for him in the future. Each inmate was told they would receive a basic wage each week even if they didn't work, but it was explained to them if they worked, they could buy more luxuries and also be out of their cell all day. The meeting dragged on for around an hour and at the end of it, they all looked drained. The addict that was going through cold turkey had been removed half way through the course. He'd started shaking, vomiting and needed urgent medical attention. Tigger told Gordon that the jail was full of smack heads; his mates had previously been in the jail and warned him all about them and their antics.

"They're low life fucker's mate. As soon as ya backs turned they'll be in ya cell robbing anything they can get their hands on to get a quick fix." Gordon looked shocked at what he'd heard and had to ask him what he meant.

"How can they get drugs in here?"

Tigger looked at his face and thought he was joking at first, but as he looked at him, he knew he would have to explain further.

"There's more drugs in here mate, than on the fucking streets. Once I'm settled and I know the script, I'll be getting a few parcels in, so I can make some decent money. Do ya fancy a bit of work in here or what?" Gordon looked at Tigger and nodded slowly, he didn't know what he meant by his words but just went along with him anyway. This was Gordon's first time in the nick and in reality, he was quite naive as to what prison life entailed. The thought of earning extra money interested him and he would definitely speak to Tigger later to find out exactly what he meant. He was game for anything that could earn him a few quid.

The prisoners left the room in single file. Gordon and Tigger were escorted back to their cells. Once the door was closed behind them, they both collapsed onto the bed. Gordon now looked around the room and examined every nook and cranny. The years he would spend inside these four walls would be long and hard. He predicted that by the time he'd finished his sentence he would probably be able to tell you just how many bricks were used to build the whole prison. His mind ran away with him as he lay down. His muscular arms were folded under his head and he was struggling to get comfy. Remembering the conversation earlier with Tigger he sat chewing on his finger nails. Waiting only a few seconds he got straight back onto it and asked his pad mate more about his plans to make big money inside the jail.

Tigger whispered as he leant towards Gordon's bed making sure nobody was listening.

"When I get my first visiting order, I'll send it to my mate. He'll smuggle some brown in to sell in here. He's done it loads of times for my mates in the past so he's bang on for getting stuff in." Tigger held his head back and smirked. He loved that he had his pad mate's full attention. "He'll just brings some girl with him and pass it over to her once he's been searched. All I have to do is kiss her at the end of a visit and that's when she drops it into my gob". Tigger bolted up from his bed and dragged his fingers through his hair, he looked distressed. "I hope she's not a fucking minger, I better tell him about that bit, fuck that I'm not sucking faces with no dirty skanks". Taking a deep breath he lay back down on in his bed and spoke in a casual manner. "Anyway I'm just gonna swallow it straight away so the screws won't clock fuck all. All that's left then is the waiting till I have a shit to get the parcel back." Gordon looked shocked and scratched his head as he asked more questions.

"Won't you overdose on it if ya swallow all that heroin in one hit?" Tigger held his belly as he laughed out loud.

"Nar, ya fucking muppet. Don't you know fuck all about prison life mate? They put it in balloons for ya so there's no way it can leak into ya body". Gordon dipped his head, he looked embarrassed as Tigger continued. "The worst part is getting the drugs out of ya shit. I'm not looking forward to that part of it, but it's a money maker and needs must innit". His eyes focused on Gordon now as he smirked at him. "So are you in or what?" Gordon nodded his head slowly and loved the sound of making some money. He knew any cash being sent into him from his family was a joke, none of them had a pot to piss in. They barely had enough money to live on themselves, never mind sending him postal orders.

The rest of the day went slowly and both the inmates were stuck in their cell for most of the time. The only time they left the pad was for their dinner and tea, but that was only for a short time and they were banged up straight afterwards. The toilet in their cell was situated at the side of Tigger's bed and the sound of the water running through it kept them amused for many an hour. That was until Tigger decided he needed to use it and the smell from his arse filtered through the cell walls. Gordon heaved into his pillow as the smell reached his nose. Choking sounds could be heard before he started shouting abuse at his pad mate.

"You dirty bastard. What the fuck have you been eating? It stinks like the sewers in here. You'd better spray something to get rid of that rancid smell." Tigger started laughing as he squeezed his head and added some farts to his amusement as he sat on the toilet. His cackling laughter filled the cell.

"Sorry mate, it's my guts they've been right off these last couple of days. It must be all the stress I've been under lately. I'm not usually a smelly cunt." Gordon listened and heard him sniggering to himself but he kept his head sunk into the pillow until the smell subsided.

The two inmates were issued with their first visiting orders and one basic prison letter. Gordon looked at the lined piece of paper in front of him and knew he would have to write to Francesca. He still needed her in his life as she was his only hope of getting a visit from the outside world. His feelings for her had changed so much lately, he could barely stand the thought of her being near him, she made his skin crawl. He secretly blamed her for losing the love of his life. Francesca was a hindrance and once he was a free man he planned to kick her to the curb forever.

The words were hard to write as Gordon lay thinking on his bed, a pen hung from his mouth with his fingers twisting it. The cell walls had been engraved with people's names and messages over the years, he look closer at what previous inmates had written. Gordon started to read one of the messages, his eyes squinted together as he tried to read the small writing, it said, "Sheila I'll love you forever, love Ged". He wanted so much to take his own pen and scrawl how much he still loved Misty, but he knew nobody must know his feelings because when he was released his plans to make her pay would be put into action and he didn't want any connection with her at all.

Gordon finally wrote his letter to Francesca, all he could write was for her to hurry up and to come and see him. He told her he missed her and couldn't wait until they were together again, he just hoped she believed him and didn't see through his cunning plan. Tigger told him that jail mail was always sent to their loved ones; he boasted that pure bull-shit was always written in these kinds of letters. After all, the prisoners had to keep their wives and partners sweet until they returned home, so most letters were full of promises they knew they'd never keep once they were freed.

Tigger loved writing letters and spent hours lay on his bed writing to some girl he had started seeing just before he was arrested. Gordon wondered what on earth he could write about as he struggled to write just one page. Tigger laughed and told him he was a bit of a player on the out and told him that the women loved all the shit he wrote to them. He started to read out one of his letters and they both giggled at some of the things he'd written to them. Tigger told Gordon that he'd asked his girlfriend to rub her fanny all over the letter before she sent it back to him, so he could smell her juices. Gordon laughed out loud and called him a dirty fucker, but he admitted he admired his cheek. He wished he'd been so happy go lucky as Tigger, because at the moment he just seemed to be under a dark cloud of depression and couldn't shake off the torment he felt inside.

# Chapter Three

Francesca looked into a broken mirror that hung on the wall opposite her for the last time. She was ready to set off on her journey to Strangeways. Checking the clock on the wall she sighed, she knew she had to leave early because she didn't have the bus fare in her tattered old purse. The walk to the prison would only take her half an hour if she hurried. Francesca felt excited at telling Gordon she was carrying his child and couldn't wait until he took her in his strong arms and told her how much he loved her. With this in mind she grabbed her coat from the arm of the chair and set off.

The walk wasn't as bad as she first thought, the weather was quite pleasant. The sun was still shining even though the winter months were fast approaching. Francesca set off down Rochdale Road and knew if she cut through the estate, it would shorten her journey. As she passed the Milan pub, she knew it was over half way there and picked up speed. As she walked on, her eyes focused on the landmark of Strangeways tower.

A large red brick tower now stood tall from all the other buildings in the area and it reminded her of a Disney film she'd watched when she was a little girl. In her mind she could picture a prince climbing a tower to rescue his distressed princess. If only she could have a life that was so simple, she thought as she carried on walking. All she wanted to be was loved and cared for and to be happy with the man of her dreams. Francesca knew in her heart she was a million miles away from the truth and doubted whether Gordon had ever really loved her, but she lived in hope. He was all she had in life that meant something to her. She placed her hands inside her long black leather coat and struggled to keep warm. Francesca had spent hours that morning trying to find the perfect outfit to go and visit Gordon and in the end she decided to wear her knee length, black boots and a tartan coloured skirt. Her looks were now a shadow of their former glory. The hair that used to shine like the sun in the sky was like a lifeless ball of fluff and her skin was covered in more spots than a Dalmatian dog. Francesca blamed her skin troubles on her pregnancy but if she had been honest with herself, she had let herself go a long time ago. The cocaine she'd been hammering had gradually stopped when Gordon couldn't provide it any longer and she struggled every day without the drug in her body. Francesca could barely afford money for food anymore, never mind the cocaine she once loved so much. She had decided there and then that the child she was carrying meant more to her than any drugs in her life and promised she'd never sniff again.

As Francesca entered the prison, she looked about at all the other visitors. She could tell by their faces that life was hard for them too. She watched one woman in particular chase her small child round the visitors centre. He started screaming as she pulled him away from the glass sliding doors. You could see in the woman's face that she wanted to slap the kid to make him behave, but in front of the visitors, she smiled and tried to remain calm as she tugged at his clothing. Francesca handed all Gordon's belongings inside the hatch where the screws were, he'd requested this in his letter. This ranged from socks, trainers and even a new pair of slippers. His orders were to make sure she brought everything he wanted, even though she didn't have the money to buy them. Francesca had to borrow money for his stuff and was already in debt yet again with the local loan shark. The visitors centre consisted of around fifty tables and a small children's corner with a few toys scattered about in it. The place itself looked clean and the sky blue walls helped to give off a fresh clean look.

Francesca waited for about ten minutes and finally they shouted out the name for her visit. Quite a few other people were shouted at the same time and they all made their way to the main entrance of the prison. Once inside Francesca was shocked as she watched the process she had to go through to gain access to the prison. First, they stamped your hand with some kind of invisible ink and she wondered what the fucking point was of it all. The next step was to walk through a security check and once you came through there, a female prison warden searched your body and clothing. The screw looked at Francesca and gave her the signal with her hand to come in front of her. Once she was there she frisked her all over. She made her take the ponytail out of her hair to see if anything was concealed inside it. Once that was over, Francesca had to wait until her bag had come through the other security check machine. It was all taking so long and she looked frustrated, all she wanted to do was see Gordon. All the visitors felt the same about the checks and one woman who was stood nearby shouted out that they weren't prisoners and didn't need to be treated like this. The male screw looked at her as he heard her ranting and slowly approached her. His face looked stern as he stood tall in front of all the visitors.

"Listen love, you're all searched to protect yourself. You won't believe what people try and smuggle in for prisoners, so relax and understand we're only doing our job." The woman made no reply and looked embarrassed as all eyes focused on her, her face was blood red. As the officer left her side, she mumbled under her breath and you could tell she felt disgusted by the whole episode.

Once everyone was searched, they were led to glass double doors. The doors finally closed, and the other side slowly opened leading to a large set of stairs. Everyone walked up the staircase and the sound of a dog barking could be heard. It wasn't until they reached the top of the stairs that they could see why the dog was present.

The guard walked slowly past the line of visitors and explained what was about to happen. He told them not to stroke the dog or even look at it. They had to remain completely still while it walked between them. The Springer Spaniel now circled the people and wagged its tail furiously as it mingled between the visitors. Luckily, everybody was fine and nobody was found to have drugs concealed. The last step was to place their hand under some ultra violet light and the stamp they'd had done previously showed up underneath it. Apparently, it stopped inmates escaping. Francesca sighed as she placed her hand under the light, she couldn't see all the need for so much security.

As she walked nearer to the large room, she could see all the inmates sitting down at the tables. The visiting room had hundreds of tables in rows. The prisoners all wore red bibs over their clothing and you could tell they were anxiously waiting for the visits to begin. The screw now walked up to the main door and told the visitors the rules before they entered. He told them they could buy inmates drinks and sandwiches from the canteen and other luxuries, his hand pointed to the left side of him. He also told them that they weren't permitted to go and sit at any other tables. Everybody was pissed off at the whole episode and felt relieved once the doors were opened and they could join their loved ones.

Francesca searched for Gordon, she stood up on her tip toes. It took a while before she actually saw him at the far side of the room; he was waving his hand in the air. Gordon looked thinner than before, but apart from that, he was still the man she loved with all her heart. Francesca walked to where he was sat, and leaned over to kiss him. Gordon immediately pulled away from her and told her to go and get him some food from the canteen, he looked flustered. She instantly felt neglected but followed his orders to keep the peace. As he watched her take her place in the queue his eyes wandered to where Tigger was sitting with his visitors. He knew today was the day Tigger had planned to get his drop of drugs and secretly watched his every move. Tigger had been shitting himself when he heard the dog was on duty today, but apparently, his mate had some kind of special spray that he put on his clothing to deter the dog from detecting any drugs that were concealed, he was a clever fucker.

Gordon winked at Tigger from across the room. They both knew the first part of the plan had run smoothly. Francesca returned from the canteen and threw the food on the table in front of Gordon, she looked stressed. He looked at the sandwich in his hands and pulled his face. "Since when do I like fucking egg mayonnaise butties?" Francesca sighed and took a deep breath.

"Fucking hell, that's all there was, so stop fucking moaning. I've just queued up for five minutes so be grateful for once in your life." Gordon slowly peeled back the plastic from the sandwich and took a small bite from it as Francesca watched him, she was eager to break her news. Her fingers were in her mouth and she was chewing on her finger nails. Gordon seemed distant from her and she could tell he didn't really want her there. Her eyes focused at the other inmates as she sat cracking her knuckles. Francesca watched how the convicts cherished the people who'd come to see them. A couple on the next table were kissing passionately and she felt jealous of the affection she was being denied. Gordon sipped his brew and Francesca knew it was the right time to tell him her news. The secret had been bubbling inside her all day and she couldn't hold it in any longer. Slowly, she reached across the table, took hold of his hand, and stroked it slowly.

"Gordon, I've got some good news to tell you. Hopefully it will bring a smile to that miserable face of yours." He looked at her for a second and tried to figure out what she had to tell him, he was pre-occupied with watching Tigger and his visitors and he couldn't concentrate on anything else. After a few minutes, he urged her to reveal her news. "Come on then spill the beans, what's this big secret you've got then." Francesca could see he was getting frustrated at the wait. Taking a deep breath, she started to speak in a low voice.

"You're going to be a daddy. I did a pregnancy test last month and it was positive. I'm so happy, we can be a family now can't we?" Gordon's face went white and all his facial expressions froze. She could tell he wasn't very happy. He grabbed her arm from across the table and pulled her closer. Looking directly into her eyes he snarled at her as he clenched his fist on top of the table.

"You fucking idiot. How the fuck, are you going to look after a baby! None of us has a pot to piss in. I'm in prison for fuck sake. How do you expect me to be a dad?" His fists were banging slowly onto the table as he shot a look at her. "Take your head from up your arse will you, and think about this properly!" Francesca's eyes filled with tears and a lump came to the back of her throat. Her hands gripped round her neck, you could see them trembling. She looked like she was suffocating.

Gordon shook his head and dragged his fingers through his hair. He knew she was upset and tried to calm her down. He had to make her see sense and get rid of the unwanted child. Shaking his head his eyes looked towards the ceiling. He was one hundred percent sure he never wanted any kids with Francesca. Pulling her hands towards him he tried to sort things out. Gordon held a cunning look in his eyes as he whispered to her from across the table.

"Francesca I do love ya, but the timing's all wrong innit? Think about it. We've got all the time in the world to have kids" his eyes were staring at her and he was looking for the answer he wanted to hear. "When I'm released, we can have a baby and look after it together. You know it makes sense don't ya?" Francesca pulled her arms away from his and held them around her body. This was meant to be a happy time but now her world and everything she'd dreamt about was slowly being broken in two and her body felt like it was going to collapse. The screw passed them and Gordon pulled her body to him hoping to calm her down because it was obvious she was upset. He held her across the table and gently kissed her forehead as tears streamed down her face hoping to calm her down.

"I'll tell ya now Francesca. I don't want this child and if ya don't get rid of it, we are fucking over. Are you listening to me, I said over!" his eyes burned into her from across the table. Francesca remained silent, nodding her head slowly like a small child. There were few words spoken after this and the visit soon ended. The screw's voice could now be heard shouting for all the visitors to start to say their goodbyes. As Francesca stood up to make her way to the exit, she looked stressed. Before the final call, Gordon bent over to her and whispered into her ear. His face looked mean as he spoke. "Get rid of the baby, otherwise don't bother coming to see me ever again." His words felt like knives being plunged into her heart and she wanted to scream at the top of her voice but her lips seemed locked. She nodded her head as she started to tremble and slowly walked away from the table. Francesca looked like her world was about to end. She had to make the biggest decision of her life now and her head was in bits. Her head looked heavy as it sank deep into her chin. She made her way to the door waited to leave.

The visitors stood at the exit and waved at their loved ones. Francesca turned her head slowly and looked for the last time at Gordon's face, he was still snarling at her. She was sweating and she looked like she needed to be sick, her hands were gripping her throat as she sucked in deep breaths. Francesca needed fresh air as quickly as possible. Her legs looked like they were going to give way. Holding the wall for support she hurried to the exit.

Everybody's mood was low as they left the prison, you could see sadness in all their eyes, especially the young children. It was so hard for them to leave the people they loved behind and one woman even shed a tear. Francesca rushed into the open air and held her body up against a small wall situated at the side entrance. One of the other visitors could see she was struggling and asked if she was all right, Francesca waved her hand in front of her face and blew her breath. "Yeah, love it's just the heat in that place, it knocks me sick." she lied. The concerned passerby remained with her for a few moments more looking at the young girl's face. "Are you sure, you're alright." she asked again. Francesca jerked her head forward. The woman started to speak, she placed her hand on her shoulder. "Is it your first time here love? It will get better you know." Francesca sucked on her lips and tried to hold the tears back. The woman now spoke about her own life and told her all about the prisons she'd visited in the past while being married to a criminal. The visitor had bleached blonde hair and her figure was round and flabby. She looked as rough as a bear's arse and the tattoos on her arm made her look like a big butch lesbian. Francesca's colour now started to come back to her face, she thanked the woman for her concern and watched as she waddled off into the distance.

Francesca started her walk back home now. Nothing seemed real around her and everything seemed to be moving in slow motion. The visit with Gordon had left her feeling exhausted, and she couldn't wait to get home to chill out. Her home at the moment was living with her auntie, but she knew once the news of her pregnancy was out she would be definitely kicked out onto the street. Her auntie was strict and she knew in her heart that she wouldn't want anything to do with her if she'd been that daft enough to let herself get pregnant.

The weather changed and rain started to fall. The black clouds in the Manchester sky seemed to understand her heartache. The mascara she'd taken hours putting on her eyes that morning poured down her face like black tears. Francesca felt like calling into a nearby pub to drown her sorrows but she didn't have a penny left in her pocket. Her head was spinning and she knew her world was crumbling before her very eyes. The choices that lay ahead of her were breaking her in two and she looked like she had the worries of the world on her shoulders.

Francesca's legs were aching when she reached home, as quickly as she could she yanked her boots from her feet and massaged her toes with her fingers. She stood thinking for a minute then she rushed to find some writing paper. Drawers could be heard slamming, Francesca was mumbling under her breath. Finally she found what she needed to write her letter and scraped a chair out from the dining table. Tapping her fingers and chewing on the end of the pen she began.

The letter was five pages long by the time she'd finished it. She put her heart and soul into every word she'd written. Francesca told Gordon of all the benefits of having a child and how good he would be as a father. She ended the letter by writing 'Gordon I love you more than life itself, and it would break my heart to lose you, just think of all the things we've been through together. I hope you change your mind and make me the happiest woman alive. Please try to be as happy as I am about our child."

Francesca read the letter for the last time. Holding it to her heart she closed her eyes and it looked like she was praying as she pressed it onto her chest. Finally her shaking hands slid the letter inside envelope and placed it on the table, Francesca just sat staring at the letter now. She was twisting her hair in her fingers rapidly. Her next step was to tell her auntie the news of her pregnancy; she hoped and prayed she would take the news better than Gordon had.

Francesca's auntie sat watching Coronation Street as she entered the front room. She was a glamorous woman and looked after herself every day. Her hair and makeup was never out of place. Francesca could see her auntie was enjoying the programme as she sat on the edge of the chair with her eyes glued to the TV screen. Her auntie loved the single life and was never short of male attention. Men were in and out of her life constantly and that's how she liked it – no commitments. The house where they lived was like a show home and the cream carpet in the front room was her pride and joy, she was always on her hands and knees rubbing at the slightest stain. She loved the cleanliness of it all and hated any build up of dust in the place. All the furniture was polished daily and not a speck of dirt could be found anywhere in the house.

Francesca eventually sat down facing her auntie. She looked nervous as she was tried to find the right moment to tell her. Sylvia knew she'd been to see Gordon in prison and casually asked how it went. She made no secret that she hated Gordon with a passion and hoped Francesca would get rid of him now he was in the nick. Sylvia secretly blamed Gordon for the downfall of her niece and knew he was bad news from the moment she set eyes upon him. She'd met his type one hundred times before and knew he was a wrong un. Francesca fidgeted about as she began to tell her about the visit. She told her all about the security checks she'd gone through and how big the prison was inside. Her auntie now searched for her cigs down the side of the chair. She was talking in a high-pitched voice. "He's nothing but a wanker, the sooner she got rid of him the better." Francesca's emotions now burst and she couldn't hold her in any longer, she stood to her feet.

"Well I know I've been a dickhead with him, but it's too late now I'm pregnant, and guess what?" her body was folding up where she stood and her face sank as she threw her hands out in front of her. "He doesn't want me or the baby, so yes, you're right. He's a no good bastard." Her aunt watched as Francesca turned to leave the room, she quickly ran behind her.

"Well don't think you're staying here with a bastard baby. Gordon is right for once in his fucking life, fancy thinking you can look after a baby, are you having a laugh or what". She held her head back and laughed in a sarcastic tone. "You can't even look after yourself, never mind a fucking baby." Francesca screamed as she ran up the stairs trying to get out of the way of her, but as she turned her head, she could see her following. Francesca threw herself onto the bed as Sylvia flung open the bedroom door behind her. She was lived and looked white in the face. Bending down towards the bed, she rammed her fingers into Francesca's head.

"Well lady, you better find yourself somewhere else to live, because you won't be staying here a minute longer." She backed away from her now and stood nearby with her hands held on her hips. "How many times have I warned you about using protection? You just think you know it all, don't you? Well look at the mess you're in now missus fucking know it all. You're a silly little bitch!" she was back in her face now and looked furious. Francesca was pulling the covers over her face for protection but Sylvia grabbed at them and screamed into her face. "You have until the end of the week to find yourself somewhere else to live because after that you are on the streets. I've wiped my hands of you and want nothing more to do with you." Francesca didn't reply because she knew her auntie wouldn't think twice about hitting her. She remained silent and hid her head under her pillow until Sylvia left the room. The bedroom door slammed and nearly came off its hinges. Francesca could still hear her shouting insults as she went downstairs.

Dragging her hands at her hair, tears rolled down her cheeks. "Fuck fuck, fuck," she whispered under her breath.

Francesca waited eagerly for the reply from Gordon. When she finally saw the white envelope addressed to her on the hall floor, her heart missed a beat. It had been nearly a week since she wrote to him and she thought he was never going to reply. Slowly she picked the letter up and ran upstairs holding it tightly in her grip. Francesca didn't open it straight away, she knew whatever was written in the letter would change her life forever. She was praying he'd written how sorry he was for the things he'd said and how much he really loved her. Her days with a roof over her head were numbered and in two days time she would be homeless.

Slowly she sat on the side of the bed. Her fingers peeled the letter open and she began to read it. At the top of the page it stated his prison number and the address of the prison. His handwriting stared at her and she sighed deeply as she began to read his words.

'Francesca,

I still stand by everything I've said to you. Get rid of the baby and everything will be fine between us. The decision is yours, but either way I'll never be a father to this baby, and I'll never call it my child.'

Francesca sobbed her heart out as she read on; she knew there would be no point in trying to change his mind now, it was obvious his mind was made up. Gordon was a very stubborn man and once his mind was made up he wouldn't change it for love nor money. Francesca ripped his letter into tiny pieces and launched it on the floor. "Bastard, cunt, bastard!" she sobbed. His words were harsh and not once had he said that he loved her. This was a time in her life when she felt so alone and didn't have anyone to turn too. Dark days lay ahead of Francesca and she knew that more than anyone, she just hoped she could find the inner strength to fight her way through.

True to her word, Sylvia threw her niece onto the streets. Francesca went to the homeless shelter for help; she was at her wits end. The place itself wasn't that bad but Francesca couldn't wait until she was settled in her own place. The people at the homeless accommodation were very helpful and told her they would help her furnish her new home and help the best they could once they found her somewhere permanent to live.

Lots of young women were residents in the refuge. Some had two or three kids with them. Looking at all the different characters, Francesca knew they all had stories to tell and couldn't wait to find out why they had all ended up in this situation. One woman sat with Francesca in the family room and told her of her fight to leave her violent husband. As Francesca looked closely at the woman, she could see dark blue bruises all over her arms. The woman told her there was a new place that had just opened that helped people just like her. She told her that the people who ran it were very good and very understanding. "I tried that place first before I come here." The woman whispered as her eyes shot to the door making sure no one was listening. She went on to tell her that the people there were very helpful and phoned around all the homeless sites in Manchester to make sure she got somewhere to stay. The woman pulled a small piece of paper from her pocket and passed it to Francesca. "Here's the address of it, if you ever get stuck again." Francesca folded the small piece of white paper and slid it into her pocket. The woman told Francesca all about her life, she held nothing back.

This was the first time the woman had ever been without her husband in many years, and she felt petrified of starting her life again. She told Francesca she had been married for thirteen years and for most of them, she'd been unhappy. Her husband treated her like a slave and beat her regularly until finally she couldn't take it anymore. The woman lowered her voice as she spoke. "My nerves have been playing up lately, and I wasn't thinking straight at the time. It's the best thing I've ever done leaving that worthless piece of shit. I could kick myself now when I look back at what I put up with." The woman raised her eyes to the ceiling and folded her arms in front of her. "Well, let's see him cope now on his own. I hope the dirty fucker rots in hell for what he's put me through." The woman smiled as she lit a cig and offered Francesca one. She looked about fifty years old and her frail figure made her look anorexic. Her hair was thin and you could see her scalp through her fine red hair.

Life in the homeless accommodation was hard for the first week. Francesca found it hard to settle but she had no other choice but to hold out until they finally offered her a house. She thought of going back to her aunt's and begging her for forgiveness, but she knew deep down that her mind would already be made up and her decision would be final. Francesca had called round to her auntie's a few days before and Sylvia had flung her mail at her. She told her to get her address changed as quickly as possible because she didn't want people thinking she still lived there. Francesca's mother had also left a message and Sylvia couldn't wait to tell her. "You're mam said never to darken her doorstep again. You're a disgrace to the family she said." Francesca didn't reply and stood looking at her aunt. She'd never got on with her in the past and the message from her mother was like water off a duck's back.

Francesca's mood was low as she walked upstairs to her designated room in the refuge. The smell of the place reminded her of wet dogs. The building itself must have been a hundred years old, as the ceilings were massive and the old cornice was still in place. The temporary accommodation had three flights of stairs and Francesca's room was right at the top. As she held the wooden banister to walk up the stairs, she could hear the noise of people talking from different rooms. The sounds she heard were people who were just like her, people who were at their wit's end and had nowhere else to go. The screams from a small child suddenly made her stop dead in her tracks. Shaking her head she knew parenthood was going to be hard. As she reached her room, a woman stood smoking a cig at the opposite end of the corridor, she was leaning out through an open window. Francesca smiled and tried to be pleasant, but the woman looked stony faced and carried on smoking with her back turned away from her.

Opening the door to her room, Francesca froze. The room was a shit tip and a million miles away from the house she'd just came from. Slowly she edged inside the door. The room felt cold and small goose-pimples started to appear on her skin, rubbing her hands slowly she plonked onto the bed. Her eyes were all over the place. The bedsit was small and the cornice was painted a soft yellow colour. The wallpaper at the top of the ceiling was peeling off due to the damp and as she looked closer, she could see black fungus growing all over it. The accommodation had a small window on the back wall. The only view was of an alleyway and nothing worthwhile could be seen from it. Francesca sat thinking on the bed and then she remembered the letters she'd picked up from her auntie's. Reaching over to her plastic bags at the side of her she searched for the letters. Her eyes scanned at each letter in detail. The one that took her interest was handwritten; she immediately recognized Gordon's handwriting. Her heart raced as she sat up on the bed just staring at the letter. "What the fuck does he want?" She mumbled. Half of her wanted to rip it open as quickly as could be and the other half wanted her to leave it sealed forever. Taking a deep breath Francesca lit a cig and stared at it, her fingers were itching to open it.

Francesca lifted the letter to her nose, her nostrils flaring as she inhaled deeply. As she started to read it, her hands trembled as she tried to make sense of it, her face looked confused. She was gasping her breath as she read each word over and over again. Gordon had written that he wanted her to move in with his brother Tom until his release date. Francesca felt mixed emotions about the letter and didn't know what Gordon was playing at. As she read the words again, she realised that Gordon now wanted her and the baby. He told her in the letter that he'd been so mixed up at the time that he couldn't think straight. Francesca stared about the room and thought about the prospects of moving in with Tom. He wasn't the cleanest of blokes, she knew that, but it was better than being in the homeless shelter, surely. Francesca decided the following day she would go and see Tom and see what he thought of her moving in with him. A smile filled Francesca's face as she pulled the bedclothes over her body. Things were looking up at last.

Tom was a funny kind of bloke, but she got on well with him and didn't seem to mind his filthy habits. Tom was a drug addict and he'd been using heroin for many years. The drugs ruled his life and Francesca knew she'd have to make sure her few possessions were always locked away from him if she ever decided to moved in with him; he was a thieving bastard without a shadow of a doubt. Gordon had put a visiting order in the letter he'd sent to Francesca and wanted her to come and see him as soon as possible. Her body melted onto the worn mattress, her head spun with thoughts and her heart started beating again knowing that Gordon still loved her.

Francesca tossed and turned all night long as she heard a child crying its eyes out in the next room. His mother was trying to comfort him but she finally lost her temper and smacked him, leaving him in a worse state than before. Francesca checked the clock on the wall and her eyes squinted together as she tried to make out the time. She was wide-awake now and thought about her next visit with Gordon. Tom's name was also on the visiting order and she felt safe knowing someone would be there to comfort her if he started his usual abuse.

The time came for Francesca to leave the council's accommodation and she started to gather her few belongings together. All her possessions could now be contained inside three plastic bags. As she stared at them, she looked sad. Three bags of clothing were all she had to show for her life. Francesca knew she had to change her life from this day forward and she hoped moving in with Tom would help get her back on her feet again. Making her way to the small stainless steel sink, she washed her tired face. Dipping her head into it she splashed the icy cold water all over her skin trying to make herself feel clean. The bed she'd slept in the night before had left her feeling itchy and dirty. She was constantly scratching at her head and arms.

Francesca said goodbye to the people in charge and thanked them for their help. They'd offered her breakfast but she refused, as she wanted to get to Tom's as soon as possible. Her stride quickened once she hit the fresh air. She set off towards Collyhurst flats where Tom lived. Her fingers started to throb as she carried her belongings and she prayed her journey would end soon.

## Chapter Four

The flat where Tom lived was on the twelfth storey. They faced a local shopping precinct called Eastford Square in Manchester. Francesca raised her head as she approached the tower block searching for any sign of him. Opening the main door to the building, she headed for the lift. The stench in the entrance made her gag. It smelt of piss and she could actually see puddles of urine as she walked in. Her nostrils were flared as she pulled her coat up over her nose to avoid the rancid smell. Her scrawny fingers pressed the dirt ridden button in the lift and she waited eagerly for the doors to close. It seemed to take forever and that was when a notice caught her eye, placed on the nearby wall.

'OUT OF ORDER'

Her temper was about to explode and she felt like life wasn't worth living anymore. "For fucks sake!" she ranted under her breath. As she entered the stairwell, she could see light fittings hanging down from the ceiling and loads of graffiti scrawled across the walls. As she looked up, the grey concrete staircase seemed to go on forever. Francesca was breathless when she reached the fifth floor; she promised herself that she would have to stop smoking, because her chest was wheezing. Taking a minute, she held her hands on her knees and dipped her head. Sucking in mouthfuls of air she blew from her mouth. Reaching the twelfth floor Francesca was in tears, as if life wasn't stressful enough without the lifts being out of order, she looked at the end of her tether. Placing her bags on the floor she wiped the sweat from her brow with her sleeve. "Thank fuck for that." she sighed. Music was being played loudly as she stood at the front door. Rapping the letter box several times she knew she'd have to shout. Her knees slowly bent down as she shoved her mouth inside the silver grubby letter box.

"Tom!" she yelled at the top of her voice. She continued shouting him three or four times but still no one came. Francesca hammered her clenched fist at the door and nearly smashed the glass window. Eventually she could see the shadow of a man making his way to the front door.

"Fucking hell! What ya knocking like that for. I thought it was the dibble ya daft cunt." Tom walked slowly back into the living room wearing nothing but his piss-stained boxer shorts. He kept walking and shouted behind him for Francesca to hurry up and get her arse inside the flat before she let all the heat out. Tom walked into the living room and turned the music down. His puny body plonked across the shabby settee. His eyes pointed at a chair at the side of him and he nodded at Francesca for her to sit down. Tom's skin was like a pint of milk and all his ribs could be seen sticking out from his rib cage. She couldn't help but notice the dark bruises running up his arms. Her face screwed up as she focused on the collapsed purple track marks. Flinging her body onto the chair, she released her bags from her grip and stretched them out to ease the pain. As she looked at Tom again, she couldn't help but notice one of his bollocks hanging out of his boxers. She tried not to look, but this hairy prune was looking straight at her and she found it hard to conceal her amusement. Tom reached for his tobacco and started to roll a cig for himself and Francesca. Passing her one he stretched his arms above his head and he scratched his knackers. .

"Get the kettle on then," he chuckled as he sniffed the hand that had been down the front of his boxers..

Francesca laughed, "Fuck off, you do it. I've just climbed twelve flights of stairs, I'm done in." Tom sneered at her as he passed her a cig.

"Here get this, my new pad mate," he laughed loudly and started to tell Francesca about his orders from Gordon to look after her. Sitting up from his horizontal position he sucked his lips around his cig and blew a big cloud of smoke out in front of him.

"Ay, our Gordon's given me loads of rules for you to abide by. He's like a fuckin sergeant major. He said no going out with ya mates, no drinking, and that you have to suck my cock whenever I ask." Francesca nearly choked on her cig as Tom tried to keep a straight face.

"Nar seriously he said if I need anything like a suck or a wank, just to ask you." Francesca huffed as she looked at the bean sprout frame of the man in front of her. Tom had always had a great sense of humour and despite his drug use, he was a top lad. She now faced him and sat forward in her chair, leaning towards him.

"Listen mate, I won't be sucking any cocks. So get that thought right out of ya mind. Anyway if it's anything like ya brothers it would get caught in between my teeth so don't bother." Tom and Francesca laughed together as she kicked her shoes off and threw her legs over the arm of the chair. After she stubbed her cig out, she headed into the kitchen to make them both a brew.

Entering the kitchen she was gob-smacked at the state of it. Pots and pans were piled high in the sink and the smell from the cooker made her heave. The flooring was all ripped apart and you could barely see the pattern on it. The wallpaper was brown with grease and all the tiles around the sink were covered in splashes of food and other mysterious liquids, it was disgusting. Scraping her finger along the filthy work top she screwed her face up.

"Fuckin hell Tom!" she yelled, "It looks like a bomb has hit it in here. When was the last time you cleaned up ya scruffy twat." He now came to the kitchen door, he looked angry.

"Why what's fuckin up with it? I cleaned up last night you cheeky bastard." Francesca tutted as she filled the battered kettle up with water. The kettle had layers of grease all over it and she knew at that moment that she wouldn't be having a brew, at least not until the place was cleaned up properly. Searching the sink she finally found a cup and rescued it from the filth. The cup was supposed to be white, but as she looked closer, it had dark circles inside, it was a disgrace and should have been thrown straight into the bin.

"You're such a scruffy bastard, Tom. How the fuck you're not dead with all these germs amazes me. You must have some strong kick arse immune system to fight them off, because I know I would surely be dead if I ate anything cooked in this shit hole." Tom rubbed his head, and felt a little embarrassed but he defended himself well as he spoke.

"Ay! Ya cheeky bitch. If ya don't like it fuck off to where you've come from and see if ya life's any better there, because from what I've heard you don't even have a place to live at the moment do ya. So shut the fuck up?" Francesca knew she'd hit a nerve with Tom and tried to make it into a joke hoping he would calm down.

"I'm just saying you need a woman's touch around this place that's all. So don't ya get on ya high fucking horse with me?" Tom headed back into the front room mumbling under his breath. The music was turned back on and Francesca was deafened by his tunes. Plonking himself back on to the sofa he tapped his feat to the beat of the music and nodded his head.

Francesca felt like she was treading on eggshells as she returned, because Tom had a face like thunder as he lay on the settee. She passed him his brew and he barely raised a smile as he took it from her grip. The room was filled with music and Francesca couldn't hear herself think. Waving her hand to get Tom's attention she mouthed her words. "Will ya turn it down, my head's banging." Tom pressed the remote for the stereo; his finger kept tapping at the button until the volume was turned down completely. The room was quiet now and you could have heard a pin drop. Francesca sucked on her lips and finally broke the silence, hoping to build bridges with her house mate.

"So has Gordon told you you're going to be an uncle?"

Tom's faced changed instantly and a smile filled his face as he turned to face her. "Yeah, I'm buzzin' for ya. Hope it's a lad yanno then it can carry on the family's name innit."

Tom looked surprisingly handsome as he smiled at her, and for the first time she noticed his sparkling eyes. They were so much like Gordon's and they twinkled like stars as he spoke. His hair looked untidy and he was in desperate need of a haircut. Francesca already knew he had a girlfriend but as far as she was concerned it was an on-off relationship and had been like that for as long as she could remember. They both sat chatting for a while and sorted out which room was going to be Francesca's and the baby's when it was finally born. As her eyes scanned round, she knew that everywhere would need a good clean before the baby came along and planned to start as soon as she got the chance. Tom started to look very edgy and small droplets of sweat started to fill his forehead. His words were slurred and she could tell something was wrong with him.

"What's up with you? Are you okay?" Francesca asked in a concerned voice. Tom managed to stand to his feet and looked into the mirror. Looking at his face he knew his Lord and master was calling him again for yet another fix. Scraping his hand across his head he blew a laboured breath.

"I need to score. I don't supposed you've got any money till I get my giro have you?" Francesca shook her head slowly. Her heart went out to him as she watched him roasting. Gathering all his clothes together from the chair, he started to get ready as quick as he could.

"Well looks like it's a walk to Conran Street market for me then innit. See what I can have away." She watched him quivering as he got ready to leave. Her heart went out to him knowing he couldn't survive without the heroin his body craved.

Tom had been addicted to smack for as long as she could remember. At first, he thought he could just take it every now and then, but the drug got a grip of him without any warning and took over his whole life. He secretly wished he could get off the gear but no matter how hard he tried, he always found himself looking for the next fix. His girlfriend didn't help any, she was also a bag head. He didn't mind at first because she shoplifted to fund her own habit and always made sure he got a share of the proceeds. As time went on, he'd told her he wanted to get off the drugs, but she always made sure the temptation was right in front of him knowing he couldn't refuse his body's craving.

People thought of Tom as a low life and he was known all over the place. Every time he walked the streets in Harpurhey, someone could be heard shouting 'smack head' from a distance. It was mainly the young kids who shouted after him. He always tried to ignore them but it cut him up deep inside. Tom had done some bad things while he was on drugs and often felt ashamed of what he'd become. His mother never had time for him before his addiction, so when she found out he was a prisoner to heroin he was shunned from the family home and warned never to come near the front door again. Tom's mother hated the thought of her neighbours talking about her and when they saw him in the area they would always make sure everything was locked up out of the way as they knew he wouldn't think twice about robbing from them. He'd stolen from his own family in the past; nothing was safe when he was around.

Tom pulled his grey padded shoplifting coat from the side of the chair. The jacket had loads of different pockets in it and made him look twice the size he really was.

He told Francesca he would be home later and to do whatever she wanted while he was out. He didn't wait for a reply and slammed the door behind him.

Francesca sat staring at four walls for a few minutes before she decided to try to clean the place up. Cups were scattered all about the living room and ashtrays were over flowing with cig ends. The front room was small and the furniture in it was old and worn. Francesca knew she'd have a task in front of her but she couldn't stand living in a shit tip. She walked in every room and looked at the job in front of her. As she opened the toilet door, the stench hit the back of her throat and she heaved. She could see the toilet hadn't been flushed and a big turd was sticking out of the pot. Francesca wretched as she covered her face with her hands and rushed to flush the toilet. As she did, she noticed that the newspaper that someone had used to wipe their arse on was causing a blockage. She tried one last time to flush it before she finally gave up. The smell had made her feel sick and she decided she'd wait until Tom returned for him to tackle it.

Francesca gathered what cleaning materials she could find and started cleaning the front room. She pulled the big cushions from the settee and started to sweep the food and bits and bobs from it. The settee was red velour and the arms were ripped from wear and tear. She'd always been good with a needle and cotton and decided later on she would fix them and try to make them look half-decent. The carpet on the floor was red patterned with gold flowers running through it, it smelt like something rotten. She yanked the carpet from the floor and seen it had vinyl tiles underneath it. Surely, they would be better than the stinking carpet she thought and started on the quest to pull the rest of it up. Once she started cleaning, she got stuck right in. She removed the stained netted curtains from the windows and wiped the furniture with some pine gel she found in the back of the kitchen cupboard. Once the carpet was up from the floor, she rolled it all together and dragged it into the lobby for Tom to shift when he came home later. The floor was swept and mopped and the place already looked so much better, she looked about and was proud of the changes she'd made. Francesca went on to strip all the beds and placed quilts covers into the washer hoping to free them from the cheesy smell of Tom's feet. The bedroom which Tom said was hers was probably the worst in the house. Car radios were scattered around it and magazines were spread across the floor. She'd even found old used syringes left scattered about. The curtains were closed in the room and once she opened them, the true state of the place was visible and she nearly fainted with the shock. "Scruffy twat," she whispered under her breath. Francesca could have sworn she'd saw a mouse run across the room, but couldn't be sure if her eyes were playing tricks on her. "Where the fuck do I start", she sighed, as she tried to move all the clothing from the double bed where she sat.

Francesca was on a mission and carried on cleaning until darkness fell. She'd hung all the bedding and curtains on the balcony outside and watched as they swung freely on the piece of rope that was the washing line. She hoped Tom would appreciate her efforts when he returned; she's worked her arse off. All the rubbish was placed in black bags and dragged to the front door. There was one other job left for Tom when he came in and that was to sort the toilet out, and then that would be the house completely cleaned. The bedding and curtains were ready within the hour and once they were dried, she put them back in place. Her body now collapsed onto the settee she felt completely exhausted and needed a rest. Francesca must have nodded off as she snuggled up on the sofa and it wasn't until she heard the voice of Tom's girlfriend Jade laughing that she woke up.

"Fuckin hell, Cinderella has really gone to town on this place. It looks so fucking clean."

Francesca lifted her head and met Jade's eyes as she stood next to her. "Fuck me; what drugs have you been on? I've tried so many times to clean this place and it never looks any fucking different."

Francesca smiled as Tom stood in disbelief looking all about the front room. He seemed stuck for words and walked round the rest of house looking at all the work she'd done. Francesca sat up and Jade came to join her on the settee.

"Fuckin hell, Tom looks like he's gonna cry doesn't he?" Jade laughed as she lit a cig. She'd been right about Tom because when he returned he looked choked up with emotion. He sat in the chair and looked at Francesca with an emotional look in his eyes.

"You've made this place look mint. I've always wanted a nice clean place but things have just got on top of me lately and I've let things slip." Francesca felt a little embarrassed and told him she was glad he liked it. Jade watched them both and noticed how they looked at each other. Jealousy gripped her instantly and she looked sick inside. Jade took an instant dislike to Francesca knowing she could be a threat to her relationship with Tom. Jade's head pumped with sweat as she pulled swag from the big shopping bag in front of her. The bag was black and white and had two wooden handles to support the weight it was carrying. She placed everything she'd nicked onto the small wooden table and smiled at Francesca. Within minutes, the table was covered with razor blades, packets of bacon, cheese, and several electric toothbrushes. Jade went through them all adding up how much they would get off each item. In her head she calculated that they should earn at least thirty quid from the stolen goods. Jade pulled her fat arse up from the chair and told them she was going to the Two Hundred Pub in Harpurhey to sell her knock off stuff. This was usual for Jade after she had been out grafting. People would wait all day until she came in the pub to grab their bargains at rock bottom prices. As she neared the front door, she shouted to Tom that she would get the gear on the way back but he didn't reply, his eyes were focused on Francesca. Once the door was shut Francesca asked Tom what gear Jade was getting, thinking it might be something for tea, because she was starving. Tom dipped his head and looked to the floor as he spoke.

"She means smack. That's what Jade does once she's sold everything." Francesca stared at him with sympathetic eyes and began to speak hoping he might listen to what she had to say.

"Tom, why don't you try and get off that shit. I know what it's like being addicted to drugs. I was on sniff before Gordon got put away and it got a grip of me too, I can tell ya. Can't you go to the doctors and get some methadone and wean yourself off it. That's what a lad done that I know?"

Tom looked at her and knew she was talking sense. Roasting was every drug addicts nightmare and he was nowhere near ready to put himself through the torment of sleepless nights and vomiting and shaking. Cracking his knuckles he tried to defend himself.

"I do want to get off the shit, but I'm not fucking ready yet. I don't think I could get through it on my own though and I know Jade wouldn't help me." Francesca felt a warm feeling run through her body as she sat listening to him. The man just needed support and she was more than willing to help him.

"Tom you're not on your own. I'm here now and I'll help ya. You're gonna be an uncle soon. Do ya want the baby to see you like this?" What she said hit a nerve with Tom and he knew she was right but for now, he changed the conversation unable to deal with the earache from her.

Time passed quickly and they enjoyed getting to know each other. Tom munched on a bar of chocolate he'd found on the side. With a gob full of food he spoke to Francesca "What day are we gonna see our kid? Have you booked a visit yet?"

Francesca had forgotten all about booking the visit, her face was white and she struggled to speak. "Orr fucking hell, I'll have to do it tomorrow now, he's gonna go mad isn't he?"

Tom chuckled. "Fuck him, what's another day gonna do, he's not going anywhere is he?"

Francesca looked relieved, "Yeah you're right, I'll just say there were no visits left."

"Problem solved." Tom giggled. Francesca started to tell Tom about what Gordon had said to her regarding the baby at first, but stopped dead in mid-conversation as she heard the front door open. They both listened carefully and they could hear Jade returning.

Jade walked in the front room, her face was dripping in sweat. She gave Tom the eyes to follow her into the bedroom. Francesca knew she'd brought drugs back into the house and presumed they were both going for a fix. Filled with disgust she left them to it and shouted to them both that she was going to the chippy. She held her last fiver in her hand and knew food was a priority as she felt weak. Francesca shouted to Tom and Jade in the bedroom if they wanted anything from the chippy. Jade opened the bedroom door and handed her a tenner.

"Get me and Tom chips and gravy each will ya and make sure they put loads of salt and vinegar on it." Francesca could see Tom slapping his arm through the bedroom door, he was getting ready to inject. She quickly hurried away and cringed at the sight of Tom getting his fix. As she grabbed her coat, she shouted to them that she wouldn't be long, they never replied.

Francesca felt alone and lonely. Her family had disowned her and the one true friend she had was lost due to her own jealousy. She'd always thought that sleeping with Gordon was wrong, and wondered if somehow this was her punishment for the way she'd treated Misty. She'd been a good friend to Francesca and she knew in her heart she'd never find a best friend like her again. Sadness twisted inside her as her eyes filled with sorrow. Francesca zipped her coat up as she came out of the flats. The night was cold and there was a winter chill in the air. Kids were shouting in the distance and it was obvious they were up to no good.

The take away was packed as she reached it. A few youths stood inside it and she could tell they were pissed by the way they were acting. As she watched them closer, she noticed one lad looking her up and down. He looked around seventeen years of age and was dressed in a black Nike tracksuit. Francesca smirked as she looked at the group of youths because the dress code was all the same.

Black trackie bottoms, black coats, and they all wore similar baseball caps. This was the dress code for most teenagers these days and they all held that teenage attitude spread right across their faces.

Francesca felt the stare of one of the young lad and turned to face him. As she looked at him closer, she noticed he was the younger brother of a lad she used to see years ago. Before she could speak, the youth started bouncing round shouting insults at her.

"Dirty Francesca. I thought I fuckin recognized you. Are you still shagging anything with a pulse, ya fucking dirty slag?" All his mates were laughing out loud and she felt her face burning with embarrassment. The teenager had caught her off guard and she knew she had to fight back quickly before he got the better of her. The other customers in the queue all stood staring at her, waiting to see what she was going to say. Francesca placed one hand on her hip and screwed her face up as she defended herself.

"Ay, ya little nobhead, shouldn't you be in bed at this time. Stop showing off in front of ya mates before I tell them about you pissing the bed every fucking night." Francesca looked at him and could tell he was angry as all his mates started laughing. "Ar pissy arse" his side kick shouted at him. Everyone in the chippy laughed knowing the yob had met his match. He bounced out of the take away holding his chips and curry in his hand and shouted more abuse at her.

"Ay! Everyone listen up. If anyone wants a quick gobble, Francesca is the girl for the job; she sucks two at a time and is up for anything. She's like a fucking rabbit, her nicknames sperm bank. So if you want to make a deposit, get a grip of her." Francesca turned to him and laughed as he left. "Little pick" she snarled as she watched him leave. One of the other customers loved the way she'd stood up for herself and couldn't wait to tell her.

"Tell ya what love; you shut that dickhead up big time. I wish I could speak to the cheeky fuckers like that, but I know they would probably hit me or something." Francesca smiled and told the woman he was a cheeky little twat and too gobby for his own good.

Francesca was finally served and left the chippy. As she stepped, she scanned the area for the lads but couldn't see them anywhere. She looked relieved and she carried on her journey home, looking forward to her scran. The night was quiet and just a few cars were on the road. She thought it might be quicker to take a short cut through the local park and changed her direction to save time. As she walked, she could hear shouting in the distance but never gave it a second thought. The area she lived in was well known for gang fights and people arguing. This was just another normal night in the area. Francesca's steps quickened as she reached the park, it was only then that she saw the gang of lads from earlier.

Francesca tried to cut through without bringing any attention to herself, but the youth spotted her and within seconds was by her side. His hands were held out in front of him and he was ramming his finger into her face.

"Think you're smart do ya? Well have that you dirty twat." Francesca could feel her face burning as the teenager rubbed his chips and curry into her face. His grip was strong and he held it there until he heard her screaming out with pain. Francesca finally managed to push his hand away from her face.

"Bastard," she screamed. She could see all his friends laughing, as they looked at her face covered in curry. The cocky teenager still wasn't satisfied with her humiliation and swung a punch right into the side of her face before he finally ran off. Her heartbeat quickened and she felt like she was going to die as she struggled to get her words out.

"You little fucker. You daft twat, just wait till I get my hands on you. Ya fucking little wanker." The lad continued to run, shouting more insults and laughing with his mates. She could feel her face burning and her eye immediately started to swell up. Nobody had come to help her during the attack and even the people who'd stood by and witnessed it just walked by without a care in the world. That was the trouble these days, no one wanted to get involved. The generation of youths were ruthless and wouldn't think twice about attacking anybody who stuck their noses in where it didn't belong.

Francesca found the plastic bag containing her food. All the gravy had seeped off the trays and was floating around in the bottom of the bag. She kept holding her hand onto her face, it looked on fire.

Francesca felt so helpless. She felt tired and if she didn't eat soon she felt she would collapse where she stood. Seeing the block of flats in front of her made her feel safe. She seemed to have been walking for hours. As she entered the building, she remembered the lift was broken, and that was the straw that broke the camel's back. Francesca entered the stairwell and her body dropped onto the cold concrete stairs. Her eyes poured out weeks of stored up emotion and once she started, she cried like she'd never cried before. Francesca had always been such a tough nut, and nothing had ever bothered her. These last few weeks had been so hard and she felt like she was sinking into a black hole with no escape. Every stair she climbed seemed like twenty and by the time she reached the top floor she could hardly move. Her trembling hands knocked at the door and within seconds, Jade opened it like a starving animal.

"Fuckin hell. Where ya been, I'm starving, bet its fuckin cold now. What the fuck took ya so long anyway?" Her words made Francesca see red and she opened fire, stopping at nothing.

"Listen ya lazy bitch. I've been ages because some nobhead in the chippy just attacked me. So next time you want something to eat, get off ya fuckin lazy arse and go ya self." Jade looked at her and her face told her how angry she was. She just gripped the food off her and went into the kitchen mumbling under her breath. Jade looked at the food and wanted to complain about all the gravy floating about in the bottom of the bag, peering back into the front room she knew to keep her mouth shut.

Francesca walked towards the bathroom and noticed Tom lay on the bed with the syringe still stuck in his arm. He looked as if he was just staring into space and his body was lifeless. She retched at the sight of him and couldn't get to the bathroom fast enough.

The cold air in the bathroom made her shake as she threw up into the toilet bowl. Nothing was coming up but her body still heaved all the same. Looking in the mirror, she could still traces of the curry on her skin and began to wash it off with a worn, discoloured face cloth. As she stood up from the toilet she hoped this wasn't the start of things to come, she hated being sick. Ever since she'd been a small child, she hated the thought of it. She started to remember when her mother used to rub her back and comfort her if she felt poorly but that was such a long time ago. At that moment, Francesca thought about her mam. She'd never missed her or needed her in her life until now. She'd have given her last penny to be at home with her parents and feeling loved.

Francesca made her way into the living room and Jade slid her food over to her. It was some sort of peace offering and she hoped she'd calmed down. Jade shouted Tom several times but he didn't answer. Francesca looked concerned but she told her that he was always like that after a hit and not to worry. Looking at her face, Francesca felt sick as she watched her ram her food into her mouth. Her eyes could barely focus on her fork and it seemed to take forever for her to get any food into her mouth. Francesca knew now that if she ever wanted to get Tom free from drugs she'd have to get rid of his girlfriend first. She was everything he didn't need in his life at the moment and she would always be a junkie.

Jade was a well known smack head and thief. Rumour had it that she would pull a few tricks down Cheetham Hill when she was on her arse. Cheetham Hill was a popular place for prostitutes and Gordon had once told Francesca he'd seen Jade stood there one night touting for business. Gordon never told his brother about it because he knew he would have been gutted. Jade's belly hung down between her legs as she sat on the edge of the chair. Francesca couldn't keep her eyes off it and wondered if this woman had ever seen her own fanny. She looked like a big butch lesbian and her hairstyle didn't help her look either. It was kind of a crew cut with a big greasy fringe splattered across her forehead. Her skin was dirty and round her mouth were big yellow inflamed spots. As Francesca looked at her closer, she couldn't help but think that she had the spots through sucking dirty cock down Cheetham Hill. Jade was a total wreck and Francesca wondered what Tom ever saw in her.

Jade seemed to be staring at Francesca, scraping her teeth with a finger nail she began to speak. "What you doing for money now Gordon is locked up?"

Francesca hunched her shoulders and rolled her eyes. "Nowt, I'm skint, I'm sick of not having a pot to piss in." Francesca's giro wasn't due for ages yet and she knew she would have to bum money from somewhere just to get her through until pay day. Jade was in deep in thought as she sat chewing on her lips.

"Why don't ya come out grafting with me? I'll do the work, you can just watch my back."

Francesca nearly choked. "What me, shoplifting? Fuck off; I would be shit at it. I've never nicked anything in my life. My face would give me away." Jade chuckled and rubbed her hands together thinking of a new business venture.

"Listen, you don't do anything. All ya do is block the camera when I'm shoving all the gear in my bag. Just lean over me as if you're getting something and before ya know it I'll be gone with the swag. What do ya think?" Francesca was fidgeting about and looked uncomfortable. Jade continued. "I think it's a great idea especially now you've got a baby on the way."

Francesca sighed deeply and told her she would think about it. "Me, a shoplifter? Fucking hell what next?" Jade faced dropped and she looked sad as she continued to speak. She flicked her fringe from her face and Francesca noticed a single tear trickling down her cheek.

"My two kids are in care you know. I haven't seen them for time now. It was the drugs that fucked me up. They got a grip of me big time and my kids suffered because of it. I know they're better off without me, but

I still can't stop thinking about them every fucking day."
Jade twisted her fingers about in front of her and looked
towards the ceiling. "Their dad was a right cunt and an
even a bigger smack head than me. He didn't give a shit
about his kids and fucking leathered me in front of them
most nights." Francesca wanted to go and comfort her
but she remained in her seat listening to every word she
said. "That's when social services got involved; when they
saw the state I was in they took the kids straight off me."
Francesca felt her heart breaking in two as she listened
to the sad story. Jade appeared so happy go lucky and she
didn't realise all the pain she held inside her heart.

Jade rolled two cigs from a crumpled packet of tobacco
that she pulled from her tracksuit pocket. Her hands were
shaking rapidly as she started to roll the first cigarette.
Her hands looked deformed, they looked purple and sore.
Francesca couldn't help but ask what was up with them.

"Fucking hell Jade, your hands are like balloons.
What's wrong with them?" Jade carried on rolling the
cigarette and didn't lift her head up as she answered her.

"It's the drugs love. I'm injecting into my hands
now and the bastards have become infected. My arms
are fucked. My veins have collapsed with all the shit I've
rammed into them over the years. Sad really isn't it?"
Francesca couldn't help but pull her face at the sight of
her hands, they were a mess.

"Why don't ya get off the brown then? Look what's
it's doing to you, you've lost ya kids and probably lost all
your self-respect haven't ya?" Jade's head sunk and you
could see she'd heard it all before. Francesca's words were
like water off a duck's back and Jade changed the subject
quickly without answering.

"Fucking Rip Van Winkle can't half sleep can't he? I

better go and see if he's getting up for summit to eat. Bet his chips are fucking freezing now."

Francesca watched her as Jade waddled back to the bedroom; she was picking her knickers from the crack of her arse. The woman she saw in front of her must have only been in her thirties but the life she'd chosen to lead had aged her. Such a crying shame, she thought as she heard Jade trying to wake Tom up.

The hours flew by and as Francesca sat watching telly, tiredness filled her body. She turned off all the lights in the front room and headed to bed. She just hoped she'd be able to sleep as her mind was doing over time.

## Chapter Five

Morning light crept through the bedroom window as Tom's hoarse coughing woke Francesca up. His cough was harsh and he sounded as if he was choking to death. Pulling the duvet over her head she tried hide herself away from the morning light. Tom could still be heard spluttering his guts up as he passed her bedroom door. He sounded like an old man who'd smoked a hundred cigs a day all his life.

Francesca lay awake now unable to fall back to sleep. She looked about the bedroom and knew that as soon as she got any money she'd decorate the room to her own taste. The wardrobe door was hanging off and nothing but a small hinge kept it in place. The whole room needed a revamp and she put it on her 'to do' list as soon as she got some cash. Francesca slid her hands onto her stomach and stroked the life growing inside her. Even though it was early days she could notice a big change in her waist size. Her breasts had doubled in size and they felt incredibly tender. Half of her was happy about the pregnancy and the other half felt sadness because without the baby, Gordon would still love her the way he used too. She had so many mixed feelings about him now. Did he really want the baby, or was he just keeping her sweet so she'd come and visit him in the nick? Time would tell, she thought. Francesca decided there and then that if she saw any signs of him not wanting the baby she would leave him to rot in jail and try to be as far away as possible by the time he was released.

Francesca felt her bladder ready to burst and made her way to the toilet. The smell inside it was still bad but not as rancid as the day before. Sitting on the toilet Francesca thought she would never stop pissing. It went on and on forever and just when she thought it was over another trickle would start again. The smell of toast filtering through the walls made her feel hungry. She could have eaten a scabby horse the way she felt. As she walked past the kitchen door Tom smiled at her and told her to go and sit down. "I'm making your breakfast, so park ya arse." he shouted to her. Making her way into the living room, she opened the balcony door and let some fresh air inside. Francesca turned the television on and pulled her legs up to her chest as she plonked onto the chair. Feeling the cold chill she yanked her t-shirt over her knees to keep warm as the cold air hit her bones. As she listened carefully, she could hear Tom stirring the cups of tea from inside the kitchen. Francesca felt happy that someone was making her breakfast for a change. Gordon had never did a tap for her in all the time she'd spent with him and he would often kick her out of bed each morning to make his breakfast, so this was a nice change for her.

Tom walked in carrying two brews in one hand and

a plate of toast in the other, you could tell by his face he was struggling as his steps quickened.

"Fucking hell quick, grab hold of the cups. They're burning my fucking fingers." Francesca pissed herself laughing as she sat up and tried to help release the cups from his looped fingers. As he bent down to the small table their eyes met and he smiled at her as she released the burning cups from his grip. Tom placed the toast on the middle of the table and told her to help herself. The pile of bread was massive and at least seven pieces made up the tower. Francesca smiled as she took a slice. The butter was dripping from it and it was still hot as she sunk her teeth into it.

"Fuckin hell watch ya fingers greedy bollocks." Tom joked as he watched her eat as if she'd been starved of food for days. Francesca looked embarrassed.

"I'm starving, can't you tell?" she sniggered. "It's this baby making me hungry all the time. Imagine what I'll be like in a few months. You'll have to put a bolt on the fridge to keep me out of it." Tom agreed and nodded his head. He folded his toast in half and shoved the lot into his mouth in one go. The television was low and Francesca was struggling to hear what was being said. She looked for the remote control and spotted it on the settee next to Tom. Without thinking, she bent over Tom and tried to grab it. Tom seized his opportunity for a bit of fun and grabbed her, tickling her wildly. She eventually fell across his lap and screamed for him to stop. Her laughter filled the room and she shook her body wildly trying to free herself from his grip. The fun only stopped when Jade entered the room with a look that could kill.

"What's fucking going on here then? You two have just woke me up, ya daft twats." Her face was red with anger and she never took her eyes off Francesca. Jade watched her return to her seat trying to straighten her t-shirt. Tom reached for his tobacco and avoided eye contact with Jade as he spoke.

"Fucking hell we're only have a bit of a laugh ya miserable fucker." Jade screwed her face up as she responded instantly.

"When was the last time you done anything like that with me?" She protested, waving her hands up and down in his face. "Am I too fucking fat for a bit of fun, ay love?" Tom giggled as he tried to make light of the matter knowing she'd seen her arse.

"Ay, I hope you're not getting jealous. Ya know I love you. It was only a bit of fun and if that's what you want." He now reached for Jade and started tickling her trying to make her laugh but she remained stern and pushed his hands away from her body. Tom stared at her and could see she was still upset and a full-blown argument started. Tom was shouting at the top of his voice.

"See, I try and have some fun with you, but you're a miserable cunt," Tom yelled louder, "you need to loosen up and chill out. To tell ya the truth I'm getting pissed off with your mood swings. One minute you're all right and the next you're in a world of your own. So you better sort it out, otherwise you can fuck right off." Jade's mouth was wide open and she couldn't believe Tom was treating her like this.

"I'm fuckin miserable because you sit on ya arse all day leaving me to go out grafting for your fucking drugs," Jade screamed as she thrust her finger into his face with tears in her eyes. "I must be a right nobhead putting up with you. Let's see where you'll get your drugs from when I'm gone." She stormed into the bedroom and slammed the door behind her as she left. Tom knew she was right and had to think quickly before she left. He quickly stood up, looked at Francesca, and turned his eyes towards the ceiling.

"Fucking women! I better go and see if she's all right. She gets like this sometimes and she blames it on missing her kids but I just think she's just a moody fucker." Tom hovered for a moment debating his next move. "Oh well, better see if she'll forgive me hadn't I?" Tom tried to break a smile as he left. He slowly closed the door behind him so Francesca couldn't hear his quest for forgiveness.

As he entered the bedroom, Jade was slumped on the bed with her face hidden away. He could hear her sobbing into the pillow. This was something Tom was used to and he knew exactly what he have to do to bring her round. Sitting on the bed next to her, his hand stroked the side of her head; she tried to shrug him off. "Fuck off will you," she moaned.

"Jade, ya know I love ya. You're my special girl and I don't want ya to leave me. It was only a bit of fun. Francesca was down in the dumps and I was only trying to cheer her up. Fucking hell, it's my brother's bird and she's pregnant." He gripped her shoulder to try and see her face. "She means nothing to me; she's not a patch on you." Jade rolled over and her face was wet with tears. Her lips quivered as she started to speak.

"Do ya fancy her? Because if you do. I'll leave right now. I know I'm a big fat twat, so I don't blame ya if ya do. I just don't want it thrown in my face." Tom reached for her, and pulled her close as he kissed her forehead. He knew he'd have to lick arse and try to make her feel special if she was going to stay. He began to speak with softness in his voice.

"Jade, how could I not love you? You're the best thing that has ever happened to me. You look after me and no one will ever take your place." Her eyes lit up and she looked at him wanting him to continue. "I know it's been hard for you. I can't imagine what you're going through. Your kids will come and find you as soon as they're old enough." She put her head into Tom's chest and held him close. At that moment, Tom knew he'd won her over and his panic stopped. "Come on love, I've made some toast. I'll do ya a nice brew to go with it if ya want." He quickly grabbed her hand and pulled her from the bed. "Come on, let's get you something to eat, my princess."

Tom went straight into the kitchen and Jade returned to the front room. When she entered, she shot a look Francesca and felt quite embarrassed about her previous behaviour. Francesca passed her a cig and that helped break the atmosphere. Francesca lit her own cig and passed the lighter to Jade. She smiled softly at her hoping she'd calmed down.

"Sorry about before Jade, but it was only a bit of a laugh. If ya want me to leave, I will ya know." Jade felt stupid at what had just happened, and tried to make a joke out of the matter. She held her head back and chuckled.

"Oh don't you worry about it. He always gets a bit cocky in front of people. He's apologised now and told me how much he loves me." Jade watched Francesca's face as she continued to tell her exactly what Tom had said in the bedroom. It was her way of telling the little bitch to keep her hands off her man. Jade knew in the future she'd have to watch her every move with Tom because she could sense the attraction between them both. She'd met her sort many times before and it would only be a matter of time before she tried to get her claws into her man. Jade was ready for whatever she had up her sleeve and once Francesca made her move on Tom she would land on her like a ton of bricks. Jade sat with a cunning smirk across her face, nodding her head slowly.

Tom walked back into the front room smiling as he carried a cup in his hands, he passed it to Jade. As she turned her head to place the drink on the table Tom stuck two fingers up behind her head causing Francesca to smile from cheek to cheek. The conversation started again when he sat down and they began to plan the day ahead. Tom rubbed his hands together.

"Right we need some cash today ladies, so who's up for doing a few runs on Conran Street market. There's a few new stallholders on there who don't know me so it should be quite easy to do a graft today." Tom was a well-known thief on the market and he'd got quite friendly with a few stallholders. It was funny because they all made deals with Tom, that if he kept away from their stalls, they would tell him who the new people were on the market. That way he'd be able to clear them out within minutes without them even noticing. Jade slowly sipped her drink and threw her legs onto the settee across Tom's body. She watched Tom's face as she spoke.

"I'm gonna take Francesca out with me today and show her the ropes. She's a fresh face and she'll take the heat off me once I've put my disguise on and that." Jade had been arrested many times before and all the shops knew her face well. She had many disguises and wigs that she would put on to go out shoplifting and even Tom didn't recognise her when she had her stuff on. Francesca felt them both looking at her waiting for a reaction. She fidgeted about on the chair pretending she was looking for a hair clip and hoped they'd leave her alone, but she knew by their faces the conversation hadn't finished there. Jade asked the question again and she felt pressured to answer.

"Me! Shoplifting? Behave! I'd be so on top. My face would give me away, straight away, you're better off on ya own." Jade scowled at her and knew she had to work her magic. Shoplifting was getting harder day by day and she desperately needed to raise some cash for the drugs her body craved. Jade bent her body over the arm of the chair and looked straight into Francesca's eyes.

"Listen love you'll be fine, I'll look after you. You're gonna need all the cash you can to buy things for the baby aren't ya? Trust me you'll be okay." She grabbed her hand and squeezed it softly. "We'll only hit a few shops today I promise ya. You'll be back before ya know it." Francesca gasped her breath and nodded. She knew Jade was right, she didn't have a pot to piss in and she needed money desperately if she was going to have any chance of surviving. Tom checked the clock on top of the television and stretched his bony body.

"Have you booked a visit for our kid yet? Bet he's going mad waiting to see ya?" Francesca smiled and told him she would sort a visit out for the following day. Gordon was the last thing on her mind at the moment and the task of shoplifting scared the life out of her. As they planned the day ahead, Francesca felt physically sick and dreaded the part she had to play. Everyone finished their brews and started to get ready.

When Francesca first saw Jade in her disguise, she started pissing herself laughing; she rammed her hands between her legs so she didn't piss herself. "Fuckin hell Jade you look like a transvestite." Francesca held her belly and laughed as Jade walked to the mirror. Jade was turning from side to side in the mirror.

"I don't look that bad. I think I look quite respectable," she huffed. "Anyway, if it keeps the security off my back, who gives a flying fuck what I look like." Jade was wearing a jet-black shoulder length wig, and a pair of gold-rimmed glasses. The dress that hung from her body looked like a maternity dress. The horizontal pattern on it made her look like a beached whale and twice the size of her original body shape. Francesca wiped her eyes through laughing and tried to keep a straight face as she spoke to her.

"You look fine. I was only joking and like you said if nobody recognises you, who gives a fuck as long as you get the job done." Francesca walked to the bathroom to comb her hair but she was still sniggering to herself knowing how much of a twat Jade really looked. As she combed her hair in the bathroom she could hear Tom laughing his head off from outside the room. She could tell by Jade's tone that she was getting upset. As Francesca left the bathroom, Tom grinned at her and began to speak.

"She looks a right cunt doesn't she. I've told her to leave them on for bed tonight as a bit of spice up for our sex life but I don't think she's having any of it." Jade sneaked up behind him and squeezed his bollocks as hard as she could until he screamed with pain, she was fuming.

"Listen fuck face, does it matter what I look like as long as I'm earning. You should count ya self lucky that I'm not sat in here all day dossing, because that's what I can do if you carry on taking the piss out of me." She released his nuts from her grip and grabbed her coat from the side looking like she could kill someone. Her teeth were clenched together.

"Come on love, let's get out of this shit hole and

earn a crust." She turned her head back behind her and shouted to Tom. "I'll see you later nobhead, that's if I can be arsed coming back." Tom ignored her and rubbed his nuts as he followed them both to the door.

"Right, let's see what today brings then. Good luck and Francesca don't forget to phone a visit for our kid." Tom headed down the flight of stairs as the girls waited for the lift. You could tell Jade was in no mood for talking, her face was like thunder.

The lift stank of piss as usual. As the door closed, the stench hit the back of their throats and they both covered their mouths to avoid inhaling the putrid smell. Once the doors opened, they both gasped for air and quickly made their way to the exit. As the fresh morning air hit them both, Jade started to speak.

"He does my fuckin head in, him. He knows how it makes me feel when he takes the piss out of me. He never learns," Francesca nodded in agreement and sided with Jade to keep the peace.

"That's men for ya. I think they're from a different planet to women, don't you?"

Jade made no reply and waited at the bus stop looking down the road for any signs of a bus approaching, she looked edgy. "Fuckin buses take forever don't they, especially when you're in a rush." Francesca watched Jade as she paced up and down. The signs of her roasting started to appear on her face. Jade needed a fix and she seemed to change within minutes.

"Fucking hell. Come on let's start walking, it's only about ten minutes away."

Jade set off like a speed walker. They crossed the busy road to head for Harpurhey shopping centre. Her body was shaking and she wrapped her coat around her tightly to comfort her body's craving for smack. Not a word was spoken between them until the shops were in sight and that's when she told Francesca for the first time what she expected her to do.

"Right we need to be in and out of here as quick as possible. I don't want to be fucking about for ages. All I need you to do is bend over me when I'm shoving the stuff in my bag. Are ya okay with that?" Francesca nodded nervously but felt like her arse was going to fall out. It was too late to bottle out now and she knew she would have to see it through.

The shop was crowded as they walked inside. The checkout girls were busy serving customers and didn't give them a second look. Jade walked straight up to a row of jeans and gave Francesca the nod to cover over her. She quickly rolled the jeans together and placed them in a large bag she'd brought with her. Within seconds, the clothing was in the bag and you could see the top of the coat hanger sticking out from it. Jade quickly swung her coat off and threw it across the top of the bag and nobody could see what was inside. Covering her mouth with her hand she whispered to Francesca.

"Right let's get the fuck out of here before we get clocked." Francesca didn't speak a word and followed Jade like a lost sheep. The walk out of the store seemed to take forever and Francesca's feet didn't seem as if they were moving forward. The assistant was still dealing with a customer and didn't even raise her head as they left the shop. Once they were outside Jade hurried to the toilets in the local super store and checked exactly what she'd stolen.

"Fucking six pair of jeans that's not bad for a morning's work is it?" Jade looked happy. "Right we need to get these sold as quickly as we can so we can carry on." Jade stood thinking for a minute and knew exactly where she was going to sell the clobber. There was a lady she knew who lived on Kesteven Road in Harpurhey who bought almost anything from shoplifters. She always gave a good price for whatever she bought so with that in mind they quickly headed down Rochdale Road. Jade was sweating like a paedophile at a children's party. She seemed to have one thing on her mind as she dodged the cars to cross the road. She held a desperate look on her face. Francesca had dabbled in drugs before, but nothing as strong as smack. She'd sniffed cocaine in the past but now Gordon was away in prison she could never afford it on her own. Reaching the house where the buyer lived, Jade knocked on the door and started to pull the jeans from the bag. The house looked quite posh and there was a smell of Dettol coming from the doorstep. Jade knocked again and lifted the letterbox to shout the woman but as she did the door opened and an attractive blonde woman stood in front of them.

"Fuckin hell I shit myself then!" Jade laughed as the woman cast her eyes over Francesca.

"Got some smart jeans if ya interested Irene? I've got six pairs and I only want a tenner each." Irene invited them in and they stood round the kitchen table as she examined the goods. Francesca looked about the house and loved the whole set up of it. It reminded her so much of her auntie's house. Everything was neat and the smell of vanilla seeped through the air. Irene looked uneasy as she didn't know Francesca. She didn't wait a moment longer to find out who she was. Placing the jeans back on the table she spoke to Francesca.

"I've not seen you before, hope you're not the dibble."

Francesca raised a smile and told her she was a friend of Jade's. Once Irene had given Francesca the once over she seemed to relax and carried on inspecting the knocked off stuff. She zipped the jeans up and down and checked all the sizes on them.

"I'll give you forty quid for the lot. The sizes might be hard to get rid of, but I'll take the chance on them." Jade shook her head and smirked at her.

"Tell you what love; you don't half do well from me. Fuckin bargains galore you get." Irene tried to keep a straight face. Jade needed the money quick so she accepted her offer with little argument. Irene pulled a bundle of cash from her lacy pink bra and counted out forty quid. Everyone who was selling anything always came to her because they knew she'd always have the money on standby waiting for them. Jade grabbed the money from her hand and listened to her request for further items she needed. She laughed out loud when Irene told her she wanted a new hoover. The girls said their goodbyes to Irene and Jade headed straight off to the phone box on the side of the road. She was digging deep into her pocket for change to make a call. Francesca listened outside the phone box and it was obvious Jade was phoning her dealer. Jade bounced out of the phone box and watched every car that went by. She was looking for the one that would satisfy her craving. Francesca had to book a visit for the following day and took the opportunity to use the phone. As she dialled the number, a black car pulled up with a middle-aged man driving it, she watched as Jade ran to the side of it.

The phone call lasted around five minutes and they took the details from Francesca to book the visit. Jade paced up and down outside the phone box now looking like death warmed up. Her skin looked grey and her eyes were rolling to the back of her head. Her need for heroin was obvious. Once Francesca's phone call was over, Jade sighed with relief, she was urging her to hurry up outside. Francesca gasped a deep breath; the following day was going to be hard without a doubt. She hadn't seen Gordon for a while now and predicted he'd still want to rule her life even though he was locked up.

Jade hurried to a block of nearby maisonettes that was just across the road from where they stood. She told Francesca she wouldn't be long and left her sitting on a brick wall. She never mentioned where she was going but Francesca had a gut feeling she was going to get a fix. She watched Jade running into the maisonettes. Jade looked like she'd shit her knickers. Once she was out of sight, Francesca placed her hand on her stomach. The baby growing inside her was all she had in life now. Her mind started to think of days gone by. She sat thinking about her old friend Misty and wondered how she was doing. The guilt was crippling her inside for the things she'd done in the past. Gordon was an out and out bastard and Misty should have been glad to be rid of him, but the only downfall was that now, Francesca had taken over her old friend's life. Gordon ruled Francesca's just like he'd ruled Misty's. She had thought about leaving Manchester a few times and even starting a new life without him, but she knew the money in her purse wouldn't even get her a bus ride into town never mind a trip to another city so for now, she'd have to grin and bear it and take the shit he threw at her.

Jade re-emerged from the building with a smile on her face. You could tell the drugs were now deep in her veins. Her pupils looked like small pinholes and her words were shaky as she spoke. "Come on love let's get back to it. The day's still young yet and we need to be earning some more cash." she grabbed Francesca's arm and pulled her closer. "Ay, we can go into the baby shops and start you off with some baby clothes. What do ya say to that?" Francesca smiled at her new found friend and nodded her head.

The shopping precinct was busier than before and they found it hard to walk as people stood about chatting and laughing. Harpurhey was kind of a meeting place for friends and families on different days of the week especially if the market was on. A mini fairground sat in the middle of the precinct. It had a few rides on it and mothers queued up to get their kids on the rides. It was funny, Francesca thought, because everyone you looked at seemed to be eating something. Some were eating pasties and some were eating chips. A burger van was situated at the side of them and a large queue of starving people waited patiently to order their scran. Harpurhey looked like one big, happy community. Francesca turned her head to see a little kid scream at the ice-cream van, demanding this and that from his mother. You could see the woman had lost all her patience with her child and looked at the end of her tether. The woman's hand now swooped across her child's head she was yelling into his face. "I can't afford fucking food never mind an ice-cream," she snarled at him with her teeth clenched together. The boy fell to the ground kicking his legs up and down. "It's not fair, I want one." he screamed.

Jade let on to a few people as she passed them on the market, you could tell she was well known. Other groups of smack heads let on to Jade and told her where they'd nicked stuff from. It seemed like a code amongst smack addicts that they told each other where they could get a good graft from. The druggies even knew what time the security breaks were and what time was best to hit the stores. Francesca looked uneasy as Jade spoke to the junkies, she hated being associated with them, but times were hard and beggars couldn't be choosers. Francesca stood swinging her arms as Jade spoke to them. One man now pulled out two legs of lamb from his coat and about eight packets of cheese. Jade looked about anxiously. She snapped and told him to stash the goods before he got them all nicked. Francesca was gobsmacked at all the things they'd stolen. She never thought in a month of Sundays that they would nick something like tins of corned beef and tuna. Jade could tell she felt uncomfortable and told her mates she would speak to them soon in the Ark Royal. The Ark Royal and Two Hundred pubs were places all the wheeling and dealing took place in the area. If you ever wanted a bargain, they were the places to be. Many of the punters came into the pub just to get knock off goods. You could get clothing out of there and even packets of bacon at rock bottom prices thanks to the smack heads who came in there.

Walking into the baby shop, Francesca's heart melted. All the clothing looked so small and cute. She picked up a small babygro and held it up as Jade watched. "Orr, look at the size of this, it's mint innit. I can't believe I'm going to have a baby this small." Francesca got carried away with the moment and started to rock the babygro in her arms as if a baby was inside it. "Do I suit being a mother or what?" she said twisting her body to face Jade. Francesca felt embarrassed and went red in the face when she looked at her friend. Jade was nearly in tears and Francesca quickly realised she must of been thinking of her own children. Francesca quickly threw the babygro in a nearby basket and gripped Jade's arm. "Sorry love, I just forgot how hard it must be for you, losing your children and all that. It must be so hard. I don't know how ya cope, because I know I couldn't do it." Jade bit her bottom lip and confided in her as she pulled her to a quiet spot in the shop.

"I've looked at babies in their prams loads of times. I just want to nick one while their mothers aren't looking" she covered her mouth with her hand and whispered. "I nearly done it once but the mother came out of the shop and gave me a right earful, she was onto me." Jade looked hot and pulled her dress from around her neck "I haven't tried it for ages, but my time will come and I'll have another baby." Francesca looked concerned as she spoke and thought she must be joking, but as she continued she realised how serious she really was.

"I want someone else to feel like I did when they take your child away, I wanna see how they fucking cope. It's hard I can tell ya, but ay life goes on doesn't it?" Francesca's spine shivered at the thought of Jade nicking someone's baby. She scanned her face in detail and wondered if she was capable of stealing someone else's child. As she studied her more, she realised she had some serious issues and could never be trusted around anyone's baby. Jade wafted her hand in front of her face to stop the tears.

"Come on let's fill our bags," Jade whispered under her breath. Looking down at the bag, baby clothing and bottles were bulging out from the top of it. Francesca felt a buzz as they walked from the shop without a care in the world. She knew this would be her life from now on. Jade made it all seem so easy and Francesca knew she could earn the money she needed to keep her head above water.

The day carried on much the same and the things they nicked were unbelievable. Jade did exactly what she'd said she would do earlier and walked out of a superstore with a brand new hoover under her arm. Once they'd sold all the stuff they headed back to the flat for a well-earned rest. Francesca's back was aching and she needed some food to stop herself from shaking. The two girls were on a high when they headed back into the flats. Jade joked about wearing her wig and glasses in bed that night for Tom. They both giggled like schoolgirls as they made comments about her outfit she was wearing. Jade knew Tom would shit himself when he lifted the duvet in bed revealing her sexy new look. Jade held her belly as she howled laughing.

"Shame I haven't got tan coloured tights like my nana used to wear innit? He would definitely go under once he'd seen them dangling from my fanny." The laughter echoed the concrete corridors as they entered the lift. The day had been a strange one and somehow Francesca found herself warming to her newfound friend.

Opening the front door, they could hear music blasting out. They both looked at each other and a blank look was across their faces. It was quite unusual for Tom to be playing music at this time of the day. Usually he'd shout at Jade for pumping the tunes, and tell her to turn it down if the volume level was more than fifteen. Walking through the hallway, they could hear Tom singing the words to a UB40 song at the top of his voice. Opening the door, they saw him in his boxer shorts lying flat out on the settee. His hand was down his shorts and you could tell they'd just walked in before he'd started masturbating. Francesca clocked his penis was stood to attention and ready for use. Tom bolted up from his position as they entered the room. He was frantic and searched for a nearby cushion to hide his manhood. Francesca's eyes focused on his penis and she couldn't believe the size of his pride and joy. Gordon's penis was only half the size of Tom's and she realised why he was called Gordon's 'bigger brother'. Her eyes couldn't stop looking at it, and she felt embarrassed as Jade launched her fist into him. Her face was red and she was livid.

"Ya dirty fucker. You was getting ready for a wank until we caught you wasn't ya." She stood with her head bent towards him and her hand on her hip as she growled at him. "No fucking wonder ya can't get a hard on for me, if ya wanking all day long." Tom laughed nervously as he tried to fight her off. Jade was on one now and wouldn't leave him alone without saying her peace.

"Fucking joke I tell ya. I hope you've earned some fucking money today, because ya getting fuck all from me ya dirty wanker." Francesca couldn't hold herself back any longer and burst out laughing and surprisingly Jade joined in. They both started singing at him as he sat there with a smug grin on his face.

"I'm a wanker, I'm a wanker and it does me good like it jolly well should. I'm a wanker I'm a wanker and I'm always pulling my pud." The pair laughed as Tom searched for his pants. As he pulled his jeans on, he looked at Francesca and smiled as he tucked his manhood into his trousers. Tom could tell she'd liked what she had seen and kept staring at her longer than he should have.

Eventually the three of them all sat round the table and shared the money out from the graft. Tom had about sixty pounds waving about in his hands. He laughed out loud as he told them of the chase he'd taken from one of the market stallholders earlier. His face looked serious as he continued to talk and you could tell he'd had a close shave.

"There I was with loads of razor blades in my pocket and the stallholder fucking clocked me just when I was putting the last few in my pocket. The bastard looked at me and tried to dive over the stall to grab my hands but I was too quick and done a burner through the market." Tom's hands were waving about in the air. "Some of the market traders were laughing their nuts off as I ran past them and I found it hard not to laugh myself." He gasped and wiped the sweat from his forehead. "As I looked back over my shoulder, the fucker was nearly up my arse and I had to turn on the turbo speed to dust the cunt off." Tom was running on the spot now acting out his misfortune. "The bastard didn't give up for about ten minutes. I was knackered by the time I finally lost him." Jade took hold of him in her arms and held him like a mother would hold her son. She began to speak in a sarcastic voice.

"Oh my little soldier, you've been through the mill today haven't ya. Told ya you need to start working out because you're gonna get caught one of these days." Tom looked at her and removed her arms from his body you could tell he felt embarrassed. He was back up on his feet pacing the living room.

"Fuck, they won't ever catch me. I'm like shit off a shovel when I get going." He now tensed his muscles and shoved them into Jade's face shouting at her at full pelt. "Kiss the muscle. Kiss the muscle," he chuckled. Francesca gazed at him and started to see him in a different light. She felt a strange tingling between her legs and knew the old Francesca was still alive and kicking in there somewhere. Francesca wanted to dive on him there and then. She slowly licked her top teeth and thought of how good he could be in bed. She wondered if he would be better than his brother and smirked. Francesca was feeling so horny right now and if Jade hadn't have been there she would have most definitely ripped her knickers off and shagged him within an inch of his life. Her hormones were playing up now and she'd never felt this horny in her life. If she carried on like this, she would be in bed with Tom before the week was over. She was longing for a man's touch.

The money was counted out and it was a good day's earnings for them all. Tom gave Jade the look that meant he'd got the drugs, he patted his pocket and smiled. The heating in the flat was turned on full and the sound of the boiler burning up travelled throughout the flat like a brass band playing. Francesca pulled all the baby clothes from the bag in front of her and looked at them individually. Tom watched as she rubbed the velour lemon jacket across her face. He looked amazed at the size of them.

"Fucking hell, look at the size of that. You wouldn't think a baby was that small would ya?" Francesca held it up and agreed. Jade started to reminisce about her own children when they were babies.

"Orr pass me a babygro love." She held it out in front of her. "That's how big my kids were when they were younger, I can't believe they're gone ya know. I'd of been a good mother." Tom raised his eyes to the ceiling as she continued. "It was just such a bad time I was going through back then but the bastard social worker didn't listen to a word I had to say. One day they'll be back with me ya know."

Tom nodded in agreement. "Yep they sure will."

"I'm gonna wait till I've earned a few quid and try and get em back." Tom hunched his shoulders at Francesca and tried to change the subject. Jade could still be heard babbling on about her children.

"Did ya book a visit for our kid for tomorrow?" Tom chirped in. "Bet he'll be buzzing when he sees you and your little bump." Francesca didn't want to tell him her fears and raised a smile at him. She'd been thinking about the visit all day and felt stressed thinking about the first time she saw Gordon's face. Jade was rubbing her stomach as she stood up.

"I'm fucking starving. Shall we get a pizza from the takeaway or what?" Tom and Francesca licked their lips and started to decide which topping they wanted on it.

"I'll want spicy beef," shouted Tom. Francesca requested the cheese and tomato, it was her favourite. Jade looked at them both and told them that she wasn't going for it, so they'd best decide between themselves who was leaving the warm flat to make the journey to Rochdale Road take away. Francesca held her tongue and hoped Tom would offer as her back was now troubling her. Jade looked at him for an answer and within minutes he agreed. "Fuck it, I'll go." he moaned. His only demand was that when he got back he could watch the football match between Manchester United and Arsenal. Jade pulled her face but eventually agreed because she needed to feed her fat face plus it would give her time to get her kit on for a night of passionate sex. She smiled and imagined the look on Tom's face when he lifted the bedclothes – she knew tonight was going to be bags of fun.

Tom threw his black leather coat on and straightened his hair in the mirror as the girls turned on the television. Francesca kicked off her shoes and placed her feet up on the arm of the chair trying to make herself comfortable. Jade spread her body across the settee like a super sized slob. Her breasts seemed to fall apart like the Red Sea; one was nearly over her shoulder at one stage as she wriggled about trying to get comfy. Jade's hair had more grease on it than a chip. She just swept it back from her face without a care in the world. Francesca wondered about the stories she'd heard about her selling her body and waited for Tom to leave before she asked her. The sound of the front door slamming could be heard. Francesca wasted no time in finding out about the life of the woman who lay in front of her. She stretched her arms over her head as she began.

"So are the rumours true that you do tricks when you're skint or what?" Francesca yawned and then continued. "Or is it just the gossips from round here making stories up?" Francesca's tilted her head to the side. "Because I know what they're like round here for making things up." Jade rolled over onto her side and screwed her face up like a bulldog chewing a wasp before she spoke.

"Funny how things around Harpurhey get turned about. People need to get a grip on their own lives before they start chatting shit about other people." Jade bolted up from the sofa and faced Francesca. "I've never been on the game so I don't know what they're going on about." Francesca could tell she was lying by her blood red face and her body language. Jade now sat back and started to quiz Francesca about her own life. They'd only known each other a short time and Jade wanted to find out as much as possible about her, so she knew what she was facing when the time came to put her in her place.

"So how long are ya planning on staying here then? You'll want to get your own house soon wont ya? This is no place for a baby." Francesca sat twisting her hair as she listened to her. "Imagine the noise when me and Tom start arguing, it will be like a war zone. You wouldn't want that would you?" Francesca took the hint and chewed her bottom lip. She knew Jade was telling her in her own way that she wasn't welcome for much longer. Francesca shot a look at her and knew the gloves were off. Jade was a fat overweight slag and Francesca knew she'd eat her for breakfast once she got back on her feet. Both girls sat chatting.

Francesca now told the story of how she met Gordon. When she told Jade that Gordon had previously been her best mate's man she nearly choked as she tried to light up her cig. Jade made no secret about the way she felt. "Fucking snidey mate you, aren't you? If you'd had been my mate, I would have hurt you big time," she inhaled deeply on her cig and darted her eyes at Francesca. "I'm not being funny love but that's the lowest of the low, a downright liberty if you ask me. What did ya mate do when she found out?" Francesca blew her breath hard as she spoke. Her arms were waving about her body.

"Gordon loved me and wanted to be with me. Misty was just a mistake, so it's not really my fault if he fell out of love with her is it?" Jade took a deep drag of her cig and shook her head from side to side.

"Dirty bitch." she mumbled under her breath.

Tom returned with the pizza and placed the boxes on the table as he dragged his coat off. "It's fucking freezing out there. My balls are like a brass monkeys." Jade ignored him and opened the box containing the food. The heat from the box filtered through the air and each of them grabbed a slice of pizza.

Francesca felt tired and knew the next day would be challenging. What would she do when she saw Gordon's face for the first time? Would she still love him as she did before? Or would he turn her stomach? She regretted ever allowing herself to get pregnant. Francesca hoped the next day that Gordon would welcome her warmly into his hands and love the fact they were now going to be a family. Somewhere deep inside her she knew not to expect fireworks, he just wasn't that kind of person and he'd never change the way he was.

Once Francesca had eaten her food she decided she needed to go to bed, her eyes looked heavy. She watched Jade pull out a small plastic bag of brown powder from her jeans and knew she couldn't stay a moment longer while they both injected themselves with heroin. Francesca stood from the chair and stretched her body, she gave Tom a disappointed look and left to go to bed.

Tom felt ashamed of his drug use. Drugs meant so much to him in the past and was all he had to keep him going. He lived everyday craving for the drug and never imagined himself without it until now. His eyes watched Jade as she tied a shoe lace round her arm. The silver needle now surged deep into her veins. Tom couldn't say no to the needle, no matter how much he wanted to.

The heroin took them both to a place they loved. Two bodies now lay on the settee. It seemed as if they were staring into space and their eyes held no pain. Tom left the needle hanging from his arm and traces of dark red blood trickled down it. Looking about the room, he tried to imagine life without drugs. This was Tom's dream and he knew while Jade was by his side his nightmare would never end. After hours had passed, Tom sat up as if he'd had an electric shock injected into his body. He was slurring his words as he made an announcement that would change his life forever. "Jade, Jade wake up. I wanna tell you summit." He was ragging her body about on the sofa. Holding her head in his hands he spoke.

"Tomorrow I'm going to the doctors to get sorted out. I've had enough of this shit. Everyone looks at us like scumbags. Do ya know that?" Jade slowly turned her head to look at him, not taking in what he'd said, she was out of it. He continued and pulled at her legs trying to make her understand. "Are you listening or what? What do ya say? Shall we get off this shit together?"

He now bent towards her and looked deep into her eyes. As he stared at her face, she looked like she was in the most peaceful place ever. He blew his warm breath onto her face to try to make her listen. Sitting next to her on the sofa he twisted his hands together.

"Listen Jade, with or without you I'm gonna sort myself out. Just think if you do it, you might even have a chance of getting your kids back. We can be a proper family together." Jade rolled over and ignored him. She looked like she was staying there for the rest of the night.

Tom walked to the toilet and he could see a light still on in Francesca's room. He froze for a moment and tried to walk past the bedroom but it felt like Francesca was a magnet on the other side of the door and she was drawing him closer. Tom managed to go to the toilet but on the way back, he knocked softly on her door. He didn't wait for Francesca to reply and slowly pushed the door open. The bedroom looked so much fresher. The way she'd changed it was unrecognisable to him. Francesca pulled her t-shirt over her pale white legs as he walked towards her. She looked slightly embarrassed at his visit and fidgeted about on the bed as he got nearer.

Tom sat at the end of the bed and picked up a white babygro she'd been looking at. He held it up and smiled at Francesca.

"Orr I'm well chuffed for you and Gordon. I can't wait to be an uncle." There was a moment's silence before Tom carried on talking. "Well this baby's gonna be proud of its Uncle Tom, because as from tomorrow I'm sacking the shit." His head was dipped low as he spoke. "I hate the life I'm leading and know that things aren't gonna get any better till I get off the smack." Francesca leant over and gripped his hand in hers. She could see the pain in his eyes. Somehow, she believed every word he said to her and knew he was desperate to get off drugs. Tom continued in a low voice. "I'm going to the doctors tomorrow to see about getting a methadone script. Loads of people are on meth and I know it will work for me if I stay strong." Francesca told him how proud she was of his decision and said she'd help him all she could. The days he had to face would be hard, but if it meant him getting off heroin, Francesca was willing to go the extra mile for him.

The bedroom door opened like a gale force wind had just come in. They both lifted their heads up, and there she stood, ready to explode. "Jade." Tom gasped.

"Don't you listen to a word that nobhead is telling you Francesca. I've heard it all before. He's full of shit. He's just after some attention," she walked closer towards Tom clenching her fist at the side of her. Grabbing his shoulder she pulled him towards her. "Anyway what the fuck are ya doing in here prick?" Francesca released his hand from her grip and Tom sprung up to face Jade. His face looked distressed.

"I'm in here because you don't fucking listen to me. I was only telling her that I'm getting off the gear and sorting my head out." Jade laughed out loud and jerked her head back.

"I've heard it all before. You're a fucking smack head, so deal with it. You're just the same as me." Jade spoke directly to Francesca now. "No matter what shit he's telling you love, he'll be begging me for heroin before the week's out, trust me, he always does." Tom shook his head and told Jade that he was serious this time; she was having none of it. "Fucking bullshit, pure bullshit." she whispered under her breath. Jade could tell she'd hurt his feelings and tried to make friends as quickly as possible by making a joke out of the matter.

"Tell ya what Tom, if you get off the gear, then good luck to you, but don't ask me to do the same. Heroin is the only thing that keeps me going each day without my kids," she rubbed Tom's arm. "I'll try to help you all I can but don't start stressing with me over it." Francesca lay flat on the bed and she caught Jade looking at her slender legs. She stretched them out full length and curled her toes. Jade knew Tom was slipping away from her and tried to speak to him before he barged past her out of the room.

"Do you fancy parting your girlfriend tash tonight or what? I've got a surprise for you when we go to bed." Tom pushed past her and she followed him with a sheepish look in her eyes trying to make amends.

"Tom," she shouted as he stormed out of the bedroom. He completely ignored her and threw himself onto the bed. Jade walked in the bedroom and sat beside him on the bed as he stared into space. He was fuming and she knew he was angry with her. She gripped his face in her hands.

"Listen love, I'll try to help you get clean. It's just that when I see you sat talking with Francesca, my blood boils. I can't help the way I feel about you. I just get jealous that you're talking to her about things like that, when it should be me." Tom lay lifeless and couldn't be bothered listening to her shit. The only hold Jade had over him now was supplying his drugs, but now he'd said he didn't want them anymore she knew it would only be a matter of time before she was kicked to the kerb. Her night of kinky sex had been thrown out of the window now and the slut who lay in the next room was probably laughing her head off. As she watched Tom fall asleep, she started to think of a plan that would get Francesca out of her hair for good.

## Chapter Six

"Come on ya lazy fucker," Tom shouted as he entered Francesca's bedroom. "Let's get ready to go and see that fucking ugly brother of mine." Francesca rolled over and pulled the duvet over her head. She was moaning at Tom telling him to leave her for a while. Tom now walked over to the bed and ripped the blankets from her body. She was trying to hold onto it for dear life. He pulled with all his might and eventually freed it from her grip. Francesca lay on the bed with a smile on her face. As he looked at her, he could see her black lacy knickers. She followed his eyes and struggled to pull her t-shirt over her legs. His eyes were wide open as he grabbed at his crotch, he was excited. Tom was only ever used to seeing Jade's big passion killers and the sight of some black lace made his cock stand to attention. He knew then he wanted her more than ever. Tom left the bedroom quickly before his cock poked him in the eyes.

Francesca reached for the duvet from the floor and dragged it back on the bed. The bit of a frolic had left her feeling aroused. Checking the door was shut; she slid her hands down into her knickers and started to pleasure herself. She needed a man now more than ever and she needed to orgasm to relieve the frustration she felt inside. Within minutes Francesca was masturbating. The person she thinking about was Tom.

Francesca slid out of bed and threw on an old t-shirt on before she entered the living room. Tom was already stood with his coat on and ready to go out. Her eyes shot to the clock on the wall and she asked where he was going. Tom spoke with a timid tone.

"I'm off to the doctors aren't I? Today is gonna be the start of my new life without drugs." Francesca hurried to his side and hugged him. He seemed very edgy and in a rush to leave her side. Tom's was shaking as she held him. She knew it was his body calling out for drugs yet again. Francesca watched his every movement as he made his way to the front door. He was shouting before he left. "When the dragon wakes up tell her where I've gone. I shouldn't be long so tell her to have some breakfast ready for me for when I get back," he winked at Francesca as he closed the door. He was gone. Francesca rubbed at her arms; she felt warmth riding through her body. There was no doubt about it, she was falling in love with him.

Francesca looked rough that morning. The smell from the cigarette stubs in the ashtray nearby made her heave. She picked it up, held it at arm's length from her and headed to the kitchen. Once she had emptied in the bin she washed it out and left it on the draining board to dry. Looking round the kitchen she decided that she would cook breakfast for everyone. Bending down she searched the fridge for any food. As she opened the fridge door, all she could see was a tray of eggs. There were also a few tomatoes. As she looked at them closer she could tell they'd been there for months, they had fur growing on them. Francesca decided she would make scrambled eggs and toast for everyone. The sound of cupboards doors opening could be heard as she searched for a pan. Francesca hadn't cooked eggs for ages and the role of a housewife appealed to her now. It was a far cry from the life she'd previously led. She was such a party animal in her day. Sometimes she missed going out with her friends and getting pissed each night. Francesca knew it was her time now to start growing up. She had to start thinking of her own child, because when the baby was born, nobody but herself would be looking after it.

The eggs were done as were the cups of tea. All that was left to do was to wake Jade and tell her of her accomplishment. As she opened the bedroom door she had to hold her hand over her mouth to stop her from laughing. Jades big fat arse was hanging out of the bed and all her cellulite was showing. No wonder Tom needed drugs, she thought. Tom needed a medal after sleeping with Jade, she was a proper minger. Her ripples of fat covered her waist and her hair looked like she'd back-combed the lot of it. Francesca was just about to close the door when Jade opened her eyes and faced her.

"What do you want?" Jade lifted her head up from the bed and searched for the clock on the bedside cabinet. "What fucking time is?"

Francesca whispered and felt slightly embarrassed as Jade pulled the duvet back over her blubber. "I've made you some breakfast if you're getting up." Francesca's voice was animated. "I've made you scrambled eggs on toast if you want some." Jade muttered under her breath and told Francesca she would be in for her breakfast soon. As

Francesca started to leave the room she heard the biggest fart she'd ever heard in her life. Covering her mouth with her hand she ran towards the kitchen so Jade couldn't hear her fits of laughing.

Jade waddled into the living room wearing one of Tom's t-shirts. It barely covered her arse cheeks. Francesca told her that her breakfast was on the side in the kitchen. Jade watched as Francesca started eating her own food.

"Yeah I'll get it in a minute. I just need a cig first before I do anything." Francesca carried on scranning her breakfast as she watched Jade coughing and sputtering as she lit a cig.

"Where's Tom?" Jade asked in a concerned voice. Francesca told her where he'd gone to and her face dropped.

"Fucking wanker. I told him last night I would have gone with him." She dragged her fingers through her hair. "See what I mean about him, he's all for his fucking self." Francesca carried on eating and tried to ignore her but what she said next knocked Francesca for six.

"Francesca, while we're on our own I need to get something off my chest." Jade sat on the edge of the sofa. "I'm just gonna say it how it is. I hate the way you're getting on with Tom. You're walking around the place with only a fucking t-shirt on showing all your arse." Jade's face was cocky as she continued. "I think you should have some respect for me and cover up, not prance around like a fucking dog on heat." Francesca was quick to reply and didn't hold back as she bolted up from the chair.

"You cheeky cunt. Prancing round like a dog on heat, my fucking arse. Get a grip will ya. The reason I'm in a t shirt is because I've got no fucking clothes." Francesca was in her face now waving her hands about. "Get ya story straight before you start accusing me of fancying your fella." Francesca remained standing tall in front of her. Jade started to throw more insults and wasn't holding back.

"Me and Tom are going through a bad patch at the moment and you're not fucking helping the situation one little bit. Can't you go back to your auntie's or summit?" Francesca let rip.

"Listen, Tom asked me to stay here. I didn't ask him. So when he tells me to go that's when I will, so fuck off out of my face and stop getting on my case just because your relationship is falling apart – you can't blame me for that you daft twat." Francesca flew into the bedroom and slammed the door behind her. Her temper was exploding and she wanted to run back into the front room and kick the shit out of the fat cow. Francesca paced the bedroom floor, her teeth were tightly gritted and her fists were clenched. Blowing her breath she tried to calm down. "Daft fat slag," she mumbled.

About half an hour later, Tom returned from the doctors carrying a bundle of leaflets and a small brown bottle of medicine. Jade was still sat on the settee when he returned and smoking like a trooper. Tom took his coat off and threw it on the back of the chair. He sat down and started to read the leaflets about a drug free life. Looking up he smiled at Jade.

"I've got a methadone script now. So hopefully if I stick to the plan they can wean me off the gear over time." Jade raised a struggled smile but he could tell she didn't give a fuck. He carried on reading without giving her a second thought. When he finished reading the pamphlets he checked the time and asked where Francesca was. Jade looked uneasy and told him she must be getting ready.

She never mentioned the events that had taken place in his absence. Jade smiled and told him his breakfast was on the side in the kitchen. "Just warm it up." she shouted after him. She never told him Francesca had made the meal and made out that the feast was all her own work.

Tom sat down with his food as Francesca walked back into the room. He tucked into his food and thanked Jade for his lovely breakfast. Francesca snarled at her and shook her head. Tom spoke with a mouthful of toast.

"Won't be long now, I've just got to have a quick wash and then we can set off. We can have a look round Cheetham Hill Shopping Fort before we go if you want." The new shopping centre was just across the road from Strangeways prison and Francesca knew it was a good idea to pass some time before the visit. Jade quickly sprung to her feet and couldn't hold her tongue.

"What about fucking me? Oh, I forgot, you're on methadone now and don't need a fucking fix, so it's fuck Jade and let her fend for herself is it?" Tom scowled at her and told her she could go to the doctors and get a script just like he'd done, but she didn't listen to a word he said and stormed into the bedroom. "Selfish bastard," she shouted behind her. Francesca rolled her eyes at Tom and told him he should get fucking rid of her. She told him she was nothing but trouble and she'd only drag him down. The sooner he realised that the better. Tom knew Francesca was talking sense but still felt like he owed Jade, he couldn't just desert her could he? He followed her into the bedroom and told her he'd come shoplifting with her till she had enough money to score. Jade smiled and thanked him. As Tom returned back to Francesca he told her that Jade would be coming with them. He could tell by her face that she wasn't impressed. "Last time honest!"

He whispered as he squeezed her waist on the way past her.

The three of them walked down Rochdale Road toward Cheetham Hill. The silence was uncomfortable between them and you could tell something was wrong. Tom could sense an atmosphere between the girls but put it down to hormones on both their parts and left them to it.

The shopping fort was hammered and the shoppers were out in full force. Jade spoke in a soft voice to Francesca and asked her would she'd cover her back in the shops. Francesca thought about it for a minute and told Jade that if she was taking part in the shoplifting she wanted a cut of the cash. Jade sighed and nodded her head. She hurried Francesca into the shop whilst Tom waited outside. They were only in the shop a few minutes and Jade had a batch of blouses rolled together in her bag. She looked at Francesca and let her know it was time to leave. Jade didn't have her disguise on today and clocked the security guard looking at her in more detail. Quickly she passed the bag to Francesca and told her to get out of the shop as fast as she could whilst she tried to keep the store detective busy. Jade was right and the security left Francesca to walk out of the shop and continued in his quest to follow her. She made him follow her about the shop and played a game of hide and seek whenever she could. Eventually she left the store with her hands in her pocket and a smile on her face leaving the security guard looking bewildered.

Once outside, Jade scouted the area for Tom and Francesca. She could hear a loud wolf whistle from the other side of the road. Her head was twisting about trying to look for them. Walking slowly, she finally clocked Tom hiding away. Sweat was pumping from her forehead. Jade ran across the busy road dodging the traffic. She had one thing on her mind and nothing else seemed to matter. Reaching the others she ragged the bag from Francesca's grip and dipped her head inside. Her face was red and she was licking her cracked lips.

"Right see you two later. I'm gonna sell this lot so I'll meet ya back at the flat."

Francesca reminded her that she wanted her share of the money too. Jade scowled at her but agreed to sort her out later. Tom and Francesca watched as she left. She was sweating like a pig's arse hole as she waddled up the road. Tom chuckled.

"Looks like she's shit herself doesn't it!" Francesca laughed as they both watched her disappear into the distance. She looked like she was touching cloth. Francesca giggled and nudged Tom playfully.

"How do you feel today?" She looked concerned. "I mean you must feel better without any of that shit running through ya veins, surely?" Tom looked agitated.

"I'm alright at the moment. Jade doesn't fucking help. Just watching her leave knowing she's going to score does my box head in." His words were low as his head sank to his chest. "The first few days are gonna be the worst. I'm just glad I've got my meth and I don't have to do a roast." Tom rubbed his arms, he looked cold. "I've heard pure shit about going cold turkey and I'm not afraid to say, it would be my worst nightmare." His face looked serious as he grabbed Francesca's arm. "One of my mates went through it, and he fucking shit his pants. He said he was just lying there shaking on the floor. He felt like the walls were closing in on him," he gasped his breath and shook his head in disgust. "The doctors only gave him painkillers to help him. Fuck that for a laugh, if I was roasting my bollocks off, I'd want loads of medication to get me through it all. I can tell ya." He stared at Francesca and she could see the fear in his eyes, he continued. "Imagine all that spewing ya ring up. I couldn't do it like that, no fucking way in this world could I." Francesca looked at him and her heart melted, he was definitely trying to change his life. She knew Jade was going to be a big problem in his quest to break his addiction. How was he going cope when she was there tempting him all the time? Francesca came up with an idea and hoped he'd like it. Coughing she cleared her throat.

"Tom, I'm not being funny or owt but don't you think it's best if Jade has drugs while she's out of the house." Her face was serious, "you don't need all the temptation there do you?" Tom knew she was right and they both hatched a plan to tell Jade the new rules about a drug free house. It was going to be hard when he told her; there would be fireworks for sure. Francesca knew this would be another nail in Jade's coffin and held a cunning grin on her face.

Tom and Francesca both sat in McDonalds to pass some time before the visit. They ordered two Big Mac meals. Francesca sat down at the table and Tom went to fetch their food. Francesca sat near the windows and watched the traffic flying by as she waited. Through the glass panel she could see the big tower of Strangeways. Her heart churned at the thought of facing Gordon again. Looking down at her jeans she popped her finger in her mouth and tried to wipe the stains away. She'd planned to wash them the night before but she knew they'd never have dried in time for the visit. Tom returned to the table and sat right next to her. He placed the large red tray on the chair and started to pass her food to her.

"Come on fatty get this lot down your neck. Our little baby in there must be starving." Tom placed his hand on the small of her stomach and started to ask questions about the pregnancy.

"Do ya want a boy or a girl?" he tilted his head to the side thinking for a moment. "I suppose it doesn't really matter does it, as long as it's healthy and all that." Francesca smirked as he carried on talking about her pregnancy. "I'd shit myself if I was a woman. Imagine ten pounds worth of baby coming from ya minge. I'm nearly crying when I'm constipated so I know if I was a woman I would be definitely shitting myself." Tom noticed Francesca's face change and he could see she was anxious. "I'm sorry for scaring you but I was only joking, you know what I'm like." He pulled her towards him and cuddled her. "I get carried away some times. It can't be that bad because women have kids all the time. Anyway you get some kick arse pain relief so you won't feel a thing." Francesca smiled at him but secretly she was terrified of what lay ahead. The thought of being alone and giving birth on her own made her feel sick inside. Francesca had nobody in her life that cared about her. Tom was the closest thing to family that she had. Chewing the side of her finger nail she spoke.

"Can I ask you something Tom? You can say 'no' if you want." Tom nodded at her as he bit into his burger. "When the time comes for me to have this baby Gordon will still be in prison won't he?" Tom jerked his head forward. Francesca took a deep breath and continued. "Would you be my birthing partner when the time comes to have the baby?" Tom nearly choked on his food. The colour drained from his face. She could see that perhaps she'd asked too much of him. "No worries, I just thought

I'd ask that's all." Tom stopped her dead in her tracks and told her he'd do it. Francesca turned her head and stared at him. "Really Tom, orr I'm buzzing now, thank you so much. You don't know how worried I've been." Francesca started to eat her burger and thought she'd have a little fun with Tom regarding the birth. "Ay, I hope you're not just coming in just so ya can see my fanny." Tom burst into fits of laughter and held his stomach. Francesca continued to wind him up. "Ay if I see ya getting aroused when I'm giving birth, you can get right out of the room. You'll have to sit at the top of the bed with me and keep your eyes away from my Jack and Danny," she held a finger in the corner of her mouth. "Do you think they make knickers that have a big hole in the crotch for the baby to come out?" he collapsed laughing on the table.

"You're off it you are." he giggled. Tom loved the way Francesca made him laugh. The feelings he felt emerging inside, scared the life out of him. He was falling in love with his brother's girlfriend. It was written all over his face. Tom tapped his fingers on the table. "We can't tell Jade about this, she'd go off her head. Can we keep this our little secret for now?"

Francesca nodded, "No worries."

The time came for them to set off for the visit. As they walked outside the heavens opened. Neither of them had brought an umbrella. Tom didn't have to think twice, he pulled his coat off and draped it over their heads. Francesca linked his arm and they jogged towards the prison. By the time they reached their destination Tom's jeans were piss wet through and Francesca looked like a drowned rat. Tom's twisted the bottom of his t-shirt in his hands and drop of water fell from it onto the floor.

As soon as they reached the visitors centre, they could

see everyone else was wringing wet too. All the women's hair that they'd obviously been styling all morning had gone as flat as a pancake. Everyone looked miserable as Tom went to the main desk to book in. Francesca sat at a table with a young woman and her small child. When she started talking to her she realised she'd come all the way from Liverpool to visit her partner. Tom came to join them and he joined the conversation. Tom noticed the small boy in his push chair at the side of him. He was moaning and trying to break free from his pram. Tom pulled at the child's foot making him laugh out loud. He continued to play hide and seek with him leaving his mother to have a well earned five minute break.

The officer stood up and started shouting out all the names out for the visits. Both Francesca and Tom helped the lady with her child. Tom carried him towards the main prison and was throwing him up in the air. As Tom walked ahead the woman covered her mouth and whispered to Francesca. "You've got a good one there; my fella's a lazy bastard and never does fuck all with his kids." Francesca smiled but never told her Tom wasn't her boyfriend. They both stared at Tom playing with her son.

It seemed ages before they went through all the security checks in the prison. When they finally reached the visiting area everybody looked relieved. Francesca took a deep breath and tried to stop herself from shaking. Her nerves were getting the better of her and she felt sick. Tom was the first to spot Gordon and made his way to his table. Francesca went straight to the canteen to get some drinks and chocolate before the queue started. The visitors scattered to their loved ones. Francesca ordered the refreshments; she could feel Gordon's eyes burning into the back of her head even though he was some distance away. As she picked up the drinks her hands shook uncontrollably as she made her way towards them. Francesca placed the drinks on the table and sat down. Gordon's eyes never left her face. When she was seated, Gordon spoke his first words to her. The sound of his voice sent shivers down her spine.

"How's my little darling. Hope you have been behaving?"

Francesca raised a struggled smile but didn't reply. Tom continued talking to his brother and told him all about the local news. Gordon was agitated with Tom and you could tell he wanted him to leave whilst he got Francesca alone.

Tom knew his presence was unwelcomed. After about half an hour he told Gordon he would leave them alone to chat for the rest of the visit. He stood up and reached over the table to shake his brother's hand. Gordon waited till he was near the exit before he lifted his hand in the air and waved, Tom was gone. His eyes burned into Francesca as he chewed on his bottom lip.

"Hope you're behaving young lady. I don't wanna be hearing stories about you when I get out of here." Francesca looked at him and hate seeped through her veins knowing he was still the tosser he had been before he was locked up. Gordon saw the cockiness in her eyes and dragged her face towards him across the table. His eyes quickly scanned the area for any screws. He knew his actions would go unnoticed. His warm breath could be felt on her face.

"You know I don't want this baby don't you?" he flung Francesca back across the table and snarled at her. "But it's here now so it's just something I'll have to get use to innit?" He looped his arms above his head as he rocked back on his chair. "I've thought about being a dad, and I'm kind of warming to the idea now, but there's one thing that's bothering me." Francesca was hanging on his every word. He punched his clenched fist onto the table.

"If I ever find out you've cheated on me while I'm in here, I'll fucking kill you." His eyes looked menacing. "The thought of you with another man makes my blood boil. I can tell you now, if you're unfaithful to me, I'll do fucking life for ya," his hands swished rapidly across his face. "I'll slice your face up like a piece of bread. No one will ever look at you again. Do you hear me?" His voice got louder. "I said do you hear me?"

Francesca looked into his eyes as they danced with madness. He was waiting for her to reply. She placed one hand around her neck as she struggled to breathe. She knew he had a bad temper but this kind of behaviour was new to her. Francesca felt fear in her body like never before. "I hear you," she whispered. Gordon carried on speaking and his words seemed strange and completely out of character. Each word he spoke seemed to last forever.

"Remember sweetheart if it has a beginning, it must have an ending. So think on before you start playing about. Are you listening?" Francesca sighed deeply. She'd had enough, after all he was the prisoner, not her. She let him have it.

"Listen prick, I'm here aren't I, so get a grip and sort ya neck out. If you carry on treating me like a nobhead you can get someone else to come and visit you. I don't have to put up with this shit, especially in my condition." Gordon looked shocked at her courage. He dragged her forward from her seat and gritted his teeth into her face.

"Listen cocky arse, what have I told you about the

way you speak to me. Don't think because I'm in here you can talk to me like shit, because I'll be over this table like shit off a shovel and sort you right out. Do you understand me?"

Francesca wriggled free and sat back in her chair. Her eyes rose towards the ceiling. "I don't believe this!" She mumbled under her breath. Francesca looked about the room at the other inmates. She watched how they cherished the moments they had to spend with their loved ones. Gordon knew at this moment he'd over reacted. He stretched his long arms across the table and beckoned Francesca to take hold of them. He checked nobody could hear him and whispered under his breath.

"I know you love me Francesca, but while I'm in here you have to understand my head's up my arse. When I'm out of this shit hole, we can be a family and everything will be fine. I just need reassuring that you won't fuck about on me." Francesca held his hands and softly stroked her fingers across them. The thought of being a family made her heart melt. She was listening to every word he said and believed him. The visit was ending and Francesca felt a little happier inside. She looked at Gordon's face and took in every line and wrinkle. At that moment she remembered why she'd fallen head over heels in love with him, he made her heart skip a beat. Gordon told her he was hoping to earn a few quid whilst he was in the nick. He giggled as he told her about his new pad mate; she could tell he liked him.

The screw walked slowly up behind Gordon and tapped him on the shoulder. He told him to end his visit. Gordon's eyes saddened as did the rest of the convicts. This was a time all the prisoners hated. They now had to watch their loved ones walk away – it was heart wrenching. All the men put on a brave face and tried to control any emotions they felt inside, but you could see the heartbreak all over their faces. Gordon finally stood up from the table and walked to Francesca's side.

"Come on then, give us a kiss." Francesca smiled and wrapped her arms around the firm shoulders of the man she loved. As he kissed her he bit her bottom lip softly and reminded her about being true to him. Francesca carried on kissing him. Gordon now placed his hand on her stomach, Francesca's heartbeat quickened. This was the first time he'd ever shown any love towards their unborn child. Her eyes filled with tears as he gripped her closer and whispered sweet nothings into her ears.

Francesca left his side and walked with the other visitors towards the exit. Everyone must have felt the same because hardly anyone was speaking. They all hung their heads low. One woman couldn't hold back her tears and cried her eyes out as they all left. The man who was with her put his hands around her shoulders and tried to console her, but this seemed to have no effect. The journey of leaving the prison now started. This did Francesca's head in. She hated that they were treated like shit by the prison service. As they entered the final door Francesca could see Tom's smiling face waiting for her on the other side. The screws said goodbye to the visitors with a sarcastic tone. No one replied to them.

Tom looked bored to death as she met him. He told her about the other visitors he'd been speaking to whilst he was waiting for her. There was a woman standing not far from them waiting to go on a visit. Francesca noticed her smiling at Tom. Tom nodded his head at Francesca. His voice was low as he covered his mouth. No one could hear what he was saying.

"Fucking hell Francesca, what a place to meet a woman! They're like flies round shit I tell you," he directed his eyes to a female not that far from them. "That woman sat over there has just given me her phone number. Her fella is doing a ten stretch," he chuckled and stood tall. She's made it quite clear she wanted a shag from me,"

Francesca nudged him in the waist. "Stop lying ya muppet." Tom dug his hand in his pocket and found the small piece of paper with the telephone number on it. He forced the paper into Francesca face.

"There you go then, if ya don't believe me take a look at that." Tom passed the paper to her. Francesca looked at it briefly before she screwed it up and threw it on the floor. Her eyes shot at the woman stood with her back against the wall.

"Fuckin slapper? Her man's in the nick and she's giving her phone number out. The dirty bitch!" Tom laughed out loud and enjoyed his moment.

"Fucking fanny magnet, aren't I? The women all want a bit of my loving, can't say I blame them though can you? Just look at me," Tom stood tall, waving his hands up and down his body, "I've got the body of a love god". Francesca ignored him as they walked away from the prison, she was jealous. Tom was still on a high as they headed home. Francesca tested the water to see what he'd do with another woman.

"Ay fuckin lover boy, what would you have done if I hadn't have thrown that slag's number away. Would you have phoned her?" Tom bounced about on the spot, he knew she was jealous.

"What are ya asking me that for? Do I detect a bit of jealousy?" Francesca told him to get a grip and started to laugh, "Ay I'm fed up, not hard up mate!"

The walk home took about half an hour. The cold wind made them walk with their heads dipped low. Tom saw that Francesca was shivering and told her to link his arm as they walked up the hill. Anybody who didn't know them would have thought they were a couple, they looked in love. Tom's face looked grey. He told Francesca he was struggling with his drug habit and felt his body calling for a fix. His methadone was in the house and he thought he could get by without it until later on – how wrong he was. Francesca squeezed him tightly. She told him they would soon be home but she could tell he was sweating and desperate for his medicine. "You run on then, and get sorted. I'll be okay." Tom didn't need telling twice, he was off on his toes.

Once he was gone she could see the back of him sprinting up Rochdale Road toward the flat. She hated seeing him like that and couldn't wait for the day when he was free from drugs. Her thoughts should have been about Gordon and their visit but she couldn't stop thinking about Tom and the way he was making her feel at the moment.

Tom rammed his key into the front door with trembling hands. He ran to his methadone in the front room. As he entered he froze as he saw Jade sat on the chair just about to inject her body with heroin. His eyes focused on the needle in her hand and she knew this was her chance to get him back on the gear, and more importantly back in her grip.

"Are ya having some of this or what? You can start getting clean tomorrow. Just one more hit ay?"

Tom shook with indecision. No matter how much he wanted to say no he just couldn't help wanting to feel the rush one more time. Before he knew it Jade passed him the leather belt and he was tightened it around his arm. Tom rocked his body to and fro as he watched Jade sink into the chair, her eyes were rolling at the back of her head. He couldn't wait any longer and yanked the needle from her arm. Tom was breathing heavily as he sunk the silver pin deep into his veins. Within minutes he was lay on his back as the drug took control of his body. The heroin had won yet again. Tom was back to square one. Jade opened her eyes slightly and saw him lying next to her. A smile filled her face, he was back on smack.

Francesca climbed the stairs to the flat. The lift was broken yet again. Her mood was more than low as she neared the last flight. Reaching the top her breath was short and she felt quite light headed. As she entered the landing, she noticed the flat door was left wide open. Pushing the door open with her hand she felt the heat from inside grip her face. The flat was in complete silence and she thought it was strange that Tom hadn't turned the television on. Walking into the front room she nearly collapsed where she stood. Tom was sprawled on the floor with Jade was by his side. Her mouth dropped, she didn't need to be a scientist to realise that they both just had a hit. Francesca felt her blood boil and she wanted to jump on Jade for giving Tom the smack. Her fist clenched and her knuckles turned white.

She walked past the two bodies and turned the television loud. Francesca sat down and lit a cigarette. She could see Jade stirring near her feet. Francesca was more than ready for her and sat forward in her seat. Their eyes locked.

"What the fuck are you giving him that shit for when you know he's trying to keep clean?" Francesca's nostrils were flaring and her face was blood red. "You're a silly fat cunt and care only about yourself." She leant in to her face they were nose to nose. "What is it, are you sick because he's sorting his head out and leaving you behind?" Jade rubbed at her eyes and dragged herself up from the floor. She was livid, spit hung from the corner of her mouth as she spoke.

"What the fuck has it got to do with you?" she slurred, "He's my man not yours so keep out of things that don't concern you. You free loading little slut." Francesca dived from the chair and whacked Jade right in the eye. Jade screamed out in pain. They both rolled about fighting. Tom opened his eyes and couldn't believe what he was seeing. Francesca was now on top of Jade, she was dragging her about like a rag doll. Francesca was shouting at the top of her voice.

"You dirty, sweaty, bitch. That's why your kids have been taken off you, because you're a worthless piece of shit. You're not happy destroying their lives, you want to fuck everybody else's life up as well don't you?" Tom dived at Francesca and pulled her from Jade who was struggling to breathe. Tom was shouting at the top of his voice for it to stop but when Jade broke free world war two broke out. All Tom could do was to try and keep them apart. Jade was bouncing about the room with her finger pointed at Francesca.

"Don't think I don't know that you fancy Tom. I could tell from the moment you met him you wanted him for yourself, you dirty little cunt." Tom was stood in front of Jade and protecting her from Francesca grip. She was yelling from behind him. "Well he's my fucking boyfriend so get use to it. I'm not like your mate Misty who let you get away with nicking her boyfriend, I'll fucking do you in before you think you can take him.

Do you hear me shag bag?" Francesca ran at her again and Tom stopped her plunging her nails deep into her face. He held Francesca as tightly as he could. He was screaming at Jade to leave things alone until later. She knew he was right but still ranted at the top of her voice. Grabbing her coat from the side she nursed her bleeding lip.

"Tell you what. I'll go Tom, but I want that little tart gone before I come back. Things were fine between us until that mixing little boot came along. I'm not coming back until she's gone. Do you hear me?" Tom agreed and nodded his head at speed urging her to leave. Francesca was breaking free, her strength was unbelievable and he knew he couldn't hold her much longer. Before she left Jade walked up to Francesca's face and spat into it. Tom screamed for her to leave again this time she knew he meant business. Jade hurried away knowing that if Francesca got her hands on her she would be a dead woman.

The sound of the front door slamming could be heard. Tom sighed with relief. He stood in front of the door for a moment then released Francesca from his grip. His back now pressed firmly behind the door. He told her there was no way in the world he was letting her chase Jade. Francesca paced the front room like a wild woman. She was dragging her fingers through her hair as she tried to calm down. Tom stood at the door shaking from head to toe. He asked Francesca to light two cigs up. He secretly hoped that nicotine might calm her down, but as he looked at her she was still pacing the front room ignoring every word he said.

"Please calm down, think about the baby. It's not good for you all this stress is it?" Francesca snarled at him and headed towards the table where the cigs lay. As she popped one in her mouth her hands shook with temper. Tears filled her eyes and she folded in two on the floor. Tom's heart melted and he left the doorway to be by her side. Reaching her collapsed body he took the cig out of her mouth and placed it on the table behind him while he tried to console her. He squeezed her in his arms and kissed the top of her head. Francesca cried like a baby as she spluttered her words out.

"Why did you have to have the drugs, Tom? I thought you meant it when you said you were getting clean. You're full of shit, just like your brother. I don't know why I ever listened to any of you." You could see a lump forming in Tom's throat. It was like years of emotion had finally caught up with him.

"I know I'm full of shit Francesca, but it's so hard to get off the brown. When I ran home I was going to take my methadone honest, but it was there right in front of me and I was weak and couldn't say no." He dragged at his clothing and screwed his face up. "I'm a drug addict Francesca and you don't know how much I want to change. Don't you think I hate what I've become? My own mam and dad have disowned me for fucks sake. Nobody lets me in their house because they know I'm a smack head. How do you think that makes me feel?" he sank to his knees and cradled his head in his hands. "I know it's my own fault but believe me I'm trying to change. It's just so fucking hard." Francesca thought for a minute and slowly placed her arms round his head. Her hand stroked his greasy mop. The feelings she felt inside were so mixed up at that moment and she wasn't sure what her next step would be.

The scene was heart wrenching. Tom lifted his head up

and the tears were visible on his cheek. Francesca slowly wiped them away with her sleeve. Her lips quivered as she told him she would help him any way she could. Tom thanked her and placed his hand on her face feeling her peach like skin. Their eyes met and slowly he pulled her head down towards his. Tom didn't kiss her straight away and he rubbed his nose softly against hers. That moment would remain with Francesca forever. Tom's tender lips touched hers. It felt so right and she couldn't fight the attraction any longer. All the men she'd been with before had just used her for a quick shag, even Gordon was the same. The kiss was soft and his lips felt like velvet. They both got lost in the moment and shared a long, loving kiss. Tom knew he held feelings for Francesca, he knew from the very first moment he set eyes on her but she belonged to his brother.

Tom stoked her face and moved the piece of hair that had stuck to her cheek through crying. He looked deep into her eyes and tried to find any signs of her feeling the same way towards him. Francesca felt the connection too, she knew she couldn't hold it back any longer. No words were spoken as they held one another in each other's arms. They both knew this was the start of something special and wanted it more than ever. Tom held Francesca's hand and guided her to the bedroom. He locked the front door and joined his new love on the bed. Francesca wasn't like she used to be. In the past her knickers would have been off in a flash but today she lay with her clothes fully intact as he came to join her.

Tom held her in his arms. He knew that what was about to happen would be a betrayal of his own flesh and blood. He kissed Francesca's head and his choice was made. She was everything he'd ever dreamed of. He knew his brother didn't really care for her he'd told him loads of times in the past; she was just a bang he'd said. Tom knew this woman could change his life. His mind was made up and the betrayal began. He slowly began to kiss Francesca's neck. His nostrils flared as he inhaled the fragrance of a real woman, her skin felt so soft to him. Jade's body was hanging and nothing to write home about. Sex with her was like shagging a wet lettuce. This was the real deal for Tom and he'd never been as excited in his life.

Francesca helped him as he pulled her clothing from her body. Their love making began. Tom caressed her nipples and suckled them. His other hand slowly pulled up her skirt and stroked the top of her lacy pink knickers. Francesca felt his hand on the top of her pubic mound and her toes curled. Even though she knew it was all wrong, she couldn't help the urge to feel him inside her. Tom kissed her passionately; they both knew that they wanted this more than ever. Before long they both lay on the bed naked. Tom slowly mounted her and kissed her ripe breasts. Francesca could feel his man hood between her legs and jerked up against him wanting more. Tom knew now there was no going back and before he entered her he looked straight into her eyes and asked the dreaded question.

"What about Gordon?"

Francesca made no response and grabbed the top of his shoulder pulling him deeper inside her. The connection was made and Francesca groaned with pleasure. Tom's penis was so much bigger than his brother's and he knew exactly what to do with it beneath the sheets. There was no wham bam thank you mam with Tom. Oh no. He took his time and made every stoke count. Francesca held on to him and felt like she was going to explode. Tom slowly guided himself too and fro and made every stroke long and hard. Unlike his brother he wasn't a selfish lover and made sure he'd pleasured Francesca before he came. She was now on fire underneath him and she felt like he'd awoken the woman inside her. She climbed on top of him and slowly grinded her body on top of his. The sweat from his body turned her on, her hand glided over his flat stomach. Within minutes they'd both found heaven. They struggled for breath as their bodies shook with pleasure. Tom looked straight into her eyes as he ejaculated. He whispered her name softly.

They lay entwined in each other's bodies on the bed. Tom squeezed her into his arms knowing he could never let go. This was his dream and it was about time he had some luck in his life. Gordon was locked up for a long time and by the time he was released from jail he would be strong enough to fight him. Tom knew in his heart that from this day forward he would die for this woman. No one would ever hurt her again, not even his brother.

Words didn't come easy for either of them. Francesca felt so safe in his arms. She knew he would do anything for her. She was in love.

Later on that evening, they discussed what had happened between them. They both decided they would keep it a secret. Tom told Francesca he would end his relationship with Jade as soon as he saw her. He gave his word that no drugs would ever pass through his veins again. It was going to be hard but with this woman at his side, he knew he could conquer anything that stepped in his way. Francesca told Tom she had an appointment at the doctors in a couple of days to discuss her pregnancy. Holding her hand in his he kissed her fingertips and told her she didn't have to face anything on her own again.

He would be by her side from this day forward. Night time fell and they slept in each other's arms knowing that the next day would be hard. Francesca knew Jade would not give him up that easily. She'd have to watch her back constantly because she knew Jade would have more than one trick up her sleeve when she discovered they were together.

Hours later, the pair bolted up from the bed. Someone was hammering on the front door. Tom looked at his watch and rubbed at his eyes. "Who the fuck is this at this time?" he sat on the edge of the bed listening to the letterbox being flicked constantly. Francesca opened her eyes, "Who is it? Is it the dibble?" Tom hunched his shoulders, "Dunno." Jade's voice could be heard shouting from outside. Francesca dived out of the bed and looked frantic. Tom looked at her with shock in his face and rummaged about on the floor for his jeans. He grabbed Francesca's arm, "Go in the front room. It's my mess, and I need to sort it out." Francesca stood for a minute thinking. "If she starts one bit of shit with you though she's getting it." Tom urged her into the living room. "She won't do shit, trust me; just get out of the way for now."

As he came out of the bedroom he could see Jade's round face squashed up against the front door panel. She continued to knocking until Tom shouted that he was coming. Opening the door Jade assumed she could just walk inside; it wasn't till Tom placed his foot at the door that she knew she wasn't welcome. She snarled at Tom, and tried to get past him.

"What are you holding the door for you nobhead. Let me in."

Tom shook his head slowly and licked the side of his lip.

"Listen Jade it's over. I want to sort myself out and get off the gear." His fingers were turning white with the grip he held on the door frame. His eyes started at her, "whilst I'm with you that will never happen, so I think it's best if we call it a day." Tom waited for a reaction and it wasn't long before Jade exploded and tried to barge past him.

"What do you mean it's over? Stop being a wanker and let me in." Tom stood tall as she tried to get past again. He could see the madness in her eyes and all hell broke loose as she tried to set about him.

"You dirty no good fucker. All the things I've done for you and now you think you can get rid of me just like that." She held her hands on her hip as her lips trembled. "Don't I mean fuck all to you anymore?" Tom tried to explain that things had changed but she lost the plot and pounced on him sinking her teeth deep into his arm. Tom dragged her away from the front door towards the stairs. His face was sweating and he was struggling to fight her off.

"Listen Jade, I've told you once it's over. I don't want to hurt you, so just fuck off and let me sort myself out." Jade screams echoed down the corridor. Tom pushed her away and headed back to the flat. Jade was screaming behind him, she was a broken woman.

"Think you're a smart arse do you? Well let's see how long you last without me. You're a smack head just like me. Once a bag head ,always a bag head." Jade fell to her knees and pleaded with him trying to make him see sense. "It's only since that little tart has come along that you've changed." She dragged herself from the floor and spat towards him. "Well don't come crying to me when you need a fix or money. Let your little slag sort you out because I'm finished with you, do you hear me? Finished. You're a using bastard." Tom watched as she flew down the stairs. Just when he thought she'd left, she shouted her final words. "Oh tell the slapper to watch her back. As I told her before, I'm not Misty and she'll pay big time for splitting us up. Mark my words bollockhead she'll pay!" With that Jade was gone. Tom rubbed his arms as the cold morning air hit his puny body. He quickly headed back inside the flat, relieved that he'd told Jade it was over. Francesca looked concerned as he entered the front room, she ran towards him. She could see his wound and quickly removed his hand from it to get a closer look. Her mouth dropped.

"Fucking hell, Tom, let me see that, has she broken the skin?" Francesca examined it closely as Tom tried to pull it away from her.

"It's nothing, just leave it. Honestly I'm okay." Francesca looked at him and told him straight.

"Listen, you. If you hurt so do I. We're a team now and we share everything. I'm not ending up like I was before so let me help you." Tom reached for her and squeezed her tightly, that was the nicest thing anyone had ever said to him. He still couldn't believe that he had a chance at life again. They both sat and spoke about the days that lay ahead.

Francesca felt sadness in her heart and missed her best friend Misty. She needed her now more than ever, she was falling apart. How had she ever ended up in this mess?

## Chapter Seven

Misty stood before the full length mirror and pulled her top tightly around her stomach. She could now see the shape of the baby that grew inside her. Misty was seven months pregnant and her heart was in her mouth every time she felt a pain in her stomach. Her pregnancy had been filled with fear throughout. She couldn't help but think this would be the day that she would lose her baby. The child she had lost so long ago was never far from her thoughts. Misty felt guilty that if she carried this baby full term that her other baby would have known and blamed her for his death. Stupid I know, but that was how she was thinking. Misty was on edge all the time, and until her child was in her arms she couldn't relax.

She hadn't bought a single item of clothing for her unborn child. She was so superstitious and thought she would tempt fate even if she bought one single vest. Her body hadn't changed much since she'd been pregnant but she put that down to all the worry. Dominic was still her rock and told her every day how much he loved her. He was doing well – his business had taken off and he was raking in the cash. His work kept him out until late each evening. Misty hated being alone but he told her straight they needed the money for their new baby and their future.

The refuge was still being managed by Sue. Misty called in every day even though she was supposed to be at home resting. Sue and her fiancé John had finally set the date for their wedding. In one weeks time Sue would become Mrs Power. Misty loved her work still and every woman that came through the refuge doors was helped as much as they could be. Misty still couldn't let go of her past and she saw herself in every young girl that walked through the refuge doors. Gordon was her past and even though he was locked up, he still haunted her dreams every night. She knew one day he would want what belonged to him and she'd have to face her demons when he was released. Her own secret was held close to her chest. The baby that grew inside her would never know that the man who nearly killed her was a part of its life in more ways than one. The truth lay heavily on her lips. There were times when she was sat with her friend Sue that she just wanted to blurt out the truth. But she bit her tongue hard. Nobody must ever know the secret she held inside.

Misty lived in a four bed roomed house in Chadderton. The area where she lived was quite up market and much sort after. Every room in the house was painted in ivory white. It looked so refreshing and clean. Dominic's parents had found them the property. Both Misty and Dominic had fallen in love with it the moment they set eyes upon it.

Dominic's mother had never got used to her son marrying a council estate girl, she wanted so much more for him. She always thought he was too good for her and never hid the fact to her friends. Misty's family came from a rough area and her family was well known on the estate. Misty had also broken her son's heart a long time ago. Sheila hadn't forgotten the tears she saw her son cry. She always kept a close eye on his new wife. Dominic's mother tried her best to like Misty and now she was carrying her grandchild things seemed to be getting better between them. Sheila hated it when Misty's mother Lisa came to visit them. She couldn't wait to get her in the front door away from the neighbours. Sheila hated Lisa's car being parked on the front drive, it was an old banger and everyone stared at the rust bucket.

Sheila had bought many things for her new grandchild over the last few months. She hid them all away from

Misty's eyes though because she knew she'd have gone mad if she'd seen them. Sheila was up her own arse at times and thought nobody should stop her enjoying buying clothes for her new grandchild, not even Misty. Dominic's father Ted was the complete opposite of her; he was rough and ready and bent as a nine bob note. Sheila didn't know half the things he got up to and would have dropped down dead if she ever got a whiff of his dodgy dealings. Dominic's parents lived in Chadderton too and Misty knew that was why they'd urged Dominic to seek property there.

Dominic wasn't a mummy's boy but Sheila had a lot to say about any choices he made. She was a cunning old fart sometimes and Misty could see right through her. When she didn't like a decision Dominic had made she would take to her bed and blame it all on the worry of his choices, knowing he would change his mind to please her. Once she'd got what she wanted she would make a miraculous recovery and free herself from her sick bed.

The day Misty moved into her new home, Sheila stood with a clipboard in her hands making sure all the furniture went into the correct place. Misty and her mother Lisa laughed as they watched her pecking everyone's head. Lisa had threatened to shove the clipboard right up her arse on more than one occasion. Misty had been on a short fuse with Sheila all day but she knew she had a heart of gold and wouldn't hurt a fly, she was just so annoying. The first night Misty spent in their new home felt quite weird. The house felt so lonely and empty. She missed the sound of noisy children running about and the family arguments. Misty had already decided she wanted lots of kids in the future, she couldn't stand being alone.

Misty climbed the stairs to bed. She felt like a queen

as she floated along the wide stair case. Who would have thought it, Misty Sullivan living in a house like this, she giggled as she gazed around her surroundings. Dominic was fast asleep when she entered the bedroom. She sneaked in beside him trying not to wake him. Night times were her worst time of the day. Once she lay in bed her mind would takeover and the torment would begin. Every night was the same. The past years were always there to fight with her thoughts whilst she tried to find sleep. Sometimes she wondered if she'd ever feel normal again. The time she had spent with Gordon had stolen years from her. She should have had lots of good memories from her youth, but all she had was dark stories and the memory of his reign of terror. Every time she closed her eyes, his face was there, grinning and smirking at her.

Misty rummaged for her note pad from underneath the bed to write a poem for the refuge. She wanted something that would stick in the minds of the women who came there to try and make them remember the lives they'd left behind. She always found comfort in poetry. Once the pen was in her hand, she seemed to drift away and find peace and tranquillity in the words she wrote. She started writing.

> *Feeling his fist across your face*
> *Feeling your heart step up a pace*
> *Knowing the beating that lies ahead*
> *Knowing that this time you could be dead*
> *He digs his fist deep inside your chest*
> *Until you are beaten, he won't rest*
> *Nobody to hear the tears you cry*
> *To cover your bruises you will lie.*

*The life you've chosen won't get much better*
*Expect your pillar to get wetter and wetter*
*Your confidence has gone and won't return*
*Look at your life, won't you ever learn?*
*Remember the days when you laughed so much*
*And longed to feel your partner's touch*
*Those days are gone there in the past*
*Let's hope you learn your lesson fast*
*You will survive without this violent man*
*And with some help you can plan*
*A better life filled with peace*
*Self confidences returned and end your grief.*

Misty read through the words she'd written with the pen hanging from her mouth. The words touched her own heart and she hoped it would touch others. Dominic opened his eyes as she turned the pages on her notepad. He could see she was restless. He looked at her face and his heart melted. He knew she was having trouble sleeping again and moved closer towards her.

"You still awake Princess?" he whispered as he looked at her tired eyes. His hands stroked her face softly, "You should try and get some sleep. These late nights will catch up with you sooner or later and what will happen then?" He snuggled his head into her breast. "When the baby comes you'll need all the sleep you can." Misty nodded slowly and kissed the top of his head before she spoke.

"I know you're right but until this baby is born, I won't rest. You know what happened last time. It's always in the back of my mind every minute of every day."

Dominic sat up, he took the white piece of paper from her hand and began to read what she'd written. His eyes filled with tears and he knew it was more than the baby keeping her awake at nights. Gordon still had a hold of his wife even though he was locked up. Dominic knew more than anyone the terror he'd brought to her life. He just hoped she could get over it, but deep down inside he knew the child she was carrying inside her would be a constant reminder of the bastard he hated so much.

Dominic turned the small side light off at the side of the bed and held Misty tightly in his arms. He was her protector now and he'd fight to the death to make sure she was never hurt again, no matter what the cost would be. Misty dug her head into his chest and felt the security he offered. As she drifted off to sleep Dominic could feel the life inside her moving about. His hand moved across her stomach and he stroked the unborn child, hoping to settle it. He too had his own doubts on whether he could love another man's child. Everyone round him talked about the baby being born and he played his part of a devoted father well. His mother had already dug some photographs out of her attic ready to compare to him when it was finally born. His mind tried to settle as he closed his eyes. He knew what lay ahead would be hard and just hoped he could be the father to the child without anyone discovering their dark secret.

Misty rushed about the kitchen trying to get breakfast ready before Dominic left for work. The toast was made and as she put the milk into the coffee Dominic entered the kitchen. He always kissed Misty each morning and this day was no different. He spoke about the day ahead and told her he wouldn't be home until late that evening. Misty hated the thought of coming home to an empty house and couldn't hide her disappointment as her face dropped. Seeing her sadness Dominic stood behind her and tickled her neck as she stood buttering the toast.

"You know I have to work late love. Do you think for one minute I enjoy being sat with two boring bastards all day long." He twisted her around to face him, "this is a big deal and if we get this land, we'll earn a fortune." Misty smiled and knew his words were wise. Everything he'd for them in the past was for their future. She just had to learn to take the good with the bad in the type of business he was in. Dominic helped carry the food to the table. They both sat chatting as the phone rang. Dominic listened to it ring for a few minutes and couldn't take it any longer. They both knew who was on the other end of the phone. Sheila phoned every morning at exactly the same time. Dominic reached for the phone and raised his eyebrows at Misty.

"Hello mum." Misty watched him as he spoke to his mother and knew he was already bored with the conversation. Dominic held the phone from his ear and pulled funny faces at her. Misty nearly fell off the chair with laughter as he rubbed the phone on his arse. Listening to the conversation all you could hear was Dominic saying, 'Yes mum', 'okay mum' and you could tell it was another morning lecture about whatever had bothered her the night before. Dominic loved his mum to pieces. He knew more than anyone that she could be hard work. He also knew how she felt about his wife. He told her straight that if ever heard her bad mouthing Misty to her friends she would be out of his life forever. Dominic's dad had been so patient with Sheila over the years. Dominic couldn't understand why he hadn't strangled her, because he knew, had she been his wife he would have left her moaning arse years ago. The conversation ended after five minutes and Dominic returned to the table with a smile across his face.

"Fucking hell, she still thinks I'm a baby you know." He was waving his hands up and down. "She's telling me to wrap up warm and the fucking traffic news for the day." Misty chuckled and started to call him mummy's little soldier. "Fuck off winding me up." he chuckled. Misty had decided that today she would go and visit the refuge. She knew nothing would be wrong there but she still felt the urge to go. Anything would be better than sat in the house all day on her own and plus she had her poem to take.

Dominic left for work and Misty started her housework. If the truth was known the house was spotless but she still felt the urge to keep busy. Misty finished her brew and turned on the radio. She loved listening to the music as she cleaned and it always put her in a good mood.

Once her chores were done, Misty got ready and headed to the car on the driveway. She loved driving and thought it was one of the best things that she'd ever achieved. The day she'd passed her driving test, Dominic bought her a new car. She remembered how he'd tied a great big pink ribbon around it and covered Misty's eyes as he took her to see it. That day would stay with Misty forever. Her husband was so generous towards her and she wanted for nothing. Misty twisted her wedding ring around her finger and she knew Dominic was her life. The sacrifices he'd made to be with her were enormous. He even put her before his mother. Sheila had told him in the past to make the choice between them both, and after days of arguing he finally told his mother that Misty was his life and there was no choice to be made. His mother finally come round to the idea of them both being together in time and slowly forgave Misty for breaking her son's heart. She still held a grudge against her but knew her son's happiness came first. She tried her best to accept Misty back into her life.

Misty picked up the post at the front door of the refuge. The noise from the bedroom upstairs caused her to stop and listen more carefully. As she listened, she could hear Sue shouting loudly and could tell she was distressed. Misty waited a few more minutes and made her way upstairs towards the bedroom. As she reached the top stair she could see a middle-aged woman carrying her bags towards her. Sue looked out of her mind with worry and she could tell there had been a heated argument between them both.

"What's going on?" Misty asked. Sue ran to her side and dragged at her arm.

"Misty please talk to her and try and make her see sense. She's going back to her husband after all he's done to her." Misty came to the woman's side and tried to console her. She was shaking like a leaf. Sue now joined them and placed her arms around the woman's shoulders. Sue pleaded with her again.

"Please just stay for ten minutes more. There's so many reasons why you shouldn't go back home." Sue sighed deeply. "Please just let's talk for a while before you make any hasty decisions." The woman lifted her hands to her head and yanked at her hair.

"He's told me if I don't come back to him he'll kill me and the kids." Her hands were shaking as she wrapped them around her body. "I haven't got a choice. He's fucking mental and I know he means what he says." The women huddled together. Sue finally convinced her to have a chat before she left. Sue started to make her way downstairs to the kitchen and Misty and the woman followed slowly behind her. They sat in a small room just off the corridor. Sue came into the room now holding three cups. She slowly bent her knees and placed them on the small glass table. Silence filled the room for a minute. Sue eventually spoke and brought Misty up to date with the circumstances that had brought the woman to the refuge. Sue's voice was calm as she started to speak and Misty held the woman's hand as she sat next to her.

"Beverley has been staying with us for two days now Misty. She came to us in a right mess. Her husband has led her a terrible life." Sue's face dropped and she shook her head. "I can't let her walk straight back to him we need her to see sense." Misty looked into Beverley's eyes and saw a look that told her she'd been through a lot of hardship. Looking at the woman's bony wrist she noticed she had bruises all over them. Beverley needed help before it was too late. Misty passed her cup of tea and watched as her hands shook uncontrollably as she tried to take a sip from the cup. Both Sue and Misty looked at each other and knew she was in a bad way. Misty started to speak and asked Beverley to tell her what had happened for her to come to the refuge in the first place. Beverley was silent for a moment. She dug her hand into her pocket and searched for her cigs. Once she'd lit one she took a deep drag, her cheeks sucked in. Her face looked stressed as she began.

"He said he'd never hurt me again. He promised me, and I believed him." Beverley's head sank onto her chest. "It's ever since he lost his job. He just snapped at the slightest thing." Misty held her hand tightly and urged her to continue. Beverley sucked on her cig as if it was giving her the strength to continue. "The final straw came when he came home pissed the other night. I was in bed fast asleep." Her eyes were wide open and she twisted her hair in her hand. "I felt water or something trickling on me. As I opened my eyes, there he was, stood right over me squirting lighter fuel all over the bed. I didn't realise what was going on at first until I saw the lighter in his hand. I fucking shit bricks and jumped up as quickly as I could." The tears streamed down her face. Her hand gripped her throat and she looked as if she was struggling for breath. Blowing deeply through her mouth she continued. "I told him not to be a silly cunt, but he kept flicking the lighter with an evil look in his eyes. I tried to calm him down and finally got him to sit on the bed." She paused for a second and chewed on her bottom lip. "He looked like he was in a world of his own. I could tell he wanted to hurt me badly, I could see it in his eyes. Anyway, he left the room and I could hear him pissing in the bathroom. I thought he'd calmed down, more fool me to think that because when he came back he had the iron in his hands. I fucking watched him plug it into the wall. I didn't know what I thought at first, but I just sat there." She stubbed her cig out in the ashtray. "I suppose I thought he was going back out to a nightclub or something. I just presumed he was ironing a new set of clothes. I never dreamt in a million years what he'd planned for me." Misty shivered as she continued goose pimples were all over her arms. Misty knew exactly what the woman had gone through. Beverley now asked for a tissue and wiped her eyes as a waterfall of tears landed on her lips.

"The bastard needs locking up. Look at my legs what he's done." She now rolled up her black nylon skirt and revealed the shape of the iron marks on her legs. The burns looked infected and she looked in pain as she pulled her skirt back down over her legs. Beverley rocked to and fro in her chair. "He's not a well man. He just needs some help that's all. I'm all he has in this world and if I give up on him he'll definitely do himself in." Beverley now sank her head into her hands and looked like she had seen a ghost. Her bottom lip trembled as she stood up and picked up her bags. At first she just froze, her eyes looked towards the door. Misty and Sue shot a look at each other and tried one last time to make her stay. Misty stood near the exit and blocked her path as she started to speak.

"Beverley, I'm so worried about you love. Stay for a while longer and just think things through. It's obvious your husband needs help, but so do you. Please let's sort this mess out together." Beverley's mind was already made up and she made her way passed Misty with her head hung low.

"Thanks Sue for all you've done, I know I'm a fool going back to him, but he needs me right now." Misty sighed and knew she was fighting a losing battle. A ball of emotion now travelled to her throat as she reached to hug Beverley. She told her she could always come back if the situation got any worse. Misty knew inside that this woman was too much under her husband's spell, she would be at his beck and call forever. The women stood at the front door and watched Beverley quickly run down the road towards the bus stop. She looked so weak and her hair was stuck to her head with grease. It was so sad how life had dealt her a hand of cards that she couldn't deal with. They knew nothing would ever change in this woman's life because she needed her violent husband just as much as he needed her.

They closed the front door and looked deflated. As they walked back to the hall Misty held Sue and told her they'd done all they could. The refuge was full of residents and Sue had helped many a women on the path back to recovery. It was women like Beverley that would always remain in her thoughts though. Sue would worry herself to death wondering how things would turn out for her; she was just so much of a caring person. After a few minutes, Sue and Misty sat on the brown leather chairs and stared at the bare walls. Sue gasped a breath of air and shook her head.

"Fucking shame it is. I can't stand it when that happens but I know we've all been there haven't we. I suppose when you're involved in a violent relationship you don't see the wood for the trees." Sue sat gasping her breath. "You just look at everything with rose tinted glasses don't you? I know I did in the past." Misty agreed and held her stomach as the baby kicked her. Sue was on one now and tilted her head to the side.

"My mam once told me, 'once a bastard always a bastard' and she were right yanno. Very few men change once they've raised their fist to you. It's just a matter of time before you realise that you're not happy with them and move on." Her face turned to Misty. "What bugs me though is once you've left them they realise what a twat they really were, and promise you the moon if you come back to them." She held her hands up in the air. "Why do they always realise when it's too fucking late." Misty reached into her bag and handed Sue the poem. Sue sat back in her chair and crossed her legs as she read it Misty sipped her brew. After Sue had read what she'd written she looked at Misty. "You should try and get this published. You've got such a talent for writing."

Misty shook her head. "Have I eck, it's just a few daft words that's all."

"Misty," Sue snapped, "you need to start believing in yourself more. You have a talent girl and you shouldn't let it pass you by. If I had a talent like that I would most definitely do something about it." Misty searched the drawers in the room and looked for the empty picture frame she'd seen there some time ago. Once she found it, she slid the poem inside it and looked at the finished article.

"I was thinking about putting it up in this room, what do you think?"

"Yeah, it would look good in here." Sue replied.

Sue stood up and searched the drawers for a small nail. Lots of things were inside it and Sue was sure she'd seen a small nail in there.

"Is that straight Sue?" Misty shouted as she held the picture frame on the wall.

"Up at the left a bit love then I think it's straight, mind you my eyes are bent as a nine bob note, so you'll have to have a look at it once it's up." Misty used her shoe to knock the small nail into the wall as Sue stood laughing.

"Fucking hell Misty, what are we like? We're right cowboys aren't we."

Misty chuckled. "When Dominic comes, I'll ask him to check its safe, just in case it falls on somebody's head." Misty covered her mouth with her hand. "That's all we need a woman coming here for help from us and a picture frame falling on her head. She'd end up with more bruises than she came in with." They both giggled and decided it would be a good idea for Dominic to put the picture frame up next time he visited. Misty propped the frame up on the side.

Sue took Misty to the small side office now and

checked her emails on the computer as Misty gazed about the room. The refuge was looking so good these days. The walls were painted a soft lemon colour that made the place look fresh. Sue and Misty had now got the funding from the local council to improve the refuge. Things that seemed only a dream in the past were now possible for the girls. The family room had a dark brown leather settee in it and a television. The chocolate carpet looked so fluffy and welcoming. Misty always wanted to lie on it and stroke it with her hands. The place itself was very homely and any family would have been proud of it. For many people staying at the refuge this was a luxury compared to where they'd come from. The games room for the children was incredible and it had lots of different gadgets for the children living there. The PlayStation was the main attraction and the one that caused all the arguing. Sue went into the room weeks before and discovered two lads rolling about the floor fighting over the control pad. They were really going for it as well as she watched in disbelief. The biggest lad, who could have only been thirteen, was sat on top of the smaller one. He was pummelling his face with great force as the other boy screamed out at the top of his voice.

"Get off me ya daft twat. It dunt belong to you. It's here for all of us, not just you, so get the fuck off me." The other lad shook him about like a rag roll and only stopped when he saw Sue stood there. He quickly dismounted his victim, leaving the other lad free to get up and challenge him once again. All hell broke loose then; they both ran at each other with full force looking like two raging bulls. Sue had to jump between them. They tried to punch and kick at each other. One of the kicks landed right on Sue's shin and she yelled with pain. It was only when a parent heard the screams from another room that she was rescued. The parent alerted the other boy's mother who was seated in the family room. They all came running to help. The two mothers of the boys dragged their children apart by the scruffs of their necks. The older lad's mam clouted him right across the head and shouted at him in a stressed voice.

"Do you think I fucking need this at the moment? I've had enough fucking violence in my life to last me a life time. I don't need you starting it as well. What the fuck are you fighting for anyway?" Her son opened his mouth and the words trailed off his tongue like an express train leaving the station. He didn't even stop for breath as he tried to get his side of the story heard. The injured boy's mother was nursing her son's wounds as she tried to listen what had gone on but with all the shouting in the room she couldn't make sense of anything anyone was saying. Sue shouted for everyone to be quiet and the room filled with silence. They'd never seen Sue like this before and they knew she meant business. Sue bent towards her leg and rubbed at her shin as she tried to calm the situation down further.

"Right," she said to the eldest boy who was stood with a cocky look on his face next to his mother. "Are you going to tell me what the hell is going on here or what?" The other lad started shouting his bit of evidence out and Sue snarled at him before telling him to be quiet. The boy started to speak with his mother at his side. Her flat palm was stretched out and ready to wallop him if he got lippy. The teenager nodded his head as he spoke.

"I had the control pad first and that little nobhead thinks he can walk in and chat shit to me. I told him to wait his turn but he still stood there pecking my head."

The boy held his head back and smirked. "He wound me up and now he's got his arse kicked because of it." His victim was chomping at the bit to speak. Sue finally gave him the go ahead. The young boy held his arms out at the side of him as he spoke and jumped about in his space as if he had a stone in his shoe.

"Nar, no way was it like that, ya muppet," he yelled, "I was on it first and he came over and tried to nick it off me thinking I was just gonna give it him." The other lad grinned at him and remained at the side of his mother. Sue now moved the other housemates to another room and asked both women to stay with their sons to sort the mess out. There was still some shouting for a while until Sue raised her voice again and told them all to sit down. Sue had learnt to deal with these kinds of situations on a course she'd just completed. This was her first chance to put her knowledge into action. She started with the youngest boy first and stopped any reply he tried to make. She remained calm throughout the talk and at the end of it the two lads shook hands. Both parents apologised to each other and a new rota was made for the use of the PlayStation. Each child in the refuge had a designated time for it now and the system worked well.

Misty listened to the story and laughed. They'd both come so far since they'd met. Sue was getting married the following week and all her dreams were coming true. John had been everything Sue had ever wanted he was her soul mate. The days that lay ahead was going to be so stressful for her but Misty promised her she would be by her side all the way.

Misty looked through the window and gazed at the grassy area outside. Everything looked so peaceful and tranquil and her thoughts wandered off to a place when she'd felt happier. This pregnancy had really played with her emotions. One day she'd be happy and the next she'd be sat in tears. This baby inside her was a constant reminder of her past and she wondered if she could ever love it the way she was supposed to. She tried to imagine the baby in her arms so many times before and her stomach turned at the thought of it. Misty kept her thoughts to herself though, because who could she ever confide in and tell the dreadful truth. Sue finished her emails. They planned to spend the rest of the day trying on her wedding dress and having Misty's bridesmaid dress altered. Misty looked like a pumpkin in her bridesmaid dress. The colour peach did nothing for her complexion but it was Sue's big day and she didn't want to moan about the choice of dress.

They both left the refuge and headed for Sue's home. Sue looked like a bag of nerves as she drove through the traffic. She was yelling at the driver in front of her to get a move on. Misty smiled, "Calm down, you're a bad stress head, you need to relax."

Sue tapped her fingers on the steering wheel, "I know, but come on that driver a fucking wanker." Sue pointed to the car in front of her.

Sue stood in her crisp wedding dress in the front room. She twirled about like a princess showing off her new gown to its full beauty. Sue looked amazing; her dress was like something Misty had only seen in the movies. It slid off her shoulders like butter melting from a piece of toast. The ivory wedding dress had lots of diamond sequins sprinkled all over it. At a glance, it looked like snowflakes had landed on it. The dress maker pulled a tissue from her pocket and wiped her eyes as she looked at the bride in her dress. Misty felt emotional and swung her arms around her friend's shoulders to congratulate her.

"You look amazing Sue," Misty whispered. Sue squeezed her with all her might in her grip. The words were few and they both tried to hold back the tears. Sue lifted her head and started to speak.

"Orr fucking hell, look at us we're a couple of emotional wrecks aren't we? Imagine us on the wedding day." The tears now turned to laughter and even the dress maker started to chuckle at the state of them both. The wedding was to be held at St Malachy's church in Collyhurst. This was a place chosen by John. He was brought up in the area and still lived there till this day. John's parents were the owners of a local pub in Collyhurst called the Robert Tinker. The pub itself was situated on a hill in the middle of a council estate. John had spoken endlessly to her of the times he'd spent growing up there. She could tell by the stories he'd told her that he'd had a happy childhood. Sue remembered he'd told her of a place called Bob's Hill at the back of the pub. He always spoke about the adventures he'd there. Bob's Hill was somewhere he'd promised to take Sue hundreds of times but as of yet he hadn't kept his promise.

Sue had been to the pub several times and met John's parents. They seemed like nice people and they made her feel part of the family straight away. The Robert Tinker was always filled with local residents. Some of them were lively characters. Sue felt a little bit intimidated by them at first but that was until she'd got to know them better. Sue had met a lovely old couple in the pub who only lived across the road. She loved the stories they told her of days gone by. Apparently, Peggy and Sydney had moved to the area when it first was built. They'd seen all the changes as they happened. The couple had seen some hard times in the past and their seven children had suffered due to their poverty. Sydney was a bit of a wheeler and dealer. In his day he had to make ends meet the only way he knew how. He was very distinctive looking man. His hair was a strawberry blond colour that he combed back from his face. Sydney's hair looked like he'd applied some thick kind of gel to it. Not one stand of hair was out of place, no matter how much he moved it about. Sydney was a tall man and always looked smartly dressed. When he was pissed he'd always keep the pub amused by playing old songs on his comb. Peggy was a character by herself. Her little scrawny legs seemed like they'd carried years of disappointment on them. She always looked like she had the worries of the world on her shoulders. Every line on her face told a different story. Peggy was also dressed smartly. She often wore a floral dress with a dark brown fur coat covering it. Her hair was a dark brown treacle colour. The rollers she placed in her hair the night before always left imprints in her hair. Peggy's eyes always had a glazed look about them, as if tears were trapped inside. They seemed to hold so much sadness from the years that had passed. Sue found herself warming to Peggy within minutes of meeting her. She felt like she'd known her all her life. The two of them spent hours huddled together in the corner of the pub every time Sue visited. They never shut up talking.

John's parents had previously asked them both to consider having the wedding reception in the Robert Tinker. Sue had been against the idea at first but once she'd been in a few times and got know everybody she gave them the go ahead. A few of the regulars had been invited to the wedding. Peggy and Sydney were among them. When Sue told them both they were invited to her celebrations they nearly fainted. The old couple were so chuffed and thankful for their invite. You would have thought they'd been invited to the Queen's birthday party the way they were going on, they couldn't thank Sue and John enough.

John's parents were older than Sue had expected. Maureen was fifty and Tony was fifty-seven. They both looked great for their ages. Maureen always dressed like she was going out for a night on the tiles. Maureen had told Sue that she was getting a private company in to dress all the tables in the pub. She'd also planned for waiters to serve the food. Sue knew Maureen would do her proud on her big day and never give it a second thought.

Misty stood like a prize vegetable as the final alterations were made to her dress. She felt ugly and fat. The heat in the room made her face sweat and she felt sick. Her eyes looked down at the silk dress as it clung to her body like it was holding her for dear life. She didn't look happy. Misty's shoes were lower than all the other bridesmaids. Her feet had swollen tremendously and she found it hard to get any shoes that fitted her elephant like feet.

★

The day of the wedding finally came. All the bridesmaids sat in Sue's parent's front room waiting for her to come down the stairs. Altogether there were four bridesmaids and each of them looked beautiful. Sue's mother was a nervous wreck, she kept pacing the living room floor like she'd lost something. Sue's dad was sat on the arm of the chair. He was smoking like a chimney. He kept pulling at his shirt and telling his wife that it was doing his head in. Sue's dad was dressed in a light grey suit with a white shirt. As he stood to look out of the window, he pulled at the crotch of the pants and chuckled to his wife.

"Fucking hell love, my knackers are squashed to death in these pants. I told you I should have got a bigger size," he yanked at the pants and lifted his jacket up to show his wife the back of the trousers. "If I get run over or something today love, they'll have to cut these fuckers off me because they feel like my second skin. How the fuck am I meant to go to the toilet in these bollock stranglers. I'd have shit myself before I could get the fuckers down." Everyone in the room laughed out loud. His wife went over to where he stood and clenched his arse in her hands, she whispered in his ear. "Ay that perky bum is turning me on, you'd better watch yourself." They giggled like school children. The relationship between Sue's parents was so funny to watch, they were like a double act and constantly had everyone in stitches.

The noise of the stairs squeaking made everyone turn towards the living room door. As it opened Sue walked in. At first, she stood still like a statue; she was waiting for the reaction of everyone seeing her dress for the first time. Her family was gobsmacked at the princesses that stood in front of them. The room was in silence.

Sue's dad stood up from his seat, his bottom lip was quivering. He seemed stuck for words for the first time in his life. Sue looked amazing and he couldn't believe that today he would be giving her away to start her own life. Tears forced their way from his eyes; he had no control over them. No matter how much he tried, his words stuck in his throat and he couldn't speak. Sue's dad moved toward her in slow motion. Everyone watched as they all felt the moment too, snivelling could be heard. Sue's dad touched the side of his daughter's face and stroked it softly before he spoke. Sue's mother was already an emotional wreck and wiped her eyes with a crumpled tissue as she watched her husband.

"You look stunning love," he whispered. "I can't tell you how proud I am to be called your father," his nostrils flared as he sucked in a deep breath. "You look like an angel love. John is such a lucky man to be marrying you today." Sue opened her eyes wide and tried not to let the tears spoil her makeup, her hand was wafting rapidly in front of her face.

"Orr dad what are you doing to me? My makeup will be all over if you don't stop it." Sue's dad pulled away slowly. She smiled at him telling him how much she loved him. Her mother could now be heard shouting. "The cars are here, let's move our arses otherwise were going to be late."

The bridesmaids and the bride's mother left first. Sue and her dad were sat alone in the front room. Her father went into the kitchen and came back with two large glasses of whiskey and a big smile across his face. He passed a glass to Sue. "Here, get that down your neck. It will sort your nerves." Sue gripped the glass, her hand shook as she necked the lot of it in one quick gulp. The minute the alcohol hit the back of her throat she felt a warm feeling passing through her body, she shook. Her dad was right; the drink calmed her right down. He coughed loudly and cleared his throat.

"Listen, Sue love. If ever things don't work out with you and John, you can always come back here. There'll always be a bed for you at our house." He sighed and shook his head, "I know before you met John you went through some bad times." He chewed on his bottom lip before he continued. "I could kick myself now for not helping you more, but that's the past isn't it. I promise you this time love." He clenched his fist in front of him and his knuckles were turning white. "If John ever lays a finger on you I'll do time for him, I promise you."

Sue held onto her father. His words touched her. She knew he meant every word and thanked him from the bottom of her heart. "I love you dad, thanks." Sue walked to the window as she checked the time.

The wedding car arrived and honked its horn outside. They both knew it was time to leave. Sue looked one last time in the mirror and straightened her lace veil. The house was securely locked up now and they both sat in the back of the car. Sue's dad was still pulling at his pants constantly. His fingers were yanking at his pink tie all the way to the church. Sue didn't speak a word; she just sat in silence twisting her fingers. Gazing out of the window she closed her eyes and tried to imagine her life once she was married.

The photographer captured every movement on film. The camera could be heard as Sue and her father got out of the wedding car. The bridesmaids stood waiting for her on the steps at the church's entrance. Misty was getting the girls in position as Sue came to join them. Misty held Sue's hands. "You look stunning Sue."

The organ played the traditional wedding march song. The bridesmaids glided down the aisle as if they were floating on air. Sue and her father now looked at one another and knew it was time to make a move. As they started to walk, her dad pulled at his pants one last time and brought a smile to his daughter's face. "Fucking stop messing with them pants dad." Sue chuckled. The church was packed with friends and relations. Everyone's face looked at the bride to be. It wasn't until she got half way down the aisle that she saw John looking nervously towards her. Dominic was by his side.

Once she'd reached the altar, the bridesmaids seated in the front row of the church. John didn't look at Sue at first but when their eyes finally met he whispered under his breath. "You look amazing love."

Sue seemed to be in a world of her own as the priest began to speak. Her eyes were focusing on the beauty of the church. The pictures set around the altar seemed to be so real. Her eyes were drawn to a statue of the Holy Mary. The sculpture looked so alive and the Virgin Mary looked so real. Secretly Sue prayed to her and asked her for happiness. The church seemed quite old. Lifting her eyes towards the ceiling, she could see where the paint had peeled off due to damp. Sue felt her heart slowing down as she looked at the priest.

The man in cloth took the rings from Dominic's hand. He placed them on a red velvet cushion edged in gold piping. The vows were exchanged as everyone listened eagerly. As John declared his everlasting love for Sue, the sound of snivelling women could be heard behind him. John placed the ring on Sue's quivering finger. He slowly reached over now to kiss his new bride. All the guests cheered with delight. Misty's shoulders were shaking up and down and tears were streaming down her cheek. Dominic came to her side to comfort her.

Sue and John both walked out of the church that day with love in their hearts. They knew they'd made a commitment to love each other forever. The crowd followed behind the newlyweds. Everybody was on a high and they all cheered as John lifted Sue up to pose for a picture. Sue's dad remarked that if anyone took a picture of his pants they would be in deep trouble. He knew more than anyone that he looked a complete idiot in them. His trousers had been a standing joke all the way through the photographs. Everybody got a picture of them on their own private cameras unbeknown to Sue's dad. The party now moved to the Robert Tinker. John and Sue walked inside the pub and they didn't recognise the place. Maureen and Tony had done them both proud. The reception looked fit for a king and queen.

The champagne was passed about and everyone had their glasses ready for when the speeches began. The first person to speak was Sue's dad. He kept it short and sweet. He had people doubled over laughing at some of the things he said. Dominic stood up next and tapped the side of his glass for silence. His voice was quiet at first but as the minutes passed his confidence grew. Misty held his shaking hand as he spoke to the guests. He smirked as he told the tales from John's younger days. Sue raised her eyes at John when the story of him losing his clothes one night on a pub crawl came to light. John soon regained his faith in his friend when he told the wedding party of the love he'd found once he'd met Sue. Everybody raised their glasses and toasted the new couple's happiness. The noise was deafening, as everybody got ready to eat their roast dinners. Laughter could be heard throughout the pub.

Misty was quiet throughout the meal. She looked exhausted as the day progressed. It had been a long few months for her and she was glad it was all over. Dominic placed his hand around her shoulders; he could tell she was tired. Misty's eyes looked black underneath and her complexion  was ghostly. The baby growing inside her was taking every ounce of energy she had. She couldn't wait for the day when she'd be back to her normal self again.

As day turned into night at the Robert Tinker pub, the DJ started to set up his equipment for the night ahead. Lots more people arrived at the function. The corner of the room was full of gifts and cards from all their friends and relations. Peggy and Sydney had brought them a gift and Sue nearly broke down as Peggy passed it to her. She dipped her head low as she told Sue it wasn't much. Sue knew that whatever it was held in the silver wrapping paper would have come from the heart. People like Peggy and Sydney were real people and Sue knew she'd found friends for life in the two of them. She knew if she ever needed anything the couple would have give their last penny to help her out.

The night was amazing and even Misty found a second wind to strut her stuff on the dance floor. The songs the DJ played put everyone in a good mood. The cheesy tunes even got the older people up doing a few dance moves. Sue made her way over to Maureen and squeezed her tightly in her arms.

"Thank you so much for all you've done. This place looks amazing and the food has been incredible," before Maureen could reply John swayed over to them both shouting the name of his new bride.

"Mam isn't she gorgeous," his arms swung round Sue's neck. "I'm such a lucky man ya know. I'm gonna be the best husband you could ever wish for," he now looked straight into Sue's eyes. His words slurred and he struggle to stand up straight. "I love my new wife." John laughed out loud and shouted over to Sue's dad who wasn't far from them. "Ay, fucking Tom Jones let's have another look at your pants before you bin them." Sue's dad rammed his two fingers in the air and giggled. He bent over and shook his arse in their direction. He loved all the attention his pants had brought him throughout the day, they were a standing joke. Sue's mother now appeared at his side of her husband and started to shout back at them.

"These pants are staying on all night I can tell you. He's promised me he'll keep them on in bed!" Sue's dad now grabbed her and threw her body back as he kissed her neck. They looked like something out of the movies. Everyone roared laughing as they watched the couple nearly fall to the floor.

The time came when Sue and John had to leave the party. They were jetting to their honeymoon destination in the Maldives. John made his way to the small stage and pulled Sue to the side of him. He began his speech thanking everybody for a great day. His body was rocking about as he held the microphone to his mouth. Sue took over as he draped over her shoulder.

"I would like to start by thanking you all for a great day. We'll remember this day forever. Thanks for all your gifts and cards and a special thanks to both our parents for all the help and support in making this one of the best days in our life." John gripped the microphone from Sue's hand.

"I would like to thank Tom Jones and his extra tight trousers for attending today and giving us all a good fucking laugh," before he could continue Sue's dad was shouting at the top of his voice, and shaking his arse for all the guests to see. Everyone clapped as he started to sing "It's Not Unusual" he was swinging his hips in a sexy manner.

Before Sue left the function, Misty made her way over to her. She held her in her arms and told her she'd miss her every day she was away. Sue was pissed and hugged her best friend, nearly squeezing the baby from her body. Misty could tell she'd had way too much to drink and listened to her words with a smile on her face.

"Misty you're my best friend; I love you with all my heart." Sue's bottom lip began shaking. "Shit has happened in both our lives, but look at us both now, onwards and upwards ay girl, what do you say?" Misty nodded her head and kissed Sue on her cheek. John came to join them. All the guests came out of the pub now to wave them off. As they sat in the back of the taxi John put his face to the window pulling funny faces on the glass. The car started to drive off; Sue was waving from the back window. The day had been so long and Misty was ready for bed, she was yawning. As soon as the newlyweds were out of sight Misty and Dominic also left the party. The party was in full swing as they left and in true Collyhurst style it was set to be a long night.

When she got home, Misty kicked her shoes off and rubbed at her feet. Her body plonked on the bed. They were swollen beyond belief and even Dominic commented on how big they were. Dominic helped Misty get her dress off. He could see she was struggling with the zip at the back of it. He decided there and then to make his move on his wife and started kissing her neck hoping she wasn't feeling too tired for a bit of slap and tickle. Misty welcomed his touch and turned her head to meet his lips. It had been weeks since they'd last had sex. Once her dress was off, Dominic led her back to the bed and made sure she was comfortable. Sex was hard for them now and most positions were uncomfortable. Dominic positioned himself between her legs. Misty took a deep breath before he began to lick the side of her inner thigh. Her body melted into the bed as his silk tongue entered the side of her knickers. His fingers carefully lifted the side of her briefs and he dug his head inside the small gap. The smell of her scent made his body tense. Misty lifted herself up as Dominic slowly rolled her knickers down. He was like a cat with a saucer of milk. Her hands now cradled his head as he looked up at her with longing eyes. He knew exactly what made her tick and teased her as he knew she was about to come. Her breathing was deep and her toes curled as she knocked on the door of that heavenly feeling she knew so well. Dominic continued only a few more minutes and heaven arrived for Misty. Dominic slowed down his tongue movements and his fingers moved only slightly to help her achieve maximum enjoyment. Once she'd finished her breathing settled down. Misty sat up and twisted her body down towards Dominic's crotch. His penis stood up like a missile ready to launch and she knew her work wouldn't be long. His body hung over her face as she lay on her side. Her mouth was warm as his throbbing penis hit the back of her throat. Misty's tongue teased the end of his penis and she could taste his excitement in her mouth. His manhood was rock solid and she found it hard to take it all to the back of her throat. Her hands now gripped the side of his shaft and she stoked it as if she was stroking a dog. Dominic's body looked as toned as ever. His bulging muscles looked massive. His body was amazing and Misty knew how lucky she was to have him as her husband. Dominic now made a grunting noise and she knew that was her signal to complete her task. Her tongue and hands now moved in sequence. Dominic reached down to her face and kissed her passionately. He spoke softly.

"I love you so much Misty," he whispered. He

returned to his position while she caressed his penis further. Within seconds, he'd ejaculated. A shot of sperm went into Misty's eye. Although she needed to remove it straight away, she kept still until he'd finished coming. Dominic fell onto the bed with a gasping breath. It was obvious he felt fulfilled with the blowjob she'd just given him. As he tried to focus, he could see Misty wiping the bed sheets on her eye, she looked stressed. "Are you okay, what's up?"

Misty raised a smile as she tried to keep a straight face. "I've got come in my eye," she smirked as he sat back up to look at her further. His face looked concerned and he didn't really take onboard what she'd said until she showed him her eye socket. Her eyeball was red raw and the whites of her eye had all red lines going across it. It looked like someone had poked her in it. Her eye was streaming. Dominic tried to stop laughing but couldn't control it. His shoulders were shaking and his hand was over his open mouth. They both roared laughing. Misty held the sheet to her eye to stop it watering.

"No way can I go to the hospital to let them have a look at it." She pulled the sheet from her eye revealing the injured eye socket. "Imagine if they ask me how it happened. I would die a thousand deaths with embarrassment." Dominic dragged himself up from the bed and went to the bathroom. Glancing about the room he located a small white flannel on the side of the bath. He ran the cloth under the cold water and brought it back into the bedroom. Placing it on Misty's eye he screwed his face up as he watched her face change. "It's freezing." she moaned. Dominic plonked on the bed at the side of her. Holding his head to the side he smiled.

"Imagine it Misty, the headlines in the paper." He

waved his hands out in front of him. "Woman blinded by demon semen."

She dug her fist into his waist, "Orr stop it, I'm in pain you know." Dominic continued to joke with her and they both fell back onto the bed giggling. When she eventually took the flannel from her eye it looked like the watering had stopped. All that was left now was a very sore looking eyeball. The couple both lay back together on the bed. They were talking about days gone by. Life had turned out really well for Sue and John and they both wished them all the happiness in the world. Dominic cradled Misty in his arms and her eyes closed instantly. Before she drifted off to sleep she could hear his soft voice telling her how much he loved her. She snuggled into his warm body.

Dominic lay for a moment and thought about his best mate now being married. He and John had built up a great business between them both. They were on the road to becoming very wealthy men. The business had started off quite small, but with blood, sweat and lots of long hours it was on its way up. Dominic was the brains behind it all, and with help from his dad, he'd learnt how to get things done on the cheap. Land was quite hard to come by these days and if you got a nice plot of land, you knew you'd be able to build on it and earn thousands of pounds. Dominic's father knew a few hooky characters to say the least. He'd set them up with some corking deals which had given him the start they both needed. Dominic's eyes now flickered with tiredness as he kissed the top of Misty's head.

"Goodnight babes."

The time Sue was away on her honeymoon was a lonely time for Misty. She pined for her return like a dog missing its owner. Misty had been in and out of the refuge for the last two weeks helping out. Everything was running smoothly. Another woman was working in the sheltered accommodation now, her name was Claire. She's also been in the same situation as many of the women she was dealing with, but she was lucky to have got out of it, before it was too late. Claire had studied for years and got all the qualifications she needed to become a support worker. She was twenty-five and a single parent. Claire had spoken quite a lot about her previous life. She was a determined woman and Misty liked her from the moment she met her. Claire had such a pleasant look about her and her voice was always soft and caring. Many of the women in the refuge would spend hours speaking to her discussing their problems. She was always patient and helped them as much as possible. Claire had many connections in the social services departments, and she'd often call upon them for help when a woman needed more than they could give.

Claire often sat chatting with Misty and she knew there was a lot more to this woman than met the eye. She could tell Misty had a problem, but just couldn't put her finger on what it was. Claire knew when the time was right Misty would confide in her and unburden the truth she hid inside. Misty felt the same as everyone else about Claire. She could talk to her for hours. Misty was sat chatting with Claire on one day in particular and nearly told her all her darkest secrets. She stopped just in time though and kept her cards held close to her chest. It would take more than a shoehorn to make her uncover the truth.

Sue returned to work two weeks later and she looked like a sun goddess. She was a lovely golden brown colour and her teeth looked pearly white next to her dark skin. The holiday had been amazing and Sue told them all about the holiday destination. She was holding her belly as she laughed about the amount of sex she'd had whilst she was on her honeymoon. Sue closed the office door and whispered as she told them about John's attempt to jump from the wardrobes onto the bed. Apparently, he'd climbed up on top of the wardrobe and positioned himself to land on the bed, but due to the fact he was slightly intoxicated he missed his landing spot and fell head first onto the marble floor. Sue told the story so well and Misty nearly pissed herself laughing as Sue acted out the next part. She told them he was lay flat out on the floor and seemed not to be moving when she approached him. When she finally lifted his head from the floor, he looked at her and tried to speak.

"Crash landing love. Phone mountain rescue!"

Sue laughed as she continued and held her stomach remembering every detail of her new husbands fall. When she'd finished telling them the story everyone was hysterical and came to the conclusion she'd had a whale of a time on her honeymoon.

The months passed and Misty's baby was due. Francesca's visit to the refuge still played on her mind. Gordon had escaped from prison during a court visit and let his fist lose on Francesca once again. As normal she'd forgiven him and went back to him once he'd been arrested. Gordon had only escaped for two days, but it was enough to put the fear of God into Misty knowing he could be searching for her and the money she'd stolen from him.

Misty never expected her labour to start the way it did. One Saturday afternoon her waters broke in the middle of Asda shopping centre in Harpurhey. Lisa was there with her at the time and they were both doing a little bit of shopping for the weekend. Misty had been experiencing a few pains over the last couple of weeks but she never thought in a million years that this would be the day she'd give birth.

Misty and Lisa walked around Harpurhey market before they went inside the Asda store. They were stood talking to a friend of Lisa's at the front entrance for a few minutes before they entered the shopping centre. Misty was constantly complaining that her lower back was aching. She held her hand on the side of her back and her face looked stressed, Lisa told her to stop moaning and continued talking to her friend without giving her a second thought. Ten minutes passed and Lisa finally said goodbye to her friend. "About time." her daughter moaned. Misty was pushing the shopping trolley at first and Lisa noticed that she was resting her body on the handle quite a lot. Her face looked concerned and she asked if she was okay. Misty just nodded and continued to do her shopping. By the time, they'd reached the second aisle Misty's face was like a beetroot. She quickly loosened her shirt from her neck and looked stressed. Lisa took the trolley from her hands thinking it was too much for her. They both carried on walking a small distance and Misty got a sharp surging pain deep in her lower back. The pain was something she knew only too well. Fear set in and her face drained of any colour, she was white as snow. Lisa saw her daughter was in trouble. She dragged the trolley out of her way to get to her daughters side. Lisa's eyes shot to the floor, she could see a pool of water near Misty's feet. At first Lisa didn't click what had happened, but as soon as she saw Misty holding her back, the penny dropped. Lisa realised her waters had broken. "For fuck sake." Lisa screamed. Misty was frozen where she stood, her hand rested on a nearby shelf. A trickle of clear liquid streamed down her legs. At first, Misty thought she was pissing herself and wanted to die on the spot. Her head sunk in shame.

A few people who were shopping near them both noticed the puddle round Misty's legs. One of them pulled a strange faces as she slowly passed her, "Dirty bitch." she whispered to her friends. A teenager and his mate made no secret that they'd seen what they thought was a woman pissing herself. He was waving his hands about his body, bouncing about. He shouted at the top of his voice for everyone to hear.

"Ewwww she's fucking pissed her knickers, the dirty cunt." Misty shot a look at them both and dipped her head low. Lisa quickly informed the staff about her daughter's situation. Within minutes, they were trying to get her to move to a side room away from the nosey customers who'd gathered at each side of them. As soon as they left the area, the cleaner was there putting a warning sign around the wet floor.

The room where the staff led her too was a small office; it was just at the side of the entrance. As they entered, all she could see were pictures of the stores employees staring at her from the wall. They led Misty to a chair in front of a large wooden desk. The woman, who'd brought her to the office, looked concerned and quickly phoned an ambulance without any hesitation. Lisa fussed round Misty and helped her to loosen more of her clothing. Misty looked like she was on fire.

The pain deepened in Misty's back and her face screwed up with the pain as she folded in two. She squeezed her eyes tightly trying to deal with the contractions. The pain she felt took her back to when she'd lost her first baby. She knew now the demons she'd feared for months had come to greet her for the second time in her life. Her heartbeat doubled and her breath was like a dog panting on a hot summer's day.

Everyone in the room looked about anxiously as another pain surged through Misty's body. This time there was no holding back. She yelled out like never before, her mother held her hand as she stretched her body horizontally. The employee looked at Lisa and knew that this young woman could have her baby at any minute now. Everyone watched on with sympathetic eyes and Lisa wished she could swap places with her daughter. The assistant paced the floor and kept opening the door slightly to check whether any help had arrived, but there were still no signs. Misty stood to her feet and with one hand resting on the wall. She paced the floor slowly.

Suddenly there was a knock at the door and everyone was relieved to see that the ambulance staff had arrived. They knew instantly Misty was in labour and tried to put her in wheelchair. Misty's hand came up to her face and she snarled at them. "I'll walk, thank you."

The journey to the ambulance seemed to take forever. Misty had to stop a few times and breathe through the pains, she was exhausted. Finally, the ambulance doors could be seen and Misty knew she could have some kind of pain relief once she got there. Her pace quickened as Lisa walked at the side of her. Just as Misty stepped up into the back of the ambulance the labour pains started again.

The ambulance man quickly passed her a plastic tube. "Put that in your mouth sweetheart and suck it in hard through your mouth." Misty placed the tube inside her mouth and sucked it as hard as she could. The contraction lasted around three minutes. The tube now hung from Misty's dry lips, she looked as high as a kite. Her eyes were rolling as she was smiling.

"Fucking hell mam, this stuff is great do you want a go?"

Lisa blushed as the ambulance man smirked. "Don't worry love," he whispered in a cheeky voice, "you should hear what I've heard when they're on that stuff. They say some strange things believe you me." He popped his head from the door to check nobody was listening. "One woman told her partner that he would never have sex with her again." Lisa raised her eyes up and listened to his every word, she loved a bit of gossip. "Mind you they all say that, and years later there still hear having another baby, so it's not all bad is it?"

Lisa nodded. "Yeah, I said the same thing, and ended up with four kids." They both chuckled. Lisa turned her head from the medical staff, she was sure he was flirting with her. She was more concerned about her daughter's welfare now and turned her back on him letting him know the chit-chat was over. The ambulance arrived at North Manchester General Hospital fairly quickly. As soon as they pulled up a nurse came to greet them. The nurse looked at Misty and demanded she sat in a wheelchair. She held her head high and told her straight that she had no time to be arguing. Misty sank into the chair, the nurse wheeled her up some long grey corridor towards the delivery suite. The hospital looked gleaming; the floors were shining like an ice rink. Misty was rushed into a medical room. The nurse quickly determined how many centimetres her cervix had opened. Lisa took this opportunity to go and phone Dominic and to also have a sneaky, well-earned cigarette, her nerves were shattered.

The female nurse reached for some disposable gloves from a nearby table. She stretched them out fully to make sure they were a good fit. As she placed them on her hands she explained to Misty what she was doing. Misty didn't need to know what was happening. She knew exactly what was going on through her own personal experience. Her body tensed her body as the nurse slid two fingers deep inside her vagina. A contraction now started, the nurse told her to breathe through the pain and kept her fingers still until the pain had passed.

A midwife now entered the room. She was dressed in a navy blue overall with white collars. She scanned the patient's notes at the bottom of the bed. The nurse now confirmed that Misty was eight centimetres dilated. She smiled and held Misty's hand. "It won't be long now; the contractions are coming faster now aren't they?" Misty nodded. The midwife carried on reading Misty's medical file. As she read on she discovered Misty had had a stillborn baby several years before. Her face looked serious and she knew how important this baby must be to the person who lay in front of her. The midwife wanted to get things moving as quick as possible. She started to prepare for the birth.

Once all the examinations were over, Lisa returned with a very nervous looking Dominic at her side. His face focused on all the different equipment scattered about the room. He slowly edged to Misty's side. Another pain erupted and Misty gripped the pain relief in her hands. She sucked frantically on the plastic tube at the side of her. Dominic looked white as a ghost as he watched his wife melt into the bed. The hour passed quickly, it was time for Misty to push her baby into this world.

Misty's face looked like it was on fire; sweat was pumping from her forehead. She slowly dragged her body up from the bed and prepared herself for the next contraction, she was exhausted. The midwife now gave her instructions to follow for when the next pain started. She told her firmly if she listened to what she had to say, she would lessen her chances of any tearing or stitches. Dominic took his position at the side of the bed and gripped his wife's hand. Lisa was at the other side of the bed and was rubbing her daughters hand at speed. "Come on now Misty, it's nearly over." Lisa was holding back the tears and her bottom lip was trembling, she shot a look to Dominic and jerked her head forward. "Get ready; this next push should do it." You could see Dominic swallowing hard. The midwife positioned the overhead light right between Misty's legs and they all waited for the next contraction to begin. Misty's face screwed up and she let out a deafening scream from the pit of her stomach. The nurse positioned herself at the bottom of the bed and raised her voice. Dominic wobbled at the side of her and had to regain his balance. He looked like he was going to faint. The midwife took over.

"Right my lady, breathe through the pain. When I tell you to push, I want you to push with all your might." Misty brought her legs up to her chest, and let out a scream like someone had poured boiling water onto her body.

"Pant, pant, don't push for a minute just pant." The midwife instructed.

Dominic and Lisa were now at the side of Misty. They

were both panting with her. Dominic told Misty to be brave for a little longer. His heart was in his mouth as he watched her and he felt so helpless that he couldn't take the pain away.

"I can see the head," the midwife shouted. Lisa moved to the bottom of the bed. She now shouted with the midwife. Misty seemed to get a second wind and sat her body up fully on the bed. The next contraction came and her face screwed up as if she'd eaten something sour. "Push, push." they all shouted at the top of their voices. Lisa could see the baby's head emerging. "It's here, its here." she yelled. All you could see now was a mass of black hair and a screwed up face. The baby looked like it was covered in lard.

"Misty I can see the baby's hair," Lisa shouted. She beckoned Dominic to come and have a look but he remained at Misty's side, holding her hand. The midwife now wiped a wet cloth around the baby's neck and told her that if the next push was a good one, her baby would be born. Misty looked like she had no energy left. She didn't seem to have the strength left for the final push. Dominic wiped her brow with cold water and told her that she couldn't go to sleep yet as she had to do one last push. Misty groaned and attempted to position herself again. Her body was weak and she was struggling to keep her eyes open. Dominic now took control and helped her to sit up on the bed. His voice was strong and firm. "Come on babes, you can do this." Misty sobbed as her head twisted from side to side.

The nurse now shouted in a wild voice. "Push girl, push. One last good push and it will all be over."

Misty tried her best and used her last bit of energy to free the child from her body. Howling screams filled the room and Dominic sunk his head into his wife's shoulder. He wasn't coping well; he was chewing onto his white knuckles with his teeth showing. The sound of a baby crying caused him to lift his head. Misty sobbed as they placed the little baby onto her arms.

At first she looked scared as the baby wriggled about on her bare chest. Misty hesitated to touch her baby. Lifting her head up slowly she realised everyone's eyes were on her. Her hands trembled as she slowly peeled back the green blanket they'd placed the new born baby in. Dominic was by her side, eagerly waiting to see the infant for the first time. As she folded the blanket back all she could see was a mass of black hair and the side of the baby's face. Tears trickled down her face and her lip shook as she struggled to speak. Dominic could see the sex of the baby and burst with excitement.

"It's a girl!" he screamed. Lisa danced about the room as if she'd won the lottery; she was kicking her legs out in front of her. Dominic leant on the bed with one hand holding the steal headboard. He reached down to his wife and slowly kissed her cheek. His emotions got the better of him now; he shook his head and he couldn't get his words out. Misty couldn't take her eyes from the infant. The midwife now needed to get the after birth out from Misty. She urged Dominic to take the baby for a few minutes. His face went white and you could see he didn't feel confident holding such a tiny baby. Lisa didn't need asking twice, she stepped in and took the baby to a small chair at the side of the bed.

Lisa was cuddling the baby in her arms. She could be heard introducing herself to the baby and she was telling her she was her nana. Lisa held the small infants hands and stroked each little finger with a tiny stroke. What everyone didn't know was that she was counting each digit to make sure they were all there. Her mouth was moving but no sound was coming out.

Misty's eyes never left her child. She held Dominic's hand while the nurse finished cleaning her up. All the pain she'd felt moments before had completely left her body. If someone would have asked her how bad her labour was at that moment, her answer would have been that she couldn't remember, her memory had blanked it all out. Everybody was overjoyed with the new arrival and it was Lisa who asked what the baby would be called. Misty now turned to Dominic and gave him an endearing look. She knew how much he'd wanted to call the baby Charlotte. As she spoke, she gripped his hand in hers and announced the baby's name for the first time.

"Her name is Charlotte." Lisa ran the name across her lips a few times and nodded her head in approval. The full examination of the baby now started and Lisa compared Charlotte to Misty when she was a baby.

"She looks just like you love when you were born." Lisa tried to find a resemblance of some feature belonging to Dominic, but the more she looked she couldn't find one thing that was identical to him. Lisa felt a little sorry for Dominic as she could see he was hanging on her every word. She lied and said she could see Dominic in the child around the eyes area. He smiled at Lisa and went along with her finding, but deep down inside, his heart broke in two. He knew Gordon's blood was running through Charlotte's veins and not his.

Misty looked at her new baby with endearing eyes. She loved her already with all her heart and couldn't imagine life without her. As she looked deep into the baby's eyes a shiver passed through her body. The eyes that looked back at her made her heart miss a beat, they were Gordon's. There was no denying he was the father of her child. Dominic had already seen the resemblance in the infant's face. He looked at Misty and they both raised a smile, they both knew Charlotte was a double of Gordon without any of them saying a word.

The nurse came into the room and told them that Misty and Charlotte was now being taken up to the ward. Misty looked exhausted and welcomed the thought of being able to sleep. Lisa kissed her new granddaughter. She now bent down and kissed Misty's forehead before. Her words were emotional as she pulled out a crumpled tissue from her pocket.

"I'm so happy love. You've made me so proud." Lisa clutched at her daughter as the words fought their way from her mouth. "If your dad was alive he'd have been so proud of you too" Lisa couldn't speak any more as her emotions took over. She kissed Misty one last time and stroked the baby's head. She was gone. Dominic knew that he didn't have a lot of time left with his new family; he could see the nurse waiting patiently at the side of the room. His voice was low.

"I'm so happy Misty. Charlotte is beautiful just like her mother. I promise you both I'll always protect you and do my best."

Misty lowered his head into her breast. Her heart broke in two, and she knew how hard this was for him. He was her rock and somehow, whatever happened, as long as he was by her side nothing else seemed to matter. Kisses were exchanged and they looked so in love. Dominic left the room but still hovered near the exit not wanting to leave. Lisa now appeared from outside the door and grabbed at his arm. "Come on, you need some rest too."

Dominic's eyes looked as if they were ready for closing; he looked mentally and physically drained.

Misty sat in a wheelchair. Charlotte was passed to her wrapped in a small pink blanket. The nurse started to wheel her through the doors heading towards the lift. The night air was whistling through the hospital corridors. Misty held Charlotte close to her chest, protecting her from the cold. As she peered down into the blanket, her heart melted at the little face that looked back at her. Charlotte was now a lovely pink colour. When she'd first been born, Misty had panicked and asked the nurse about the colour of her baby because she looked yellow. The nurse immediately put her mind to rest and explained that most babies were born that colour. She told her it usually meant that the baby had a bit of jaundice but it was nothing for her to worry about.

The ward was strangely quiet and all the beds had the curtains drawn around them. Misty was led to her bed. The baby was placed in a small transparent cot at the side of her. Once Misty was comfortable, the nurse brought some bottles of baby milk to her bedside. She told Misty that once her baby woke up she would need to feed her straight away. Misty looked horrified and twisted her fingers in her hand. She'd never fed a baby before and wondered if she would be capable. The nurse saw her distraught look and chuckled.

"Listen love, everyone's the same at first. Once you've done one feed they're all much the same after that. If you need any help just give one of the night staff a shout, I'm sure they'll be willing to help you." The nurse checked the baby one last time in the cot and wished Misty good luck in parenthood. Misty thanked her and watched as she closed the curtain behind her.

Misty lay like a scared animal looking round at her surroundings. Her body shook with the cold night air filtering through the small window above her head. Pulling the checked woollen blanket over her body she snuggled inside it trying to keep warm. Misty positioned herself so she could see Charlotte's face in her cot. It was amazing how long she just stared at her for. Every now and then, she would reach over and feel the infant's chest just to make sure she was still breathing. Misty finally gave in to her body's needs and closed her eyes for sleep. This was her first night's sleep as a mother and she felt like she was going to take to the role like a duck to water.

The sound of a crying baby woke Misty. When she finally focused she realised it was Charlotte at the side of her. Her heart jumped about in her chest as she reached for the small bottle from the bedside cabinet. Once she had it in her hands, she hesitated a few minutes before she took the baby from the cot. Charlotte's screams pumped about in her ears. She'd never heard anything as piercing in all her life. She placed the bottle in the baby's mouth and held her away from her body, she looked petrified. The baby found the teat to the bottle and sucked at it with incredible speed. Misty immediately panicked thinking she was going to choke and pulled the glass bottle from her mouth. Within seconds, the whole ward was in uproar. Charlotte's piercing cry startled the patients and nurses. The nurse on duty heard the infants crying and immediately came to assist. As the female nurse pulled the curtain from around the bed, she could see a distraught mother looking for help. The nurse took the baby from Misty's arms and sat on the green leather chair at the side of the bed. Charlotte was crying now at full pelt and she looked like she was going to pop, her face became redder and redder. The nurse remained calm and started rubbing the baby's back while holding her hand under her chin, Misty looked on with concerned eyes. Within seconds, Charlotte gave out an almighty burp and Misty looked shocked, she was chewing on her finger nails. The nurse now took the remainder of the bottle and carried on feeding the baby without a care in the world. She made it look all so easy. Misty's eyes filled up and she started to speak as her tears started to flow.

"I feel such a gawp, why has she stopped crying for you? Have I done something wrong?" Misty was dragging her fingers through her hair. The nurse had seen this so many times over the years and Misty wasn't the first woman to think she was a failure as a mother. The woman now leant forward with the baby still on her lap and faced Misty before she spoke.

"Of course you haven't done anything wrong. Babies are funny creatures, once you get use to feeding yours, you'll be fine. Trust me, everyone's the same." The nurse chuckled. "Babies don't come with instructions; a lot of it is trial and error. She most probably had wind, and that's why I started rubbing her back. When you feed a baby you should really stop half way through and wind her, because believe me if your baby's got wind, say goodnight to any decent sleep." Misty wiped her eyes and the nurse passed the baby back to her. She still remained at the side of the bed and stood observing Misty coping with the baby. Misty smiled when Charlotte burped again and looked at the nurse in surprise. The medical staff clapped her hands softly. She now reminded her that her baby's bum would now need changing. The woman stayed with Misty for a few minutes longer and just watched as she completed the task of changing a nappy. As she watched closely, she knew Misty would have no further problems dealing with her baby. She left her bedside.

Charlotte was now back inside her cot and Misty plonked on the bed. She turned her eyes to a small clock that was situated on her bedside cupboard and realised it was two o'clock in the morning. The day had been so long. All her fears of her baby not surviving the birth had disappeared. The nine months that had passed had been torture for Misty and she now felt like a dark cloud had been lifted from her shoulders. The days ahead looked bright and filled with happiness, and now Charlotte was in her arms the world seemed a brighter place.

The tea trolley came round the ward at six thirty in the morning waking Misty from a deep sleep. The hospital staff pulled the curtain from around the bed and a mature woman appeared asking her if she wanted a cup of tea or coffee. Misty sat up and tried to straighten her hair. It looked like someone had rubbed a balloon all over it.

"Yes please" she answered in a soft voice. "Can I have a cup of tea with one sugar?" The woman took a large silver teapot from her trolley and struggled to lift it up. She started to fill the small white cup in front of her with shaking hands. Misty felt as if she needed to get up and help the woman, but her legs felt like someone had tied pieces of iron to them and she struggled to move. The brew was placed on her bedside cabinet and Misty thanked the woman with a smile on her face. The cup of tea was just what she needed at the moment, as her mouth felt like a badger's arse. The first sip squished around her mouth as she tried to wash the horrid taste away. Misty blamed the gas and air for her breath and hoped nobody would come near her until she had at least brushed her teeth. Looking about the ward, she looked at all the new mothers caring for their babies. Misty's heart melted as she looked at the little bundle in the cot at the side of her. She couldn't wait till she was awake again so she could hold her in her arms.

All the curtains from around the beds were opened fully now. She could see other women fussing about. The woman in the next bed was a lot older than Misty. Her face was hidden by the big blue balloons tied to her bed frame. Misty needed the toilet as her bladder felt like it was going to burst. One by one, she struggled to lift her legs down from the bed. With a final effort she managed to regain her balance. Holding one arm on the bed she looked like she was going to faint. Taking a deep breath, she rocked her body from the bed, standing to her feet. At first, she had no idea where the toilets were, but with a quick question to a nurse, she started to make her way down the hospital ward. The sanitary towel rocked between her legs as she quickened her pace. Another minute more and she would have definitely pissed herself. Yanking her knickers down, she felt relief almost instantly and gasped her breath. She seemed to be there for ages and wondered how much her bladder could possibly hold. Once it was over, she reached for the toilet paper and started to wipe herself. As she did she could see masses of blood and bits of clots on the tissue paper. Misty didn't worry at the sight of it, she'd been through this procedure once before and knew it was normal. Once she'd finished, she replaced her sanitary towel and pulled her knickers back up. Her legs were still wobbling as she walked back to her bed. Misty looked weak and her body was calling for food. The window that overlooked her bed had a great view of the hospital car park. As she sat on the edge of it she could see could see all the comings and goings of hospital life.

Breakfast came at eight o'clock. Once it was placed in front of her she ate the scrambled eggs and soggy toast as if she'd not been fed for weeks. Just as she'd finished her last mouthful of food, super lungs Charlotte began to cry. Misty didn't panic; she took her time and got the bottle ready. Slowly she lifted her from her cot.

"Come on my little darling, are you hungry?" Misty whispered.

Charlotte continued to scream until the bottle was firmly in her mouth. Misty giggled thinking how impatient her daughter was. This was the first day of motherhood and she kissed the top of her baby's head as she fed her. Looking down at her, Misty examined every part of her face. Her ears had little blonde hairs on them and the shape of her face was round like an apple. Charlotte's eyes were wide-awake as she gulped her bottle. It was uncanny how much she could see Gordon in them. Misty stroked the top of Charlotte's head and knew this child would bring her so much happiness. Today was the start of her new life. She knew she had to leave her past behind her as from this day. She'd wasted so much time thinking about ifs, buts and maybes during the last few months. Misty made a conscious decision there and then to live her life to the full without any more thoughts to the man who'd nearly killed her.

A sea of pink balloons now came floating through the main entrance. Misty could just about see the smiling face of Dominic behind them. Lisa was at the side of him and her pace quickened as soon as she saw her daughter sat on the bed. A few of the other new mothers could be heard remarking about the collection of balloons, they were envious of them as they looked at their own collection.

Dominic passed the pink balloons over to his wife and kissed her on the cheek. Lisa wasted no time and placed her head in Charlotte's cot to kiss her. Dominic plonked on the chair at the side of the bed, and reached for Misty's hand. He looked drained. Misty smiled at him. "You look done in, did you get any sleep." He shook his head.

"How could I possibly sleep after seeing my daughter being born? It was the happiest day of my life. Every time I tried to close my eyes, I just couldn't stop thinking about you both." He moved forward in his chair. "I love you both so much and I can't wait till your home so I can enjoy Charlotte as well." His eyes shot to the baby lying in the cot. Misty stroked his cheek softly and told him that she might be coming home the following day if everything was fine with her and the baby. You could see by Dominic face he was relieved. Lisa was eager to get Charlotte out of her cot. Misty snarled at her and told her to leave her where she was until she'd woken up. Lisa moaned at her decision but she knew it made sense. That's all Misty needed, everyone picking the baby up and unsettling her all the time. She started as she meant to go on; Charlotte remained asleep in her cot. Lisa pecked Misty on the cheek and told her that everything would be ready for when she got home. The pram she'd ordered was still in the shop and now everything was fine with the baby Misty gave the go ahead for Dominic to go and pick it up. Dominic's parents had wanted to come up to see Misty and their new grandchild but he'd told them that he wanted to be alone with his new family for the first time. They would have gone ballistic if they would ever have found out that Lisa was at the hospital too. Everyone at the bedside was sworn into the circle of trust and it was agreed not to tell his family.

The visiting time ended and Charlotte was still fast asleep, much to Lisa's disappointment. Misty still looked exhausted and was looking forward to a rest when they'd left. Lisa stood up and paced slowly towards the cot. She looked one last time at her granddaughter and smirked at Misty. Throughout the ward, you could see all the visitors leaving the bedsides. Some of the mother's children were hysterical because mummy had to stay in the hospital with their new brother or sister and had to be carried out screaming from the ward. Dominic squeezed Misty one last time and told her to get some rest. Lisa kissed her daughter on the cheek, and stepped away from the bed. She walked a few steps and paused.

"Don't forget your butties I've made you. I know what it's like in hospital. The food is usually crap, so get them eaten before you starve to death." Misty took the bag from the bottom of the bed and she could see a large pile of sandwiches wrapped in tin foil. As she dipped her head further inside the bag she could see several bars of chocolate. Misty lifted her head up and began to unwrap one of the bars of her favourite chocolate bars.

"Thanks mam, trust you to think of food at a time like this." She looked to see that none of the staff were listening and spoke in a low voice behind her hand. "The foods not been that bad up to now, but I've only had breakfast. Thanks for these though." Misty patted at the food parcel on the bed. Lisa knew she was appreciated and walked down the ward towards the door. Dominic made funny faces at Misty as he walked behind Lisa telling Misty to make sure she ate all her sandwiches in a sarcastic tone. They were gone.

Misty peered out of the window for few minutes hoping to see Dominic and Lisa leaving the hospital grounds. Her eyes scanned the area and she thought she saw someone else that she knew. Her hands gripped the window sill and her knuckles turned white. As she looked closer, she watched a woman holding a baby wrapped in a blue blanket. The nurse at the side of her was opening the car door so she could get inside the vehicle. Misty placed her hand over her mouth and her chest was moving in and out at speed. She quickly moved back from the window hoping no one had clocked her. "Francesca." she whispered.

Francesca looked like she'd been dragged through a hedge backwards. Misty recognised Gordon's brother Tom talking to the nurse as he watched Francesca wind down the car window to listened to them both. Misty couldn't watch any longer and sat on the bed with her mind working overtime. Did she see right? Francesca had given birth to a baby boy. Her face looked stressed as she sunk her head into her hands.

"What a fucking big pile of shit this all is." she mumbled under her breath. The secret she held inside now seemed bigger than ever. And to add fuel to the fire, Charlotte had a half brother.

# Chapter Eight

Jade scratched her arse as she knocked on her friend's front door. Times had been hard for her since Tom had ended their relationship. She now earned her money by selling her body. The drugs that ruled her life still meant she didn't have a care in the world. The heroin seemed to numb any emotions she felt inside, even about her children and the man she had lost. Jade continued to rap at the door. Eventually a scrawny woman opened it wearing nothing but a small discoloured t-shirt that barely covered her arse. Jade moaned as she pushed past her. "Where the fuck was you, I've been knocking for ages." The woman looked spaced out and closed the front door without replying. She slowly trudged behind Jade into the front room. Jade plonked herself onto the settee. Her eyes clocked some cigarettes on the table. Leaning over she grabbed one and stuck it in the corner of her mouth.

"I'm fucking gasping. I've been all the way to Newton Heath jobcentre to try and get a crisis loan off the fuckers but they're having none of it. They sent me marching back home without a fucking a carrot." Jade lit her cig and shook her head.

Dawn sat on the chair facing Jade and tried to cover her skinny legs with her t-shirt, she pulled her knees up to her chest. The house was a disgrace and smelt of sweaty socks. None of them seemed to care; all they were bothered about was where their next fix was coming from. The settee was covered in chocolate draylon. The cig burns in it stuck out like a sore thumb. Even the light from outside barely brightened the place up. It all just looked grim and dirty. The portable television in the corner of the room was buried beneath hundreds of old letters, most of which remained unopened.

Dawn Hacker was a well-known smack head in the area. Everybody knew she would do anything to get the drugs she needed, no matter what it was, she was a dirty skank. Her hair was a strawberry blonde colour and her body looked like it would have snapped in half if a strong gust of wind would have come along. Dawn looked gaunt in the face and the spots round her mouth looked inflamed. She'd had met Jade several years before, and they got on well. The drugs they shared kept them friends. Dawn had been selling her body for such a long time now that all the kids on the estate nicknamed her 'bucket fanny'. You could always hear the teenagers shouting insults behind her no matter where she was. Jade sat smoking her cig. Her cheeks sucked in at each side as she took long, deep drags. It was obvious she had something on her mind. Jade didn't tell Dawn what had happened to make her feel so low and tried to keep it to herself. On her way to the jobcentre she'd seen Tom and Francesca pushing the new baby about in a navy blue pram. Her temper broke when she saw them and she wanted to run over and punch Tom right in the mouth. She watched them both from afar and saw her ex boyfriend draping his arm round Francesca's neck. It was obvious they were now together. Jade sat watching them like a German sniper, her face was red and her fists were clenched tightly. Gritting her teeth together she snarled at them both as she mumbled under her breath.

"Oh you think you're smart do ya. Well trust me, you pair of snidey bastards, I'll make you both pay," she was shaking her head from side to side. "Nobody takes the piss out of me and gets away with it." Jade twisted her fist into a nearby lamp post and banged her head on the side of it. "I'm gonna hurt you both so bad, you fucking cunts. Let's see whose laughing then ay." Jade stayed behind the bus shelter until they were both out of sight. She looked like a lioness getting ready to pounce. The new couple looked so happy together and Tom looked like a new man. He'd put some weight on his face since she last saw him and his clothes looked smart and clean. Jade could tell he was off the drugs now. His face looked full of colour and he no longer carried the look of desperation in his eyes. Jealousy ran through her veins as Jade carried on the rest of her journey to the jobcentre. She couldn't get the picture of them both together out of her head. Jade finished her cig and stubbed it out in an empty can of coke at the side of her. Lifting her head up she scanned Dawn's face.

"Fucking hell Dawn, what the fuck have you been on? You look wrecked love."

Dawn tried to focus and turned her head slowly towards Jade. Her words were slurred.

"I couldn't sleep last night so I took eight Tamazapans to try and get some shut eye. They've fucked me right up." Dawn gasped her breath and held her head back on the chair.

Jade shook her head. "You better sort yourself out for tonight; we need to earn some cash desperado. We're on our arses ya know." Jade stretched her body out across the settee and lifted her leg up as she farted. She expected Dawn to laugh as she usually did, but she was on cloud nine and away with the fairies. Jade looked tired, she looped her arms behind her head and lay staring at the ceiling. The sound of someone coming into the house could be heard. Jade lifted her head up and listened. She could hear Dawn's boyfriend talking, he was with his mate. As soon as they came into the front room he clocked Jade stretched out across the settee. He began his usual abuse.

"Fucking hell Jade you fat bastard. The settee wasn't built for slobs, get ya fat arse off it before it snaps in two." His mate now joined in the banter, as Jade tried to defend herself.

"Ay, ya boney twat. I might be fat but at least I'm fed and watered. You look like you're fucking anorexic and need a good meal down ya neck. So don't fucking start calling me." They all laughed out loud. His eyes were drawn to Dawn who was still sat on the chair looking like she was a step away from death.

"What the fuck's up with her, she looks like death warmed up."

Jade told him about her taking too many tablets. He stepped to her side waving his hand in front of her face. "Fuck me, she's out of it." He chuckled as he walked away from her. Jade twisted her body now and watched as Phil and Neil emptied their pockets on the table. Her eyes enlarged when she saw they had drugs. Phil counted the money they'd earned from a graft and started to get the smack ready to inject into their bodies.

Everybody used Dawn's house to dig drugs deep into their veins. The neighbours had tried several times to get her off the estate in Harpurhey but without any success. The residents of Kesteven Road had seen the comings and goings of the drug house and were sick to death of all the traumas Dawn had. One neighbour had lost her temper with Dawn a few months earlier. She'd gripped her by the throat when she'd found signs of drug use in her garden. Dawn had tried to fight with the woman, but she'd punched her in the eye before she got chance to fight back. The woman warned her there and then that if she ever found needles in her garden again she wouldn't be responsible for her actions.

Phil and Neil had their fix and lay in the front room in silence. Neil shared his drugs with Jade too. Once he'd injected himself with the heroin he passed the remainder in the syringe to Jade who quickly dug it deep into her veins. Drugs ruled the four lives in the room. They all just melted into the furniture like ice melting in front of the fire. Heroin had been on the streets of Manchester for years and the four of them had just started using it to see what it was like. Nobody had ever told them how addictive the drug was when they first started taking it. They all thought it was just like smoking weed and they would be able to take or leave it. How wrong they were. The years had passed since the very first time they'd used heroin and each of them had deteriorated beyond belief. If they've had had their choice over again, I'm sure they would have never have gone within an inch of it. But now they were prisoners to heroin and their morals had gone through the window, as had all their self-respect.

Their parents could only look upon them now with sadness. Philip's mam and dad had tried many times to get him clean but the story was always the same – he couldn't live without the drug. They'd put him in rehabilitation centres several times. He only ever lasted a couple of days before he'd end up climbing through the window to escape. The call of heroin had always been stronger than any love for the people who cared about him. He just seemed to be lost forever. Philip's parents had banished him from the family home several years before. He wasn't allowed near his family once they found out he'd nicked his sister's jewellery. He'd stolen endless things from his family; he even sunk as low as selling his mother's clothing. When Phillip was desperate for cash, he would often go to the post office and wait for his mother to come to collect her pension. He knew when she saw him roasting his nuts off she couldn't stand him shaking and sweating in front of her. He'd destroyed such a nice family and caused endless arguments between his parents regarding his drug taking. His mother always felt like they'd let him down in some way and blamed herself for his downfall. Phil's father was quite the opposite of his mother and he'd wanted to lock him up in the garage to make him go cold turkey but his wife had always stopped him, telling him he couldn't treat his own flesh and blood like an animal. His father told her straight that she was soft in the head, and wiped his hands from his son.

As darkness fell, Dawn woke up but she still looked spaced out. The girls began to get ready for a night on the streets. Jade didn't look any different once she'd got ready. The only thing that had changed was her hairstyle. Jade usually wore her hair down but tonight she'd decided to put a bobble in it to keep it away from her face. Her make-up was also limited; a hint of colour was on her top eyelids. She'd applied a sky blue eye shadow with her finger and wiped the remainder of the powder on her pants when she'd finished. Jade never used soap and the smell of stale sweat lingered about her body constantly. Jade shouted for Dawn to hurry up from the bottom of the stairs. Jade pulled at her skirt, she never usually wore one, but due to her selling her body she'd put on a long, black gypsy style skirt. She said it made it easier to get her knickers off when she got a punter. She was a proper minger. Dawn walked into the front room and Jade scowled at her.

"Fucking hell hurry up will ya, otherwise we'll miss all the punters. You know what those sperm banks are like down there."

Dawn turned her head and looked at the crooked silver clock on the wall. She realised it was nearly nine o'clock, "Oh fucking hell!" she mumbled. Jade was right, if they didn't get a move on the other prostitutes who worked on the same patch would take all the decent punters. If that happened they would be left with the usual dirty perverts.

They both walked down Rochdale Road and into town. It took about twenty minutes. The wind was howling and caused them to huddle together. Dawn was wearing high heels and she was struggling to walk in them, they were crippling her feet. She'd made much more effort than Jade to look good and wore a short black leather skirt with black fishnet stockings. Dawn made sure her breasts could be seen through her red netted top. She always tried to make the effort because she knew she'd get the better punters if she looked sexy.

The lights on Sackville Street were dim and the area had an eerie feeling about it. The girls walked to their usual spot. A few of the other brasses were already there and nodded at them as they passed. Dawn left Jade's side and stood on the other corner of the street where she could still see her. The wind was causing her to lose her balance. Dawn wrapped her arms round herself to keep warm, her teeth were chattering together.

About fifteen minutes passed before Dawn's first punter pulled up. He parked the car at the side of her and turned his engine off. Jade could see Dawn and felt a bit down that she didn't have a punter yet. Dawn rubbed her arms and stood at the side of the car waiting for the man to open the window. Once he did she hung her breast inside and began to talk to him as she slid her tongue along her top lip.

"Hello sweetheart, are you looking for business." The eyes of the Asian man focused on the perky breasts in front of him. He reached over to open the door and let her in. Once she was inside, he drove off at speed to get out of the area. Dawn nodded her head at Jade on the way past. The man's body odour stunk as she sat beside him. Her nostrils were flared as she inhaled his musky scent. The punter drove for about five minutes and took her to a place near the river Irk in Collyhurst somewhere underneath some arches. He pulled up and turned his engine off. Dawn felt uneasy at first, but continued to do her job.

"Right love, tell me what ya want and I'll tell you how much it is." She tilted her head to the side and snarled. "By the way I'm not doing owt till the money's in my hand, because I've had so many men ripping me off lately, so I have to be careful don't I?" The man looked at Dawn in a menacing way and she thought she was in danger at one stage. He now spoke in a Asian accent.

"I want a gobble, and I want you to rub those big tits on my cock while you're doing it." She smirked and turned away so she didn't burst out laughing.

Dawn told him her prices. He dug deep in his nylon pants and passed her the money without hesitation. The man yanked his trousers half way down his legs and pulled his seat back so he could stretch out his legs. Dawn began, as soon as his cock entered her mouth she wanted to heave. The taste was horrendous and it smelt like rotten cheese. His moans could be heard as she plunged his penis to the back of her throat. The punter pulled at her hair as his arse lifted up from the driver's seat. He now asked for a Bombay roll. He was ranting that he wanted her to put his member between her tits and to rub it all about. Dawn gave into his demands. Her body was now leant over him. Minutes later, he was shouting again for her to suck his cock. Dawn got back into position and knew this job would be over pretty soon. She placed his sweaty dick back into her mouth and rammed it in and out as quick she could. It was all over. The man had tried to make her swallow his come by placing his hands firmly on her head, but she pulled away before it was too late. The punter groaned with pleasure and spoke in a foreign language as he shot his load. Dawn was dying to laugh at his ranting but left him until he'd finished ejaculating. She was dying to know what he was saying but didn't dare to ask just in case he took offence. Perhaps he was telling his wife how sorry he was for having his cock sucked off by a prostitute; she smirked as she watched him yank his pants up. Once he'd wiped the windows from the steam he pulled out from the arches with a smile on his face. He took her back to the other prostitutes. Once they'd reached Sackville Street he pulled up at the end of it and looked at Dawn, he nodded his head and looked at the door. She didn't say goodbye. When she got back to her original place she noticed Jade wasn't there. She scanned the area for a few minutes and then went up to a working girl who was close by.

"Have you seen Jade?" she asked another girl. The brass chuckled and started to tell her that back door Bob had just picked her up. They both started to laugh out loud and Dawn nearly choked as she lit her cig. Back door Bob was a well-known character to the prostitutes. They called him that because he only ever wanted anal sex. Bob was about twenty stone and had a bald head that shone like the moon on a dark night. He was a nice enough fella but the girls only went with him as a last resort. Dawn giggled, she knew Jade had never experienced him before and couldn't wait for her to get back so she could take the piss out of her. A car now pulled up and the woman who she was speaking to got into the car leaving Dawn alone. Dawn's face looked sick. She stood wiping her mouth with her sleeve. The taste of the man she'd just sucked off was still in her mouth and no matter how much she tried she couldn't get rid of the taste of sweaty cheese. "Dirty twat." she mumbled under her breath.

Jade could be seen walking up the street about half an hour later. She looked as if she had been riding a horse, her legs were spread apart. Dawn had to bite her bottom lip to stop herself from laughing at the sight of her mate. Jade's face was a picture and you could tell she wasn't a happy bunny.

"Where have you been? You've been fucking ages,"

Jade made her way to the doorway in silence. She was shaking like a leaf. Dragging her hair back from her face she huffed. "Give me a cig will ya, because what I've just been through you wouldn't want to know." Dawn passed her a cig and started to enquire what had happened with a hidden smile on her face.

"Are you okay, you look like your gonna be sick?" Dawn sniggered. Jade lit her cig and collapsed onto the floor in the doorway. Dawn covered her mouth to stop the laughter escaping. Jade sighed and shook her head.

"My arse hole is fucking killing me. Talk about the ring of fire or what. The man I fucked off with was an arse bandit and only wanted anal sex." Dawn tried to look shocked. "I tried to work a gobble on him but he was having none of it." She sucked on her cig. "He just wanted my rusty bullet hole. I told him to fuck off at first but when he shown me two twenty pound notes I couldn't turn it down, could I?" Dawn shook her head, as Jade continued. "I told him to be quick but the fat fucker was there for ages and now my back doors have well and truly been kicked in."

Dawn pissed herself laughing as Jade told the rest of the story. It was just the look on her face that made her double over in fits of laughter. Jade looked so serious and quite shocked that anyone would dare ask her for anal sex. Dawn now told her about the punters nickname and they both giggled as Jade held her arse cheeks in her hands.

The rest of the night went well and before long, they nearly had enough money to go home. They bought a large bottle of vodka between them both and swigged at it as they waited for more punters to come along. Life on the game was hard and as the night came to an end both girls had had enough of selling their bodies. Dawn was the last one to come back from a punter and they decided they should call it a night. They were both pissed out of their heads and Dawn still joked about Backdoor Bob all the way home. Jade had seen the funny side of it in the end and said that her farts smelt of sperm thanks to Backdoor Bob. Dawn could hardly walk now and she dragged her shoes off her swollen feet. She swung them round her fingers as they headed home.

As they walked down the garden path they tried to keep the noise down. Jade was a right loud mouthed bitch though and it was hard to keep her quiet. Dawn searched her bag for her keys. Rattling noises could be heard as she opened the front door. When they both got inside they could hear the television from the front room.

"Oh Philip must be in" Dawn whispered. The front room was dark and the light from the television let them see the shape of Philip's body on the settee. As Jade switched the main light on they could see he was in some kind of trouble. His lips looked blue. Dawn looked concerned and knelt to where he was. His arm still had a belt wrapped round it and a syringe was still stuck in his arm.

"Philip," she shouted, but still he didn't respond. She pulled the needle from his arm and got Jade to remove the belt that was tightly fastened around it. They both started to shake his body up and down from the settee, but he still remained lifeless. As Dawn touched his face, his skin felt cold. Panic now took over them both and they sobered up within minutes. Dawn was hysterical and shouted at Jade to ring for an ambulance. Jade froze at first but as Dawn screamed into her face, she ran for help as quickly as she could.

Phillip was pronounced dead at three o'clock that morning. Once the ambulance came they took his body straight to the hospital, he never regained consciousness. Dawn sat outside the hospital when she found out the news and screamed like a banshee at the top of her voice. Jade sat by her side and tried to comfort her but she was hysterical.

Philip's parents came to the hospital as soon as they got the call. When they came out of the room where their son lay dead they were heartbroken. Jade tried to console them but her words were wasted. Phillip's mother approached Dawn like a loose cannon and it was only her husband that stopped her from killing her there and then. Phillip's father held her tightly in his grip as she screamed into Dawn's face.

"Are you happy now? My son's dead because of you lot!" she gritted her teeth at the girls. "You're nothing but dirty no good smack heads. Why didn't you throw Phil out, he would have come home and still been alive today if you had." She clenched her fist and pummelled them into the wall as he husband tried to stop her. "You're nothing but a low life scum bag Dawn. I wish you were dead as well. You dirty fucking junkie." Phillip's mother was dragged away kicking and screaming. Everyone in the room could hear the abuse. Jade placed her arms around

Dawn's neck as they sobbed together. Philip's mother was right, she was a dirty junkie and she knew that more than anyone, she dipped her head in shame.

The morning of Phillip's funeral arrived and Dawn tried her best to look respectable. His mother said she could come to the funeral as long as she kept well out of her way. Dawn obeyed her request and stood at the back of the church to pay her last respects to her boyfriend. Six members of Phillip's family carried the coffin inside Blackley crematorium. The song he once loved played aloud as his funeral began. The song by Coldplay, called 'Fix You', seemed to express all the thoughts Phillip's family had about his life. As Dawn heard the words, her heart shattered into a million pieces. She realised just how much drugs were ruling her life. Each word of the song felt as if a hot poker was being plunged deep into her heart. The priest began the service as Phillip's coffin lay facing them. The wooden benches in front of her were filled with his family. There wasn't a dry eye in the place. The crematorium was a beautiful place and somehow Dawn felt at peace sat in there. All the stories were told of Phillip in his younger days and how he once had a great life in front of him. The priest spoke about how drugs had changed such a nice man with everything to live for. Dawn sunk her head in shame knowing everything he said was true.

Phillip's sister now stood in the pulpit and started to begin her speech about her brother. His sister looked so pretty, her blonde hair was clipped back from her face by a black flowery slide. As the mascara ran down her eyes, she rubbed a crumpled tissue at them. Phillip's father stood at the side of his daughter as she spoke, you could see his hand gripping hers as he held his head low. As she spoke, she told the mourners about their times together as children. You could see Phillip's mother nodding her head in agreement. Her next sentence sent shivers throughout the crematorium. They all looked shocked at each other until she'd finished.

"I'm glad my brother is dead," she paused for a moment and chewed on her trembling bottom lip. "He is no longer suffering and I know he can be at peace without drugs in his life." Her body was rocking from side to side. "My brother was lost to our family years ago and all that we had left was the shell of the brother we all knew". Her father draped his hand around her shoulders, they were shaking vigorously. "Phillip got caught up in a life of crime and drugs and I don't think he knew how much it broke our hearts. He was ill you know". Tears trickled down her face now and her body shook as she tried to finish the speech. She said she owed it to her brother to set the record straight and this was her last chance to let people know that he was a good lad and never really meant to hurt anyone. As she finished you could have heard a pin drop. She now looked towards the coffin and made the sign of the cross across her body. "Goodnight our kid. Missing you already, goodnight, God bless." Her father kissed her head and pulled her closer. Dawn and Jade sobbed at the back of the church, because Phillip's sister had hit a nerve inside them both. She made them think of all the bad things they'd done to their families and the people they cared about.

The red velvet curtains finally closed and Phillip's body disappeared behind it. The funeral song was played. It was songs by The Verve called 'The Drugs Don't Work'. As everyone listened to the words they shook their head at the wasted life of yet another drug addict..

Philip's family left the crematorium huddled together. His mother could barely walk as she passed the two drug addicts. Dawn stared at the red curtain. The man she loved was gone forever. Dawn was shivering and her teeth were chattering together. Once they went outside the cold air crippled her body. Dawn was rattling now and small droplets of sweat were visible on her forehead. The look in her eyes told you she wouldn't be staying at the funeral for much longer, she was agitated. Jade was roasting too and her arms were gripped tightly about her chest. They both left the cemetery; Dawn looked over her shoulder at Phillip's family before she left. She could see the misery that the demon drug had caused.

As the weeks passed, Dawn hit an all time low. On several occasions she'd tried taking her own life, but always pulled through. Jade was at her wits end and she knew sooner or later she would find Dawn dead. Jade was the only one who'd been earning any money at this time. She was funding two addictions. She'd even gone back to shoplifting to try and earn some extra cash.

One particular morning Jade left the house to go to Harpurhey Market. She was desperate for cash and the market was a place she could earn a quick few quid. What happened next was all spur of the moment and once she'd started she knew she couldn't turn back. Jade was on the market stalls looking at what she could have away, when from the corner of her eye she saw Tom and Francesca. At first, she felt sick in the pit of her stomach. A cunning look was in her eyes and at that moment she knew how she would pay them both back. Creeping around the market stalls, she could see them looking at some jumpers. Her eyes shot to the pram at the side of them, they'd left the baby unattended. The noise on the market was loud and you couldn't hear a word with all the people talking. The vegetable man was shouting at the top of his voice, "Come on ladies, bunches of bananas only a pound, come and get them before they're all gone."

Jade positioned herself at the side of the stall and as soon as a crowd of people were walking past she joined them. Her hands were trembling as she pushed Francesca's baby with her. Jade looked white in the face and her white knuckles clenched the pram as tight as she could. Her heart pounded in her chest and she knew she didn't have long to get away. Her plump legs ran and ran and within minutes she was heading for Dawn's house not far from the market. As she neared the house, sweat poured down her face, and she was chuckling to herself. "Let's see who is laughing now bitch!" she mumbled under her breath.

Francesca turned her head from the market stall and didn't realise her baby was missing at first. It was only when she went to put a jumper under the pram that she realised her baby was gone. Francesca looked around the market and couldn't speak, her lips were locked. She started to run up and down the aisles now shouting at the top of her voice.

"Has anyone seen my baby, please has anyone seen my baby?" Tom now ran to her side and realised the baby was gone. People on the market started to ask questions of one another and the market was up in arms looking for the missing child.

"What colour is the pram?" one woman shouted. Francesca fell to her knees and dragged her hands through her hair.

"It's, it's, it's… fucking navy blue with cream on the side. He can't be far we've only just turned our backs to look at the stall." Everyone on the market passed the news round to one another and they were all looking for the missing baby. Francesca dived to her feet and started running round like a headless chicken. She was looking in every nook and cranny. One of the stallholders phoned the police and the area was already being searched.

A policewoman came to assist Francesca. She needed to get as much information about the baby as possible to pass on to her colleagues. The officer asked what the baby was wearing. Francesca struggled to remember. Her body was shaking from head to toe, her hand gripped her neck and she looked like she was struggling to breathe. The police officer asked the question again and Francesca snapped.

"I can't fucking remember, can I? My baby's gone missing and my mind won't let me see further than that, for fuck sake." The policewoman gave her a few moments to calm down and watched Francesca pace the small market office. Tom was trying to calm her down and reminded her that policewoman was only trying to help. He now tried to jog her memory in the hope that she'd remember something. Francesca closed her eyes slowly, her nostrils were flaring and she was twisting her fingers at speed. She bolted forward and dragged at the officer's clothes.

"A blue jumper with a train on. That's what he had on. I bought him the clothes from Asda, so I remember." Francesca shot a look to Tom. "It was his light blue pull up bottoms and the jumper that had a red train on."

Tom nodded his head. "Yeah that's right."

The policewoman asked lots more questions. She asked whether the baby had been fed or not, and what time his next feed would be. Francesca folded up in two. "I want my baby back, please help me, please." Tom stood over her and tears fell from his eyes. His voice was shaky as he told the policewoman what she needed to know. He knew exactly how many bottles were on the pram because he'd made them that morning. Tom always put in an extra bottle on board just in case they were out late. The policewoman went outside the room and relayed the information to her colleagues. Francesca sobbed as she heard her son's name being mentioned over the radio. Rico was only five months old. "He needs me, they don't know anything about him." Francesca sobbed.

Sirens could be heard blaring all over Harpurhey. The police helicopter was out searching the area. The residents were all in shock and they kept their own children close by at all times. The police started to do door to door enquires almost straight away. The press were also there trying to get an interview with the parents. Tom and Francesca weren't ready for them yet and told them straight to fuck off.

Unfortunately for Tom and Francesca, day turned into night and Rico was still missing. The local news channel was already at the market telling the story of the missing baby. The news reporter gave out a phone number on TV for anyone knowing the whereabouts of the baby. They all hoped and prayed that somebody out there would have seen something because at the moment nobody had a clue where Rico was.

The police questioned Francesca and Tom, and they both felt like they were suspects. One of the officers knew Tom and didn't hesitate asking him if he was still using heroin. Tom went ballistic and told the officer that he'd been clean for ages. "What the fuck has that got to do with the disappearance of my nephew." Tom snarled at him. The police asked who the baby's father was. Tom's

Black Tears

licked his cracked lips and told them it was his brother's child.

The officer held his head to the side and tapped his pen on his front teeth. "What's the arrangement between you and Francesca?"

Tom looked uncomfortable and chewed on his finger nails rapidly. "We just live together, our kid's inside. I'm looking after her innit?"

The police officer screwed his face up and stepped closer to Tom. "What, your brother's locked up in jail and you're living with his girlfriend. What kind of set up is that?" Tom found himself getting angry and started to lose his temper as the officer carried on with his interrogation. The next question hit Tom for six. He realised now how much of a secret he shared with his brother's girlfriend. The policeman continued, his eyes were burning into Tom's face watching his every movement. "Are you having a relationship with Francesca?" Tom blew a struggled breath as he searched his mind for the right answer to give. He didn't want to lie, but he didn't know what Francesca was going to say so he paused for a minute trying to banish the question. Tom waved his hands about in front of his body and paced the floor.

"What the fuck has that got to do with my nephew being missing. This is about a missing baby, not mine and Francesca's fucking relationship." The policeman realised he'd hit a nerve and looked at his fellow officer with concern. Tom kicked at the floor. "Fucking hell, just help find Rico will ya?"

Francesca was sat in another room. She too was being questions. The police hadn't arrested either of them yet but the way they were speaking to them made them think they were prime suspects. The same question was now asked to Francesca. The policewoman asked what her relationship was with Tom. Francesca looked anxious, and asked for a drink of water. Once she'd quenched her thirst she looked directly at the officer.

"We live together that's all. I had nowhere to live and Tom put me up till I got myself sorted." The woman looked at her for a bit longer than was necessary and carried on with some more questions. She asked her where the father of the baby was. Francesca nearly died on the spot. "He's in Strangeways doing a five-year sentence." The room was in silence. The whole episode now seemed to be turning against Francesca and Tom. The police woman left the room leaving Francesca alone.

★

Jade took Rico from his pram and greeted him with a smiling face. "Hello there little man," she whispered. He looked so cute and reminded her of her own son who was in care. Jade's son was a lot older now, but she remembered him when he was a baby. Rico made a slight whinging noise when he saw Jade's ugly mush for the first time. She started talking in a soft babyish voice now, and he started to smile. Jade searched the pram and found a black baby bag that contained two readymade bottles and several nappies. As she rooted through more, she also found some baby notes for the health visitor and started to read them. Her fingers flicked the pages slowly.

"Oh so you're called Rico," her eyes looked at the baby. "You're a lovely little fella, aren't ya? It's such a shame your mother is a dirty little slut innit." Her voice still remained soft as she spoke to him. Jade knew she'd have to keep Rico out of sight from all the neighbours. She'd already made up a story to tell Dawn regarding the new house mate. Jade decided she would tell Dawn that an old friend was in serious trouble and needed to get away for a few days but couldn't take Rico with her. So that's how she'd ended up with the baby. She knew Dawn's head was up her arse at the moment and didn't worry too much about what she'd say. Jade played with Rico for hours and loved being a parent again. She missed her own children so much. It had been years since they'd been taken from her and not once had she tried to turn her life around and prove she could be a good mother. Jade was laughing inside and knew the pain Francesca must be feeling inside. She felt no remorse for her actions. Jade wanted Francesca to feel pain just like she had when she'd lost Tom. She never thought about the consequences of her actions and to tell the truth she didn't realise how much trouble she'd be in if she ever got caught. Jade was living for the moment and decided she would cross that bridge when she came to it but for now she felt happier than she'd felt in years playing with the little baby sat in front of her.

Dawn now joined them in the front room and asked who the baby belonged to. Jade's story seemed to satisfy her and no further questions were asked. Dawn was a complete mess and was secretly hoping to die, she couldn't face life anymore. She popped pills all day long and she didn't even know the names of some of them. Other smack heads gave her tablets to her to try to help her sleep, but nothing worked anymore. Her mind was tormented every time she closed her eyes. Jade knew her secret was safe for now and thought about how she would care for Rico in the future. She knew she needed clothes for him and she was desperate to get hold of some baby milk. Jade only had two bottles of feed left and that wouldn't see him through until the next morning. She had to think of a plan and fast.

★

Francesca and Tom finished answering all the questions and were told to go home. A police woman was sent with them and she tried to keep them informed of any updates regarding their missing baby. The flat felt so empty once they entered it. Francesca couldn't rest knowing her baby was still missing and she stood pacing the floor all the time. All scenarios were running and she couldn't concentrate. Francesca sank her head into Tom's chest and cried like a small child. "Why Tom, why?" she cried. Tom felt her pain and his head was about to explode with all his thoughts. Rico was a big part of his life since he'd been born. He always treated him like his own son. Tom loved Rico with all his heart and would do anything to make him happy. Since he'd been born he was the one who got up in the middle of the night and fed him his bottle. Francesca couldn't have wished for a better father figure for her son and sometimes she wished he was Rico's real father. Their own relationship was like a fairytale. They didn't have a pot to piss in but they were rich in love. Tom treated Francesca like a princess and his day was planned around her needs. They both loved each other dearly, and they'd even thought about telling Gordon the truth about their love affair while he was still in prison.

Tom shivered at the thought of telling his brother that he loved Francesca. Gordon had always had this power over him that made him feel worthless. But those were the days when Tom had been dependent on heroin and was scared to say anything to anyone. He'd changed so much since then. Gordon didn't scare him anymore.

He was ready for whatever he had to throw at him. The policewoman made cups of tea for everyone. They were all sat around waiting for some news. Nobody had heard a thing up to now, and any leads were extinct.

"Somebody must have seen something," Tom whispered. "How could someone just push a pram away and not be seen by nobody, it just wasn't possible."

★

Jade decided she had to go and get Rico some baby milk and nappies. Her only option was to put him inside her coat where no one could see him. There was no way she could push the pram about when everyone was looking for it, it was on top. She decided she'd go to a different shop where she wasn't as well known and set off up Moston Lane. She didn't have a lot of money and she hoped what cash she had would cover all the stuff she needed for the baby.

Jade shot her eyes around the shop and found the baby milk. The shop was quiet and the shopkeeper was reading a magazine at the till. As quickly as she could, she shoved the baby powder in her large coat pocket and made her way to the nappies. The shop owner now looked up and left his magazine open on the counter. He seemed to be watching her every move she made. He now came from behind the counter and started to rummage about in the store. Jade picked up a packet of nappies and made her way to the till. She didn't know if they were the right size, but anything was better than nothing. Rico now started to wriggle about inside her coat and she knew she had to be quick before the shopkeeper became suspicious. She held a five-pound note in her hand and quickly passed it to him. The Asian man seemed to take forever in giving her the change. At one stage she thought he was going to ask what she had under her coat and looked anxious. As soon as she got out of the shop, she pulled Rico's head to the top of her coat, and began to talk to him.

"Hello, have you been asleep?" Rico's eyes were wide open and he gazed at the night sky like he'd never seen it before. Jade gripped him tightly and dipped her head low as she headed back home. As she walked down Moston Lane, she saw a few lads who she knew from the estate. She quickly crossed the road before they got sight of her.

Once she was safely in the house, she locked the front door and closed the threadbare curtains to keep away prying eyes. Dawn was still upstairs and she couldn't see her coming down for the rest of the evening. Jade started to wash the two dirty bottles from earlier and started to make fresh ones. Rico rolled about on the kitchen floor. The floor was manky, and bits of food were scattered all over it. Jade didn't pick any of it up; she just kicked it away from Rico's reach. The bottles were now made and it was now time to change his bum. It had been so long since she'd changed a nappy and she had to gather her thoughts before she began.

Rico wriggled about on the floor as she tried to change him. Jade had to put one hand on his stomach to stop him wriggling about. As she took the nappy off, her face screwed up. "Oh you dirty little bastard." she ranted. Jade was heaving and looked like she was going to spew up. Rico had shit all up his back. His vest was completely covered in it. Jade panicked and knew she would have to take all his clothes off. As she pulled his vest over his head, she could see his fair hair was now caked in it as well.

"Oh for fucks sake," she moaned. Jade carried Rico upstairs like she was holding a newspaper under her arm.

As she rested on the toilet seat, she started to run the bath. She cautiously held Rico away from her body. The smell from his arse was rancid and she kept heaving as she covered her nose.

Rico lay flat on his back in the bath. He was kicking his legs as he lay in the warm water. Jade knelt at the side of him and hung her head into the bath. She was splashing water all over his body. Jade scrubbed his soiled vest and put it onto the nearby radiator. As she lifted the baby up from the bath he screamed from the top of his voice. At first she thought she'd hurt him, but as she watched him she realised it was because he'd been taken out from the bath.

"Oh you little mard arse. You can't stay in there, you have to get out." Rico still screamed as she wrapped the crusty towel round his body. The clothes he'd worn throughout the day were now placed back on him. The bottle Jade had made earlier was now shoved in his mouth to stop his high pitched screams. "Sssshhhhh," she whispered. Jade cradled Rico in her arms and tried to comfort him. She knew the baby was missing his mother and prepared herself for a sleepless night. Dawn now came into the front room. Her face was like thunder as she fronted Jade.

"Hope that little brat's not gonna be crying all night. I thought he was going home?" Jade put her finger to her lips and hushed Dawn to be quiet with a screwed up face. Rico had just closed his eyes and looked like he was going to sleep. Jade stood up and moved towards the pram at the side of her. Slowly she placed the baby down and covered him with a blue blanket. Jade had forgotten how tiring being a parent actually was. Now the baby was asleep she flaked out on the settee. Rapping could be heard on the front door. Dawn dragged herself up from the chair once she knew it was Neil. Neil had been looking after Dawn since Phillip's death. He was now a regular visitor at the house. He was giving Dawn everything she needed, including sex. Neil would often supply Dawn with drugs.

Rico was restless all night and his screams echoed throughout the house. Dawn could be heard shouting from her bedroom to shut the little bastard up and Jade finally lost her temper with him. Dragging his body about she yelled at him.

"Right, shut the fuck up. You've had ya bottle. What else can I do for ya. I've done everything I can." Rico was hysterical and she tried to rock him in her arms to calm him down. Her night was horrendous and she hardly had a wink's sleep.

By morning, Jade was like a corpse. She knew the child had to go back, there was no way she could cope with him. The heroin was now calling her and she needed that more than any revenge on Francesca. She decided there and then that later that day she would dump the baby outside some shops to get rid of him.

★

Francesca's eyes looked like she'd peeled a thousand onions. She hadn't slept a wink. In her hands was Rico's teddy and she kept lifting it up to her nose smell her son's scent. Tom was by her side all the time. Between them, they'd smoked hundreds of cigs. The policewoman had stayed with them all through the night, and still there was no news of Rico's whereabouts. Francesca's mind had tortured her the whole night. She'd imagined her son was dead and he was somewhere freezing in a ditch. She'd cleaned the flat a hundred times over and she knew if she stopped and sat down her nerves would take over.

The police had informed Gordon of his child's abduction. He'd tried to get a day's release to be with Francesca, but the authorities wouldn't allow it due to his escape on his last court appearance. The prison let Gordon use the phone to speak to Francesca. She was at the police station when she spoke to him. Her heart raced when she heard his spine chilling voice at the other end of the phone.

"Find my fucking son, you daft bitch. How can he have gone missing? Why weren't you watching him?" Gordon was going sick on the other end of the line. "Tell ya what, if anything has happened to my boy they'll be hell to pay, bitch." Francesca froze as his screaming voice yelling down the phone. She dropped the receiver not able to cope with his threats. Tom snarled and picked up the phone. Gordon could still be heard shouting as Tom began to speak.

"Gordon, its Tom." All he could hear now was Gordon shouting for him to put the daft slag back on the phone. His brother's voice reminded him of times when he'd also been at the end of his fury. Goose pimples appeared on Tom's arms. He slowly passed the phone back to Francesca obeying his brother's command. Tom closed his eyes and cringed at the hold his brother still had over him. His fists were clenched tightly at the side of him as his nostrils flared. Francesca held the phone in her hand, she was sobbing. Gordon didn't let up on her; he just told her straight that if anything happened to Rico he would hold her personally responsible. The policewoman had witnessed Francesca's tears and quickly took the phone from her hands. She now spoke to Gordon. Her voice was calm and she explained to him that Francesca wasn't to blame. I don't know what he said to the police woman but within minutes she'd hung the phone up on him and walked away muttering under her breath. The policewoman now came to Francesca side and hugged her. She told her that she should ignore anything that Gordon had said. The prisoner had secretly scared the officer half to death, and she could tell he was a dangerous just by listening to his voice.

Tom looked deflated. Gordon still ruled him, no matter how much he didn't want to admit it. He found it hard to show any emotion to Francesca. He'd wanted to hold her in his arms and take away her pain but the police were watching his every move. The abduction had been all over the news. Members of the press were outside the flats trying to get the full story.

A male officer now walked into the flat. He nodded his head to his colleague who'd stayed with the parents all night. Taking her into the hallway he spoke in a low voice so no one could hear them. Apparently the police had had a phone call that they were chasing up. The call could have been nothing to do with the abduction, but they were chasing it up any way. A woman had phoned the police station and told them of a child crying throughout the night. The informer had been worried about a child's safety and thought someone should call round to the address she'd given to check everything was alright. The woman who'd made the phone call told the police that her neighbours were smack heads and she knew one hundred percent that she didn't have any children. She also informed them that she heard a child being shouted at in a furious voice. The concerned member of the community said she'd never forgive herself if anything happened to the child and that was the reason why she was reporting it.

The policewoman sat down with Francesca and Tom. She told them that they might have a lead. Francesca fell to the ground and her shoulders were shaking as she cried her heart out.

"Please Lord, please," Tom gasped.

★

Jade managed to calm Rico down yet again, he was hysterical. Once she'd had her cup of tea, she'd decided she was dumping him outside a row of shops in Harpurhey. Jade needed her drugs more than ever and she didn't have a pot to piss in now. Dawn's face was a sight. She didn't have to say a word to let Jade know how she felt about the baby keeping her awake all-night. No words were spoken between them. Jade and Dawn jumped out of their skins when the banging started at the front door. Neil sneaked down the stairs and was running round the room like a headless chicken. Dragging his hands through his hair he looked white in the face.

"It's the fucking dibble. I've just looked through the window upstairs. They're round the back as well. Fucking hell, I bet they want me." Everyone was panicking. Neil paced up and down the front room. He was scanned his mind for what they could want him for. He chuckled now as he placed his hands down the front of his pants scratching his bollocks. "Fucking let them in. Let's see what they want. I've got no warrants out on me, so fuck knows what they're here for."

Jade's face was white with fear. She bolted up from her seat and ran in front of Neil. Her foot was behind the door stopping him from opening it. "Fucking leave 'em there. They might want any of us. We've all done shit so don't take the chance." Neil listened for a few minutes more. The sound of the knocking was getting louder and louder. At one point, they thought they'd broken the door down. Neil's face was cocky and he looked at Dawn for guidance.

"Cheeky fuckers, who do they think they are, banging like that?" His face was red with anger and he moved Jade out of the way as he went to open the front door.

As he opened the door he could see a police officer on his radio. Neil looked at him like a piece of shit. The officer finished talking and began to give him the reason for his visit. "Is this your house mate?"

Neil snarled at him and placed his hand on the doorframe, before he answered. "Nar, it's my girlfriend's house. Why is there a problem?"

The police officers who were watching the back of the house now came to join them. As they walked down the garden path, Neil lost his bottle and shouted for Dawn. "Dawn it's the police they want you." Dawn shit herself and thought about doing a runner, but she knew she didn't stand a chance. The policeman took one look at her and knew she was a junkie. He'd seen the picture so many times before and he watched as she tried to pull her sleeves over her arms to cover her injecting marks. Dawn's voice was low as she came to the door. Neil stayed by her side, eager to know what they wanted. Once they'd confirmed she was the tenant they went ahead with a few questions. Jade held her ear to the door and tried to listen to what was being said, but she was struggling as Rico began to cry. Quickly she ran to his side and shoved his dummy in his mouth hoping to soothe him.

The police asked Dawn whether she had any children. Once she answered no, they thought their visit had been wasted. They seemed more concerned with Neil and knew he was an active thief in the area and began to quiz him. Neil laughed in their faces and told them he'd turned over a new leaf. The officers looked at the bag of bones in front of them and knew he was lying through his teeth. The police were just about to walk away from the door when Rico started to scream from inside the house. Jade placed her hand over his mouth, but there was no stopping him, he was screaming at full pelt.

Almost immediately, the police asked who was crying. Dawn told them it was some baby her mate was minding. That was like music to the police officer's ears and his face lit up. He asked if they could come inside and talk further. Dawn was reluctant to let them in at first, but once she knew she was safe and not under arrest, she headed to the front room. They followed behind her.

Jade shoved Rico back inside the pram, and as soon as the living room door opened. She dipped her head low and remained from any eye contact. Jade told Dawn she was going out. The officer's eyes lit up when they saw the pram she was pushing. They knew it matched the description of the one that the baby had gone missing in. The officer stood firmly in front of the pram.

"Is this your baby?" his voice was firm. Jade panicked and sweat was rolling from her body as she stuttered.

"Nar, it's my mate's baby. I'm taking him home now. I was just minding him for a bit, as a bit of a favour." The police officer now placed his head into the pram and looked at the baby further. Once he'd seen enough, he knew this was the baby who'd gone missing he grabbed Jade's arm. As he started to place the handcuffs on her, he started to read Dawn her rights as Neil looked on in total shock. Jade was trying to break free.

"I'm arresting you in connection with abduction. You don't have to say anything, but if you do it may be used in evidence against you at a later date." Jade screamed and kicked her legs out. The officers had her twisted up in minutes. She was lying flat on the floor and was unable to move. Dawn and Neil were speechless.

Once he'd regained his composure, Neil started to shout at Jade as they ragged her through the front door. "You fucking crazy bastard. What the fuck have you done that for? Is there something wrong with you? Ya fat slag." He was bouncing about behind the officers trying to see her face. "Fancy nicking a kid, you're fucked in the head." Dawn was speechless and she thought it was some kind of mix up. Jade wouldn't abduct a baby, would she? She watched them throw her in back of the police van.

Jade hurled abuse at the police and kicked the doors from inside. "Let me out you bastards," she ranted.

Dawn and Neil were now questioned about the baby's abduction. It was obvious they didn't have a clue what was going on. One of the officers took Rico from the house and he was now being checked over by a doctor before he was reunited with Francesca.

When Francesca was told her son was found she collapsed on the floor and needed urgent medical attention. Tom stood over her as she fell to the floor and really thought she was a goner. Shock was a terrible thing and when Francesca came round her body was shaking from head to toe. A cup of hot sweet tea was passed to her and she sipped at it with trembling hands. Once she'd got over the shock, she wanted to see her son straight away. All the questions were in her mind but for some reason her lips were frozen. Tom was the one who started to ask the questions and Francesca sat at the side of him still shivering.

"Where did you find him? Who had him?" The questions rolled off his tongue at incredible speed. The police officer turned her head as they headed for the car.

"I don't know much at the moment, but all I can tell you is that he has been taken to the hospital for the doctors to have a look at him." Francesca screamed out and pulled at Tom's arm as he sat beside her on the back seat of the car. "Why the fuck has he been taken to hospital. What's happened to him? Oh my god! If anyone has harmed him I'll fucking kill them?"

Her face was white with fear. She pulled at her hair as she banged her head on the car window. The policewoman tried to calm her down. She told her it was procedure and she shouldn't be too worried. The officers sighed her breath; she just hoped she was right.

The hospital was crammed with patients as they walked into the main entrance. Everyone looked at Francesca as she stormed through the doors like a hurricane. The policewoman went to the main desk and after a few minutes Francesca and Tom were escorted to a small room through the waiting area doors. Francesca stood shaking as she entered the room. Tom held her as she wriggled to break free.

"Just leave me alone will you. I need my son back here where he belongs. He's my baby and I want him back." Her eyes filled with tears, her patience had run out and she gripped Tom by his coat. The policewoman came over to them and she tried to calm down the situation. She gently took Francesca's hand and slowly removed it from Tom. To look at Francesca, it looked like the policewoman had hypnotised her. She was stood with a vacant look on her face. The room was hot and clammy.

Four chairs were left vacant in the corner of the room as they all paced the room waiting for some kind of news.

Five minutes later a nurse came to the room and asked if they wanted anything to drink. Francesca snarled at the nurse and spoke in a fierce voice. "The only thing you can help me with is bringing my son back. Do you know where he is?" Francesca was in her face now, with her hand on her hip. The young nurse dipped her head and her face burst with embarrassment. She must have been only eighteen years old.

"I'm sorry I don't know anything. I've just started my shift." The medical staff looked at the policewoman for support. Tom jumped in to save her from any further embarrassment.

"Francesca, as soon as they've done their checks, Rico will be back in your arms. The police and doctors are doing everything they can to help us. You want to make sure Rico's alright don't you?" Tom stared at her waiting for an answer. Francesca knew what he was saying was true, she slowly back-pedalled.

"I'm sorry love. My head's up my arse at the moment. I can't think straight. I apologise if I sounded rude." The nursed raised a struggled smile and left the room. It was obvious she wanted out of there as soon as possible and accepted Francesca's apology.

The wait seemed like years before Rico was returned to her. The police came back to the room for another quick chat. As they entered the room, they took their hats off and placed them on the table. Both of the men looked quite young and could have only been in their early twenties. Tom looked worried and slowly seated at the table with Francesca at the side of him. The silence round the table was daunting. The police man spoke.

"Do any of you know a lady called Jade Harrison?"

At first, Francesca shook her head and wondered where the questions were leading. Tom's face told a different story and he placed his head into his hands. "She's my old girlfriend." Francesca looked puzzled and didn't know what the question had to do with her baby's disappearance. However, as he continued her eyes nearly popped out of her skull. She couldn't believe her ears.

"Your son was found with a Jade Harrison this morning. She's refused to tell us anything about him being there. I just hope you can help us put the missing pieces to the puzzle." Tom began to fidget and he looked at Francesca as he began.

"She is my ex-girlfriend. I've not been with her for ages though have I Francesca?" Francesca shook her head. "We split up on quite a bad note though. I haven't seen her in months." Francesca listened to his words carefully, and all of a sudden, the penny dropped. She exploded without any warning.

"The fucking mental bastard! Is it Jade who took my baby? Please tell me, because if it is God help her. I'll fucking kill her." Francesca punched her clenched fist onto the table. Her teeth were gritted as she snarled at Tom.

Tom looked at the officer in hope he could tell them the truth. By the look on his face he knew Jade was the accused. Francesca darted up from her chair. The things she was threatening to do to Jade when she got her hands on her were horrendous. The officers now tried to calm the situation down. They told Francesca that her son had come to no harm. She was still in a rage and if the door hadn't opened at that precise moment she could have caused harm to anyone in the room. It looked like Tom was in the firing line.

As she turned her head to the door, her heart melted as she saw Rico for the first time. Her heart stopped and for a moment her legs seemed stuck to the floor. As the shock left her, she ran to the officer holding her baby. She grabbed him out of his hands. Francesca squeezed him with all her might. She kissed his head hundreds of times.

"My baby. Oh! My baby. Where have you been? I've missed you so, so much. I'll never leave you again I promise you with all my heart." Everyone in the room felt the emotion and the policewoman who'd been with them throughout their ordeal gripped Tom and hugged him. Tom now came to join Francesca and kissed Rico on the cheeks. As he kissed him Francesca turned her head and snapped into his face.

"It's your fucking fault. It's your mental fucking girlfriend who's done this to us. I hope you're satisfied?"

Tom looked gobsmacked and tried to hold them both, but she pushed him away. "Fuck off, will you. Just fuck off." The police officers felt his pain and wanted to leave them alone for a moment. They could see he was already starting to break down and hoped she would calm down once they were gone.

Francesca sat on one side of the room and Tom was left alone on the other side. He was smiling at Rico and he was trying to escape to get to him. Tom left it for a few minutes and walked to where Francesca was sitting. His voice was low as he knelt by her side.

"Francesca, please don't blame me for what Jade's done. You know she's a fucking crank. I love you and Rico more than anything in this world and I'd do anything to make you both happy. Please don't block me out."

Francesca's knew her actions were wrong and pulled

Tom towards her. He was right. Jade was a crank and she knew that by her own previous dealings with her. Jade was a vindictive bitch and one buttie short of a picnic. Francesca's family was now back together now and she held them tightly in her arms. She loved them both so much and for now that was all that mattered.

Francesca and Tom still couldn't come to terms with what had happened and every time Francesca thought of Jade she cursed her and promised revenge once she'd seen her. Francesca and Tom returned home.

★

Jade sat with her knees up close to her chest in the police cell. The room was hot yet her body was rattling. The walls of the holding cell were familiar territory to Jade. She'd spent many an hour sat in them after she had been caught shoplifting. This time it was different though because she knew there was no way on this earth she would ever get bail. The doctor had been to see her and give her painkillers for her drug withdrawal. The codeine tablets didn't even touch the pain she was feeling inside. The walls looked like they were closing in on her and she was hallucinating. Jade's screams were checked constantly by the officers on duty. They knew it was just another smack head withdrawing from drugs and left her alone to deal with her roast. The police station had seen so many drug addicts pass through its doors in the past. It was a normal day for prisoners to be roasting behind their cell doors.

Jade had been interviewed earlier that day. She'd used the on call duty solicitor to represent her. To all the questions she replied 'no comment'. The police were use to this from habitual criminals. Jade was remanded until her case was due in court. The solicitor was the one who informed Jade that she would have to stay in custody. She was up in arms when he told her. She grabbed at his arms in desperation.

"What do you mean, staying in custody? Get me the fuck out of here. I'm roasting my tits off. What am I being charged with anyway?" Her grip loosened as he pulled her away. He could see the menacing look in her eyes and rang the bell for assistance. He spoke quickly.

"Jade you have been charged with the abduction of a baby. No law in this world would ever allow you to walk free." The solicitor watched her face as his words sunk in. "You will have to be patient until you appear in front of the courts and things might change," he now spoke in a low voice trying to calm her. The solicitor couldn't wait to leave the room. As soon as the door opened he flew out of the door with a gasping breath. Jade was one crazy bitch, he thought and he hoped she'd never walk the streets of Manchester again. He himself had small children and he couldn't believe she would put any parents through the trauma of kidnapping their child.

Jade punched and kicked the cell door all night long. Her body plonked on the floor behind it. She was banging her head on it repeatedly. "Let me out, please." she sobbed. There was vomit all over the floor and she'd shit her knickers - the stench was unbearable. All her body functions had now shut down. She seemed to have lost all self-control. Eventually Jade fell lifelessly onto the cold cell floor. Her body rolled about for the heroin she craved. Her hair was caked in vomit and her eyes rolled to the back of her head.

The future was set in stone for Jade. She knew her freedom would be taken from her for a good now. She still didn't think her crime was that bad and couldn't see what all the fuss was about. After all, the baby was back with his mother unharmed. Jade had only wanted to scare Francesca and surely, when she told the judge that, he would have mercy on her.

Francesca couldn't wait to get Rico in the bath once they got home. She wanted to wash every trace of Jade's scent from his body. The thought of that woman touching her son made her heave. Tom started to make Rico's bottle in the kitchen. He leant on the kitchen side as he waited for the kettle to boil. His head shook slowly from side to side. He still couldn't come to grips with Jade's actions. The whole situation had unsettled him and he started to think of the years that lay ahead. He knew Gordon wouldn't be inside forever and he knew he would have to face him once he was freed. Tom hadn't spoken to Francesca about any plans for the future but he knew in his heart he couldn't give her up. Questions rolled about in his mind and the torment of losing her sent chills down his spine. He stood thinking about the situation as he poured the water into the bottle. Tom decided there and then that once Rico was in bed he would talk to Francesca about her plans. He knew the timing was all wrong, but the way he felt at the moment was like someone had just tied a brick round his heart and he needed to know what the future held.

Rico lay on the double bed and kicked his legs into the air. Francesca rubbed talcum powder all over him. He looked so clean and happy. Francesca kissed his belly as she placed a clean nappy on him. Rico seemed to look much bigger than he had before. He'd definitely had a growth spurt. Francesca's son looked so much like Gordon. In fact, it was just like looking at a miniature version of her boyfriend. It freaked Francesca out from time to time just how alike they were.

Once Rico was asleep Francesca lay next to his cot and wouldn't leave his side. Tom had been in the room to ask if she was joining him in the front room but she told him straight that she was never leaving Rico alone again. Tom understood and went to join her on the bed. As he lay next to her, he held her hand and squeezed it tightly. He ran over in his mind what he wanted to say and kept taking deep breaths trying to get the words out. Somehow, he couldn't bring himself to say anything. Francesca was his world. More than that, she was his life. He snuggled deep into her breasts whispering how much he loved her.

Tom's drug use was nearly over now. He was still on methadone but only needed a small amount each day to get him by. His drug worker had told him that after this last course of methadone he would be completely off heroin altogether. The councillor was a former addict himself and told Tom that he should take every day as it came. He told him he'd worked with so many drug users in the past and it always seemed as soon as they had a trauma in their lives they'd search for the comfort in the drug that nearly killed them. Tom looked like a strong man and the drug worker had every faith in him. Life could change at the drop of a hat and he didn't want Tom to become a user again.

Francesca lay on the bed and watched every breath Rico took. Every few minutes she would stand up and check he was alright. Her heart seemed to be ticking at incredible speed and she couldn't relax. Even when she went to the toilet, she made sure Tom didn't leave the room. Tom couldn't wait any longer his head was exploding with the torment; he had to get it off his chest.

"Francesca, can we talk for a moment, my head's in bits. I need to set the record straight between us." Francesca turned to face him and looked into his eyes as he spoke. His voice was shaky and his face was filled with love. "Francesca I know the timing is probably all wrong to start talking about this, but after Rico went missing I've realised I could never lose either of you again." Francesca never let him continue and kissed his lips softly telling him he was special. Tom sat up and looked down at her face and continued. "My heart is breaking Francesca, because I don't know what will happen when Gordon is out of the nick. I class you and Rico as my family now and if…" he chewed on his lips as tears filled his eyes. "When he comes home if I'm gonna lose you I would rather know." Francesca had thought about this question hundreds of times before and still she didn't know the answer. She knew Gordon would come home and want to claim his family back no matter what. She'd imagined telling him in her head time and time again and the outcome was always the same. She'd never have the bottle to tell him the truth. The thought of it scared her to death. Tom had also thought of telling Gordon but, like Francesca, he knew how dangerous his brother was and feared for his life if he ever got to find out the truth.

The pair of them lay entwined in each other's arms and tried to come up with some kind of plan that would mean they could be happy together, but each scenario came at a cost and none of them would put their neck on the line for it. Gordon had ruled Tom from an early age and he seemed to have a secret power over him. Tom had always tried to please his brother in the past and he knew now his brown nose days were well and truly over. He loved Francesca and he would have to stand up and be counted. He just hoped his strength and love for Francesca was enough to set her free from Gordon.

They finally finished talking at about three o'clock in the morning. They had decided once Gordon was released from prison he would come and stay at the flat with them. Tom and Francesca hoped that before long Gordon would get sick of family life. He would never in a month of Sundays settle down to a family life and become the father Rico needed. He was selfish and would never change.

★

Once Gordon found out his son was safe, he lay in his cell and ran over the abduction in his mind several times. His mind was doing over time and he'd wondered why on earth Tom's girlfriend would take his son. No matter how much he thought about it, the answer always came back the same. She was trying to her hurt Francesca. It all mapped out in his brain and the answer came to him. It all made sense now.

"The dirty bastards," he ranted as he paced round his cell. Tigger lay on his bed and shot a look at him and wondered if he'd lost the plot.

"What the fuck are you on about mate. Who's a dirty bastard?"

Gordon sat on the edge of his bed cracking his knuckles. He ran the whole story by his pad mate as he pumped with adrenaline. Tigger knew what Gordon was saying made sense but tried to calm him down.

"Listen mate. You don't know for sure they've been

shagging each other do ya? It's your brother you're accusing don't forget that." Tigger folded his pillow under his head and lay on his side facing Gordon. "He's done ya a favour mate. Francesca would be on the streets if it wasn't for Tom. His girlfriend has probably read it all wrong and got the green-eyed monster. You know what women are like, they're crazy fuckers. Just chill ya beans and wait until you have got some kind of evidence."

The more Gordon thought about it, the more he knew Tigger was right. He thought about Tom and knew he wouldn't have the bottle to shag his girlfriend. Gordon smiled confidently knowing he was worrying over nothing. Tom had always been a shit bag where his brother was concerned and he'd never put himself in any danger of winding his brother up, no matter what.

The friendship between Tigger and Gordon was solid. As the years passed they were like brothers in arms. They supplied the jail with drugs and anything else they could get their hands on. Their friendship was that strong that Gordon confessed all his troubles about Misty to him. At first Tigger was concerned at the things Gordon had done to Misty, but as he continued to fill him in he realised that the bitch had stolen his money and got what she deserved. Night after night the two inmates spoke in depth about Misty. Together they plotted a revenge that would teach her never to mess with the big boys again. Tigger was a clever man and the contacts he had on the outside were extensive. Men would do anything for him and he knew he could call in a few favours to get their plan to work. The convicts plotted every night and day. Payback would be so rewarding. The time was nearing to make Misty wish she'd never been born. Gordon rubbed his hands together with excitement and smiled at the thought of her falling flat on her face.

## Chapter Nine

After Sue's first child was born things started to change drastically in her marriage. John had been excited about becoming a father at first but when the baby finally came along he seemed to change. His temper had took a turn for the worse and on one or more occasions he'd lashed out at Sue. She had been devastated about it at the time but forgiven him, giving him one last chance. Sue felt so much of a hypocrite being the victim of domestic violence yet again. She'd told her husband straight that if he ever raised his hands to her again she would phone the police.

John didn't do a tap regarding the baby. He was lazy and hated Sue attending to the baby all the time. In fact, if you looked at him closer you could see he was jealous of the attention the baby was getting, he was a right smacked arse. The date for the christening had been set. It was to be held at St Patrick's Church in Collyhurst. John's mother thought they should have had it at St Malachy's but Sue stuck to her guns. St Patrick's seemed like a step back in time. The floors were marble and the paintings on the ceilings reminded you of Roman times. Everything about the church felt so peaceful. The after party was left to John's parents as usual and The Robert Tinker in Collyhurst was the venue. Sue didn't mind because she knew everything would be perfect.

Misty and Dominic were asked to be the godparents of the child and they took their role seriously. Since they'd been told, they had attended mass every Sunday making sure they knew about the Catholic faith. The role of a godparent was to raise a child with good values and make sure they abided by the Catholic faith. Misty and Dominic were already Catholics but hadn't been to church in years.

Sue wanted everyone to have Holy Communion on the day of the christening. This meant everyone would have to go to confession first. Confession was a way of cleansing your soul and asking God for forgiveness before you could accept Holy Communion at the altar. On the day that the confessions were to be heard, everyone laughed before they went in to see the priest. None of them wanted to go in after John because they said his sins were endless and they would be waiting all day to get their turn.

Misty was the first to go and see the priest. She looked nervous as she played with the cuff from her coat. As she entered the small dark room the smell of old wood hit the back of her throat. The light from behind the small curtain showed her where she should kneel. The netting was black with small holes in. You could just about see the outline of the priest's face as he sat in the next room getting ready to listening to your sins. Misty remembered her childhood when she knelt down and started to read the small prayer that hung over her head on a small piece of paper. When she was a child, life had been so much easier, her sins were so simple, and nothing like the ones she had to confess today. The prayer was over and silence filled the room. Misty searched her mind for the words to start her confession. Within seconds, she started to confess the sins that crippled her each night when she lay alone. Her voice was low.

"Bless me father. It's been many years since my last confession." The priest's voice was deep. "Yes my child."

Even though Misty had gone to confess her sins, the truth she hid away remained stuck to her lips. She looked ashamed of the things she'd done in the past and struggled to confess them. The priest's voice was low and she could see the side of his face nearing the netting on the other side. Misty hung her head low and sighed as she shook her head slowly, she was twisting her fingers rapidly. The darkness in the room hid her identity well. She began to whisper her sins to the man in cloth knowing she was safe.

"Father, I've stolen money from my old boyfriend. I know that's bad but I did it for a good cause." Misty flew through her other sins that weren't as bad and hoped the priest would forgive her for stealing the money. The room held an eerie was silent. The priest could be heard clearing his throat. Misty closed her eyes and held her head in her hands.

"My child, you have sinned. I think you know how to right the wrong you have done, without any help from me. May I suggest you think about your sins and try and give back the money back." Misty wanted to shout out that the person she'd stolen the money from had tried to kill her, but she remained quiet and listened to her penance. As she watched the priest make the sign of the cross on her face from the other side of the netting, she struggled to breathe. Her hand was held around her neck and she was rubbing slowly at her throat. When he'd finished, Misty felt cleansed. It was like a weight had been lifted from her soul. After she stood to her feet she rubbed at her knees. Misty left the room and headed towards the altar at the front of the church. When she came out of the room Dominic and Sue laughed at her. They asked her what penance she'd been given trying and evaluate how bad she'd really been. Misty's face blushed as she replied to them both.

"Four Hail Mary's and an Our Father. That's good going for what I've just confessed," she giggled. Misty headed to the main altar as she watched John entering the confession box.

As the priest listened to John's sins, he was quite surprised at what John had to tell him. The man he could hear in the other room could be heard sobbing as he tried to speak. The priest tried to calm him down telling him that no matter what he wouldn't be judgemental. John tried to control his tears but they ran from his eyes with a mind of his own. The priest left John for a moment and he knew in time he would begin his confession. John snivelled and wipe his nose on his sleeve.

"Father, I know what I'm doing is wrong but I can't stop. I've tried so many times but I always end up back where I started. What can I do, please help me." John's shoulders were shaking as he kept turning his head to the exit. The priest gave John words of wisdom and told him to be strong. He couldn't give him the answers to his sins, but he tried his best to make him see sense and mend his ways. John wiped his eyes and stayed with the priest for a few minutes more. He slowly stood to his feet and kept looking back over his shoulder to the priest as he left. John followed Misty to the altar to say his penance. No one noticed that John had been crying as he left the room. He raised a struggled smile at Sue as she went to confess her sins. That day when they left the church two out of the four people had big decisions to make.

The day of the christening came. Sue held Bethany in her arms like a prize trophy. She looked so proud of her daughter and loved that she was now a mother. John stood at the side of his wife and looked bored out of his head. His face was unshaven and his shirt looked like he'd worn it the day before. Sue however looked amazing. She wore a powder blue skirt and a matching jacket. Her hair was a dark red colour and it made her complexion look fresh and young. Misty and Dominic stood at the altar with John and Sue. All the guests looked upon them eagerly. The priest finally got to the part where he poured the Holy water over Bethany's head. She screamed like no one's business, refusing to calm down. John face was a picture as he listened to his daughter high pitched screams. He quickly reached over to Sue and dragged the baby from her arms. Everyone looked on in disbelief, she could see them whispering.

"Cry, cry, cry. Is that all this kid ever does?" John kept his head low. Sue snarled at him and gritted her teeth. Misty shot a look at Dominic and they both wanted the floor to open up and take them away. It looked like World War Three was just about to kick off. The priest came to the rescue and broke the atmosphere. He told them that all babies cried at that part of the service. Sue backed down and pretended she was okay; her cheeks looked red and flustered.

As the christening finished they all made their way to the pub to celebrate the special day. As soon as they walked through the door, John headed for the bar and helped himself to a large glass of Brandy. Sue ignored him and went to sit with Misty and Dominic who sat in the corner. All their friends and family now turned up and the day was set to go on late into the night. The disco was up and running and the DJ was playing some great tracks that got everyone in the mood for partying. The atmosphere was electric and everybody seemed to be having a great time. The buffet was set out across the back wall of the pub. Once it was opened it was like feeding time at the zoo. Sue scanned the room for her husband; she hadn't seen John in hours. The day passed and now it was time for Maureen to take Bethany upstairs to bed, she was whinging and tired.

Night time fell and everyone in the pub looked pissed. The regulars in the pub were now allowed inside. Peggy and Syd were the first to come through the doors. They'd been invited to the church but said the day would have be too long for them and agreed to come later on. Peggy pushed a crumpled five-pound note into Sue's hands. She told her to buy the baby something out of it. Sue looked embarrassed and told her to take the money back but Peggy insisted and refused point blank. The older woman had become such a close friend to Sue she looked upon her as family. Peggy always reminisced about years that had passed; she was a wise old woman. Sue escorted them both to the bar and made sure they were served before she found them some seats. Sue sat with them both for a while. When Peggy asked Sue where John was she looked embarrassed and ended up making excuses for him. She lied and told them he'd just nipped out and should be back soon. Sue didn't have a clue where her husband had gone and kept looking at the door waiting for him to return.

Peggy sat and studied Sue's face. She had an idea that things weren't as good as she was making out. As Sue reached over the table to get something, Peggy's eyes clocked two dark blue bruises around her wrist. She didn't want to assume straight away and waited until later on in the night to ask about them. Peggy was drinking something called pale ale and Sue commented how much it smelt like sweaty socks as she inhaled it deeply. Lifting the glass to her mouth, Sue tried a slurp. Peggy nearly pissed herself as she watched her face change. Sue spat the beer out at the side of her and remarked how horrible it was; Peggy sat back with a smile on her face and chuckled. Peggy pulled Sue toward her, and looked directly into her eyes. "Sue love," she checked nobody was listening. "Is everything alright with you and John only you seem a bit distant from each other these days." Peggy watched her face drop and knew her gut feeling was right. Sue fell onto her shoulder and began to open her heart.

"Is it that obvious Peggy?" Sue shook her head slowly. "Here's me thinking nobody can tell how much of a twat he's being, and all along everyone knows." She gasped her breath. Her eyes looked sad as her face sunk. "It's just me pretending everything is fine when it's obviously not."

Peggy gripped her arm and rolled Sue's sleeve up. "Where are the bruises from love? Are they off him?" Sue looked shocked and quickly dragged her sleeve back down. Peggy screwed her face up. "Listen my husband beat me for years and there's nothing you can tell me about covering up what's really happening." Peggy huffed and hunched her shoulders back as she continued in firm tone. "Because I did it for years." She shot her eyes over to where her husband sat and started to tell Sue about the years of violence she'd put up with.

"I've forgiven Syd now, but back then it was expected that your husband beat you up. Nobody really cared how badly they hurt you." Peggy reached for her drink and gulped a big mouthful. "My daughter went through the same thing with her husband and I've found her black and blue from head to toe before now. So I'll tell you what I told her." Peggy placed her hand on Sue's lap and looked directly into her eyes. "Phone the police and have the bastard arrested. No woman should be any man's punch bag and believe me love, it will only go downhill now he's used his fist once."

Sue choked back the tears as Misty came to join. She was pulling at Sue's hands to get her up to dance. "Orrr no, just leave me alone. I'll have a dance in a bit." Misty continued dragging at her hand and wasn't giving in. Sue finally agreed and went to join Misty on the dance floor, but before she left Peggy she leant down and kissed her on the cheek. "Thanks," she whispered. Peggy was wise and Sue knew she was right in what she was saying, but for now she put it to the back of her mind and headed to the dance floor to strut her stuff with her best friend. Misty didn't have a clue what was going on in Sue's life. She couldn't bring herself to tell her, she felt like a failure.

Meanwhile John was walking down Rochdale Road towards the city centre. The rain was beating down on his face but it still didn't deter him. The cold wind circled around his feet as if it was trying to stop him moving forward. His legs looked weak and every now and then he held onto a lamp post for support. John entered a small passageway and shook the rain from his coat. He was wobbling all over the place and staggered over to the wall for support. Taking a few minutes to gather his thoughts he slowly headed to the entrance. His hands trembled as he pushed the steel door open. The lighting was poor and he squeezed his eyes together trying to focus. The walls looked grimy and you could see the handprints of all the other people who'd used the stairs in the past. John struggled to reach the top of the stairs. He was gasping his breath and his nostrils were flaring. Another door now stood facing him, slowly he pushed it open.

"Hello Sir," the young girl said as she sat on the leather settee in the reception. The brass must have only been seventeen years of age. Her long blonde hair was tied back in two pigtails. As she stood up to get him a drink, he stared at her red silk housecoat that only came to the top of her knees. John's eyes danced with excitement. He could see her black lace bra sticking out from the top of her housecoat. He slowly licked his lips and inhaled deeply. John plonked his body on the settee, and wiped the rain away from his trousers. An older woman now came to join them. She was familiar with John as he was a regular at the brothel. The girls loved John because he was a good looking man with a great body, much better than the usual scum bags who walked through the doors.

John finished his drink and moved closer to the prostitute at the side of him. Her face was new to him and he couldn't wait to feel her young firm body against his. John slid his hand on the girl's leg and stroked it up and down slowly. The top brass knew he'd made his choice and told him he could settle up on his way out. The new girl stood up and took John's hand in hers. She had to help him up from the settee, he was falling all over the place. John's eyes looked like they were dancing. He held a cunning look in them.

The landing was dimly lit as they walked along it. The brothel was an old terrace house that had been turned into a brass gaff by one of the local gangsters. John had been using it since it first opened. As the bedroom door flung open, a double bed looked straight at him. He'd been in this room so many times in the past and enjoyed hours of fun with the working girls there. The silken sheets that were covering the stale mattress looked crusty. At the side of the bed was a small table and on it was a collection of oils and different love toys. John was a big fan of vibrators. The new Ann Summers rabbit was one of his favourites. He'd suggested to Sue to get one in the past, but she just looked at him with disgust, so he never mentioned it again. John stumbled onto the bed and he looked agitated. Looping his hands behind his head he smiled at the girl. "What's your name sexy?" When she told him she was called Toni he patted the bed with the palm of his hand and asked her to join him.

At first, John spoke of the day he'd spent at the christening and rambled on not making any sense at all. Toni looked at him and knew if she didn't make her move now, he was likely to keep her in there for hours. She had money to make and wasted no time in getting things started. Toni started by stroking his thigh. John lifted his head up towards her.

"I think you're gorgeous. I'm gonna do things to you that will blow your mind." Toni smiled at him and licked her lips. The men she'd slept with in the past were all the same. They'd talk a good fight but when it came down to the crunch their nobs would shrink to the size of a walnut whip. As she looked at John, she noticed how handsome he was and looked forward to getting shagged by someone half-decent for a change. Her usual punters were old men with disabilities; previously she'd shagged a man with a wooden leg. She'd never laughed as much as the first time she'd shagged old Albert. The first thing he would do before sex was to take his leg off and hop towards the bed. All through sex he'd shout out "fuck the Germans!" Old Albert was a dirty pervert and all the girls dreaded having sex with him he was a head case.

Toni began to kiss John's neck. She could see the swelling of his cock rising in his pants. A smile came to her face and she knew sex would be over before it even started. John peeled back her housecoat and slid his hands into her black lacy knickers. Within seconds, he'd spun her onto her back and was ramming the rabbit in and out of her vagina. Toni seemed to be enjoying it. She looked like she was allowing a punter to satisfy her own sexual needs. Usually she would completely switch herself off and become numb when she was with a punter, but John had worked some kind of magic on her and it looked like she was having sex with her own boyfriend. The sex lasted around ten minutes. It all ended when Toni sucked John's cock. He was knelt up on the bed and his hands were hung behind his head. John's sexual noises were like something you would only hear in a porn movie. His head sunk back as the pleasure stormed through his masculine body.

John collapsed onto the bed. His breathing was fast and he was blowing through his mouth. Toni fell at the side of him. The sex between the two of them was amazing. It was obvious they both felt an attraction towards each other. They'd only known each other such a short time, but John looked smitten. John's penis was still like a missile ready for takeoff. Toni looked at him with a smile on her face. Usually her punters would only get an hour with her, but as sex had happened quickly between them she knew before the hour was over, he would get a second wind and shag her brains out again.

They both sat talked for a while. John seemed hypnotised by her hazel brown eyes. Her eyes looked like they had gold glitter sprinkled inside the deep hazel colour. Toni's skin was lustrous and silky to touch. John sat chewing his bottom lip and looked in deep thought; he was wondering to himself why on earth this girl was working in a brothel, she was gorgeous. Toni looked up at John as he leant forward to kiss her. She quickly turned her head away from him. His face snarled at her and he looked angry.

"What the fuck's that about. I only wanted a kiss."

Toni turned her head back at him. She told him that kissing was all she had left to keep for the special person in her life. As she spoke, he noticed a tear forming in the corner of her eye. He left her alone for a minute; he could see she was getting upset. John checked his watch; he knew if he was going to shoot his load again he had to make a move before his time was up. He grabbed her body now and flung her about the room like a dog shagging a teddy. He loved that her body was so flexible. Sex with Sue was like shagging a corpse and he blamed her for him seeking other women's company. Once John had ejaculated for the second time he seemed to sober up rapidly. His face was covered in guilt.

He got dressed; the confident man who came into the brothel earlier had now disappeared. He was a crumbling wreck. All that was left was a man that was full of remorse and guilt. He stared at Toni who was putting her knickers back on and struggled to raise smile. She was a cute little thing and he knew without a shadow of doubt he'd be shagging her again in the near future. He just couldn't help himself. John walked back down the landing on his own as Toni disappeared inside the bathroom. Once he reached the reception area he was greeted by Nicola, the boss of the brothel. As usual, she smiled at him and asked him whether his time spent with Toni was enjoyable. John stuttered and told her she was a good. Nicola now relayed the information to an older gentleman who was now sat on the leather settee; he was waiting for Toni too. John screwed his face up as he scowled at the old pervert sat on the settee. He must have been at least sixty. His skin looked craggy. As John looked at him closer, he saw a reflection of himself in years to come, his head sank low. John said goodbye to Nicola and hurried out of the door. He jumped down the stairs two at a time and his face looked stressed. He was gone.

John finally reached the pub as the guests were leaving. His mother snarled at him as soon as she set eyes on him. "Where the fuck have you been?" she moaned. John made no reply and pushed his way past her. "Fucking waste of space!" she whispered under her breath. As he strolled into the pub, Misty grabbed hold of him and started to kiss his face telling him what a wonderful day she'd had. John smiled at her and he could tell she was as pissed as a fart. Dominic now came to rescue him. He chuckled as he took Misty's arm and started to speak with John.

"Where've you been hiding all night? I've hardly seen you." John shook his head and whispered into his mate's ear. "Sue was doing my head in, so I just fucked off for a bit. You know how it is pal." Dominic sniggered knowing exactly what he was talking about.

"Women, ay. Can't live with em, and can't live without em." Dominic smirked as he carried Misty to a nearby chair, she was rat arsed. Sue watched as John approached her. She carried on talking to Peggy watching her husband from the corner of her eye. John plonked his sweaty body down next to Peggy. She quickly greeted him and thanked him for a lovely day. Sue now turned to him with a face of thunder and all hell broke loose. Sue was livid.

"Don't bother thanking him, Peggy. He's not been here all fucking night. He doesn't give a shite about anyone but himself." Her eyes were burning into his face, "everyone's been running round like a blue-arsed fly, trying to make the day perfect, but he just sits about looking like chief black cloud." Sue reached for a cig from the table. Popping into the corner of her mouth she continued. "Well let me tell you now Peggy, things are gonna change in our house otherwise he can book his bed back at his mother's." John's face was on fire as Peggy stood up to leave. It was obvious that she felt embarrassed with the whole situation. John could tell Sue was fuming. He knew that some serious brown nosing was now in order. John sat for a moment and watched as Peggy waved goodbye. Sue now turned her head away from him and watched the couple at the side of her. John placed his hand on her lap. She snapped, her teeth were clenched together.

"Fucking move away from me! Don't waste your bullshit on me anymore, because I'm not fucking listening." John dipped his head low and looked at the woman he'd once adored. He knew the shit she been through in the past and hated himself for treating her that way. Maureen now came to join them both and she could tell they weren't speaking. Her initial reaction was to have a go at John but as she looked at him, she could tell he was in no fit state to take onboard anything she had to say. Sue started to speak and completely blanked John. He stood to his feet and made his way to the bar feeling sorry for himself. John's dad saw he was upset and came to join him throwing his arms around his neck.

"Alright son. Fucking hell, you look steaming. What have you been drinking?"

John raised a smile and flung his arms around his dad's shoulder. He felt loved again. "Mi old man. You know I love ya don't you."

His dad raised his eyes to the ceiling and listened to his son's drunken bullshit. John ordered a large brandy now and hung over the bar as he waited for it. The brandy came and he necked it in one go. His father watched in disbelief.

"Fucking hell, son! Take your time with that because you're not getting another one." John looked at his dad and smirked. He started to sing a song he knew his father loved. They were both singing at the top of their voices now.

Maureen and Sue still sat in the corner of the pub. John's mother smiled as she watched the two special men in her life singing aloud. Frank Sinatra was one of her husband's favourite artists and as he sung 'High Hopes', she remembered when he'd serenaded her with that exact song so many years ago. Maureen shot a look at Sue. She could still see the gloom in her face and tried to bring her round.

"Things will be different in the morning love. It's just been a stressful day that's all." Maureen looked over at her son with endearing eyes. "You know our John's no good with a bit of pressure. He was like that as a kid. Any sign of stress and he was off like a shot. I think I'm a bit like that as well, he must get it from me." Sue knew she was trying to make her forgive her son and stared over at John as she spoke.

"Maureen, he's let me down so much lately, you don't know the half of it." Her eyes rolled to the back of her head. "Since Bethany's been born, he's been a right twat, he won't talk about whatever is bothering him. I'm just so pissed off with him lately," she twisted her hair round in her fingers, "and I can't see it getting any better in the future." Maureen looked horrified. She hadn't realised that things had got so bad between them both. In her mind the words divorce flashed in front of her and she continued to talk with tears forming in the corner of her eyes.

"Orr love, things are always hard after having a baby. I wanted to leave John's dad every other day but we got through it. It's just one of them trying times. Things will sort themselves out they always do." Sue looked at John and hoped his mother was right. She still adored the ground that he walked on and to lose him would be devastating to her.

Sue now followed Maureen to the singing pair. John pulled Sue to his side as he sang the words of the song to her. It was funny because she seemed to put the dramas of the day behind her and carried on as if nothing had ever happened between them. She was getting good at hiding her pain.

The night ended and both Sue and John went upstairs to bed in the pub. The stairs that led to the front room were steep and Sue had to hold John up as he walked in front of her. His arse was shoved in her face. She firmly placed her two hands on his bum cheeks to push him up the last few stairs. As they opened the front room door, Jayne the babysitter sat smiling at them both. She was fifteen and the daughter of one of the regulars in the pub. John reached into his pocket and tried to search for the money to pay her for babysitting. Sue stood sniggering as all his money fell on the floor. She bent her knees and helped him try to pick it all up. Finally, after about five minutes Sue handed Jayne a ten-pound note from her own pocket. You could tell the young girl was chuffed with the babysitting money and she couldn't wait to say goodnight to them both. Sue escorted her down the stairs and told her Maureen would wait with her till her taxi came. She thanked her again for babysitting and headed back to the front room.

John was nowhere to be seen. Her eyes scanned the area. She quickly looked in the kitchen to see if he'd gone there. She could hear banging noises from the bedroom; Sue turned her body and went in search of him. As she neared the bedroom door, she could hear him laughing to himself and wondered what on earth he was up to. Slowly she pushed the door open and got the shock of her life when she saw him stood there dressed in her red underwear. John giggled and started to do a sexy dance about the bedroom, as Sue watched with a smile on her face.

"You're fucking mental you are. What on earth are you doing with my knickers and bra on?" John came towards her and caressed her face with his hands.

"I'm spicing up our love life, that's all. That's what we need a bit of filth in our sex life. What do you think?" Sue's face dropped. She looked at him in disgust.

"I think our sex life is all right. How could it possibly turn me on, seeing you wearing my fucking underwear? I'm not a lesbian you know." John looked embarrassed. All he'd wanted to do was spice things up a bit, but she'd even spoilt that. He now stood there feeling like a prize prick in her underwear. His temper was boiling.

"Fucking frigid you are! What happened to the woman I married who loved sex?" Sue stopped dead in her tracks.

"You cheeky bastard. Who the fuck do you think you are?" Sue rammed her finger into his chest and was nose to nose with him. "Let me tell you something shall I? Sex with you is boring. I get more of a thrill when I go over a hill on the bus," she chuckled. "Fucking spice our sex life up, my arse! Get my fucking knickers off and get in bed you drunken bastard."

John's face changed immediately and he gripped her hair pulling her back towards him. Spit was hanging from the corner of his mouth as he blasted his words into her face. "Sex is shite because I'm shagging you. You don't turn me on anymore. I have to fantasize about other women to get me hard." All Sue's past came flooding back to her now and she couldn't believe she was in the same situation yet again. John spat in her face. He was growling at her as he threw her onto the bed.

"Fucking frigid bitch. No wonder my head's up my arse with you. I don't know why I bother." He pushed her back onto the bed and yanked the underwear from his body as if they were on fire. Sue now bolted up from the bed and screamed into his face.

"You fucking nobhead. Tell ya what. Tomorrow you can get the fuck out of my life and do whatever your perverted mind wants to." The door slammed behind her as she left the room. He made her blood boil so much. "Fucking wanker!" She cursed under her breath.

Sue checked Bethany in the cot and pulled the pink blanket up over her. There was a single bed in the room and it looked like that's where she would be spending the rest of night. Her tears seemed to be stuck in her eyes as she stared about the room. Sue's past life seemed to have a lot to do with the way she felt at the moment. She'd had always promised herself that she would never end up like this again. As she lay on the bed, Sue knew she'd have no choice but to leave her abusive husband. How could she stay with him after the way he'd just treated her? Sue had preached to so many women in the refuge about leaving violent partners and to look at her now she was just in the same boat as them. She buried her head under the duvet and you could see her shoulders shaking.

John lay in bed and stared at the empty space where Sue should have been. He'd meant every word he'd said to her at the time but now the hours had passed he looked like he wanted to apologise. John's head was banging as he reached for two headache tablets from the side cabinet. He could hear the birds starting to tweet outside. John closed his eyes and rolled on his side. He was asleep.

Bethany woke Sue from her sleep; she was trying to stand up in her cot. It was so heart warming watching her trying to find her feet for the first time. These were the moments John was missing out on. Sue lay in bed on her side and watched Bethany playing in her cot. Sadness filled her eyes. She had to make some big decisions in the future and she just hoped her daughter wouldn't be affected by them. As she moved her pillows under her head, the door opened slightly. John appeared looking sheepish. His hair was all over the place and he looked like he'd been dragged through a hedge. At first, his eyes just focused on Bethany. Slowly he made his way to sit beside her. This was like second nature to him now and he knew he'd have to creep to his wife to try and build the bridges between them. As Sue scowled at him, her anger was still visible. She moved her legs from where he was sat. "Tosser." She mumbled under her breath.

John sneaked his hand under the duvet and stroked Sue's leg. She quickly moved him away with a flick of her foot. He turned his head to look at her and she knew the usual sorry treatment was on its way. Within seconds, she was right he started to speak.

"Sue, you know I'm sorry. I don't know what came over me. It must be the brandy, because every time I drink it I go off my head don't I?" Sue moved away from him and her back was pressed up against the wall. "I'm sorry love; I promise you I'll never hurt you again." His eyes filled with tears as he spoke. Sue stared at him and no matter how much she tried, she found herself forgiving him. John continued and his apology was on form. He should have been awarded an Oscar because this was a class act, better than any that he'd done in the past. He knew exactly how to get round his wife and pulled at all the heartstrings that would get him back in her good books. "Please forgive me Sue. I'll take you and Bethany out today for your dinner. We can spend the day as a family if you want. What do you say?" The word family spun around in her mind and she found it hard to resist. She stuck to her guns for now. She sat up in the bed and shook her head.

"Listen, I've heard it all before and nothing ever fucking changes. It's like listening to a broken record and to tell you the truth I've had enough of your shit." John panicked and grabbed her hand. The thought of losing her terrified him, even though he didn't really want her. The room was quiet and the only noise was that of Bethany moaning in the cot to get out. John sighed and tried again to win her around.

"Fucking hell Sue, it's not that bad. Why do you blow everything out of proportion, and make mountains out of molehills? Just say you forgive me and we can have a great day together, don't spoil it for Bethany." Sue thought for a moment but still didn't want to give in. Her eyes shot to Bethany in the cot, she wanted so much to make her marriage work. After a few moments, his plan started to work and Sue was under his spell yet again.

"Right, I'll forgive you, but I'm telling you now if this ever happens again I'll be off like a shot and you won't see me for dust." John flung his arms around her neck and kissed her cheek. Her reaction wasn't enthusiastic but she patted his back as not to continue the argument. John smiled and his depressive face disappeared as if by magic. He now fell to the floor and got on his knees crawling across the bedroom to see Bethany in her cot.

"I'm coming to get you," he shouted. Bethany kicked her legs in excitement knowing her daddy was coming to get her. Maureen now entered the room and was none the wiser about the trouble between them. Her face looked green and her hangover was written all across it. She was rubbing her hand in her hair, trying to flatten it.

"Oh I feel as rough as a bear's arse. I don't know about you two, but my heads banging." They both smiled at her and she clapped her hands to get Bethany's attention.

"Bethany, Bethany," she shouted. "Are you being a good girl? Don't look at your nana because she's a bit worse for wear this morning." Maureen chuckled and fastened her pink fluffy housecoat round her waist. A smirk filled her face. "I'd better go and see if fucking Frank Sinatra wants any breakfast hadn't I?" They all giggled and Maureen left the room singing the Frank Sinatra song from the night before. John held Bethany in his arms and started to sing along with the song his mother had started. Sue watched him as he spun Bethany around the room, she looked happy.

Maureen could be heard shouting from the landing. She asked them both whether they wanted any breakfast or not. John was more than ready for one of his mother's full English breakfasts and the smell of the bacon made him make up his mind. Sue rubbed at her belly. "Yeah dead right I do, I'm starving." John looked at the closed door and shouted to his mother.

"Yeah, mam. We both want breakfast. Make sure my bacon is crispy, and don't overdo my egg."

Maureen could be heard talking to her husband and by the sound of it, she was making sure he was going to help her cook breakfast for their guest. John and Sue lay together for a moment and he stared deep into her eyes. He should have been thinking how much he loved her, but all he thought about was that he'd won his wife over yet again. The day went to plan and John kept his promise and spent the day with his family. Sue was still being frosty with him, but as they day progressed she returned to her normal self.

The months that followed were more or less the same for Sue. John would use his fists from time to time to remind her that he was still the boss. Sue had become a prisoner to love and could never find the courage to walk away from her abusive relationship. Her marriage was on the rocks. Misty saw the changes in Sue; she seemed to have lost all heart in the refuge and the women inside it. She was always a positive person and found the good in whatever the problem was but these days she didn't seem to give a shit about anything or anyone. You could tell that her heart wasn't in it anymore. Misty had asked her several times what the problem was, but she always shrugged her off telling her she was tired. If the truth was known, Sue hated being in the refuge. She knew she was living a lie. Sue talked to women each day about making plans to lead a happier life without their abusive partners but she couldn't do it herself. She branded herself a hypocrite and the sooner she could leave her job at the refuge the better. The place depressed her so much lately and she found herself snapping at the slightest thing.

John's life looked great, or so he thought. He still had a wife and child at home, and he was waited on hand and foot. His meal was always on the table every night when he walked through the door, he never lifted a finger. John's love for prostitutes continued and most of his wages were spent on them. Well not so much 'them', just one in particular. Toni was his dream girl and he would see her at least twice a week. He was infatuated by her, and brought her gifts every time he went to visit. Toni loved the attention he was giving her and took him for every penny she could. When she first started seeing him, she actually thought she could get serious with him but as time went on his sexual habits knocked her sick.

One Friday, after a night on the town with his mates, John left Dominic and the lads and headed to the brothel for his fix of dirty sex. Misty was parked on Oldham Road waiting for Dominic to come and meet her. They'd arranged earlier in the evening that she would come and pick him up once the night with the lads was over. Taxis were a nightmare to get in town, and it was a usual thing between them both that they picked each other up after a night on the tiles. Misty sat in the car tapping the steering wheel with her fingers. She couldn't see any sign of Dominic and decided to drive a bit further up the road. As she pulled up, she could see John heading towards her and thought Dominic wouldn't be far behind him. As she watched carefully, she could see him disappear into a doorway. She was shocked. A few moments passed and John was still nowhere in sight. Misty had first thought he'd gone for a piss but he never re-appeared. Scratching her head, she decided to go and investigate. Locking the car she walked the short distance to the doorway. Her heart stopped when she saw the writing above the door. She looked scared and ran back to the car as quickly as her legs would carry her.

Manchester town centre was buzzing that night and she feared for her safety. Jumping back into the driver's seat she pressed the central locking. Her head was all over the place searching the area. Misty's mind was working overtime. Surely she'd got it wrong. There was no way in this world that John would have gone into a brothel. He was such a nice man and had a lovely wife, why on earth was she even thinking that? Goose pimples now appeared on her arms. Was Dominic in there with him? Her heart pounded inside her chest and she decided to investigate further. Misty jumped from the car and started to walk to the doorway again. Just as she was steps away from it, she could hear Dominic voice coming from around the corner. He saw her straight away and looked shocked as she stood in front of him.

"What the fuck are you doing waiting here? Where's the car?" Dominic was twisting his head from side to side. Misty had to think on her feet. His mates started to kiss her on the cheek. She spoke in a stressed voice.

"I've been waiting ages for you. I thought something was wrong so I decided to walk to the end of the street to see if I could see you."

Dominic picked her up in his arms and chuckled. "Orr have you missed me?"

The lads now joined in the banter. "Did ya think he'd got lost Misty? Don't worry we always look after him when he's out with us. Don't we Dom?" Dominic smirked at his mates and walked slowly towards the car.

"Later lads." he shouted over his shoulder.

Misty's mind was racing with questions about John's whereabouts as they got back in the car. She couldn't hold her tongue any longer.

"Where's, John? I thought he was out with you lot tonight?"

Dominic shrugged his shoulders and began to stutter his words, he was well and truly pissed. "John, he's a fucking waste of space. He fucked off on his own and didn't tell any of us he was going." His head fell onto the window as he looked across at her. "You see he can't handle the beer like your sexy husband can." Dominic leant over to the driver's side and tickled Misty's neck. You could tell he was in the mood for some serious loving. Misty looked shocked at what he'd just said. Banging her hand on the steering wheel she let rip.

"Well I know where he is, the dirty bastard. I've just seen him going into that fucking brothel there." She rammed her finger at the window screen. Dominic's face dropped and he knew John was in deep shit. Dominic had known of times before when John had visited prostitutes but thought he had given it up when he'd got married. He had to think quickly and make a decision. Should he lie to Misty or should he tell her the truth about John's antics. As he looked at her, he could see she meant business. He now confessed to Misty the story of John always going to prostitutes in his younger days. His face looked stressed and he was chewing on his lips. Misty was livid, she started the car's engine. The sound of the wheels spinning could be heard as she pulled out onto the main road.

"The dirty scumbag!" she ranted. Sue is such a nice woman; he doesn't deserve her, the fucking wanker." All the way home, she cursed John. Dominic just sat there knowing he couldn't defend him; he was caught bang to rights. Misty screeched up outside their house. Questions were jumping around in her mind; her head was all over the place. They headed inside the house and Misty launched the keys on the side cabinet. She turned to face him and stopped dead in her track. Running at him she gripped his arm.

"Dominic, please tell me you haven't been going as well."

He snarled at her and walked away shaking his head. "Fucking hell love, give me some credit will ya. Why would I pay for sex, when I've got you?" Misty looked at him closer. She could tell he was innocent and looked relieved as he continued. "If I was a fat ugly cunt, then yes I might shag a brass. But I'm not." He gasped his breath and waved his hands over his body. "Come on Misty give me a bit of fucking credit."

Misty believed him; she could always tell when he was lying. They made their way upstairs to bed. Charlotte was staying at Lisa's that night so they didn't have to think about keeping the noise down. Misty was annoyed and her body was shaking at the thought of John and his dirty secret. Sue was her best mate and she knew she would have to tell her no matter what. She told Dominic of her plans to grass John up. He looked devastated as he fell onto the bed and tried to persuade her to keep the truth from Sue.

"Fucking hell Misty, it would cause murders between them. They would definitely split up yanno. What about Bethany? Do you want to be the one who splits a family up?"

Misty gritted her teeth. Her temper was bursting and she hated the situation she was put in. Pacing around the bedroom she snapped. "He is the one splitting a family up. Nobody forces him to go and shag some dirty little prossies. He could give Sue a disease or anything." She dragged her fingers through her hair. "He's a nobhead and deserves everything he gets, the no good wanker." Dominic could see there was no point in defending John anymore. The silly bastard had got himself caught, so it was up to him to deal with it. Dominic lay on the bed as Misty joined him. The room had an atmosphere

"Come on love. We don't need to fall out over this do we? I'm not the one who's cheated. Come here and give your sexy husband a big cuddle." Misty knew he was right and ran into his open arms. His face now became serious. Gripping her hands he told Misty whatever she wanted to do regarding Sue, he'd stand by her. The words seemed to calm her. The first thing in the morning she was going to tell her friend the horrible truth.

Sue was flying about the refuge like a blue-arsed fly as Misty entered. The rain was pouring down outside and Misty looked like a drowned rat as she took her coat off. All the leaves at the entrance of the doorway had gathered outside the walkway and Misty knew she'd have to clear them away before someone slipped on them. Sue came to help her. The wind was howling hard and the leaves were blowing all over the place.

"Oh it's bloody freezing isn't it?" Misty said. Sue nodded her head but made no attempt to reply. Misty looked at her friend closer, she looked so exhausted. Sue had always been a glamorous girl and her makeup had always looked perfect. She was a walking wreck now.

As Sue shovelled the leaves from the entrance, Misty

took her hand in hers and looked at her with a serious face. "What's up?" Sue enquired.

Misty wanted to hug her and tell her everything was going to be all right but she needed to be somewhere private first before she told her the dreaded truth. "Do you fancy a brew?"

Sue tilted her head to the side and looked at Misty's face, she knew something was wrong. "Yeah alright then," she said with caution.

Misty went inside as the last bag of leaves was filled and put the kettle on to boil. She knew this was going to be hard and tried to go over in her mind what she wanted to say. Sue entered the room and started to wash her hands. "My hands are freezing." she complained. They both sat down now and Misty made pointless conversation as she tried to get the courage to tell her the truth.

"How's things with my bessie mate then? We haven't had a good chat for ages, have we?" Sue smiled and started to tell her about some woman who'd come to the refuge earlier that week. Misty looked frustrated and couldn't stand it any longer. She came and perched on the arm of Sue's chair. Misty's eyes filled with tears and she told her what she'd seen.

Sue was quiet and never said a word. Her eyes stared at the same spot on the floor for what seemed like forever. Misty asked her if she was okay but she just stood up and walked towards the door saying nothing. Misty ran behind her and tried to speak to her but Sue pushed her out of the way and left the room. "Fuckin leave me," she snarled.

Sue sprinted to her car as Misty followed closely behind her. Misty gasped.

"Please Sue, speak to me. I'm worried about you.

Just come back inside for five minutes to calm down." She placed her hand on her shoulder and rubbed at it softly. "You don't want to be driving when you're in this frame of mind." Sue twisted her to face to look at Misty. Her cheeks were red and she clenched her teeth tightly together.

"Don't you think I've got enough on my plate without adding to it?" Her hands were waving in front of Misty's face. "What the fuck do I do now my husband is shagging prostitutes? How the fuck do you want me to act?" Misty flung her arms around her best friend's neck as she crumbled to the floor in despair. "Come on love, let's go back inside for a minute." The tears flowed as Sue started to tell Misty the truth. Sitting in an empty room she told her all about her husband's abusive behaviour. Misty was flabbergasted, they cried together. Sue was broken in two.

"Everything seems to fit now," Sue said in a distressed voice as she stood to her feet. "That's why the bastard has been treating me the way he has," she dragged at her skin as if it was on fire. "Fucking paying for sex, I can't believe him. No fucking wonder he's not interested in me." Sue ran to the toilet, she was retching. Misty entered behind her and she could hear her being sick in a nearby cubicle. Sue now came into sight her face looked devastated.

"Misty, what the fuck do I do now?" her body folded in two as she held her head in her hands. "I know what I should do, but I'm so scared of losing him. How will I cope?" her eyes shot to Misty. "I'm a fucking walking wreck already, he's destroyed me you know, physically and mentally."

Misty cradled her as she sobbed her heart out. "You're not going home, you're coming and stay with me. We can get through this together."

Sue nodded her head. "I need to go home first for some things."

"Do you want me to come with you?" Misty asked.

Sue wiped her nose on her sleeve and chewed on her bottom lip. "No love, I need to see him on my own before I leave. I don't want you involved." Misty tried to argue with her, but she told her straight that she wanted to go alone. The two women held each other for a few minutes. Sue broke free now and looked deep into Misty's eyes. "I will be fine, trust me." The sound of the door being slammed behind Sue could be heard.

John wasn't in the house when Sue arrived home. She was like a hurricane flying. The first thing she did when she entered the front room was to phone her husband to tell him to come home straight away. John had asked what was wrong, but she just told him to get home as quickly as possible they had an emergency to deal with. John tried ringing back to find out what had happened but Sue just stared at the phone, knowing he would be on his way.

Sue began packing her husband's belongings. Tears raced down her face as she flung his clothes into the black bin liners. Bethany was still at the child minders and she knew by the time she was due home, she'd be well rid of her cheating husband.

The front door could be heard slamming downstairs. Sue could hear John shouting her name in a frantic voice. She stood like a scared animal debating her next move. John was now stood at the bedroom door looking stressed. His eyes shot to the bin liners filled with his clothes. He gasped a deep breath, shaking his head.

"What's happened love? Where are you going?" Sue growled at him and her nostrils were flaring. The bedroom had witnessed so many sad times lately and she struggled to remember if she'd ever really been happy with husband. The photo of them both together at the side of the bed now looked like a reminder of all the bad times they'd had. Sue walked slowly towards it and gripped it in her hands. Her knuckles were turning white as she laid it flat on the side. The bedroom was decorated in a soft lilac colour. All the furniture was in pine. When she'd bought the lilac carpet, John had told her it looked like a prostitute's bedroom, he hated it with a passion. Sue remembered his exact words now, he made her skin crawl.

John edged towards her. His face was white and small droplets of sweat were visible on his forehead. He slowly licked his dry lips.

"Sue what the fuck is going on, will you please tell me, because I'm getting worried now. What's fucking happening?"

Sue snapped and all hell broke loose. She pounced on him and sank her nails deep into his face. "What's happening? I'll tell you what's happening. You fucking dirty no good bastard." Her fists were clenched and she pummelled the side of his head. He was trying desperately to get her off him.

"What the fuck have I done? Please tell me." Sue bounced away from her husband and stood near the window, her chest was rising in and out at a rapid pace. Quickly she turned to face him; her body was trembling from head to toe.

"Fucking shagging dirty prostitutes. You're a dirty cunt and I hope your nob rots off. You're fucking disgusting and the sooner I'm away from you the better." John's face dropped he looked horrified. She could tell by his face it was all true. John stood lifeless and didn't know what to do. Sue gave a sarcastic chuckle. "No wonder we've never got any fucking money when you're paying for sex. I hope they were worth it, because as from today, you're on your fucking own. You can have as much scabby fanny as you want now. You're a dirty cunt." Sue started to pack hers and Bethany's clothes what she needed for her time at Misty's. John sat on the bed looking in a world of his own.

John ran over it all over in his mind. He knew he couldn't lie to his wife anymore. In a way, he was glad his secret was out. "Sue, I'm so sorry. I never planned to hurt you, but it's something I've always done since I was a young lad. It's nothing you've done believe me." Sue looked like someone had plunged a sword into her heart. In a way, she was hoping he'd denied it all and told her it was a pack of lies, at least then she could have forgiven him. John continued telling her all about his guilty pleasure. Sue looked pale; she held one hand on the wall to steady herself. Her head was spinning and she thought she was going to pass out as his words crucified her. John looked relieved.

Sue continued to pack her clothes but there were questions in her mind that needed to be answered, he owed her that at least. Her words were low as she folded Bethany's clothes into the bag. "Was sex that bad with me that you had to go and pay for it?" Sue waited for a reply, but he seemed to be thinking about his answer for too long. "Well then, fucking was it?" She screamed at the top of her voice as she slung a shoe at his head.

"Sex wasn't bad Sue. I just needed something more." Sue bolted up from the floor and hurled their picture together from the side of the bed at the wall. The glass frame shattered all about the bedroom.

"You cheeky twat. How dare you say it wasn't that fucking bad?" She huffed her breath. "It made you scream my name a few fucking times as I can recall. Well I hope you enjoy your little slappers now because I'm out of here." Her voice was firm as she paced around the bedroom looking like a headless chicken. "I want the house and I want a fucking divorce, so start talking to your solicitor." She leant into his face and pushed her finger deep into his cheek. "I'm going to take you for every penny you've got, you wanker." Sue's body seemed to have a mind of its own; it was all over the place. John made no attempt to stop her leaving the house. As she stood at the front door holding her bags in her hands she froze in her step. She turned her head slowly to the stairs; he never came to stop her leaving.

The windows in the car were steamed up. Sue had to wait a few minutes before she could see out of them. As part of the window screen started to clear up her eyes focused on the house. Her knuckles were white as she squeezed the steering wheel. "Bastard, bastard, bastard," she sobbed. The rain pelted down on the car now as the heavens opened. The black clouds in the sky seem to know about her misery and looked angry as they circled on top of her.

Sue screeched out of the driveway. The house she'd once loved seemed like something she never wanted to see again. It only held bad memories for her now and the sooner it was out of her life the better.

As she drove towards the refuge, her eyes streamed with a river of sadness. Looking in the mirror she could see black tears trickling down her face. The mascara she'd been wearing had dissolved all around her eyes. The radio played softly in the back ground and a song she'd once loved began to play. The words of Whitney Houston's, 'Where Do Broken Hearts Go' took her breath and her shoulders began to shake rapidly as her heart broke into a million pieces. Sue couldn't take it anymore; she quickly leant over and turned the radio off. As she cried she mumbled to herself.

"I'll tell you where fucking broken hearts go Whitney. Right back to where they fucking started so many years ago. I've been such a nobhead. Don't I ever fucking learn?" Sue finally reached the refuge in a panic and stayed in the car. Her body draped over the steering wheel as she cried her eyes out. Everything seemed so unreal to her at the moment and she tried to take on board everything that was happening. Sue punched her clenched fist at the dashboard. She started to blame herself for her husband's infidelity. "Why? Why?" she sobbed.

Sue crept into the refuge through a side door that led to her office. She quickly sneaked into her room and tried to wipe away any signs that she'd been crying. In the hallway she could hear footsteps approaching and panicked. Misty stood at the door and stared at Sue with a devastated face. Not wanting to be disturbed, Misty quickly pulled the filing cabinet in front of the door. Sue fell to her knees and sobbed and sobbed. Misty stood watching her friend fall apart. She couldn't find one word that would ease her pain.

"What am I going to do now Misty? John was my life. I loved him so much, and look what he's done to me." Sue pulled her body from the floor and plonked onto a chair. "You know what, it sounds pathetic but I could have put up with the odd belt here and there, but shagging tarts, it's so unforgivable." The words she spoke cut Misty in two. Why had she never told her that John was hurting her before? Was she not her friend anymore or was it that she was too mixed up in her own world that she didn't see what was happening right in front of her own two eyes? Misty looked uncomfortable and played with the cuff of her sleeve.

"Why didn't you ever tell me he was hurting you? You know I'm always here for you no matter what." Sue hung her head low as she rubbed at her arms.

"I wanted to tell you Misty, but I always thought it wouldn't happen again. Then, as time went on, I realised that I was back in the place where I'd been before." she snivelled. "How could I tell you it was happening to me again? I feel so ashamed. I'm a total dickhead." Misty swallowed hard as she realised how bad things had got for Sue. They had a friendship that went back a long way and Misty knew she'd let Sue down big time.

Misty offered again for Sue to stay with her, but she declined her this time. Sue told her she'd be staying in the vacant room upstairs in the refuge. They both hugged each other for what seemed like hours. Both of them sat chain smoking now, the room was filled with clouds of grey smoke. Their friendship was a strong one and they both knew that together they could tackle anything and anyone that ever came between them.

The months passed and Sue did as she'd promised. She divorced her husband and the house was sold, giving Sue enough money to rebuild her life. John never came to reclaim her or even to declare his undying love for her. His visits with Bethany stopped a long time ago. Everyone who'd seen John had said he'd taken to the drink big time and as far as they were concerned he was still a regular visitor to the brothels.

After time Sue felt began to feel sorry for him, but he never darkened her doorway again. She'd opened a new chapter in her life and John wasn't part of it. At the moment she wanted to concentrate on her daughter and rebuild her life. Sue had bought a small terraced house and that's where she started again. Looking at her now, you could see she was a fighter and somehow you knew she would do well in life even without a man by her side.

## Chapter Ten

Gordon stared at the calendar on his cell wall and couldn't believe his jail sentence was nearly over. Life inside the jails had been hard. He'd been moved eight months before from Strangeways to a jail in Blackpool and the final months were taking their toll. Tigger was still coming to see Gordon in prison and the plan they'd talked about so many times in the past had started to take shape. Gordon missed Tigger so much since he'd been released, and his new pad mate wasn't a patch on him. Gordon looked like he had aged twenty years. The lines on his forehead were long and deep. It looked like someone had chiselled the lines into it. The weight had fallen from Gordon once Tigger had left. The screws always joked about it saying it was because he was pining for Tigger so much.

Francesca had been to visit Gordon a few times, but as the years passed, he was lucky to see her once every six months. Rico was so big now. When he came on the last visit, it was so hard for Gordon to bond with him, it was obvious that he didn't give a shit about his son. Rico was talking now and went to school fulltime. Gordon had missed so much of his life already and he knew it was going to be so hard for them all once he was released from jail.

Gordon's love for Francesca had disappeared years before. He only sent her visiting orders because he had no one else to come and see him. On the visits with her, she was a stranger to him, and he'd noticed the changes in her behaviour towards him. Even kissing Francesca had changed. He remembered on one visit, he'd leant towards her to kiss her, and she'd pulled her head away saying her breath stunk of garlic. At the time, he was angry and wanted to punch her head in, but as the years passed, he just got used to the stale relationship.

Tigger was a top friend to have. Every time he came to visit Gordon, he'd bring some slapper along with him. The idea was that she'd kiss him and pass the drugs over. The girl who he'd brought on the last few visits was quite sexy, and before long their kisses were getting more intense. Gordon was quite turned on by her. After he'd seen this girl a few times she started writing to him and before long, they were planning a life together when he finally got out. Gordon knew his life with Francesca would be short lived once he was on the out, he was just plodding along with her for now.

On the final visit with Tigger they discussed a few things they'd already put into place. Gordon's old pad mate had many friends and was a main head about Manchester. All it took from him was to call in a few favours from his old friends and the connection with Dominic's father was made. Dominic's father loved a bit of the old knocked off stuff and bought it by the pallet loads. His latest buy was a van full of snide Prada handbags. Tigger could see him rubbing his hands together as he thought of how much he would make on each bag. Tigger also roped him into a few hooky property deals.

Tigger had worked deals with Dominic's dad for around a year now and he trusted him one hundred percent. He'd spoken of his son quite a few times in conversation and told Tigger if the right property ever came up, his son would bite his arm off for it. Tigger knew once he mentioned his son's name that his job was nearly complete. All he needed now was for Gordon to be released from prison and the months of plotting would finally be put into action. The prison visit between them both was intense and you could see Gordon hung on every word Tigger said.

Tigger was told to keep his eye on Francesca. Gordon knew something had changed between them both, but he just couldn't put his finger on what it was. He'd asked Tigger to call round to the flat now and then just to check things out and to see if anything was going on that he didn't know about. Tigger had visited Francesca a few times at the flat and tried to suss out what Gordon was going on about, he thought his mate was paranoid. On one occasion he'd gone around to give Francesca some money and felt like shagging her himself. From the moment he walked in, he was instantly attracted to her. On the day he'd gone to see her she was alone in the flat and she'd kept him stood at the front door. Gordon had still been dealing drugs in the prison since Tigger had been released and some of the money he was earning was brought to Francesca every couple of weeks.

Tigger kicked his foot at the floor and asked Francesca could he come inside and have a brew with her, she nearly died of embarrassment. However, in the end Francesca thought a bit of harmless flirting never did anyone any harm and invited him inside. Her life with Tom had fizzled out ages ago. She was bored shitless. Francesca was still an attractive woman and the slut inside her was still alive and kicking. Tom was on some training course for a new job he'd just started and she knew he wouldn't be home for at least another couple of hours. Francesca let Tigger inside the flat and began to strut her stuff.

"Tea or coffee? Sugar?" Francesca shouted from the kitchen. Tigger's voice was deep.

"Coffee please, I don't take sugar I'm sweet enough." Francesca giggled as she stood in the kitchen making the brews. As she came back into the room, she passed him his coffee. Her eyes scanned every part of his body. Tigger had all the top clothes on. Even his trainers were the latest, most sought after brand. A large gold chain swung from his neck and he had a bracelet to match. Francesca inhaled deeply as she sat near him. The smell from him was incredible. He smelt so alive and clean and she could have licked him from head to toe there and then. Conversation between them was easy. Tigger made her piss laughing as he told her a few stories about his life. His hazel eyes looked like big conkers and she was hypnotised by them.

Francesca studied him and wondered what he'd be like in bed. His tracksuit bottoms showed the outline of his penis and she couldn't help but look at it. Tigger stayed with Francesca a lot longer than he should have. He even suggested that they should go out for a drink sometime. Francesca hadn't been out to the pub in years and she looked horrified at the thought of him asking her out. Rico was still at school at this time and she knew she could keep Tigger there for at least another few hours. The old Francesca now started to reappear and it wasn't long before she had him drooling over her. Tigger liked her cheekiness and he knew he would shag her brains out given the chance. After all, Gordon no longer wanted her – he'd said as much so many times before so she was fair game. Tigger stood up to leave.

"Right sexy, I better be off. I've got things to do and places to go. Think about coming for that drink with me, ay." Francesca wanted to shout out there and then that she was ready now, but she played it cool. As Tigger stood at the front door Francesca stood behind him fidgeting. As he turned back, he pulled her towards him and kissed her cheek. He quickly gripped her arse in his hands and chuckled. Francesca's mouth dropped and she pushed him away. She giggled as she told him she was Gordon's girlfriend, but he knew by her tone she was just joking. Francesca wanted it as much as he did it was written all over her face. Tigger nodded his head slowly.

"Right I'm definitely going now. I'm here for a good time not a long time, so be good and we'll speak soon, ay?"

Francesca smiled, "Ay I'm fed up not hard up." Tigger raised a smile, he loved her cocky attitude. Francesca aroused him and he loved the way she teased him. As he left her, he squeezed his penis in his hands and knew before long she'd be sat on his throbbing member. It was obvious Francesca loved all the attention Tigger was giving her and he knew he'd be back again in the near future. He was gone.

★

Gordon's time in prison was hard. On one or more occasions he'd thought he couldn't do it anymore, he was at an all time low. Death seemed his only way out. Once his new pad mate arrived, things got a bit better and his mood lifted slightly. Gordon's new pad mate looked like

Big Daddy the wrestler. His head was bald and his eyes shone like someone had held a torch behind them. When the inmate first walked into the cell, Gordon stood up and nodded at him. The screw introduced him.

"This is your new pad mate Gordon. He's come to keep you warm on these cold nights." Gordon told the screw to fuck off and smirked at him as he tried to wind him up some more. The screw held one hand on his hip as he continued with the banter. "Ay, beggars can't be choosers. Steve is much sort after as a pad mate, aren't you?" Steve told the screw to fuck off now and dropped his belongings on to his bed. The officer didn't stay much longer and as he left he tried one last time to break both their tempers.

"You be good now, won't you ladies." Neither Gordon nor Steve responded to him and set about whatever they were doing. When the door shut, silence filled the room and it felt quite uncomfortable. Steve started to empty his big, transparent bag that contained his belongings on the bed. He asked Gordon what drawers he could use to store his stuff.

Gordon lay on his bed with his hands looped above his head. He told Steve he could have the two bottom drawers that the previous pad mate had used. Gordon watched him like a hawk as he pulled different objects from his bag. Steve had piles and piles of letters and they were all held together with elastic bands. He also pulled out lots of different objects made with matchsticks. Gordon looked amazed as he scanned them, and asked could he see one in more detail.

"They look good mate. Did you make them yourself?" Steve now sat on his bed and held each of his designs up like a trophy.

"Yep, I made them all. They took me fucking ages to do; they're my pride and joy."

As Gordon looked closer he stroked his hands across the grand piano. Steve told him he'd made the jewellery box for his daughter. Among the matchstick models there was an eagle and an aeroplane, they were amazing. The next thing he pulled out of his bag was a load of photographs. Gordon had wanted to ask who they were but thought it best to leave it until he knew him a bit better.

Steve sat on his bed once he'd finished unpacking and sighed. "Fucking hell. I'm getting sick to death of all this moving about to different jails. A fucking gypsy doesn't move as much as I do." Gordon smiled and asked him where he'd come from. Scratching his bollocks Steve replied. "Oh, a jail in Scotland. Tell ya what mate this is like the fucking pleasure beach compared to it. When they told me I was coming to Kirkham I nearly come in my pants." Kirkham was an open prison near Blackpool and prisoners came there to finish the last months of their sentences. An open prison meant more freedom for the convicts. They were allowed to walk through the grounds on their own and escape would be very easy if they wanted to leave. Gordon had a job on the farm there and loved the time he spent out of his pad.

The question of Steve's crime rested on Gordon's mind – he was dying to know what he was in for. Steve was about fifty-five years of age and Gordon racked his brains trying to think what he could have done to end up in prison. Curiosity finally got the better of him and he casually threw it into the conversation.

"So, what ya in for mate." Steve looked at him and shook his head as he sat on the edge of the bed. His big belly was hanging between his legs and nearly touching the floor.

"I was in the fucking wrong place at the wrong time mate. To tell you the truth, I think I got off pretty lightly compared to my co-accused. He got fifteen years shoved up his arse." Gordon sat up from his bed and cracked his knuckles. Steve blew a laboured breath and continued. "I'm just glad I left him before he raped her otherwise I'd have got slammed for years too." Gordon looked at him and wanted to know more. His story sent chills down his spine and he wanted to know exactly what kind of man he was padded up with.

"So what were you charged with then?" Steve rolled his sleeves up and shot his eyes to Gordon.

"Me and my mate Dave were out in our local pub one Friday night. We always went out on Fridays and had done for years. Anyway, this particular night, a young girl comes in the boozer and she's all over my mate Dave like a rash. He thought all his Christmas's and birthdays had come at once, she was fucking gorgeous." Gordon sat on the end of his bed rapt by Steve's story – it was like a drama he was watching on the telly and he rubbed at his arms as the story unfolded. "Dave bought this girl drinks all night long and it was presumed by everyone he was taking her home for a good shag. I tell ya she was one dirty little bastard. Her hands were all over his cock as he stood at the bar. She didn't give a fuck that everyone could see her. Anyway, as the night went on she asked him to walk her home. I was going that way too, so I said I'd walk with them." Steve dipped his head low and looked sad. "We'd only been out of the pub about ten minutes and we seen these two guys jogging towards us looking like they wanted trouble. My mate Dave tried to keep the peace at first, but they were having none of it. They pulled baseball bats from their coats."

Gordon was hanging on his every word and chewed on his knuckle. "No fucking way did they?"

Steve nodded his head. "Yeah within minutes we were fighting with them both. I grabbed the bat from one of them and I let him fucking have it. I might be an old cunt but you should have seen me swing that fucking bat." Gordon loved it and wanted more of the story, he was hooked. "Anyway, the girl who Dave thought he was shagging was now on his back. She sunk her nails into his eyes and tried to scratch his fucking eyes out. Dave threw her to the side of the road and carried on fighting with the lads. Tell ya what mate. We fucking left them for dead. They are lucky to be alive I can tell you."

Gordon rolled on his side and kicked his leg across the bed to Steve, "They got what they deserved the cheeky twats."

Steve sighed. "Anyway, I fucked off before the police came and headed home to get cleaned up, I was covered in claret. Dave stayed at the scene and I thought he was helping the girl from the road side." Steve sucked on his lips and rolled his eyes to the back of his head. "Dave dragged the girl to an alleyway nearby and fucking raped her." Gordon shook his head, but kept from eye contact with Steve. How could he call Dave when he'd been charged with rape as well in the past? Steve rolled a cig and popped it into the side of his mouth. "Wouldn't have been that bad if he'd just shagged her, but he abused her good style. He shoved bottles up her and shagged her up the arse. He even kept her hostage after her ordeal. When the truth finally came out in court, the little slag was involved in the whole set up. Apparently, she'd done it before to a few other fellas in the local pubs in the area. Her job was to get the man outside the pub and then the lads would come along and kick fuck out of them taking their money. The police who investigated the case only had to look at the CCTV near the pub to see what happened." Steve waved his hands about in front of him. "And here I am finishing my seven year sentence. The lad who I wasted was in a coma for weeks and now he is brain damaged. I feel a twat for what I done, but ay life goes on. What about you, what you in for?" Gordon shied away from the question and told Steve he was in for a string of offences. Steve stared at him for a few seconds but didn't ask any further questions.

Steve looked like a gentle giant. His voice was soft. He now produced some photographs from the side of his bed and started to show them Gordon. Steve came from quite a large family and he had five children at home. His wife was devastated when he'd lost his freedom but she always stuck by him, even when she had to travel all the way to Scotland to see him. The next few hours were spent talking about their life on the outside and they seemed to be getting on like a house on fire. Steve treated Gordon like a son. Steve's own lad was a similar age to Gordon and he always corrected him when he was going over the top at some topic. Steve tried to make him look at things through other people's eyes and Gordon seemed to be changing his outlook on life. Steve was older and wiser than Gordon and despite him ending up in jail; he'd always lived a good, clean life. It was like he said, he'd been at the wrong place at the wrong time, and now he was paying the ultimate price for his sins.

Gordon was still supplying drugs in the jail. He had lots of runners who did all the dirty work for him; he kept his hands clean at all times. All he would do was pass the drugs to the inmates and they'd do the rest. The screws knew Gordon's was up to something and they always spun his cell trying to find something, but each time they came away empty handed.

Since he'd moved from Strangeways prison the drugs had been much easier to get into the nick. In Kirkham people would just throw parcels over the fence for the inmates. Gordon knew a lad called Joey, who went out of the jail each day to do some work. He'd organised it so that he'd pick up drops from Tigger. Joey was on a good earner from this and the money that he earned was going to take him and his family on holiday once he was free. Joey also collected the money from the drugs on the inside and he'd take it back out to give to Tigger. Heroin was still a big seller in the jails and Gordon was surprised what the smack heads would do for one hit of it. The inmates seemed ruled by heroin and all their self-respect went out of the window to get it in their veins. Even in the canteen, you could see the junkies searching in the bins for tin foil left from Kit-Kats packets. The tin foil was used to toot off in the privacy of their cell. Gordon didn't mind because at the end of the day they were putting money in his pocket.

Tigger had arranged work for Gordon when he finally ended his sentence. He promised him they would do well together. The jobs Tigger planned were nothing big to start with, but he told him once he found his feet the big cash jobs would start to flow.

Gordon lay for the last night in his pad. The walls of his cell seemed to be looking at him. He stared at each brick that had become his friend over his sentence. The light blue walls had seen some tears over the years and if they could speak, they would have told a few stories that would have curled your toes. The one window in the pad was steamed up and the rain was banging at it rapidly as if it needed to tell him something. Steve had been asleep for the last few hours and had already said his goodbyes to Gordon before he dozed off. Steve's snoring rattled the walls but it was something Gordon had become used to over time. Even Steve's farts were loud. Many a night he'd pissed himself laughing at the different noises that came from his pad mate's arse. He'd nicknamed him Mr Methane.

Gordon closed his eyes and tried to imagine his life on the out. His head was spinning with imagines of what he was going to do. Tigger had arranged to pick him up in the morning and his first stop was to go home and shag Francesca. Gordon hadn't even thought about Rico and the time they'd missed together. He hadn't even put him into his plans when he got home and never intended to in the future. He'd missed a lot of years in Rico's life and felt a stranger towards him. Gordon knew more than anyone that he should have wanted to make it up to his son but he had no feelings toward him.

As the morning light shone into his pad, Steve was up out of bed whistling like a bird. Gordon had not long been asleep and his eyes barely opened as Steve started kicking at his bed. "Come on lad. It's your big day; you should be up, washed, and ready to go." He now started to sing "I Want to Break Free" by Queen at the top of his lungs.

Gordon chuckled calling him "a fucking nobhead."

Once Gordon was awake he pulled the bed covers from his body. He darted out of bed and stretched his body fully as he looked out of the window. The weather had calmed down from the night before and the sun shone in the distance. Gordon put all his belonging in a large plastic bag and passed on some of his property to Steve. He gave him his radio and some other gadgets he no longer needed. Gordon started to get dressed but this time he was wearing his own clothing. Tigger had bought him some new trainers and tracksuit weeks before ready for his big day. There was nothing worse than being released from prison and having to wear the clothes you started your sentence in. No one knew this more than Tigger and that's why he sorted Gordon out with new clobber for his release.

Gordon washed his face slowly in the sink. Once he was finished he started to get ready. The smell from his new clothing made him feel clean. It was a good job Tigger had got him a tracksuit because it hid his weight loss well. Gordon looked thin and drained. Once he zipped up his jacket, he looked like the dog's bollocks. Steve was sat on the side of his bed now and he looked emotional. His own release date wasn't for another three months and he envied that Gordon was going to be a free man.

Everything was packed and ready. Gordon's heart was beating ten to the dozen and his chest was rising rapidly. He'd imagined this day for so long in the past and now it was here he didn't know if he could hack it. The screw opened the door and looked at Gordon with a smile on his face.

"Come on mate; let's get you out of this gaff."

Gordon picked up his belongings and headed towards the door. Just before he left he stopped and walked back to Steve. He dropped his bags down on the floor and blew his breath slowly through his mouth. He flung his arms around him and tried to pick his large body frame up from the floor. Gordon was struggling and Steve giggled like a small child.

"Fucking hell mate, you've got no chance of lifting me."

"I know you fat twat." Gordon chuckled. Gordon shook his pad mates hand and told him to take it easy. If you looked closely enough at the convicts you could have seen tears in both their eyes but they hid it well.

The screw now hurried him. "Come on lad, get a move on." Gordon trudged from the pad dragging his bag behind him. The prison landing was hammered with prisoners and as Gordon walked down it, they all wished him the best in the future. The inmates hugged him and rubbed the top of his head as he passed them. He was like a war hero returning home.

The last stop for Gordon was the prison reception. Once he was there, the officers gave him back all the property he'd first came in with. Gordon placed his gold signet ring back on his finger and smirked as it fell off due to his weight loss. The Zippo lighter he'd been given from an old friend so many years ago still looked as new as ever. He flicked the flame on it and watched as the yellow flame blew about in the cold air. The prison officer passed him fifty pounds in cash and he shoved it straight into his jacket pocket. Every inmate there was given money. This cash was supposed to buy them food until they'd sorted out all their benefits from the government. Once all the release forms were completed, the screw told him he was ready to go. The two male officers wished him luck and told him they hoped they wouldn't see him again. Gordon rubbed his hand at his head and laughed. "Nar mate I'm not coming back in here again, not a chance." The screws had heard this so many times before and hoped Gordon was one of those inmates who really meant what he said.

The walk from the reception to the main gates seemed to take forever. Gordon looked at the fields that surrounded the prison grounds and shook his head. His breathing was struggled and he looked like he was going to have a heart attack. Gordon held one hand around his neck, his face looked white. As he reached the prison gates Tigger was there waiting. He was smiling like a Cheshire cat. The music from his silver Astra car played at full pelt and Gordon started to relax knowing he was a free man.

The screw opened the big metal gates. Gordon looked strange as he scanned the area. Slowly he walked towards the car. His feet seemed to be glued to the floor. Tigger jumped out of the car and shook Gordon's hand. Once they put all his bags into the boot they pulled away from the prison. Tigger passed him a large bottle of brandy. "Here, get that down ya neck soft lad. That will sort you out." Gordon unscrewed the lid with shaking hands and necked a big mouthful. As the brandy travelled into his body, he could feel the effects of it seeping into his veins. The music played at full volume and they were both on a high as they hit the motorway towards Manchester.

The journey took about forty-five minutes. Once they entered the city centre Gordon started to notice the changes in the area. Gordon sat in silence and looked shell shocked. Even when Tigger spoke to him, he struggled to reply. The brandy was near enough finished now and Gordon was pissed out of his head. He wound the car window down and started shouting things to women as they passed. Tigger knew exactly what it felt like on the first day on the outside. He knew Gordon would take a few weeks to adjust. Tigger had struggled himself when he'd been released and he hoped Gordon would bounce back to everyday life just like he did.

The car pulled up at the block of flats where Tom and Francesca lived. The building looked as depressing as ever. The grey bricks were now a dirty black colour and the overall appearance of the flats had poverty written all over them. Tigger grabbed his bags from the boot and Gordon walked inside the flats waiting for the lift to come. Once they were in the lift, the usual smell of piss was present. "Fucking stinks in here." Gordon moaned.

Gordon slowly knocked at the front door and he could hear Rico's voice telling Francesca that someone was knocking. Rico had been so excited that day knowing his dad was on his way home. He couldn't wait to tell him all the things he'd done in school since the last time he'd seen him.

Francesca and Tom weren't looking forward to Gordon's return. If the truth was known, they were shitting themselves. Francesca and Tom's relationship had calmed down a long time ago and they weren't at it like rabbits anymore, in fact their relationship was nearly over. All Tom's stuff had been removed from Francesca's bedroom, and there wasn't a sign left that said that they'd ever been together. It had all worked out pretty well for Francesca; because once Tom knew the score he backed away from her leaving her free to spend more time with Tigger.

Tom still loved Francesca with all his heart and he treated Rico like his own son. He wished things could have been different between them but he knew Gordon would have killed them both if he had ever found out that they were together while he was in prison. Francesca had spoken to Tom several times about the circumstances between them and at the end of many talks, they decided it was best to end their time together. Tom had thought about telling Gordon his secret many times in the past and he'd even thought about getting rid of his brother for good, but somehow his courage failed him. He knew Francesca had to go back to her life with his brother.

The knocking at the door gradually got louder and Tom finally got up from his chair to open it. As he opened the door he forced a smile and hugged his brother in his arms. Tom looked like he was dying inside. The smell of alcohol hit the back of his throat and he knew Gordon was pissed. Tigger followed behind them both and couldn't wait to see Francesca's face when she saw Gordon for the first time in months.

Gordon walked into the front room and his mouth dropped. The place had changed so much since he was last there and it looked smart. Gordon now met Francesca's eyes and smiled at her. He made his way to where she was sat. Rico jumped on him as soon as he sat down and he kissed him briefly on the cheek. He grabbed Francesca and pulled her towards him.

"Come here you and give us a kiss. I've missed you a lot." Gordon held a cunning look in his eyes.

Francesca kissed Gordon back but kept her eyes on his mate. Tigger looked like a knife had been plunged deep into his heart. He dipped his head low and fidgeted with his jacket. Tom felt the same as Tigger. His fists were clenched tightly at the side of him and his teeth were clenched firmly together. He looked like he wanted to run at Gordon and beat the living day lights out of him.

Francesca looked embarrassed at all the attention Gordon was showing her. Her cheeks were red and she looked flustered. She pulled Rico up onto her knees.

"Look how big he is now daddy; don't you think he's a big boy?" Gordon stared at his son and the love a father was supposed to feel for his child just wasn't there. He slowly grabbed at Rico's leg and told him how big he'd grown but ended the conversation there. Tom offered everyone a brew and disappeared into the kitchen feeling like his life was over. Tigger only stayed a while longer and told Gordon he would be in touch in a few days. His jealousy was hard to cover and as he left, he winked at Francesca letting her know he was still interested.

Gordon seemed to be smoking one cig after the other. Tom sat talking for a while and asked about his brother's final days inside jail. Gordon couldn't be arsed with Tom's chit chat and before long he told him to take Rico out for a walk while he and Francesca had a bit of time together. Tom agreed and helped get Rico's coat on. He could feel his brother's eyes burning into him.

Once Gordon heard the front door being slammed shut, he took Francesca's hand and led her to the bedroom. Her face looked worried and she wondered if he'd be able to tell that she'd had sex since he'd been in jail. As Gordon walked into the bedroom, he looked surprised. The room had been decorated in light pink flowery wallpaper and all the bedding was matching. Gordon jumped onto the bed first as Francesca slowly lay by his side. As she looked at him, she thought about how much he'd aged in the time they'd been apart. Gordon now stripped off and stood in front of Francesca. "I've lost some weight haven't I?" Francesca looked at him and nodded her head slowly. His legs looked so thin and his stomach was flat as a pancake. The only thing that hadn't changed was his thin penis. Gordon ordered her to get her kit off. Francesca peeled her clothes off slowly and cringed as she felt his eyes all over her body. The room was cold and she quickly walked to the open window and closed it.

Francesca lay next to Gordon and their skin touched for the first time. He felt so different – old and rough. This was the first time he'd saw her body since she'd given birth. Gordon let her know without holding anything back that her body had changed and he didn't look too pleased at what he saw. Francesca didn't look turned on one little bit by her boyfriend's touch, but she knew she'd have to go through the motions of sex to please him. Tigger was the man she was thinking about now. As Gordon leant in to kiss her, her body tensed. His kiss was passionate to start with and he wasted no time in mounting her. Once he was on top of her he inserted his erect penis. Francesca groaned and pretended she hadn't had sex for a long time. Even when he first entered her, she gave out a loud groan hoping he'd think he was hurting her, but in reality, she couldn't feel a thing. Tigger's cock was a lot bigger than Gordon's and he'd stretched her fanny beyond belief.

Gordon began jerking his body around in circular movement. He was staring at her and watched her face for any signs of enjoyment. Francesca was faking it and let him think he was a sex god as she pretended to orgasm. Once Gordon heard her moaning with pleasure his arse began to move faster and faster. She knew within minutes it would all be over. Gordon continued ramming his penis inside her but half way through it his cock shrunk and he couldn't get it back to its true size. Francesca felt his floppy member inside her and wanted to laugh her head off but as she watched his face, she knew she would have to pretend she hadn't noticed it. Gordon pulled himself up from her. Gripping his man hood in his hands he smiled at her.

"Here get this in your mouth," he chuckled.

Francesca looked at his penis with concern. It looked like a shrivelled worm. Gordon could see her face and told her that the brandy he'd drunk earlier was now playing tricks on his dick. As requested she placed his cock in her mouth and teased it with her tongue hoping to wake it up. No matter how much she tried his trouser snake still remained as small as ever. Gordon looked angry and pulled it away from her mouth. He started to wank himself off. As she looked at his face she could tell he was trying his hardest to try and come. Gordon was going like the clappers and his face was sweating. He still couldn't come.

As they lay in each other's arms, Gordon spoke about the time they'd spent apart. He wanted to know exactly what Francesca had been up to because he could tell something had definitely changed between them. They spoke of the years that had gone by and they seemed to be getting on well. Suddenly Gordon asked a question that stumped Francesca.

"Do you still love me?" he held her hand stroking at her fingers. Francesca felt her face going blood red and panicked knowing she'd have to lie.

"Why wouldn't I love you?" she said haltingly. "We have a child together don't we. I hope we can be a family now." Gordon didn't reply at first and ran her answer over in his mind. He still had the girl he'd met on the visits if things didn't work out between them but he just wanted to make sure Francesca was still in love with him. Gordon yawned and stretched his hands above his head.

"Yeah that's what I want too. I'm sick of watching my back all the time yanno. I'm gonna really try to make you both happy."

His words were like water off a duck's back to Francesca. A leopard never changes its spots, and she knew he was lying his face off. What she didn't tell him was that her plans for the future were to get as far away from him as quickly as possible. Tigger held the tickets for her new life and she was doing all she could to make it happen.

Tom returned home with Rico. He was shouting to see his daddy as soon as he walked through the door. Tom tried to keep him in the front room but he was determined to go and find him, Tom let him go. Rico walked into the bedroom and when he saw Gordon in bed with his mother his face changed, his lips were trembling. Rico froze near the door and he chewed at his fingernails for comfort. Francesca saw her son looking scared and shouted for him to come and join them but he still stood there like a statue, not liking what he was seeing. Gordon now tried to win him over and eventually Rico came to the bedside pulling at Francesca's arms.

"Mummy get up. I don't want you to stay in bed with daddy, I want you come and watch television with me." Francesca started to get up from the bed and Gordon pulled her back down as he spoke to Rico.

"Mummy and daddy are tired so you'll have to go and watch telly with Uncle Tom for a bit won't you." Rico now started wailing and yanked at Francesca's arms. Gordon watched and his temper grew as he watched the brat. Francesca looked at Gordon and told him she was getting up anyway. He growled at her.

"He's a little spoilt bastard," Gordon ranted. He told her there and then that things would be changing now that he was back at home. Francesca and Rico left the room and Gordon settled down to sleep. He looked exhausted and his eyes closed almost instantly.

Tom looked sad as Francesca returned into the front room with Rico. It must have been torture for him to be sitting there knowing she was in the next room having sex with Gordon. Tom kept his eyes on the television and didn't say a word as Francesca sat down. Rico was clinging to her for dear life and he was still upset. Tom now turned his head from the television and asked if Rico was okay. Francesca smiled at him and spoke about what had just happened in the bedroom. She was waiting for him to say it would sort itself out in days to come, but his answer shocked her. Tom scowled at her.

"Well he's right, it's like you've sold him out and you haven't got any time for him no more. You both should have spent time with him instead of jumping straight into bed together. Rico has had all your attention since he's been a baby." He waved his hand about in front of him. "You just can't change that now that Gordon is home, can you?" Francesca looked at him in disbelief. What a fucking wanker she mumbled under her breath. She knew the real reason was that it was him who couldn't stand her being in bed with Gordon and she could see the jealousy eating him up inside. Francesca lit a cig and ignored Tom. You could have cut the atmosphere with a knife.

Tom looked like a broken man as he sat there twisting his fingers in the chair. His face had held the same expression all night long. Tom had always been such a happy character but now he looked like he'd sunk into a deep depression. The night went quite quickly and once Rico was settled in bed, Francesca joined Gordon back in the bedroom. She tried her best not to wake him as she sneaked in beside him but his eyes met hers as she lay down to go asleep. This time Gordon's penis was rock hard and he rammed it in her as soon as he got her knickers off. He was shagging her like he had something to prove this time and he wasn't stopping for love nor money. Surprisingly Francesca got into it and she yelled with excitement as she too reached orgasm.

Tom lay in the next room and gripped the pillow over his head. He was once the man who'd made Francesca groan with this kind of pleasure and now he had to listen through the paper thin walls at someone else who'd taken his place. He clenched his fist together and punched them into the bed as the groans got louder. At one stage, he bolted up from his bed and was ready to go in and confront his brother. Tom walked about his bedroom with his hands placed firmly over his ears. He prayed it would be over soon. Rico was fast asleep next to him in a single bed and he even thought about waking him up to go into their room to end the sex they were having. Minutes later the sound of the bed rocking against the wall stopped. Tom removed his hands from his ears and collapsed onto the bed. This couldn't carry on anymore. He lay staring around the bedroom. His mind was working overtime and he was hatching a plan to win his true love back.

Gordon chugged on a cig as he praised Francesca on her performance. She'd always been a good ride and apart from her body being a little fatter nothing else had changed in the bedroom department. The day had taken its toll on Francesca. Once she'd finished her cig she settled to sleep looking completely knackered.

Gordon found it hard to sleep. He fidgeted in bed for a while then decided he'd get up and make himself a brew, he was hoping this would calm him down. Inside, his stomach felt like a washing machine, he looked strange. The world seemed to be passing him at an incredible speed and he knew at that moment he would struggle to cope with the weeks that lay ahead. Tom had heard a noise from the kitchen and thought it might have been Francesca. They'd always had a late night brew together and he thought she was maintaining the tradition, even though Gordon was now back at home.

Tom crept into the kitchen and his mouth dropped when he saw Gordon staring straight back at him. He knew he couldn't turn around and go straight back to bed. He casually started to speak to his brother as he watched the kettle boiling.

"I'll have a brew if ya making one, our kid. I can't fucking sleep tonight, I don't know what's up with me at the moment." Gordon added another cup to the kitchen side and prepared two cups of tea as Tom went into the front room.

Gordon entered the living room carrying two cups. He snarled at Tom, telling him to take one from his hands as his fingers were burning. Tom quickly jumped up from the chair to assist. Gordon flicked his hand about at the side of him and blew onto his fingers. Both men sat there wearing only their boxer shorts. Gordon's hands was down the front of his playing with his floppy nob, he started to talk with Tom.

"So you've sorted yourself out then? What's life like without the brown? Bet you don't know what to do with ya self now, do you?"

Tom looked intimidated by his brother; it was like they were kids again. Tom told him of his journey to become clean and the job that he'd got to make ends meet. Gordon looked at him and nodded his head. He thought he'd done well, but never told him that. Gordon now spoke about the smack heads in jail and how desperate they were when they needed a fix. Gordon could tell something had changed with his brother, but he just couldn't put his finger on it. He hated that he didn't have that power over him anymore and wanted to know the reason why. Gordon began to investigate hoping to get to the bottom of the changes in Tom. Gordon tapped his fingers on the arm of the chair.

"What made you get off the gear then? I know people who've been off it for years but have always gone back to it, what makes you any different?"

Tom struggled to answer; you could see him swallowing hard. He told him he'd had enough of living his life with drugs and wanted to change. The answer he gave seemed enough for Gordon for now. Gordon spoke about the days that lay ahead and told Tom he'd be dealing drugs for Tigger. He also told Tom he could join him and earn a bit of money if he wanted to. Tom started to sweat at the mention of heroin and turned him down point blank. "What a twat", he whispered under his breath. How could his own brother do that to him knowing he'd been an addict for so long? Gordon held a cunning smirk on his face. "Your loss, I'm only trying to earn you a few quid, that's all."

Rico now walked into the front room crying his eyes out. "Where's my mummy." he sobbed. Once Gordon told him she was asleep in bed, he started to scream at the top of his voice. Gordon tried to pick him up but he struggled frantically in his arms. Gordon snarled and placed him back to the floor. "Little mard arse," he ranted. Rico made his way to Tom for support. The child started to shout at Gordon and told him he didn't like him. Gordon looked evil as he screamed back at him telling him he didn't like him either. Tom shot a look at his brother and told him that he shouldn't say things like that to his son. Gordon huffed and barged out of the room. "He's a little fucking fairy!" he shouted behind him.

Tom stayed with Rico for a while. When he'd finally calmed down he took him back to bed. It was obvious there was no bond between father and son and Tom knew he had the love of Rico even if his mother's affection was lost forever.

The next few weeks were more or less the same. Rico hated the sight of Gordon, and his dad felt the same way. Gordon booked in to see the doctors. His nerves were shocking and he was struggling to cope with life on the out. Tigger had given him a few grafts to start with and Gordon was fine. He never knew the real reason why Tigger had given him jobs out of the area and never suspected for one moment that his mate was in a relationship with Francesca.

Gordon was bang into selling heroin now and he was earning stacks of cash from it. The money Misty still owed him was never far from his thoughts and the time was coming nearer for him to reclaim what was rightfully his. Francesca had been distant with Gordon lately. He knew the conniving bitch was up to something. One night, as Rico sat eating his tea while Francesca and Gordon watched the TV, the words his son spoke nearly made him drop down dead.

"Mummy, why don't you kiss Uncle Tom anymore?" Rico carried on eating his food as he carried on speaking. "He looks so sad since daddy has come home." Francesca's face looked like it was going to explode, she was bright red.

"What are you like? I don't kiss Uncle Tom. What are you telling lies for?" Francesca laughed and shook her head. Her eyes stared at Gordon, she could see she was going to have to do more, he looked like a ticking bomb. She started to interrogate Rico further. "When have I kissed Uncle Tom?"

Rico held his head to the side and thought for a minute. He carried on munching his food and Francesca thought it was all over until he piped up again.

"You kissed him on there. Don't you remember?" Rico pointed to the settee and Gordon was hanging on his every word. He sat forward in his chair as he watched her face turn white. Francesca's eyes were wide open as she remembered exactly what her son was talking about and panic took over her body. Rico had got up one night in the past and caught them in each other's arms. She thought he'd forgotten all about it.

Francesca looked flustered and tried to make a joke out of it. Gordon could see right through her lies and knew his son was telling the truth. His knuckles were turning white as he growled at her. His first reaction was to kick the living daylights out of her, but as he thought about it for a moment longer, he knew that wasn't the answer. It all made so much sense now. Francesca made up a corny story to keep Gordon off the scent and he laughed inside thinking how fucking cunning his girlfriend really was, he'd under estimated her. Gordon accepted her explanation and carried on eating his tea but now it tasted sour, just like his love for Francesca.

Gordon had still been seeing the girl he'd met while he was in prison and he really liked her. She was a bit of a tart but she made Gordon feel good about himself. Tigger was still trying to get the meeting with Dominic set up and he told Gordon nearly every day that the big day was only around the corner.

Gordon wanted revenge on the people who'd hurt

him in his life, and he planned to start with his own brother. How dare he think he could shag his woman and get away with it? Didn't he ever think he would be found out? Tom was going to be destroyed.

That night Francesca was fast asleep in bed as was Rico. Gordon had noticed how depressed Tom had been lately and knew the time was right to seek his revenge. Tom was sat alone watching the telly in the front room, as Gordon came to join him. Words were few between them both. Gordon now placed the heroin onto the table and started to bag it up. He knew Tom was finding it hard not to get involved, he could see him fidgeting in the chair. Within minutes Gordon had Tom sat at the side of him weighing the smack into small plastic bags. Gordon watched his brother and knew it wouldn't be long before his plan came together. He passed his brother a small bag to place the drugs in.

Gordon held the heroin up to his nose and inhaled deeply. He encouraged Tom to do it too. He watched as Tom sniffed the drugs and he could see the fear in his eyes. Gordon sat back in his chair and spoke about the buzz people got from heroin. Staring at Tom he asked him to tell him what it felt like after a toot of the brown. Tom didn't hesitate answering and remembered exactly how it felt. He told Gordon of its effect. Gordon sat munching a Kit-kat as they finished bagging the drugs. He purposely left the foil from the chocolate bar visible on the table. The amount of heroin they bagged was massive. The street value of it must have been at least four grand. Gordon had a shotgun in the flat just in case the local gangsters thought they could come along and tax the drugs from him. He'd shown it Tom in the past and told him if any bastard tried robbing from him he wouldn't think twice about blowing their brains out. Gordon yawned and told Tom he was off to bed. He asked Tom if he would finish the bagging of the drugs. At first, he said no, but as Gordon told him he'd give him a tenner for doing it, he quickly changed his mind. Gordon left his older brother that night and went straight to bed hoping his plan would work.

Tom finished bagging the last bag of the smack. He sat staring at it for at least fifteen minutes. His mind was racing and the questions were banging on his skull. Just one bag he thought and never have it again, he could do that couldn't he? Tom was off the drugs now so one little toot wouldn't do him any harm, surely. Before Tom knew it, the drug had gripped him and he had it spread on the silver foil.

Gordon got up to use the toilet later that night. As he peeped in through the living room door, all he could see was the burnt foil on the table. Tom's body was stretched out on the floor; he looked off his head as spit hung from the corner of his mouth. Gordon nodded his head and grinned with delight. "Strike one!" he whispered under his breath. Tom was now his for the taking and within weeks he knew he would be able to get him to do anything he wanted, because once a smackhead, always a smack head. Gordon smirked as he lay back on his bed, his brother was a prisoner to the heroin once again.

In the coming weeks Tom was left with the job of bagging the drugs each night. Just as Gordon had predicted his brother was a junkie again. Gordon didn't let on to Tom that he knew exactly what he was doing and he just let him think he was safe with his own little secret.

Within weeks, Tom looked gaunt and his complexion

looked grey. His weight loss was almost instant and Francesca put it down to the stress of him losing her. Never in a million years had she thought that he'd gone back to drugs.

Tigger and Francesca were in love. They couldn't wait to spend every minute with each other. While Tom was addicted to heroin, Tigger was addicted to Francesca. Tigger and Francesca had both spoken about being together properly. No matter how much they discussed it, one thing always stood in their way. Tigger could have dealt with Gordon no problem but Francesca didn't want it that way, after all he was still her child's father. If they were ever going to be together, Francesca wanted her and Gordon to end it properly and amicably. She knew things would never be that easy, and prayed each night that Gordon would come home and tell her he'd met somebody else. Gordon's fist had been back in action recently and it was normal for her to have a black eye every week or so. Tigger always cringed when he saw her bruises and many a time he threatened to kill Gordon stone dead. Tom had also heard Francesca's screams from her beatings during the night. He hid his face under the duvet to escape the cries of the woman he still loved. He too wanted to end Francesca's torment, but his body was too weak. The heroin that he'd taken sucked away any life that he had left his body, he was like a zombie.

## Chapter Eleven

Gordon's nerves were as bad as ever and he was struggling to keep himself from shaking most days. The doctor had told him that he needed to learn how to relax and offered him a bit of therapy. Gordon laughed at the doctor and told him to shove it up his arse and left the surgery with just his tablets. Tigger had earned Dominic's father's trust over the past year. He felt guilty about setting his son up, he really liked the guy. Tigger had met Dominic a few times in the past when he'd done business with his dad. The property deal Tigger had set up was to take place in an old mill in Ancoats in Manchester. Once the final touches were in place the meeting was ready for the following week.

Gordon had rehearsed this moment in his mind for years. He knew exactly what he wanted out of it. Misty owed him big time and was going to make sure the bitch paid him back in full. Dominic had never hurt Gordon but if his plan was to work, he needed be involved in it. Gordon had seen Misty a few times since he'd been out of jail and she always looked happy. Her daughter was beautiful and he wished he could have been the one who'd fathered her. When he saw Misty, Gordon hid away in the shadows and admired her from a distance. She was still attractive and he still fancied her like mad even after all these years. Misty was wearing a short red jacket and jeans with knee high boots when he first saw her. Her hair still shone like it had when he first met her. Gordon had tried to look at her daughter to see if there was any resemblance to Misty but the child didn't keep still long enough for him to focus.

Tigger had set Gordon up with the perfect plan to seek his revenge. He now handed Gordon a gun telling him that he wanted no more to do with it. Tigger knew the time and place of the meeting and passed all the information to Gordon. As he left his friends side he patted his shoulder softly. "Don't do anything stupid ay, just get ya money back and fuck off."

Gordon nodded, "Don't you worry about me mate, I'm gonna sort this once and for all."

★

Misty kissed Dominic as he left for work that morning. He told her he had a business meeting that night and not to expect him home until late. Misty was used to this and didn't bat an eyelid.

Misty's first job was to take Charlotte to school. Her daughter was so old headed and she loved the relationship they had together. Charlotte was like her wingman and each morning they would sit in the car on the way to school and sing their heads off. Charlotte knew a lot of the old songs and her favourite one was Shirley Bassey's "Hey Big Spender". Misty would laugh at her daughter face as she sang along to the tunes. Charlotte was like a mini me of Misty. They both dressed trendy and their personalities were so a like. Even the teachers in school couldn't believe Charlotte's singing talent. She always got a main part in any of the school plays because of it.

Once Charlotte was in school she made her way to the refuge. Misty and Sue had planned a girly day with all the women at the refuge and she was looking forward to it. A local beautician who Misty knew had said she would come in free of charge and teach the women how to apply make-up properly. The women in the refuge loved days like this. Previously Misty had brought her cousin Lindsay into the shelter who worked as a high street hairdresser. She'd cut and styled a lot of the women's hair for no fee just to help out.

Sue had turned her life around now and she was back on track. John had tried to win her back but it all had come much too late. Sue knocked him back, telling him their time together was over for good. Sue owned her own house now, her and Bethany were living a stress free life. Her daughter still went to see her father but most of the time he just left her in the pub with her nana and pissed off somewhere else. Sue had learnt from her mistakes and promised herself that she wouldn't be anyone's doormat again. She'd already been out on a few dates since splitting with John and enjoyed the company of other men. But for now she chose to stick with her Ann Summers rabbit. Sue laughed and told Misty it was the best thing that she'd ever invested in. She told her it didn't answer back and you didn't have to feed it – what more could a woman ask for she giggled as she confided in Misty.

"Misty I nearly collapsed the first time I used it. Believe me, you need to get one. You can orgasm in seconds, and if you want to go again," Sue held her belly as she chuckled, "there's no rest period for it, it's ready when you are. It is the commando of all vibrators I can tell you. You definitely need to get one." Misty listened with excitement. She told Sue that she wanted to go and get one too as soon as possible. Misty asked her to come with her that same day to get one. She told Sue that Dominic was working late that night and if she wasn't busy they could go into town after work to get her new love tool. Sue chuckled and agreed, "Bloody hell, okay okay. You horny woman, I'll come with you."

On the morning of the meeting, Gordon sat on the toilet trying to settle the nerves that had tormented him all night. He'd already taken some of the tablets but they didn't seem shift the jitters he felt inside. As he sat there, he heard Tigger enter the flat.

"Won't be a minute, mate. I'm just on the shitter," he shouted. Tom took Tigger into the front room until

Gordon had finished. Francesca now entered and Tigger grabbed her arse as she walked past him, he winked snidely at her. Tom was in a world of his own and didn't see what was going on; he just sat staring into space. Once Gordon came into the front room he shot a look at Francesca. His eyes told her to fuck off. Francesca huffed under her breath and knew they were talking business. Tigger darted his eyes at Tom, but Gordon gave him the okay to talk knowing that Tom was in a world of his own. Tigger checked the door and once he knew the coast was clear he whispered to Gordon.

"Right mate. It's all set for tonight at Victoria Mill at seven o'clock. Dominic said he'd be there waiting for you. He seems an alright kind of lad yanno, I don't think you should hurt him because of what Misty has done to you." Gordon screwed his face up and shook his head. He told Tigger that he planned to kidnap Dominic and use him to get Misty to bring the money. Gordon sniggered as he told him that if Misty handed over the money there would be no problem, nobody would get hurt. Tigger didn't believe a word he was saying and raised his eyebrows.

"Just hope it all goes to plan mate and you don't end up back in the nick." Tigger gasped his breath and rubbed one hand at the side of his head. "Fucking hell mate, for what you've got planned, it carries a big sentence so think on whether it's worth it or not." Gordon knew no matter what anyone said to him he was going through with it. His mind was made up a long time ago and there was no going back. Today was D day.

Francesca was shaking as she crept away from the living room door. The conversation she's heard sent fear through her body. Did she hear it right, was Gordon planning to kill Dominic and Misty tonight? She ran to her bedroom and tried to listen some more could but all she could hear was Tigger leaving the house. He shouted goodbye to Francesca as he left, she made no reply. Sitting on the side of her bed she cracked her knuckles as she stared at the floor.

Gordon was so wrong about Tom being too spaced out to hear what they were saying. He'd heard everything his brother had said. He, too, feared for Misty's safety. When Gordon returned to the front room putting his coat on Tom lit a cig. He casually asked his brother where he was going. Gordon snarled at him, "None of your fucking business beaky so mind that." Gordon tapped his finger at the side of his nose

Gordon had already been to Victoria Mill over the last week. He'd planted everything he needed to make the job a good one. He'd even taken a chair for Dominic to be tortured on, and a bag to place over his head once he'd captured him. The last thing he needed to take with him was the gun Tigger had provided. It actually looked like a toy water pistol and Gordon had questioned his friend whether it was real or not. The shotgun he had at the flat was too big for him to carry around and he knew he'd be taking a chance trying to conceal it.

Gordon started to get ready for his big day. Pulling a pair of black pants up his legs he shook with nerves. When he came out of the bedroom Francesca looked him up and down and asked him where he was going all dressed in black. Gordon had to think quick and told her that old friend had died and he was going to the funeral, he was very convincing. Gordon kept checking his watch he looked agitated.

When Tigger left the flat, his own little plan started to take shape. If it all worked out, Francesca would be his forever and he wouldn't have to worry about Gordon any longer.

Francesca quickly hurried from the flat with Gordon. She knew he was up to something as he was strangely quiet. When she asked him if he was okay, he snapped at her and gripped her by the throat. "Just fuck off out of my space, you dirty slag," he screamed at her. Gordon realised he'd over reacted and tried to calm down. He was pacing the floor. "Fucking hell every time I'm a bit quiet you automatically think there's something wrong with me. Well there's not, so fuck off and go where you're going." Francesca headed off in a different direction. She hated the ground that he walked on and she prayed he'd get caught for whatever he was up to. Francesca's mind now started working overtime. A plan was growing inside her that would rid her of the bastard once and for all. She knew exactly where Gordon was going and what he was planning to do, so all it would take was one phone call to the police to get rid of him for good.

Francesca headed into town with the money Tigger had given her. He was always bunging her cash and other gifts. She had to hide the jewellery he'd bought her, Gordon would have been on to her in a flash if he'd have ever saw it. Today she had £200 in her pocket and she was off to treat herself. Gordon had asked where her money was coming from for shopping, but she lied and told him she'd got a loan from the local loan sharks in the area, he never questioned her further.

Francesca reached Manchester city centre and got

off the bus near the Arndale. She loved the market there and couldn't wait to see what bargains she could find. Francesca walked slowly through the food hall first and the smell from the fish stalls made her heave. There were lots of other food outlets in the market and some of them even sold Chinese food. Francesca was starving at this point and thought she would grab a quick beef Chow Mein to walk round town with. As she waited to order her food her mouth watered. Once she got her scran, she slowly walked away from the stall scoffing it as quickly as she could. The town centre was busy and the amount of people walking around was untrue. It was only four weeks to Christmas and everyone was shopping like there was no tomorrow.

Francesca joined the crowds and seemed to be pushed along past all the shops. She had to stand still and make her way towards a nearby wall to try and finish her food. Once she'd eaten her Chow Mein, she rejoined the crowds to do some serious shopping. Francesca loved the thought of being able to buy whatever she wanted. She strolled into each shop as if she was a queen. Immediately a black dress caught her eye and the silver sequins on it made it look special. Francesca held the dress up and pulled it in different directions. This was her dream dress; she headed to the till to make her first purchase. Tigger had promised to take her out for a meal and this dress would be just what she needed to show off her sexy curves. His penis was going to throbbing like a sore finger when he saw her in it.

Francesca spent the day shopping. She also bought Rico some new clothes and her mood was great until she sat on the bus heading back home. Her conscience was strangling her. How could she let Gordon get away with what he planned? Misty had been out of his life for so long now, so why did he still have to punish her. Francesca gazed through the window on the bus as it travelled up Rochdale Road. Gordon was an out and out bastard and she decided there and then he wasn't getting away with it.

As she entered the flat she shouted but no one was home. Tom must have gone out. She rehearsed out loud what she going to say the police on the phone. Her stomach churned at the task in front of her and she sat down on the chair weighed up all the pros and cons. A life without Gordon would be heaven; Rico would be a lot happier too. Since Gordon had been released from jail, Rico had changed. He'd once been such a happy child but now he would sit alone in his room and keep out of his father's way as much as possible. Francesca chewed frantically on her finger nails. Her eyes were watching the clock on the wall as she lit another cig. "Fuck, fuck, fuck." she moaned. "What shall I do?"

Francesca prepared tea for later in the evening; her mind seemed all over the place. When she'd finished cooking she went to collect Rico from school. Her thoughts were muddled as she planned the phone call that could change her life. Francesca decided she couldn't use her own phone to make the call to the police. All calls to the emergency services could be traced. Walking along the street towards school she clocked a pay phone that wasn't too far from where she lived. A smile came to her face. "Bingo!" she whispered under her breath.

Rico came to the classroom door and smiled at his mother. He looked so big these days and she wondered where all the years had gone. Rico's hair was as fair as ever and he still looked the double of his father. Francesca felt sadness in her heart and wondered why Gordon had never bonded with him. He was such a lovely child and deserved to be loved by his father. Rico handed Francesca a picture that he'd painted in school and told her it was of his family. As she looked at it closer, she noticed it was the two of them together but there was no sign of Gordon in it. She looked at his innocent face as she held his hand to cross the road. Holding the picture towards Rico she asked where his dad was. Rico sunk his head low and pulled a strange face as he spoke.

"Mummy there wasn't enough paint left to do daddy."

Francesca smiled but inside it looked like someone had twisted a knife deep inside her heart. Her mind was made up now and any last minute doubts she had over making the phone call to the police disappeared. Gordon had to go and she'd do anything in her power to make sure he didn't upset her son anymore.

★

Six o'clock came and Gordon was already sat waiting at the warehouse. It was dark and very dimly lit. Gordon pushed the wooden door at the entrance and moved some old boxes from behind it so he could get in without a struggle. As he looked inside, he saw a staircase. The stairs were covered in water from the leaking roof above. His shoes were wet as he made his way to the top of them. Gordon's eyes focused on the floor and he thought he could see someone else's footprints in the dry concrete. He tilted his head to the side and he scratched at his head, he couldn't be sure if they were footprints. The stairway was made of old bricks all the way up to the top. The red paint that had been applied years before had peeled off due to the damp conditions. There was a strange smell in the air that reminded Gordon of an old tip he used to play on when he was a small boy. When he reached the top, he yanked open the two double doors in front of him. He had full view of the place. The warehouse was massive and the concrete floors let him know exactly how cold it was in there. As he walked about, he dodged the puddles of water on the floor. Gordon turned his torch on and placed it on a small wall behind him. The cold air made his body shake, his teeth were chattering together. He now got everything ready for the ordeal. His eyes looked menacing as he stuttered his words.

"Let's see your face now Dominic. All the years you and your little slut have been laughing at me, well today's the day my friend, it all stops here." Gordon cackled as he blew his warm breath onto his hands. "Revenge is sweet you pair of cunts."

Gordon plodded about the warehouse and moved things around. He was constantly checking his watch and knew the moment of truth was near. As Gordon walked the floor he continually checked the small window that wasn't far from where he'd been was sitting. The top part of it was smashed and the glass was jagged round the edge of it. Gordon crept towards it trying to see if he could make out the figure stood in the nearby car park.

Tigger remained frozen as he watched Gordon from afar. He tried to calm his breathing down but continued to pant like a dog on a summer's day. At one stage he had to cover his mouth thinking that Gordon could hear him. The warehouse had lots of places to hide away in it and anybody could have hidden there unnoticed.

Tom had also taken his place in the ceiling of the warehouse. His brother had thought he was so off his head that he hadn't heard his plans, but unknown to him Tom had heard everything he'd said. The hate for his brother seeped through his blood and he wanted to end his brother's life there and then. All his life he'd been bullied by him and now he'd taken the one thing that he was willing to die for. Francesca was his world, as was Rico. Now they were gone he had nothing to live for. Tom had thought about his brother's behaviour quite a lot lately and realised that he'd got him hooked on heroin again so he could rule his life once more. Tom curled up into a ball and looked at Gordon through the small opening he'd scraped away with his finger. His blood boiled as he watched him, he wished him dead. Tom wanted him to die a slow, painful death. Gordon's brother lay still in his hiding place and waited eagerly in a cloak of darkness.

The sound of a car door slamming could be heard. Gordon sprinted to the window. The night had settled in and visibility was poor. Gordon listened near the window and heard footsteps in the building. Sweat poured from his forehead, he was frantic as he tried to get into the best position to capture Dominic.

Tigger bolted up from where he lay and tried to see more clearly. At one point, he nearly blew his cover as a rat crawled over his leg. Tigger chewed rapidly on his finger nails. Gordon was a top lad when he was padded up with him, but now he knew him properly he hated him with a vengeance. Francesca was nearly his now and all that kept them apart was the beast he saw in front of him. Tigger had a clear view of the stage Gordon had set, and the torch he'd placed on the wall gave off enough light for him to see everything that was going on.

Gordon held his breath as he heard the footsteps coming up the stairs. He could hear someone shouting.

"Hello is anyone there?" the voice shouted. Gordon

could see a light coming to the top of the stairs and realised Dominic must have been holding a torch in his hands. Misty's husband could be heard mumbling as he reached the top of the stairs. Gordon froze like a statue behind the door waiting for Dominic to enter. Years of torment were now coming to an end and Gordon could sense his revenge was only moments away. He was out of sight and as soon as Dominic entered through the door, he would pounce on him.

Gordon whacked Dominic over the head several times with a piece of wood. The sound of each belt hitting his head turned your stomach. Gordon gritted his teeth together as he watched him collapse to the floor. His blood was boiling now and he knew he had to be quick. Gordon dragged the lifeless body of Dominic to the chair he'd positioned in front of him. He was grunting as he tried to move his victim's body on his side so he could bind his hands together. Gordon had seen this on the television weeks before and knew exactly how to make sure his prisoner was his for the taking. Dominic started to moan as he came round.

Gordon was shaking uncontrollably, his knees were trembling. He tried to light a cig hoping it would calm his nerves down. His eyes never moved from Dominic. He knew the games would begin any moment now. Dominic had grown up quite a lot since the last time he'd seen him. He was a man now, not a boy. He looked toned and in great shape. Gordon's enemy was wearing a smart black suit with a white shirt underneath. As Gordon growled at him, he realised that Dominic had done well for himself. Jealousy now set in, and he remembered how he'd lost the love of his life to him. He kicked Dominic's legs trying to make him aware of where he was.

Dominic could hardly see as his eyes began to open. His head was covered in blood and it was trickling down his face. The blood excited Gordon and he knew his plan was working. Dominic tried to focus but he was struggling to see clearly. His eyes squeezed together as he watched the shadow of someone stood in front of him.

Gordon chuckled and walked closer to his victim. "Didn't think you would see me again, did ya sonny boy?"

Dominic made no reply. Gordon got frustrated wanted him to know that his worst nightmare had begun and swung his hand back. The sound of a loud slap could be heard and Dominic's head swung to the other side of his body. Gordon walked behind the wooden chair and gripped Dominic's hair in his hands. He yanked at it with all his might and pulled his head back until their eyes met. Gordon's voice sent shivers down your spine as it echoed throughout the warehouse's walls.

"It's payback time prick. I hope you can get me what I want." He stared deep into Dominic's eyes. "Otherwise the night is going to be a long one for you."

Dominic raised his head and thought he recognised the face in front of him. It didn't click until Gordon came into view again. His chest was moving in and out rapidly when he realised who it was. Gordon grabbed the torch from the side of him and shone it directly into Dominic's face. To look at the scene you would have thought it was an old prisoner of war film. Dominic stuttered as she spoke.

"What the fuck do you want with me? Why have you done this to me? Are you fucking off it or what?"

Gordon sat on the small brick wall and growled at Dominic knowing he feared for his life. Dominic continued to speak as Gordon listened with a smile on his face. You could see he loved the power he held over him. Gordon could have killed him at any moment. Dominic was pleading for his life, but Gordon just sat cracking his knuckles.

Finally, he'd heard enough of Dominic's whining and decided to put him in the picture. He popped another cig in his mouth and chugged on it as he slowly walked up and down in front of him. Gordon blew the smoke from his mouth and you could see it circling around his head. He cleared his throat.

"I want my fucking money back. Your slut of a wife stole it from me several years ago, do you remember?" He raised his eyebrows at Dominic. "I want what's mine. Did you both think I would let it go by and let you two bastards have the time of your life on my money?" Gordon scowled at Dominic looking for an answer. He sprung from the wall and pounded his fist into his face. Dominic was helpless and could only take the blows. His eye started to swell as Gordon's clenched fist connected with it yet again. He was screaming at the top of his voice now. "Have you?" he snapped into at Dominic's face, "Have you got my fucking money, or do I have to continue beating the shit out of your fucking thick head."

Dominic knew exactly what he was talking about. His face was white; he knew the money had all been spent years ago. Misty had put all the money she'd stolen from him into the refuge and he knew for certain she didn't have a penny left. Gordon punched him in the chest; Dominic gasped for air and looked like he was choking. After a few minutes Dominic answered him.

"Fucking wanker, what can I do about your fucking money? It's gone, do you hear me, gone." He was screaming at the top of his voice. "Misty put it to a good cause years ago and there's fuck all left. The life we've been living is from my money that I have worked hard for and it's nothing to do with the money you had." Gordon wanted to end Dominic's life there and then you could see it in his face. He clenched his fist at the side of his legs and shook his head from side to side.

The conversation seemed to drift away from the money Misty owed him. Dominic noticed a strange look in his attacker's eyes. Gordon sat on the wall with his hands cupped together. He licked at his lips.

"How is the love of my life anyway? Is she missing me yet?" Dominic cringed inside and knew he'd have to listen to every word Gordon spoke about his wife. Every comment he made was like another punch in his chest. Dominic sat with his teeth clenched tightly together; his nostrils were flaring as listened to Gordon. "Does she still suck a mean cock? When we were together she couldn't get enough of it and loved it stuck in her fanny twenty-four seven." Dominic tried to break free, his temper erupted and he didn't care if he lived or died. Gordon now looked serious and stood to his feet. He spoke directly into Dominic's face.

"Me and Misty would have been happy if it wasn't for you. Fucking right little knight in shining armour aren't ya?" he flicked his finger onto Dominic's nose. "We could have worked out our problems and stayed together if you hadn't poked ya fucking nose in." Dominic rocked about on his chair trying to free his hands. Gordon didn't seem to remember the years of torment he'd put Misty through. He was a serious head case.

"You ruined it yourself mate. You treated her like shit and fucking beat her up whenever it took your fancy. So why blame me for losing her? It's your own fucking fault." Gordon rummaged in his pocket and ran at him. He pressed the pistol into his cheek.

"She'll always love me ya know. I could have her back at any time I wanted, but she's soiled goods now and I don't like sloppy seconds."

The gun barrel sunk deeply into his cheek. Dominic wondered why he hadn't shot him there and then. Misty's ex boyfriend removed the gun from his cheek and walked up and down in front of him. He looked like he was deep in thought. Gordon was pulling at his coat he looked like he was suffocating. Small droplets of sweat were now visible on his forehead. Dominic thought his life would end at that moment and squeezed his eyes shut. Gordon sat down and lit up another cig, inhaling it deeply. He knew his plan had gone out of the window and racked his brains trying to find a solution to get his money back. Minutes passed and like a bolt of lightning Gordon jumped up to his feet..

"Where's ya mobile phone," he now started to pat Dominic's jacket. Dominic flapped and told him where it was hoping his torment would be over. Gordon pulled at his coat and searched for the phone in a panic. Once he'd found it, he shoved it in Dominic's face and told him to speak to Misty. Dominic looked puzzled and asked why, but he dragged his hair back and told him not to ask questions.

Gordon searched the phone with difficulty and finally found the name Misty. He looked at the name several times and told Dominic what he wanted him to say to her.

"Tell her to come here now. Tell her its important, but not to worry." Dominic told him to fuck off at first but another punch to his face made him follow the instructions. "Tell her to be here as soon as possible."

Gordon pressed her name on the keypad and held the phone to Dominic's ear. Misty didn't answer straight away but when she did she could be heard laughing. Dominic could tell she was still talking to someone and urged her to listen.

"Misty, Misty will you listen its important." Misty now said goodbye to whoever she was talking to and gave him her full attention.

"Hi babes, what's up?" Dominic tried not to sound nervous but his voice was shaking as he told her what he wanted.

"Misty I need you to come to the old Victoria Mill in Ancoats. Please hurry it's important." Misty went into loads of questions asking why, but he raised his voice to let her know it was serious. He told her exactly where he would be in the building. Misty's voice could still be heard asking questions. Gordon dragged the phone from his ear and ended the phone call without speaking any further.

They sat in silence. Gordon was pacing the floor, he was a nervous wreck. Suddenly, a noise from the back of the warehouse made them both look at each other. Gordon grabbed his torch and ran to investigate it further. Gordon shone his torch around the nooks and crannies in the ceiling, but he couldn't work out where the noise was coming from. After a few minutes, he returned to Dominic. Tigger let out a sigh of relief having avoided being detected. A rat had crawled over his legs and he couldn't help but try and shake it off, he hated them with a passion. The commotion had nearly blown his cover and lost him his dreams. Tigger watched Gordon returning back to Dominic and realised he was safe. He slowly twisted his body about and tried to remain as still as possible.

Misty looked puzzled after the phone went dead. Dominic had sounded strange and she wondered what on earth he wanted her to go to the mill for. Moments later, she started to smile and thought she could read Dominic like a book. Christmas was only weeks away and she thought he'd bought her some kind of surprise. Dominic had done things like this in the past and he loved to surprise her. Her face lit up and she shouted Charlotte to get her coat.

As Misty placed the seatbelt around Charlotte in the back of the car her excitement took over. What could her surprise be? Then she remembered talking to Dominic earlier that day and she remembered their conversation. He'd told her he was going to a business meeting and he wouldn't be home until late that night. She laughed at Charlotte and began to talk to her as she drove with speed to reach her surprise.

"Daddy thinks mummy's daft. He doesn't know that I am on to him. I think he's got an early Christmas present for mummy, I can't wait to see what it is." Misty turned on the radio and they both sang along to some Christmas tunes.

★

Francesca watched the clock eagerly. She thought Tom would have been home to watch Rico, but there was still no sign of him. After waiting another five minutes, she decided she had no other option than to take her son with her. Rico was crying and told her he didn't want to go back out in the cold, but she finally persuaded him with a trip to the shop on the way. Francesca dragged

Rico to the lift. She knew if she didn't hurry, the police wouldn't catch Gordon in the act and her chance would be gone forever. Francesca walked at speed, she had to pick Rico up and carry him in her arms. He was walking too slowly.

The phone box was finally in sight at the end of the road. Francesca noticed a few people standing outside it waiting. Quickly she ran inside the pub across the road. There was a phone there she could use. Rico was crying, telling her he was freezing, but she didn't listen to him she had more urgent matters on her mind.

Once inside, she found the phone near the bar. She took Rico's hand and dragged him with her as she dialled the number. The voice answered almost instantly and she was asked which service she required. Francesca paused for a moment and quickly said "Police please". The next voice she heard was a man asking what the problem was. Francesca sighed and wondered if she was doing the right thing, but as her eyes shot to her son she knew she was making the right decision.

"There is a man at Victoria Mill in Ancoats and he has got a man captive. Please hurry because he's gonna kill him." The operator tried to get more information out of her, but she panicked and ended the call. She slammed the receiver down and stood with her back up against the wall. Her hands dragged through her hair and she looked stressed. Rico started to cry. He'd never seen his mother like this before and looked scared.

"Mummy what's wrong? Please don't die." Francesca bent down towards him and lifted him up into her arms. She squeezed him tightly and started to speak in a soft voice.

"Mummy's not going to die, son. In fact she's gonna

start living." Francesca smiled softly.

Rico couldn't understand what she was saying but he knew his mum was okay. He started to ask her for the sweets from the local shop. Francesca's breathing settled down and she looked like a weight had been lifted from her mind. Slowly they headed to the shop without a care in the world. Francesca knew her new life was just around the corner.

Misty pulled up at the mill. The lighting was very poor except for the two streets light that lit the whole of the car park. Her eyes scanned to where Dominic's car was parked. She gripped Charlotte's hand tightly and walked towards the entrance. Charlotte clung to Misty and told her that she didn't like the dark.

Misty pulled the entrance door open and shouted Dominic's name. She looked at the stairs in front of her and knew she'd have to make her way up them to meet her husband. Misty looked uneasy but tried to remain calm for Charlotte's sake. The staircase was pitch black. Charlotte started to cry and Misty tried to console her telling her they were going to see her daddy. When they reached the top of the staircase Misty could see some doors and started to relax. She shouted Dominic's name again and started to pull the doors open.

With the door half open, all that Misty could see was the small window in which a little light from the streetlight shone through. She stepped inside with caution and shouted her husband's name again. Misty waited with a smile on her face, she expected all the lights to go on and Dominic to jump out shouting "Surprise" but she couldn't have got it more wrong. She stood inside the warehouse and held Charlotte's hand tightly. She yelled Dominic's name one last time and a light shone in her face.

As the beam hit her eyes, she struggled to see and placed her hands up to her face to avoid the glare. Within seconds, her nightmare began and the voice she heard rattled her bones.

"Hello Misty Sullivan. Long time no see ay, bet you didn't think you'd see me again did you?" Misty panicked and turned to the door to run. Gordon sprinted to the door and stood in front of it as Charlotte screamed out.

"Mummy I don't like him. Please let's go home!" Gordon snarled into the child's face and started to speak in an animated voice.

"Mummy has to give me what she owes me first love, and then you can all go home."

Misty turned and looked for another exit but she couldn't see a way out in the darkness. She stood in exactly the same place looking horrified. Gordon dragged them both to where Dominic was sat and shone the light onto her husband's face. Misty screamed as she saw him and ran to his side trying desperately to set him free. Gordon ragged her away from him and shoved her to the ground. As she fell, she landed in a puddle of murky water. Charlotte could see her father now and melted to her knees. Misty jumped back to her feet and ran at Gordon with clenched fist.

"You simple bastard, what the fuck are you doing to him? Why have you got us here?" Misty shouted.

Gordon chuckled crazily and spoke of the man she loved as if he wasn't there. "Told you I'd be back didn't I? Have you missed me darling?"

Misty couldn't believe the shit he was speaking and

wondered if he was drunk or on drugs. "Are you fucking real Gordon? Why would I ever miss you?" Charlotte was hysterical and she pleaded with him to let her parents go. Gordon shook his head slowly and smirked at the crying child.

"Tears mean fuck all to me sweetheart. The night's gonna get much worse before it gets any better." His eyes shot to Misty. "Mind you that depends on you, Misty Sullivan." Dominic pleaded with him now and begged him to see sense, he would have given anything he owned to end their ordeal. Gordon gripped his hand around Misty's neck, his warm breath was all over her face.

"I want my fucking money Misty; remember the money you stole from me. You didn't think I'd forget about it did you?" His teeth clenched together as he spoke into her face, his nose was touching hers. "Five long years I've had to think about what you did to me and now it's payback time." Misty darted her eyes at Dominic, she couldn't think straight. She knew she didn't have the money and needed to come up with some kind of plan that would get them all out of there alive. Moving her head back from his she spoke in a soft voice hoping to calm him.

"The money's gone Gordon. I put it to a good cause and helped women who were in desperate need of help. The money changed you into someone I didn't even recognise anymore and you're better off without it." Gordon snapped again. He threw her away from him and made his way towards Charlotte. He was like a mad man as he shouted at the top of his voice.

"I've had enough of this shit. Have you got some money for me or fucking what?" Dominic was the one to answer him. Misty struggled to get up from the floor.

"I'll give you the money back, but I can't until the bank opens in the morning." The sound of the word money made Gordon's face light up. He chewed on his bottom lip and nodded his head.

"Good fucking job. If you wouldn't have come up with the money, you'd have all been in body bags by the end of tonight." Gordon lit a cig and plonked his body on the wall. He stared at Misty like she was the Mona Lisa. He still loved her and he couldn't hide it no matter how much he tried. Gordon sat cracking his knuckles.

Tigger and Tom were both watching from different sides of the warehouse and the adrenalin was pumping in both their bodies. They both sneered at Gordon and hated him for different reasons. Life would have been so much easier with him off the scene. As they looked through the darkness the light still shone on where they were sat. They could see Gordon's gloating face thinking he was the winner yet again. From the distance they saw him grab the child and wondered what he planned next. Both of them were hanging on Gordon's every word.

Misty screamed like a banshee as Gordon yanked Charlotte from her arms. Dominic yelled at the top of his voice as he wriggled about in the chair.

"Listen I've told you I'll give you the money tomorrow. Why are you taking Charlotte, she's no use to you, she's a child?" Gordon grabbed the girl. Charlotte was hysterical. She was punching and kicking trying to get back to her mother. Gordon grabbed her face and squeezed her cheeks together.

"Listen to me kid. When your mummy and daddy pay what they owe me, you can go straight back to them, but until then you're staying with me."

Misty ran at him, but he just sent her crashing back

down to the floor, as she grabbed at his ankles.

"Please don't take Charlotte, please! You don't need her; you have my word that the money will be here tomorrow. Gordon please." He kicked her from his legs and grabbed Charlotte by her hood.

"Daddy, daddy." the child sobbed. Gordon walked a few paces from them about to leave, and Misty stopped him dead in his tracks.

"Gordon… Charlotte is your daughter, please don't hurt her."

Gordon didn't turn around straight away, but stood in shock. The words he'd heard knocked him for six, and he needed to hear it again to make sure he wasn't hearing things. He twisted his head like an owl and faced Misty. "What the fuck did you just say?"

"Charlotte is your daughter."

The child now wriggled free and ran to Dominic's side. Gordon looked paralyzed and before he could reply, a loud bang was heard. Gordon fell to the floor like a lead weight.

Misty ran to Dominic and tried to free him from the ropes as quickly as she could. She urged her daughter to help. Charlotte was a complete wreck, her little shaking hands were pulling at the ropes and her face was strained as she tried to free her father. Once Dominic was free he hugged Misty and Charlotte in his arms. His body was all over the place and he struggled to stand up unaided. Gordon was on the floor and he was fighting for his breath.

Dominic made his way towards him, he urged Misty to get Charlotte out of there as soon as possible. She stood at the doors and refused to leave without him. Dominic bent down next to Gordon. He struggled at first because of his own injuries, but finally he saw the face of what looked like a dead man. Dominic panicked and he didn't know what to do. Half of him wanted to leave the bastard to rot, and the other half of him wanted to try to help save him.

The sound of sirens could be heard from outside, they sounded close. Gordon lay in Dominic's arms. His words were short as he gasped for breath. "Misty, Misty, please let me see her".

Misty looked at Charlotte and slowly looked at Dominic for support. Dominic knew the man didn't have long left and granted him his dying wish. Misty came and stood above Gordon with Charlotte by her side. Gordon lifted his head slowly and held his hands out to the scared child. Charlotte huddled next to Misty and hid her face away from the beast. Misty knew his life was at an end and held his hand as he spoke his dying breath.

"Misty why didn't you tell me I had a daughter? She's lovely and just like you. I love you, always have and always will". Gordon's body now started to shake from head to toe. Dominic knew it was all over. Gordon's eyes still focused on Misty as he sucked in his final breath. His eyes looked so sad and Misty was sure she saw tears in his eyes.

At that moment the police flew in through door. The sight in front of them told them they were too late. They gripped Dominic instantly thinking he was the one who'd killed the man lay on the floor. Dominic was in too much shock to argue. He followed the police officer's lead as he cuffed him and led him down the stairs. Misty was taken too. Charlotte was now in the police car with an officer taking care of her. After the shot was fired Tom and Tigger both left through different exits. Neither of them knew if Gordon was alive or dead as they disappeared into the night.

Francesca watched the clock all night long. She had a gut feeling Gordon had been nicked. Tom had only just come in and she tried to act as normal as possible in front of him. Tom looked agitated and she thought he was rattling. As she studied him closer she could have swore she saw tears in his eyes.

The police finally came to the flat at one o'clock in the morning. When Francesca heard the door banging she knew the house was being raided. She quickly threw on her dressing gown on and opened the front door. As she stood there looked anxious, the two police officers looked at her and asked if she was Gordon's next of kin. At first, she looked at them as if they were daft, but finally told them she was. Gordon had always put Francesca's name down as his next of kin as he never wanted the police mithering his mum regarding his personal business. The police officers asked to come inside. Francesca thought it was strange as on previous raids the dibble had just barged past her to search the flat. Tom came to join them. His hair was stuck up all over the place and he looked stressed. The DCI asked Francesca to take a seat and she looked at him with a worried face, she was twisting her fingers rapidly. Tom sat beside Francesca and they both listened as the officer spoke.

"Francesca, your partner Gordon has been found dead in an old warehouse. We're still searching for evidence regarding his death. We have two people in the cells being questioned regarding his murder, but we don't have any concrete evidence as of yet."

Francesca looked numb. Her tears didn't come straight away. She could feel everyone's eyes on her and felt like she was a suspect too. Francesca covered her eyes with her hands and began to cry. She didn't know whether they were tears of happiness, or tears for the death of a man she'd once loved. The officers believed she was upset and she played the part well. They left her in Tom's arms telling him they would back when they had any more information.

Tom held Francesca in his arms. His nostrils flared as he smelt her hair, the fragrance reminded him of their times they spent together. Gordon was gone forever from their lives and he felt a mixture of feelings toward his brother's death.

Francesca phoned Tigger and told him the bad news. He sounded shocked on the phone and told her he would be round straight away. He asked if the police had been and asked what they'd said. Francesca told him that they were questioning two people regarding Gordon's death and she didn't know anymore. Tigger told her he would be there as soon as he could. Francesca asked him to get some cigs on his way because she'd nearly smoked all hers and the way her and Tom were smoking they wouldn't last another hour.

The three of them sat in the front room and Gordon's death sunk in. Each of them felt pain for their own reasons, but they also felt freed from the hands of the man that had caused them nothing but pain.

The ashtray was overflowing with cig dimps as the morning light shone into the flat's windows. None of them had been to sleep. Gordon's body was still at the hospital and the police had asked Francesca to go and identify him. She told them straight that she couldn't go. How could she go, when deep down she felt like she'd put him there. Francesca was wrestling with her conscience.

Tom saw how upset she was and quickly stepped in. It wasn't till it was too late that he realised he was now going to see his dead brother in the hospital. His heart was pumping in his chest as he left the house with the police officer.

The hospital was empty that morning and there were only a few people on the corridors. The walls looked like they were closing in on Tom. He thought he could still hear Gordon's voice in his ear calling him a "No good wanker." As they neared the mortuary, Tom wanted to turn and run away, but his legs seemed glued to the floor. The police officer went into reception and told Tom to take a seat, telling him he wouldn't be long. His eyes looked around the small reception area and he tried to imagine what Gordon would look like now he was dead. His head dipped low and how looked feared to death of whatever lay beyond the hospital walls. The male officer returned within minutes. He told Tom they were just getting Gordon ready for them to see. Tom stood up and thought about doing a runner; his eyes were scanning the area for an escape route. The medical staff now came out and told them they were ready.

The room felt cold when Tom walked inside. He folded his arms in front of him trying to keep warm. Goose pimples were all over his arms. The smell of death lingered in the air and he looked like he was going to faint. The room was filled with lots of silver drawers on the wall. The mortician asked Tom a few questions regarding his brother and went through the process of identifying a dead body. Tom didn't speak, he just nodded his head. The mortician walked to the wall and pulled out his dead brother.

At first, Tom froze, all he could see was a white plastic

bag that was quite long and obviously held something inside it. The man now beckoned Tom to come closer. His fingers slowly unzipped the body bag. Tom nearly collapsed and his heart was going ten to the dozen. The face of his dead brother stared back at him now and he couldn't cope any longer.

Tom ran for the door as the police officer followed closely behind him. Gordon's face was there in Tom's mind and he knew until his dying day that the picture he'd just seen would never be far from his thoughts. Gordon just looked like he was sleeping but the traces of blood on his forehead let him know he was never coming back ever again.

The officer tried his best to comfort Tom but he was shaking like someone who was having a fit. The policeman had seen this so many times before and started to treat him for shock. Tom sipped some hot, sweet tea and his body calmed down. All the relevant questions were answered and Tom identified Gordon. The police officer offered Tom a lift home as he could see he was in a bad way, but he refused telling him the walk home would help clear his mind. Tom had one thing in his head at the moment and that was to get his fix as quick as he could. Heroin had always numbed his emotions. All he wanted to do was to feel no pain and drugs were the only answer.

Francesca thought she should have been more distraught about Gordon's death, but she seemed to be coping well. To look at her you wouldn't have thought her boyfriend had just been murdered. Tigger was staying with her now and he knew she'd be his forever. He'd planned in his mind for them both to move away, but for now he had to remain quiet and keep them to himself.

Misty and Dominic were both questioned about

Gordon's death and once they'd told their story, they were released without any charges. The police were now searching for the man who'd set up the meeting in the first place. When they questioned Dominic's father, he shit bricks. He gave them Tigger's name without any hesitation and told them he was the man who'd set up the whole deal. He gave them a full description of Tigger but thought it was safer for everyone to keep his second name well out of it.

Charlotte was reunited with her parents and they all held each other for what seemed like a lifetime. Charlotte's face was swollen through the tears she'd cried and Misty told her that everything was going to be alright from now on. Charlotte was asking hundred of questions on the way home but left the most important one out. Misty trembled inside and the thought of someone else now knowing that Charlotte was Gordon's flesh and blood terrified her. Even more than the experience she'd just been through. Their journey home seemed to last forever. Charlotte slept with Dominic and Misty that night as the three of them were traumatised. The poor little soul was scared out of her skin, she needed her parents by her side to try to rid herself of the experience she'd just encountered.

## Chapter Twelve

The morning of the funeral was upon them. The Manchester skies had opened with buckets full of rain pouring down from the angry black clouds. They all stood in the church and listened to the priest who tried to make Gordon out to be a saint. Francesca sat with Tigger and Tom. On the opposite side from them Misty sat with

Dominic. Misty wasn't going to attend the funeral but Gordon's mother had pleaded with her and played on her emotions to go. Misty went to the funeral just for her sake. She knew once this was all over she could move on with her life once and for all.

Francesca had packed all hers and Rico's belongings over the last couple of days. Once the funeral was over she planned to move away with Tigger to make a new life. Days before the funeral Francesca had been packing all her stuff, when she found a large sports bag that belonged to Gordon. At first, she thought nothing of it and thought she'd just leave it for Tom, but curiosity got the better of her. Francesca sat on the floor and looked inside it. At first, all she could see were old photographs. As she looked closer she could see it was all Gordon's personal letters from when he was in prison. As she came to the end of the search, a large brown paper envelope appeared. She pulled it out of the bag to look closer.

One by one, she pulled out the letters and nearly died when she saw what was written on them. The anger raged inside her body and she wanted to bring Gordon back from the dead to tell him exactly what a twat he really was. As she read the letter in her hands she felt sorry for Gordon.

Dear Misty,

*I know you'll never read this letter, but I'm going to write it anyway. This can be my therapy to try to rid you from my thoughts. I think about you every second of every day and regret the life I led you. You were my world and everything I ever dreamt about, but like a fool, I didn't see it and lost you. I know I deserve everything that happens to me and I can never say how sorry I am for the way things turned out.*

*You are such a lovely woman Misty and I never deserved you. You'll make someone very happy one day and I'm so sad that man won't ever be me. My heart is still captured by you and will be until my dying breath. Will I ever love another like I have loved you? Maybe one day we can be friends again and I can tell you to your face, but you know me Misty, I will probably bottle it up for years and never get around to it, so this is the only way I can say it. Sad isn't it, that I have to write it all in a letter that I'll never send, but believe me if I don't get this out, the way I feel about you it will drive me mad.*

*I'm living a lie as we speak and nobody knows how much I love you still and always will, but I have given myself so much of an image of this big hard man that I have to live up to it and carry on with the lie that keeps me awake most nights. This is the price that I have to pay.*

*Misty, I hope one day you will forgive me, and perhaps even be my friend. I know that I need a miracle for this to happen and believe me I'm praying each and every day. I just hope one day my prayers will be answered and you will forgive me.*

*Always Gordon xxxxxx*

Francesca read the letter and sobbed. Her body was rocking on the floor. Gordon had never loved her the way he'd loved Misty and she knew deep down she'd always been second best. Misty was his true love and she hated herself for the choices she'd made in the past. Francesca carried on reading through all the letters and they all more or less said the same thing. Half of her wanted to burn the letters, but the other half wanted to give them to Misty. She knew they would make no difference to her friend's life but she thought she needed to let her know exactly how much Gordon really loved her. This could be the closure Misty needed in her life. Francesca placed the letter back in the envelope. She looked devastated.

★

Gordon's body was laid to rest and they all gathered around as his coffin was lowered to the ground. There were a few tears shed around the grave side. Some of them were crying because they could move on with their lives and some of them were crying with tears of guilt. The people stood at the graveside, hung their heads low. Francesca's sobbed her heart out. They all thought the tears were for Gordon, when in fact the sooner they filled the hole where he lay the better she would feel. The bastard had made her life a misery and deserved everything he'd got.

As they all walked from the graveside Misty said goodbye to Gordon's parents. Just before she got in the car, she heard a voice shouting her name from behind her. Misty turned her head to see who it was. Francesca dipped her head low as she quickened her pace towards her. Gasping for breath she passed Misty a large brown envelope.

"What's this for?" Misty asked in a concerned voice.

Francesca took a deep breath and put her cards on the table. It had killed her inside to say the words she was about to speak but she knew she would never get the chance again. "Misty these are letters that Gordon wrote to you while he was in prison. He never posted them to you but I think this will help you put a closure on many things in your life. He always loved you and I was a fool to even think he could ever love me." A single tear fell down Francesca's face. "Take care, Misty, I'm so sorry for the way everything turned out. I hope one day you might be able to forgive me. I lost a true friend when I lost you. Nobody will ever step up to that mark again." Misty took the letters from her with a shaking hand. Her face was pale and she looked wobbly. Both girls sat on a nearby bench. Misty reached into the envelope and pulled out a letter.

The words Gordon wrote inside the letter brought tears to her eyes. The black mascara she'd applied on her eyes formed into black tears. They streamed from her eyes at speed. Gordon's words were soft in the letter and she felt she could hear him saying the words inside her head. Tears from her eyes dripped onto the letter. Francesca placed her arms round her neck and sobbed.

The man Misty had once loved with all her heart had finally opened up and told her how he felt inside. Her lips shook as she read each word. She always knew he had a heart. It was such a shame he'd pretended he was a big hard man to the rest of the world. Things could have been so much different between them in the past if he'd have only changed. Misty wiped her eyes and all her mascara was smudged. She placed her head onto her knees and sighed loudly. Lifting her head slowly, she began to speak with a shaking voice.

"Mad innit. I think he loved us both in his own way didn't he?" Francesca nodded and sucked on her bottom lip. "Thanks for giving me these letters; it must have been hard for you. Both our lives have changed so much since we were younger. We both made mistakes didn't we?" Francesca looked relieved as years of torment had been released. She held Misty hand in hers.

"Misty, I can't find the words at the moment. My heart is broken into a thousand pieces, but your forgiveness means more to me than anything in this whole word. Gordon loved you from day one, and I spoilt something that could have been so special. I'll have to live with that for the rest of my life. You've found happiness now with Dominic and I wish you nothing but love and happiness". The moment that passed was heart wrenching. Both Francesca and Misty stood up and held each other tightly. Somehow, after all that had happened, they still cared about each other. They'd suffered at the hands of Gordon.

Dominic's voice could be heard shouting in the distance and Misty shouted over to him to tell him she would be there in a minute. Francesca kissed her on the cheek and squeezed her one last time before she left her side. Misty stood alone for a few seconds and gasped for breath. This was what she needed. At last she had closure. She folded the letters carefully and placed them into her black leather handbag

As one door had shut, another one had opened and she knew that her life was for living. From that day forward, Misty was going to live life to the full and have no more regrets. Goodbye Gordon, goodbye past she whispered as she went to join her husband in the car.

Tom remained at the graveside once everyone had left. His words were hard to find as he collapsed at the side of where his brother lay. His shoulders were shaking as he whispered his last words to Gordon.

"Ar kid, please forgive me. I loved you brother, but you destroyed everything I had. I'll have to live each day with what I've done and I know your blood will always be on my hands. Please try and forgive me Gordon, I did it for all the right reasons."

Tom walked away and pulled his hood up over his head. He could still feel the presence of his brother by his side. Life was going to be hard for Tom from this day on. Somehow and some way you could tell he would find happiness, and start to live his life once again without the shadow of his brother's death hanging over him. The police were still no nearer to catching Gordon's killer. The investigation was still pending by the police. They were still hoping to find Gordon's murderer, but Tom had been clever. He'd covered his tracks well and destroyed all the evidence pointing to him.

Tom knew Gordon's blood still lived on in Misty's child and Francesca's. He smiled softly knowing a part of his brother still lived on in his children. Perhaps one day he would tell Rico all about his father's other daughter.

# THE END

# BOOKS BY THE SAME AUTHOR

BROKEN YOUTH

NORTHERN GIRLS LOVE GRAVY

BAGHEADS

TEABAGS & TEARS

THE VISITORS

SLEEPLESS IN MANCHESTER

FOR MORE INFORMATION OR TO
ORDER ANY OF KAREN'S BOOKS VISIT:

WWW.EMPIRE-UK.COM

WWW.KARENWOODS.NET